Gildentongue shouted something in a tongue the hobgoblin did not recognize, but that the hobgoblin assumed was a curse. The draconian dropped to his knees, attempting to roll the fires out, but instead succeeded only in picking up more oil to feed the flames.

"It's almost beautiful," said Groag, watching the aurak's agony.

"Beautiful like a dagger in the dark," said Toede, grabbing his companion. "We have to get out of here before . . ."

Groag was transfixed. "Ooooh, the fires are turning green."

Toede cursed loudly. "That means Gildentongue just died."

Groag smiled. "So he's dead."

Toede nodded. "So now he's really steamed.

Groag looked down and saw that the burning form of Gildentongue was rising from the ground in a parody of its former self. Its head had already been charred to a black-ened skull, wrapped in pale tongues of green fire. The beast began shambling up the right-hand stairs, leaving a scorch mark in its passing.

It croaked a single word from its useless throat: "Toede."

DragonLance® Saga

DragonLance® Saga

VILLAINS
Volume Five

LORD TOEDE

*Being the Death and Life and Death and Life
and Death and Life of the Highmaster of Flotsam,
his Quest for Nobility, and the Lessons
which were Learned in that Quest.*

Jeff Grubb

[Editor's Note: Although the anachronisms in this tale may seem out of place,
they are an integral part of the author's style, and therefore have not been excised.]

DRAGONLANCE®
Villains Series
Volume Five

LORD TOEDE
©1994 TSR, Inc.

All Rights Reserved.

Cover art by Jeff Easley. Interior art by Karl Waller.

First Printing: July 1994
Printed in the United States of America.
Library of Congress Catalog Card Number: 93-61464

9 8 7 6 5 4 3 2 1

ISBN: 1-56076-870-3

TSR, Inc.
P.O. Box 756
Lake Geneva, WI 53147
U.S.A.

TSR Ltd.
120 Church End, Cherry Hinton
Cambridge CB1 3LB
United Kingdom

Dedicated to
Margaret Weis and Pat McGilligan,
who dragged me back
into the enjoyable state
of writing fiction.

The City of FLOTSAM
at the time of the death of
HIGHMASTER TOEDE

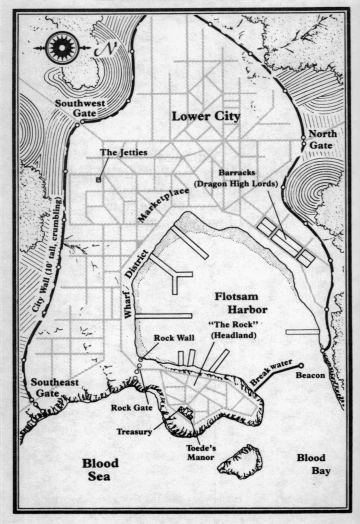

Prologue

In which we do not meet Our Protagonist, exactly, but in which we witness a wager being made in lands far from our own.

The face of the Abyss was the face of its goddess. Takhisis was the land, and the land reflected her moods. A light, pleased smile became an earthquake, a furrowed brow a new rise of mountains, a sudden irritation a thunderstorm of blood and dead creatures sweeping across her features.

And yet the face of this goddess was inhabited, for life crawled and scrabbled and clawed its way across her surface like fleas and mites across a seasoned world-traveler. Here the fiends prowled, the tanar'ri bathed in the blood of their victims, and the yugoloths capered with gleeful intensity. Here the moondarks swept low, hoping to snare some rising soul from the terrain, and the ground roiled with the passage of the bulette-liches, their bone-white carapaces knifing the soil from below. Here the pindizzers spun in their dervish-dance, the kothmew sharpened their scissorlike mandibles, and the eloda, blinded, hunted the damned by the reek of their souls.

Here in all its deadly splendor was the Abyss. For two observers, looking out on the blasted landscape, it was home.

By rights, said observers should have been working on

some soul-wrenching plot or Krynn-destroying plan, but even fiends from the lower planes take their five-minute breaks, their long lunches, their extended afternoons, hoping that their Abyssal masters do not need them (or at least do not notice them missing). Were these observers a pair of dwarven roustabouts, human idlers, or kender finders, no further notice would be taken of them, but they were not dwarves or kender or even men, but abishai, the chosen of Takhisis, the most mischievous and foul of the creations under her command. The pair resembled lizards, after a fashion, with long, fanged, crocodile heads and thick batlike wings, and they resembled men in their upright stance and cognizant eyes. Blood sweated from their scaled black hides and hissed as it struck the ground. They regarded the Abyss as servants would their master's house, with respectful awe and not a small bit of personal pride. Indeed, if not for them, who would look after things, keep matters in order, dust the odd crevice, and whatnot?

One abishai was long and lean, the result of too many turns of the rack. He had to stoop, his long knuckles grazing the ground, to bring his soft, whispering voice to the ears of others. He was one of the Abbots of Misrule, and his portfolio was to journey into the world of Krynn and dispense bad advice and terrible truths. By rights he should have been in Taladas, nosing softly into the dreams of a corrupt accountant the evening before a surprise audit, assuring said coin-counter that his embezzlement was perfect and none would catch him, so why not take a little bit more?

Instead, this particular abbot was taking a break, the dark equivalent of sneaking out to the alley for a few puffs with the mates. The tall reptilian creature surveyed the pandemonium around him and let out a contented sigh, stretching like a cat to his full height.

"Another day in paradise," he said.

His companion was shorter and more potbellied. This

abishai's task was to maintain the souls of the truly and justly damned, the most evil of the evil, to contain them and prevent any chance of rivals to their dark mistress arising in the pits of the Abyss. For Takhisis knew the deadly danger of evil turning upon itself, and brooked no competition. Making sure, that was the fat abishai's task, he who was called the Castellan of the Condemned. The weight of this task was only exceeded by the sheer spine-numbing boredom of it all. The Castellan of the Condemned did not dwell on his lot in eternity, the fact that he remained in place while his companion got to jolly-ride about, spreading bad advice. Not often, at least.

At the moment, the Castellan just grunted and waved a claw at a nearby hillock. "Looks like we have a tourist."

The taller abishai grunted in agreement. A bright light had manifested halfway up the low rise, as if a star of pure radiance had been brought to the surface of the land. Its brilliance cast hard shadows on the surroundings, and the lesser creatures of the Abyss, unaccustomed to such a glow, fled squealing from its purity, tunneling deep into lairs or tumbling downhill to darker, more secure locations.

At the center of the radiance was the glittering white and steel form of a mortal, human-sized, with a great sword of solid crystal.

"Paladin?" guessed the taller abishai, shading his eyes with his overlong knuckles.

"Seems as if," said the shorter one, squinting into the light. "Definitely not subtle."

"Storming the gates of the Abyss never is," said the other. "Here comes the first of the Heavy Brigade, representing our team."

The bright light was eclipsed, if only for a moment, by the rising form of a charging fiend. A large specimen, such fiends served as the pit bulls of the Abyss, and this one had horns that would make a minotaur blush in inadequacy.

The observers did not see the paladin move, only the bright afterimage as the crystal sword traced a lightning-like arc through the fiend. The pit-creature fell away in identical halves, carved down the center.

"That had to smart," said the Abbot. His companion grunted in agreement.

A second fiend took the first one's place and met a similar fate as the first, this one's separation being horizontal as opposed to vertical.

"Looks vorpal to me," said the squat Castellan.

The taller one nodded, though neither showed any movement toward the scene of battle. "Bet he shan't last five minutes," said the Abbot.

"Bet he can," said the shorter abishai. "He's got the armor, the sword, and the attitude. How about a cup of saint's blood against a breeze of a mortal's summer?"

The Castellan's tall companion nodded, his crocodile-like head turning the nod into an exaggerated bob. "Bet taken. Starting now."

The pair made themselves as comfortable as possible on a broken pile of smoldering rocks and watched the battle unfold. The Abbot of Misrule counted the seconds off on his fingers. Ten, then ten again, then ten again and so forth, ticking off the time.

Across the low valley, the legions of the Abyss marshaled themselves against the invader. Two more fiends tried to bring the new arrival down and were rewarded for their efforts with lost limbs and severed heads. A yugoloth met a similar fate. An abishai (for not all were malingerers) tried to sneak up from behind and aloft and was skewered for its effort.

"Was that the Padre of Pain?" asked the short observer.

"Probably," said the tall one. "He's always sucking up for attention and battlefield merits. One minute."

Two more yugoloths fell in quick succession, along with another abishai whose blood-red wings were severed from his body. A wormlike beshak wrapped around the paladin's leg and exploded in a million shards from proximity to so much goodness.

"Two minutes," said the Abbot.

The ground erupted beneath the paladin, and the chitinous maw of a bulette-liche broke the surface, seeking to swallow him in one gulp. The shining paladin jumped on the beast's snout, driving the sword deep into the decaying rot that was the creature's brain. The undead landshark gave a sharp spasm and perished immediately. The paladin retreated up the beast's crenelated back as more creatures poured out of their lairs.

"I think he's dimming," said the Castellan, a note of concern in his voice.

"That's just blood covering the armor. Three minutes," said the Abbot.

A dark wave rose as the combined mass attack of twisted creatures sought to overwhelm the paladin. The armored human took out the closest rank of the beasts, stepped backward, nearly lost his balance, took out the next rank, and retreated again, until he was perched centermost on the body of the undead landshark that was resting on an ever-increasing number of other lower planar creatures.

"What is it that gives creatures like that such power?" asked the short observer, almost in admiration.

"The power of Good," snarled his tall companion. "Four minutes. Ah, she's finally here. It's over now."

The short abishai followed his cohort's sharper eyes to the blossom of crimson on the horizon. "Keep counting," he said grimly.

By the count of ten the blossom had congealed into a great flying creature, the form of a hell-maiden in full regalia. Her flesh was shining silver, polished with the blood of her enemies, and seemed to merge with her flame-mirrored armor. She held in one clawlike hand an ebony blade of a shade so dark it hurt the eyes to behold it. Her crimson hair swept backward away from her face as she dove upon the battling paladin, a banshee scream on her lips. She was the most beautiful and frightening creature of the Abyss.

"Judith," said the Castellan, suppressing a shudder. Judith was among the Keepers of the Peace, the strong arms of Takhisis in the Abyssal Planes. She was also nominally the watching abishai's immediate superior. Both creatures shrunk back into the rocks, even though Judith's attention was fixed on the interloper.

The paladin looked up, cued to his peril only by the dark hordes themselves pulling back with Judith's arrival. A timely duck kept his head on his shoulders as the black blade, trailing ebony flames, passed through the air where his neck had been only seconds before.

Judith circled again, and the paladin began to glow more strongly, more intensely.

The hell-maiden swung her great black blade over her head with both hands as she dived. The paladin raised his sword of glowing crystal to catch the blow and turn it aside. The blades met . . .

. . . and the paladin's sword shattered into a million fragments. Judith swooped low over the land in a banking dive and turned to make another pass. The paladin staggered, his own blood now mixing with the darker hues on his punctured armor. He looked up with dull, fearful eyes as Judith returned a third time, sweeping her sword in a broad stroke aimed at the top his helmet. The Castellan saw the paladin reach for his throat and . . .

. . . the blade passed through his body just as the paladin became misty as a fog bank fading in the dawn. Judith stood where the paladin moments before had withstood the armies of the Abyss and howled in rage. The ground thundered at her shout. There was another blossom of crimson, then she, too, was gone.

"Rather fled than dead, it seems," said the Castellan. "Time?"

"Two tics short I'm afraid," said the Abbot, holding up

eight of ten fingers.

"You counted slow," pouted the short one.

"If I did, you failed to notice," said the tall one with a smile. "So it matters not. Come on, Judith's going to be haring after that paladin for a little while more. We might as well clear the scene."

The two descended from their low hillock, toward the Castellan's crypts and away from the ruins of the battlefield. Already the scavengers of the Abyss were crawling from their burrows, unconcerned about the allegiance and alignment of their meals. The Abbot had no love of such feeding frenzies and lengthened his strides. The more portly abishai had to puff and scurry to keep up.

"Why do they do it?" asked the Castellan, panting. "Why storm the Abyss?"

His taller companion sighed and slowed only for a moment. "Because they see themselves as Good and us as Evil. We're opposites, so we gravitate toward each other."

"Then what is Good?" continued the Castellan.

"Our opposite," said the other, then stopped, as if turning his attention fully to the question. "But I think I see your point. You don't see us storming Paladine's castle on a regular basis. Shouldn't the question rather be 'What is it about Good that causes those possessing it to act in such a foolish fashion?' There is probably something in the very nature of goodness that inflicts such blind stupidity."

"Stupidity and more," said the shorter creature. "There is a tangy taste to their souls. You can feel it when they die: an electrification of the air, an exhilaration of the soul, a nobility of the spirit. . . ." His voice died off as he realized his companion was now staring at him.

"A nobility of the spirit," said the Abbot of Misrule, a small smile flickering across his face. "Then isn't our question not 'What is good?' but 'What is nobility?'"

"Perhaps it is," said the Castellan, and set off again, passing the first crypts of the area under his care.

"Or perhaps not," the Abbot said. His shorter companion

could hear the shrug in his voice. "There is goodness in nobility and nobility in goodness. You cannot separate the two."

"I disagree," said the Castellan. "You should be able to have one without the other. I'm almost sure of that."

"Hmmm," said the Abbot as they reached the heated brass doors of the shorter abishai's domain. "Do I hear another wager being made?"

"It's just an idea, an experiment, if you will," said the Castellan, thinking (briefly) of how Judith would react to all this spurious betting by her subordinates. "But since you bring it up, we could make it . . . interesting with a bet of some sort."

"Not just a cup of saint's blood for an . . . experiment . . . of such magnitude," the Abbot cautioned.

"Well, I have long lusted after your freedom in the living world, advising the great and near-great. Badly, it is true, but still, such freedom." The Castellan sighed despite himself.

"And I have always envied your vaunted position as guardian of the most damned among the damned, the crème de la crème in a manner of speaking," the taller abishai replied, grinning. "But that is the fate of eternal damnation: You don't get what you want. What would the nature of this 'experiment' be?"

The Castellan swung his crypt door open to reveal steps made of burning anthracite. Without a second thought, he started down them, while his companion gingerly picked his way down among the cooler spots. "We discover if one can be noble without being Good," said the portly abishai, rubbing his leathery palms together. "I have entrusted to me the worst of the worst, hated creatures condemned for five or six eternities. We take one, restore him to life, and send him to Krynn with the command 'Live nobly.' And we see if he pulls it off."

By this time the pair had reached the bottom level of the crypt, where the worst of the worst were kept. The shelves were made of brass and glowed from the heat of the burning floor. Stacked upon each shelf, almost filling the room, were jars made of iron, white gold, and heavily leaded glass. There was the low moaning of the tormented within the room, and the smoky glass would often clear enough to reveal a mortal face, screaming in pain.

The Abbot's foot crunched on a broken shard. He picked it up and turned it over in his hands. On it, in burning gold script, was the single word: RAISTLIN.

"Have you tried this before?" asked the Abbot, turning the glass over.

The Castellan shook his head. "There are always a few who slip through the net, for one reason or another. I have a bottle for Lord Soth, but it was never filled." He gave a heavy shrug, then motioned to the remainder. "But we have such a variety to choose from: murderers, maniacs, deluded priests, petty officials. Pick one, and we'll see what happens."

The Abbot of Misrule raised a taloned hand to his lips, his eyes locked on one shelf of bottles. "Let me understand this clearly. I say that nobility cannot exist without goodness. You say that you can be one without being the other."

"That is the supposition of the experiment."

"The winner gets the loser's position, power, and portfolio for . . . say . . . a year of Krynn's time?"

"That is a fair wager."

The Abbot nodded. "I get to choose the sinner we try to redeem?"

The Castellan held out both palms in agreement. "Done," he said.

"Done," said the Abbot, and with a long arm snaked out and snagged an iron bottle from one of the burning shelves. It was a small jar, and in the mortal world it would seem a suitable vessel in which to store pickles, and small pickles at that. He tossed it to his partner.

The toss was short, and the Castellan had to lean forward

to catch it up. He turned the small jar in his short-clawed hands and brushed the dust from its surface.

TOEDE.

The Castellan let out a low whistle and swore. "You rat-bastard. You're not going to make this easy."

Chapter 1

In which we officially meet Our Protagonist, who returns to the land of the living and soon comes to regret it.

Toede awoke with the taste of ashes in his mouth. Had he gotten drunk again and slept too close to the dying embers of the hearth? No, that was years ago, another lifetime and half a continent away, in a crude cavern with his fellow hobgoblins. Before the dragons came. Before opportunity knocked and showed him a dream of great power. Much had happened since then.

Then there was another dream as well, more current, stemming from his recent slumber. Great and powerful figures—giants or godlings—striding the landscape, speaking to him. He was bound for greatness. No, not that. Nobility. He was bound for nobility. The rest of the dream tore away in small, forgotten strips as dreams tend to do, but that was enough. He liked dreams that promised good things in the future.

But where was he? Toede looked around and saw he was perched at the base of a comfortable maple tree overhanging a quietly gurgling stream. On three sides—north, east, and west—the tree-clad hills rose sharply, cloaked in the brilliant green of new foliage, but the ground of the valley floor was flat and dotted with brush. The sky was as blue as a paladin's eye.

The maple was in full bloom, and thin yellowish flowers streamed down around him on the soft breeze. Toede's nose twitched from the blooms, and he sneezed, explosively, expelling gouts of dust from each nostril.

No doubt about it, thought Highmaster Toede, sniffing. I'm in the Abyss.

Toede rose and padded down to the bank of the stream, kneeling over it and splashing water in his face, wiping the dust and pollen from his eyes. He drank a bit from his cupped hands. The water had that bitter, cold taste of freshness that always made Toede queasy, but any refuge is a relief, as his departed mother always used to say.

As the water stilled from his libations, he looked down and saw himself full in the face: a weak chin tucked beneath two blubbery lips that ran from ear to ear; a pallid complexion that would make an undead look positively perky; limpid, saucerlike eyes (now rimmed in red) placed against a sloped forehead and topped by a hairline that receded all the way to the back of the neck, bracketed by drooping ears tufted with stringy gray locks. Toede smiled, and his teeth flashed in sharp triangles, filed in the traditional hobgoblin manner.

"You handsome devil, you," said Toede aloud.

It was then he noticed his clothing. Worn finery beneath a chain and plate shirt stretched over his portly, malformed frame. Huge shoulder plates imitated the fashions of the dragon highlords. The armor had been specially made, modified from a suit that had belonged to a dwarven tax-dodger.

His hunting clothes. He had been hunting? Somewhere along the line he had lost his weapons.

And with that Lord Toede remembered the hunt, the final hunt.

It had been Groag's idea, really. Highmaster Toede, master of the city of Flotsam, had been bored with life at court, bored to tears. Nothing seemed to hold his interest, not feasts, nor entertainment, nor even the occasional interrogation of suspected rebels. Groag had been one of the hobgoblins of the court, a preening, spineless little flunky with the talent of agreeing to everything Toede said. In a rare moment of independent thought, the smaller hobgoblin had suggested a hunt.

And so they went hunting. Toede, Groag, and most of the highmaster's hobgoblin retinue, along with some human servants. Toede had left his normal mount, Hop-sloth, behind and was mounted on his jet-colored war stallion.

A pair of kender were the prey, Toede remembered, Kronin and Tal-something. Rebellious poachers. Led them on a merry chase through the woods south of Flotsam, too. Kender were a miserable, dangerous breed, and kender poachers doubly so. Toede's party had shackled the two together and still the kender ran rings around them. Over the hills, into the briars, through the woods, and at last to the cave.

A cave. That thought stopped Toede for a moment, and his brow furrowed. And what happened next?

The kender were in the cave. They went in to flush them out, and . . .

And . . .

Then it hit him, rocking his memory like a large stone dropped from a balcony. A dragon. There was a dragon in the cave. A wild and feral creature, not one of the pets the highlords kept. They had sent the dogs in, thinking the kender were within, and they had awakened it.

His bodyguards scattered under the dragon's assault. Toede tried to rally them, but by that time the dragon had overtaken him. The beast reared over him, there was the sudden white heat of the dragon's breath, and . . .

And . . .

And nothing. Absolutely nothing. Blackness, darkness, an Abyss of lost memory.

No. There was the dream—great and powerful figures looking at him, talking in unknown tongues, a gibberish

of godspeak. One message. "You shall live like a noble."
Then dawn at the edge of this unpleasantly pleasant
stream.

What happened? Had he fainted? Perhaps he blacked
out from the intensity of the heat and lay prone as the
dragon passed over him? Or even wandered off in a daze?
Maybe Groag, or some other faithful retainer, seeing his
meal ticket endangered, had dragged him to safety, then
went looking for help.

Maybe. None of the options felt exactly right. The mental block, a great icy black chunk of lost time, remained in
place, resistant to any attempts to pry it loose.

Toede thought about it for a full two minutes, a long
time in hobgoblin terms to be devoted to anything not
directly connected to violence. Well, nothing to be done
about it at the moment, mused Toede. It would come back
to him, probably when he least wanted it.

Besides, if Groag had gone for help, there was a good
chance that the courtier had become lost. Even by a hobgoblin's standards, Groag was a waste of a spot at the dinner table. All that fancy finery, the rings, the jewelry, the
snuff, was like gilding the pig, in Toede's opinion. Groag
was still a hobgoblin beneath it all. If it were not for the
fact that Groag had been so good at groveling and fawning, Toede would have tossed him to Hopsloth, or to the
sharks, a long while ago.

Toede sighed and looked at the sky. Still plenty of daylight. His gaze fell on the stream. The sharks had made
him think of the sea. And all streams run, eventually, to
the ocean. By following this one he should reach something that resembled civilization.

Heaving himself slowly to his feet, he began padding
south along the low grass of the stream embankment,
pausing only occasionally to kick the petals off a clutch of
wildflowers.

Near the sea is where my throne lies, Toede thought.
Ignoble Flotsam, a city-state of bandits and pirates and

rummies, humans and kender and less-polite races, a clearing house of corruption and thievery. Home. The first building block in what the highmaster already thought of as the Greater Toede Empire.

Long ago there had been the cavern encampments, the brawls, the savageness of his youth. He had survived by his brains, back then, by pitting one rival against another until he was regarded by all as the next natural leader of the tribe . . . after his mother died.

Toede slowed for a moment in his walk. Poor Mother. He still remembered the day when the representative of the dragon highlords had arrived, seeking battle-fodder for their wars against the outnumbered human kingdoms. Mother wanted nothing of it. "Hobgobs live free on their own and die free," she kept repeating, as if it meant something of import. The highlord's man said he would wait until dawn for an answer. They argued long into the night, Toede, his mother, and the rest of the tribe. Toede wanted to take the offer; his mother was adamant against it. At last they settled their disagreement in the traditional hobgoblin fashion.

Toede closed his eyes and imagined his mother, standing there in that ancient, uncleaned cave with a bone-handled knife jutting out beneath her heaving right bosom. Her porcine eyes had gone wide; her mouth, already filling with blood from a punctured lung, gurgled a curse. Then she pitched over backward.

Toede opened his eyes and laughed to himself loudly. A half dozen frightened frogs leapt into the stream in surprise. The look on her face! Hilarious!

Well, of course the tribe entered into the service of the dragon highlords, with the condition that Toede himself be trained to lead them in combat. This meant that most of the tribe ended up thrown away in some forgotten battle, while Toede groveled to the higher muckety-mucks safely behind the lines. A little bootlicking, and some character assassination, and soon he was one of the top flunkies in the chain of command.

It was then he noticed that most of the successful humans were like successful hobgoblins—they chose their lackeys from those who would be unlikely or unwilling to replace them. The same political skills that had served him so well in the tribe he wielded here, and wielded them so well that he became the chief aide-de-camp of a highlord himself, Old Verminaard.

Toede sighed at the memory. Those were the days. A little murder, a little spying, a little slaving—no, that particular job didn't pan out as well as he had hoped. If only he had been given decent help, maybe he could have held on to those Solace slaves: Riverwind, Goldmoon, and that gold-skinned youngster, Raistlin. If only he had held on to those slaves, then things might have been different. Ah, well.

At least Verminaard had the good grace to perish in battle with those aforementioned luminaries. A carefully phrased report, a quiet tour watching over the conquered and burned landscape, and Toede had moved on to Flotsam for a new posting.

It was the only thing the highlords could do with someone of his talent. It wasn't as if they could suddenly put him in charge of a wing command, or ask him to lead an army into battle. They *tried*, at the close of the war—a brevet command to highlord of a dragon wing, a temporary position at best.

But the real work (and real dying) was done by human subordinates, and within days the highlords found a suitable replacement on the field. No, Toede was of more use far from the action, and Flotsam was a quiet enough backwater that they risked little of the war effort by leaving him in charge there.

Of course they had to give him his own mount, a frog-dragon crossbreed named Hopsloth, and a draconian advisor named Gildentongue, and all the perks. It was a pleasant sinecure, for the most part.

Then the evil dragons fell in on themselves, and it suddenly became important to hang on to what you had. The move to remain behind, to not lead a dragon wing into combat, suddenly seemed to be puissant wisdom. Quickly the sleepy little seaport had a lot more to do with piracy and rogues and all the other evils that inhabited those later days, and more than ever needed a capable administrator.

Toede smiled again, for he had been dealt a good hand, even if he had a devil of a time getting taxes collected and keeping the human chattel in line. And those kender in the hinterlands, always poaching and raiding.

The thought of kender brought Toede back to the real world. With his own retainers and guards driven off, kender might be anywhere, lying in wait to ambush him. He was suddenly painfully aware of his unarmed status. He'd bring a pretty penny in ransom, he would, the highmaster of Flotsam.

No, live like a nobleman. High *lord* of Flotsam. That's what he should be called. With the dragonarmies squabbling among themselves, nobody would begrudge him. He liked the sound of it. It had a nice rhythm. *Lord* of Flotsam. Lord of *Flot*sam. Lord of Flot*sam*.

He already had his own court and his personal guards, though most of them had scattered before the dragon. Toede snorted again. The cowards! He'd see each one of them tortured. No, publicly flogged. Human nobles were into that kind of spectacle, and it would show he didn't play favorites among his own race.

Lord of Flotsam. Lord of *Flot*sam. Lord of Flot*splash!*

The shock of cold water snapped him out of his reverie as the ground opened up before him. Toede had stepped into a small, shallow pool of water. The vale here widened and the embankment lowered, such that the stream became a wide marsh, dotted with water-filled sinkholes. One such sinkhole had positioned itself in Toede's path, and inconveniently he had tumbled into it.

The water, only knee-deep to a normal man, rose to Toede's hips, completely soaking his leggings and boots.

With a curse, and a remonstration on keeping his mind on matters at hand, Toede scrambled out of the hole in a less-than-lordly fashion and surveyed the land ahead.

The grass grew thicker and was dotted with tails (of cat and horse varieties) as the sinkholes joined together to form a solid, impassible marsh. From Toede's (admittedly low-level) viewpoint, there was no sight of relief or dry land ahead. So much for the theory of all streams leading to the sea. With another curse, Toede turned toward the left-hand, eastern ridge and began to carefully navigate his way along the edge of the swamp.

This land would have been perfect for Hopsloth, thought Toede, with another sudden wave of emotion and nostalgia. He truly missed his assigned mount, a behemoth amphidragon the highlords had granted him when he took over Flotsam. The beast was a fat, sluggish, warty creature, a twisted melding of dragon and amphibian, inheriting the worst of both worlds. Hopsloth had a wide mouth, an insatiable appetite, a pea-sized brain, and a lazy demeanor. Not surprisingly, Hopsloth and Toede had found common ground at once, and the beast responded well to his orders even if it confined its comments to the deep-seated, belching ribbit or two.

But no, Toede had decided to take a battle stallion on the hunt (and the dark gods only knew where the blasted horse was *now*). If he had Hopsloth, perhaps he would have avoided all the rest of this mess. He hoped that the courtiers at his manor house remembered to keep his pet well fed. Hopsloth got positively peevish when he was peckish.

The land rose beneath Toede's feet, and he climbed the ridge. About halfway up, the trees began in earnest. Toede turned to look behind him, and saw that the marsh had become a swamp that evolved into a full-fledged lake, without a single sign of sentient habitation or obvious outlet. With a sigh he continued up the hillside, cursing his cowardly courtiers, his runaway stallion, the poaching kender, Hopsloth, Mother, Groag, Verminaard, slaves, and anyone else he could think of. He had reached the top of the hill when a breeze wafted a distinctive smell up toward his sensitive nostrils.

Now, Toede had all the weaknesses of a hobgoblin. Bright lights hurt his eyes, and subtle noises were lost on his battle-dimmed ears. But all hobgoblins retained their sense of smell and taste (if not good taste) throughout their adult lives. Particularly for food.

And that was what Toede smelled now, a goose, no, several geese by the strength of the scent, roasting on spits over an open wood fire (a cultured nose could tell by the amount of fat dripping down on burning logs). He had found someone, and what is more, that someone had had the good sense to cook a meal.

Toede's stomach growled in confirmation. It seemed like it had been ages since he last ate.

Toede quickly followed the scent down the far side of the ridge, careful to move with as much grace and quiet as he could manage. Just because it was food did not mean that it was friendly food. It could mean he'd found his runaway entourage . . . or poachers.

The brush and undergrowth thickened, which helped keep the small highmaster hidden until he was almost upon the encampment. He closed to within sight of the camp, then moved counterclockwise along its perimeter to a point where he could get a good view, careful not to be seen until he could determine the true nature of those within.

They *were* poachers, and kender to boot. There were about two dozen huts in a rough circle around a central fire. The huts were made of light willow saplings bent into hemispheres and covered with skins and bull rushes. A few of the kender were lolling about in typical kender fashion—dressed in shirts and leggings made of tanned hide, accented with small flourishes like feathers and bits of metal. The fire itself was a good-sized hearth of stones, indicating this was a semiregular campsite he had stumbled into. A half dozen geese had been dressed and were hanging from tripods over the campfire, their dripping fat causing the tongues of flame to spit and dance. A portly female kender was berating a slower, larger (larger to her, smaller than Toede) creature who was bringing wood for the flames.

Normally Toede would have continued around the encampment, looking for a clear trail out, ignoring his stomach's rumblings. He *would* have, but at that moment the larger creature dropped the pile of wood he was carrying, and Toede saw his face. A very hobgoblin face. Groag!

Toede was stunned, but only for a moment. Groag's face was thinner, leaner, and not as well tended as Toede remembered, but nonetheless it was his former courtier and chief bootlicker. Same lumpish head, chinless face, and beady eyes that were common to Toede and all hobgoblins, but in addition a nose that looked like it had been flattened by a rock, and a black mop of hair cut bowl-fashion at ear level. Groag's finery had been stripped of him, and the hobgoblin was dressed in worn, tattered buckskins that looked like they had been patched together from several kender's throwaways.

The hobgoblin was shorter than Toede and (in better times) wider, but his presence next to the child-sized kender made him look like an ogre-sized creature next to a human. Groag was nodding dumbly as the kender cook lectured him on some matter of wood hauling. It was then that Toede noticed the manacles on his former lackey's ankles and wrists, and the thick chains that linked them together.

A white fury exploded in Toede's heart. If anyone had the right to toss his servants in irons, it was him, not some ragtag collection of poaching kender. The insult was incredible, he fumed. He should come back after dark and free his companion. This made proper sense, since Groag would probably know the best route out of these marsh-lands.

At least he should warn Groag to expect something, thought Toede, to prepare for an escape. Careful not to reveal himself too much, Toede attempted to signal his former courtier. Fortunately, the kender cook had her back to him, and no other natives were in sight. Toede waved, trying to catch Groag's attention.

Groag looked directly at him as Toede waved, and his piggy hobgoblin eyes widened. Toede placed a finger to his lips and quickly pantomimed the sun going down, then pointed at himself, then at Groag, then made walking-finger motions to show the pair of them escaping.

Repeating the motions a few times, Toede expected Groag to nod in agreement, or at least to look puzzled.

What Toede did *not* expect was for Groag's eyes to roll up in his pointed little head, and the smaller hobgoblin to pitch backward in a dead faint, sending kindling scatter-ing in all directions. Yet, this was exactly what happened.

As he ducked back into the brush, Toede did not remem-ber if he'd cursed aloud at Groag's reaction. Of all the foolish, stupid things to do! Fainting at the first sign of rescue. There was nothing to do for it but to get out qui-etly and come back later, hopefully with a detachment of guards and Hopsloth.

Toede began backing slowly away, careful to keep as much vegetation between himself and the fire (and the cook calling for aid with a fainted hobgoblin) as possible. He thought he had cleared the area when he felt the sharp point of a dagger placed expertly between the links of his chain shirt.

"Sure and now," said a high-pitched, definitely kender-ish voice, "you wouldn't be leaving us without joining your friend." The pressure from the dagger point grew, and Toede cursed again.

Then Toede raised his hands in surrender and began walking, slowly, back into camp.

Chapter 2

In which Our Protagonist and his faithful servant have a chance to get reacquainted, and are reminded why they did not miss each other too terribly much. However, an opportunity arises before their reunion results in a homicide.

Groag awoke with a head full of bees, his face and hands still tingling from the shock. Had to have been heatstroke, he thought, grasping for consciousness. All the work, all the labor, all the pain—that was the only rational explanation.

The real world swam back into view, and he found he had been carried back to his own hut. His chains had been threaded through the iron bolt driven into a large rock positioned at the hut's center. He could move about the hut in relative ease, but any further escape was impossible. As usual.

It was still morning, evident from the slant of the light through the doorway bars, light that illuminated the other occupant in his hovel, similarly chained and shackled and securely moored to the anchoring stone.

Toede scowled at him and said, "Well, thank you so *very* much."

Groag's eyes rolled up in his head again, and the darkness reclaimed him. He pitched backward.

Toede sighed and grabbed the water bucket and ladle

placed by the door. He waddled over to his prostrate companion, pulling a ladle full of the cool swamp water. He stood there for half a moment, as if considering the consequences of his intended action. Then he drank from the ladle, set it aside, and poured the water from the bucket over his companion.

Groag awoke with a start, spitting and cursing.

"That was your wake-up call," said Toede smoothly. "Do try to stay conscious for a while."

"You're alive!" sputtered Groag.

"Ah, observant as ever," said Toede. "I can see why the poachers kept you to gather their wood. You've been out a full hour, you know. And unconscious, you're neither entertaining nor enlightening."

"I mean, you're dead," said Groag. "I mean, you're supposed to be dead."

Toede scowled deeply. "Dead! Do I look dead?"

"Well, not now," said Groag, looking hurt and ashamed. "But you were, I mean, *are*. You're not one of those zombies the necromancer keeps, are you?"

"My dear Groag," said Toede in his best axe-is-about-to-fall voice. "We are in sufficiently serious trouble as it is. Now is not the time to go delirious on me."

"I'm not delirious." Groag shook his oversized head. "I mean, I think I *am* delirious, but because you're here. I mean, I *saw* you die!"

"Do I look dead?" said Toede again, a little taken aback by Groag's vehemence on the subject.

"Well, not at the moment," said Groag. "But . . ." He let the word drift off.

A silence fell between the two hobgoblins. Then Toede sighed and said, "Let's entertain the fantasy for a moment. How did I die?"

"There were these kender . . ." started Groag.

"I remember the kender," interrupted Toede.

"And there was this dragon . . ." continued Groag.

"And I remember the dragon," added Toede.

"And the dragon breathed on you and boiled the fat from your bones!" finished Groag.

"Ah," said Toede, standing. He began to pace the small hut, the leg shackles causing him to clank in the process. By the entrance, he turned and pointed at Groag like an accuser in court. "Ah. Here's where our remembrances diverge. You saw *what?*"

"The fat being boiled off your bones," repeated Groag, more timidly.

"The *fat,*" said Toede.

"Yes." Groag nodded.

"Being *boiled,*" Toede continued.

"Uh," said Groag, "huh."

"From *my* bones?" finished Toede.

Groag shrugged. The way Toede put it, it did sound a little foolish.

"You're *sure* it was *my* fat being boiled?" said Toede sharply.

"Well, it was wearing *your* armor," said Groag defensively. "The fat, I mean."

"And from that you assumed I was *dead,*" snarled Toede.

"Well," said Groag, pursing his forehead and lips, "I think it was a fairly, uh, logical assumption."

Toede stared at his fellow prisoner in stony silence.

"Did I mention you left your armor behind, too?" added Groag.

Toede dismissed the argument with a wave of his hand. "Here's what must have happened. I must have been knocked aside by one of our guards. Loyal, brave hobgoblins they were. At least, *one* of them was."

"They had all fled by that time," said Groag quietly.

"And it was that lone courageous guard that suffered the brunt of the blast, giving his life to save me," continued the highmaster.

"There was only you left," said Groag.

"Then you fled the scene without confirming it was I

with the fatless bones, eh? Until I came to and found you here," Toede finished with a clanking flourish and smile. He did not expect applause, but it would have been appreciated.

"Then, milord, where have you been for the past six months?" asked Groag sheepishly.

The smile on Toede's face cracked and dissolved. "Six . . . months?"

"It has been six months since the hunt when you d— when someone or something that I and everyone else thought was you died," said Groag, eyes wide. "It was autumn's twilight, then, and now it is spring dawning."

Toede sat down with a clank of chains. "One mystery resolved," he muttered, "and another rises to take its place. Amnesia? Some kind of magical effect? I don't think that we're going to find the answers here. Six months, indeed. Well, then, what have you been doing for six months?"

He stressed the 'you' to accent that everything Groag said was probably preposterous.

Groag looked miserable as he was brought back to the here and now. "Well, after you, er, somebody died, I ran like the rest, and carried the news of, er, your death back to Flotsam."

"Except I'm not dead," muttered Toede, though more quietly than before. He hastened to add, "I assume there was a massive outpouring of grief."

"The festiv . . . ah, mourning ceremonies lasted several days," said Groag. Toede nodded, while his companion took a deep breath and continued.

"Then the kender started putting stories out about how they tricked you into getting yourself killed. They were mostly true." At this Toede shot him an icy glare, so Groag quickly added, "As truthful as kender ever are, of course, with their half-statements and innuendo and rumor and everything." Toede motioned Groag to continue. "I had had my fill of these tales, and at one point went after the kender spreading the lies, Talorin, Kronin's friend. Chased him into the forest, and, ah, got lost for my trouble. Couldn't find my way back and nearly starved before Talorin and another kender, Taywin, Kronin's daughter, rescued . . . er, captured me."

"Groag," said Toede, shaking his head, "you were ever the most hapless of my retainers. You could get lost in a water closet."

Groag ignored his fellow prisoner and continued. "I pleaded to be released, but they hauled me here to their camp, and I have been their most abysmal prisoner ever since." Groag held up his chains and shook them for emphasis.

Toede had an image of Groag begging for mercy, pulling every stunt, promising every devotion, and plucking every heartstring to save his hide. Yes, Groag would gladly grovel—he had done it before.

"Have they . . . tortured you?" asked the highmaster hesitantly, thinking of his own favorite amusements and wondering if the kender matched up.

"Worse," sighed Groag. "Were they merely to torture me, I would respond with good hobgoblin stoicism."

At least for the first five seconds, thought Toede, but said nothing.

Groag continued. "No, they were far, far worse. They tried to . . . tried to . . ." His face twisted as he attempted to spit out the words. "*Rehabilitate* me!"

"No!" Toede tried to look shocked.

"Yes!" Tears began to pool at the corners of Groag's eyes. "They keep talking to me about how it's not my fault that I was born into a misshapened shell with the manners of a bloodthirsty wolf and things like that. And that I should aspire to be better than I am."

"Meaning 'more like them' I suppose," sniffed Toede.

Groag went on. "And they don't really yell at me, but they do explain things real loud when I'm wrong. And they say how disappointed they are when I do something bad."

"You mean, like twisting the heads off one of their young?" suggested Toede, with a smile at the thought.

"Er, more like forgetting to turn the goose and letting it burn," said Groag quietly. "I feel horrible to disappoint them. Sorry."

Toede just shook his head.

"And every now and then Kronin's daughter comes by and we go . . ." His voice sank below audible levels.

"Yes?" prompted Toede.

"We go . . ."

"Yes?"

"Berry picking!" sobbed Groag, clutching his mis-shapened head in his hand. "And . . . and . . . she reads *poetry!*"

Toede mouthed the words "berry picking," and walked softly over to his sobbing companion. He placed a firm foot on Groag's shoulder and shoved him, hard, back-ward. Groag went flailing in a flurry of chains.

"Berry picking! Poetry! Burning geese!" shouted Toede. "You're a sad excuse for an evil humanoid, Groag! Think about it! Any other member of your tribe would have opened his veins by now in embarrassment, or tried to tunnel out of this predicament with his teeth if need be. If anything, you're even softer now than you were when you were in my court! Well, I'm not going to follow your example. I'm going to get out of here one way or another."

Muttering, Toede stalked back to the opposite side of the hut, which he already thought of, in the first day of incarceration, as "his" side. *Trapped in a small hovel with a spineless fool who thinks I'm dead,* he thought angrily. *Was dead. Yet if I was dead, why am I now alive?*

The icy block of blackened memory remained. The heat of the dragon's breath blistered his skin, Toede remem-bered that. And the shadows of the ghostly god-figures surfaced briefly, promising great things.

Toede shuddered. He glared at Groag, pulled himself back up to his seat, focused all his anger on the other hobgoblin. When it became clear that Groag was not going to burst into flame or otherwise disappear, Toede reopened the conversation, saying, "And . . . ?"

"And what?" said Groag softly.

"And did they commission a monument to me after I . . . after it *seemed* like I died? In Flotsam, I mean." The corners of Toede's mind tried the idea of death on for size, even if it was an uncomfortable fit.

"Ah, not exactly," said Groag.

"A statue perhaps? Something modest and dignified?"

"No, not a statue. . . ." said Groag.

"A plaque, perhaps, commemorating my long and just rule?"

"I'm afraid not." Groag shrugged.

Toede felt the anger building again. "Anything at all to mark my . . . passing?"

"Well, a proclamation . . ." began Groag.

"Ah, well, that's something," said Toede, softening a moment. "A memorial holiday in my honor, then."

"Not exactly," sighed Groag. He concentrated on a point beyond Toede's left shoulder. "The proclamation said that all hobgoblins were banned from Flotsam now that you were dead," he said, very quickly.

Groag closed his eyes tight, waiting for another explosion. After half a moment, he opened them to see Toede sitting there, calmly, in deep thought.

"Highmaster Toede?" said Groag softly.

"Who?" said Toede, his voice stone-level.

"Who what?" prompted Groag quietly.

"Who made that proclamation?" snarled Toede. "Who is going to die for his temerity and stupidity!"

Groag rocked backward just far enough to be out of arm's reach. "That would have been Gildentongue, your draconian advisor. I understand that he is involved with some cult or another nowadays, but at the time . . ."

Toede missed most of the words after "Gildentongue" and was already on his feet, ranting. "*Gildentongue!*" he shouted. "That cheap gold-plated draconian has *my* job? My throne? That lizard hasn't got the political savvy to tie his own bootlaces without checking with the dragon highlords! No doubt about it, we're getting out of here, and going to set that little piece of scalework straight!"

"Please, Highmaster Toede," said Groag, "your voice carries."

"That's *Lord* Toede, as in Lord of Flotsam," shouted Toede, ignoring Groag's plea for quiet. "When I get hold of that Gildentongue, I'm going to take a long pole with barbed hooks and shove it down his throat, pulling it outward so he can see his own intestines before I pop his eyes out and use them as billiard balls! And then, while he's twisting in his own blood, I'm going to call in the manor guard for some spear practice, then I'll call in a team of hobgoblin tap dancers, and then . . . and then . . ."

It was about this time that Toede realized that he and Groag were no longer alone. Halfway through his ranting someone had pulled the bolt free on the hut door, and now a young female kender stood there, framed in the morning sun.

She was frail and beautiful in the childlike way that all kender seemed—children who had run off and stayed young by hunting and fishing and living in the wilderness. She was nearly as tall as Toede and half his weight, and was poured into a stylish set of buckskin pants and a loose cotton shirt worn open to the third button. Her boots were custom-made and mud-spattered. A beaming smile dimpled her cheeks, and her fine-boned face was framed in a halo of auburn-red hair. She carried a large wicker basket at her side.

Toede hated her at once.

"Mister Groag, I see you're feeling better," she said, her voice a chirping warble, which to Toede sounded like a sliding cat trying to get purchase on a slate roof. "And your friend is in good voice, too, though he sounds a tad grumpy. Does he want to come berry picking with us?"

Toede's face flushed to the color of overripe tomatoes. "His . . . *friend* would rather have himself stripped naked and fed to wild tigers than spend one moment in kender slavery! If my hands were free I'd stretch your poaching little neck far enough to hang draperies on it! How dare you imprison me like this!"

Toede expected the kender to back up, like a tentative courtier daunted by a superior's anger. Instead, the kender held her ground, such that Toede was straining at the end of his leash, his chains taut from his outstretched arms. The kender did not seem daunted in the least. In fact, she wore a small smile.

"Now, that attitude is not going to help," chided the kender merrily. "Your companion has come a long way in the time he has been with us, haven't you, Mr. Groag?" Toede heard a mumbled agreement behind him.

Toede spat and cursed, "I am not like Mr. Groag. I am a great and powerful lord, bound for ever greater greatness! Do you have any idea, any idea whatsoever of whom you are . . . you are . . ."

Toede hesitated. He was close enough to examine her jewelry in detail, and part of his mind was already involved in estimating its net worth and use. One item caught his attention and began sending messages, marked 'urgent' to the section of his mind that controlled his ranting. Finally, the rant-section of Toede's brain took a look at the message, and then at the item hanging around her neck on a small silver chain.

"Pardon me for a moment," said Toede with sudden calmness, turning back to his companion. He hissed at the other hobgoblin. "Mister Groag, this wouldn't be by any chance Kronin's daughter that I am now addressing? The one that took you captive?"

Groag nodded.

Toede continued in a low mutter. "And is that a key she is wearing right here?" He motioned to his sternum, trying not to clatter his chains.

Groag nodded again.

"And would that be the key to these locks?" he whispered between clenched teeth, motioning as gently as possible to his wrist manacles.

Groag nodded again.

"Aha," he said, and Groag saw his former master's smile widen to the point it seemed to split his face. That had always been a bad sign in the past, so Groag began to back away from the highmaster.

Toede turned to the kender girl, his smile softening slightly, his face becoming a placid plate of contentment. "I must apologize, my dear kender. I have been under a great deal of stress recently and sometimes lose my temper. I say things I do not mean, and, well, hurt the feelings of others. I'm sorry. Very sorry. Perhaps I do merely need a change of lifestyle."

The kender's smile lit up the room. Toede felt his stomach tighten in a spasm of pain at the very sight.

Instead, he locked his teeth together, fought his own rising gorge, and continued. "Do you have any idea how much I truly enjoy berry picking? Why, I'm an old, seasoned hand at it. And perhaps, if I could be so bold, might there be some poetry as well?"

"If you wish." The kender smiled with genuine excitement. "Though I thought we might go easy your first time out."

"Oh, of course," said Toede. Groag shook his head, wondering, not for the first time, if Toede were dead, and this was some strange and bewildering spirit that had moved into his body.

The young kender pulled the key from its silver chain and began unlocking their fetters from the central bolt. Only when her back was turned did Groag see Toede's face immediately cloud and small lightning bolts of anger dance beneath his deeply creased brows. The only Toede present, realized Groag, was the one that had always inhabited that body.

Chapter 3

In which Our Protagonist and his faithful companion go berry picking and attempt to part company with the kender way of life, in the process discovering the merits and perils of bungee diving and white-water rafting.

The kender's full name was Taywin Kroninsdau, at least that's what Toede thought she said when she made introductions, making mention of Kronin's name. Thankfully neither Kronin nor Talorin were immediately at hand to discern his true identity, and Toede hoped no one caught the early part of his self-identifying rant. Taywin seemed perfectly agreeable to calling him Mr. Underhill. Were the kender to figure out who they really had tumbled upon, they might try to ransom him. And that old scaleflint Gildentongue would probably rather leave him there to rot than part with one sliver of steel.

As it was, Taywin Kroninsdau nodded brightly (she was the type of semi-sentient who did everything brightly) when he introduced himself as Mr. Underhill and gave no sign that she doubted his words.

Their hut had a kender guard posted outside, a sleepy sort who seemed lazy even by kender standards, who was to accompany them along with Taywin. Toede and Groag had their chains lengthened so they could take shortened, hopping strides, with about ten feet of chain connecting them.

Taywin led the way, the large basket in hand. The two chained hobgoblins were reduced to skipping to keep up with her. The amused kender guard, armed with a particularly wicked-looking spear, brought up the rear, alongside a shag-muzzled, honey-colored mastiff. Taywin introduced the guard as Miles and made Toede shake hands politely. Introductions were not made to the dog.

The sought-after fruit hung from low, dense raspberry bushes that flanked a small river, the probable outflow of the lake Toede had seen earlier (the presence of which had forced him to stray into kender territory). The tumbling water was too small to do the name "river" proper justice, and too large and energetic to be considered a mere stream or creek. It was a whitened cascade of water about twenty feet across, thundering over falls and cresting in hydraulics, the latter being great standing waves three feet higher at the top than at the base. The spray from the water hung like a low fog, and the omnipresent dampness encouraged the bushes to bear fruit throughout the warm months.

Toede was still seething inwardly with the indignation of his plight. It took a full ten minutes for him to switch from planning imagined revenge on all kender to assessing the situation for possible escape. The water looked too rough for a chain-bound swimmer, but could throw off the scent of a party of dogs. The spray would dampen any clear sight or bow shot past a hundred feet, and the thunder of the cascades meant that any survivors would have to crawl for help rather than count on being heard crying out in pain.

The girl seemed like no real problem, and the guard was not particularly watchful. Toede realized he would have to take him out quickly, before the dog reacted. After which, there was the matter of Groag.

Toede sighed—there always was a weak link in any plan. They had been spirited out of the hut before making any real decisions as to escape, so he had to act and hope that Groag would pick up on the momentum. More likely another large mountain would hit the sea of Istar, Toede reflected bitterly as they skipped glumly alongside the water. The path was only wide enough for a single creature, and in places was devilishly slick, even for those not hampered by iron chains.

Lord of Flotsam, Lord of *Flot*sam, Lord of Flot*sam*. He repeated it now as a mantra, not a daydream.

The sun peeked out from behind the clouds about the time Taywin chose a likely place. She looked back, and Toede beamed at her, trying his best to outshine the timid Groag. If I play this right, Toede thought, they will never know what hit them. Taywin brought out a smile that gleamed in the sun in return to Toede's, but Toede was unaware of it, his eyes riveted on the key around her neck.

"This looks like a nice spot. They should be ripe enough. Mister Groag, Mister Underhill, you can start here. I have some baskets. . . ." She fished several smaller baskets from her hamperlike carryall.

"Of course," said Toede, smiling and shoving his arms wrist-deep into the nearest berry-laden bush, wrapping his fingers around a likely collection of berries in the process. The smile froze as the bush locked around him as if it were a tooth-laden vise. Shouting, he pulled his scratched hands away.

"Oh, I'm so sorry, Mr. Underhill," said Taywin, "I thought you knew about the thorns. All raspberries have thorns."

"Of course, thorns," said Toede through gritted teeth. "I knew about them, just forgot for a moment. It's been so long since I was in the field." He sucked on a bloodstained knuckle.

"Of course," beamed Taywin Kroninsdau, "there are gloves in the large basket, with the smaller berry-baskets. Oh, and if Mr. Groag was any example, there is a difference in hobgoblin and kender taste. We like the ones that *aren't* green."

"Aren't green," gritted Toede, his jaw still firmly clenched.

"I'll make a note of that."

The three of them worked the berry patch, Toede and Groag together, Taywin a little farther down, the guard with the dog watching the pair of hobgoblins. They gathered berries for what Toede thought was half an eternity but was most likely three-quarters of an hour, until each hobgoblin had a half-full basket to Taywin's full one.

"Well, you boys had better catch up. How about if I read some poetry?" she said with a smile.

"Kill me now," muttered Toede in a prayer to the dark gods.

"Beg pardon?" She blinked at the highmaster.

"I said 'silly cow.' I was talking to Groag. He made a face when you mentioned poetry."

"Mr. Groag, I thought you *liked* my poetry," said Taywin, pouting.

"But I did, mean I do, er, I *didn't*," Groag's explanation tumbled to an eventual silence as the kender pulled a small tome from her pocket. Toede turned back to his bushes, stifling a smile.

Taywin's voice was strong and clear, and did absolutely nothing to improve the quality of the poetry. Fortunately for Taywin's feelings, it was normal for hobgoblins to hate all sorts of verses above the level of obscene limericks equally, so they failed to appreciate good poetry with the same enthusiasm as bad.

Taywin intoned in her "serious" speaking voice, dropping several octaves into a humanlike alto.

> *"The knight amount swept on his horse*
> *through bracken field and brawny heath*
> *and drew his sword of N'er-do-well*
> *to face each danger in its teeth."*

Groag and Toede were working close together now, a little apart from the female kender. "I didn't make a face," whispered Groag resentfully.

"It's all part of the plan, so don't worry," Toede hissed back.

> *"He vanquished dark and dreadful lords*
> *and proved his will to fight and fight*
> *and won the hearts of all around*
> *with his fine and lordly might."*

"But I don't think it's so bad," continued Groag.

"You wouldn't know bad if it infested your nostrils and bore young," said Toede.

"But she writes it herself. I think she's improving."

"Will you forget about the poetry for a moment?" shouted Toede breathily, trying to convey his rage without increasing his volume. Taywin halted, and the guard looked over at them, spear at the ready.

Toede clanked his chains as he waved at them. "No problem, just a tuber in the way."

Taywin returned to her declamation.

> *"And so the people of the land*
> *did seek him out to cure their woes*
> *to battle dark and dreadful lords*
> *and aid them in defeating foes."*

Groag sighed again. "You think she means us when she says 'dark and dreadful lords'?"

Toede bit the inside of his mouth. "Let's concentrate, for the moment, on escaping."

"Escaping?" said Groag, puzzled.

"Yes, escaping, as in 'finding a lifestyle involving less-heavy jewelry.' " He clanked at Groag. "I have half a plan."

> *"And so the great and powerful knight*
> *did seek the great and holy quest*
> *to find the faith and fairest flower*
> *and put himself to holy tests."*

"Got it!" exclaimed Toede.

"Stuck yourself with a thorn again?" responded Groag.

Toede glared at Groag. "Got the other *half* of the plan. Be ready to move when I say move."

"Right, move when you say move," agreed Groag. "And in the meantime?"

"Pick faster. I don't know how much more poetry I can take."

Whether spurred on by Toede's promised deliverance or Taywin's poetry, the hobgoblins filled their baskets in record time. The sun had risen high, but the vale was still wet from mist when they finished.

Then the four dined on berries and a few goose sandwiches the female kender had packed. Groag volunteered the information that he had helped grind the grain to make the bread. Toede felt his smile get more brittle by the instant.

"Well, we have to get you boys back," said Taywin at length. "There are other chores needing to be done."

"Pity, it seems so . . . idyllic," said Toede with a wide smile. Groag looked at him with a panicked glance. The nicer the highmaster seemed, the worse things usually got. "Tell me, Miss Taywin, I'm confused after all this. Are we on the east side of the stream or the west?"

"The western side," said Taywin, already gathering the baskets and the remains of the sandwiches, handing the gathered collection to the guard.

"Oh . . . pity. Well, we should be getting back," sighed Toede, rising to his feet. Groag, without much choice owing to the chains, rose with him.

"Why is it a pity?" said Taywin, her cute brow wrinkling in small dimples.

"Didn't Groag tell you?" said Toede, miming shock at an apparent breach of common sense. "The best berries are always on the eastern side. They take in the dying sun, and as such blush the reddest. It's common hobgoblin lore. . . ."

Groag started to say, "I never heard of . . ." but Toede stepped in quickly, "Perhaps he was waiting to tell you later. I'm sorry if I spoiled the surprise." Toede gave a quarter turn toward his companion, his eyes flashing the threat of holy terror.

"Well, yes," said Groag quickly, "a surprise. It was going to be a surprise.

"Perhaps next time, then . . ." said Toede. "Besides, there's no way to cross this creek."

Toede took three half-steps away, then turned. Taywin was still standing there, thinking. Watching a kender gather her thoughts made Toede think of an old rain barrel about to explode from being overfilled.

"I've never heard of that business about the eastern side," said the kender at length, "but there's a log wide enough to walk across a hundred yards or so down below. We can check it out."

For the first time the guard spoke, and Toede realized why he had kept silent—his voice cracked with adolescence. "Milady, these *are* prisoners, and . . ."

"Oh, for Mishakal's sake, Miles," said Taywin. "It will only take a moment, and Daddy will be back this afternoon so there won't be that much to have them do."

The five of them (the dog padding along in last place) weaved their way down along the banks to where an ancient maple had fallen across a narrows. It had been used as a bridge before, and most of the bark had already peeled away, leaving a smooth, straight pole between opposite banks of slippery rock.

The kender ideal of "crossable" was at great odds with the hobgoblin definition of the same, or anyone else's for that matter. The water thundered about ten feet below in a torrent, squeezing between the two rocky banks before passing over a low falls and into a series of rapids.

"Better berries, you say?" said Taywin, taking the lunch basket from the guard.

The guard shook his head, "I don't think it's wise to

take the prisoners across, milady."

"If I may be so bold," broke in Toede, "but the young man, sorry, young kender is correct. In our current condition I don't think we could make it across such a narrow crossing." He held out his chained hands and cocked his head at the young female.

Taywin looked at the cuffs as if they had just that moment entered her vision. Toede could swear steam was pouring out her ears as her brain struggled to grasp the concept that two chained hobgoblins could not cross the stream. She touched the iron key that hung around her neck as if it were a holy fetish.

Then she nodded. "Right. I'll go across first and see if the berries are truly sweeter. Then next time we'll bring more guards and do some *major* picking."

With that she turned and, with surefooted ease, started to cross the log, ignoring the fact that the crossing lacked anything resembling a handrail and was slick with spray.

Toede sighed as the young kender guard stepped up next to him. "She's real smart, she is," the kender said with a grin.

"Very," agreed Toede, nodding. "I notice how she never during the entire morning got within an arm's length of me. Not like you are now."

The kender guard was about to respond, but the words (and several of his teeth) were shoved back down his throat by Toede's iron-manacled forearm.

The guard went down like a lump of suet, and Toede reached out and grabbed his spear before it hit the ground. Then he kicked the guard for good measure, watching the kender curl up in a small pain-filled ball.

The mastiff growled and was rewarded with a hard rap across the nose from the spear shaft. The hound retreated two paces and growled again, crouching. Toede raised the spear to throw it, and the dog bolted for the woods, yipping.

The kender was still down, spitting blood. Groag

looked at Toede in shock. "Why did you do that?"

"Couldn't you see? He was about to read us a poem," snapped Toede, and started dragging his compatriot toward the fallen log. "Come on."

"But we can't get very far in these," whined the lesser hobgoblin, rattling the manacles and chain between them.

Toede turned and glared at his companion. "But *she* has the key, and there are *two* of us. Now come on."

Groag said nothing, but reluctantly followed the high-master to the edge of the thundering stream.

The passage had gotten very slick indeed at the center of the beam, and Taywin had reached out her arms to both sides to balance herself. Now she looked back for a moment and spotted Toede starting to inch along the beam, shuffling sideways along the span. That was her first clue that something had gone wrong. The second clue was the fact that he held the guard's spear, about a third of the way down from its flint-tipped head, and was using it as a balancing pole. The third clue was that Toede was smiling. It was a frightening, ear-to-ear smile.

"What's wrong?" Taywin shouted to make herself heard over the rushing water. "You shouldn't come out here!"

Toede shouted back, "The guard just took ill! Bad berries! You'd better come back." Indeed, beyond Toede on the near bank, the guard was clutching his mouth and stomach in obvious pain. Groag stood about three paces behind Toede, feeding out the chain and looking worried.

Toede saw a look of concern cross Taywin's face, and she tottered, just slightly, on the slippery log. She bellowed, "Hang on, I have to turn around! It's worse than it looks." She made a quarter-turn so she faced downstream, the opposite direction as Toede.

"Here, take my hand," said Toede, reaching out with one chained limb. The other, carrying the spear tightly like a dagger, was tucked behind him. Groag followed him out onto the beam a few careful paces.

"No, you're rocking the log," shouted Taywin. "Look . . ."

The next word was hypothetically "out," but Taywin merely screamed as she pitched backward, her large basket flying in the opposite direction and quickly disappearing in the rapids.

Toede instinctively leaped for the key. However, his hands were chained together, with a second chain leading to those connecting his feet, which were in turn chained to a similar arrangement on Groag, who did *not* leap forward, at least not voluntarily. The result was that the chains pulled taut, pulling Toede's arms and legs backward suddenly, and pitching him headfirst after the falling kender.

He dropped the spear, but did manage to catch the kender with a firm grip, snaring the top of her blouse between clenched teeth. This would normally have been an extremely embarrassing situation for both of them, but at the moment such proprieties were not the top priority.

Groag, as Toede had oft pointed out, was not the brightest of hobgoblins, but as he saw the chain connecting him to the falling hobgoblin play out, he immediately realized what would happen to him. With a quickness gained by his several-months' tenure as a servant, he dropped to the log and held on for dear life.

Nonetheless, Toede and Taywin splashed into the torrent and were immediately dragged back under the log and downstream. Toede still had his arms and legs pulled tight behind him, but Taywin was already grabbing him and pulling herself up the chain to shore. As soon as she had a firm grip on the chains, the submerged hobgoblin released his jaw-grip on her shirt-front.

Slowly and painfully, Taywin clambered back up the sheer rock to where Groag stood. The hobgoblin on shore shouted encouragement and put out his foot for her to grab on to as she pulled herself up the final few feet.

Taywin swept back her matted hair and spat water, trying

to force air back into her lungs. "I owe you two my life," she said between pants.

Groag replied, "It was nothing, I . . . Oh! Toede!" and with that started hauling on the chain that had disappeared into the swirling white water and (presumably) was still attached to his former master.

"Toede?" said Taywin, shaking her waterlogged head. "As in Highmaster . . ."

"Gotcha, you rat!" shouted the kender guard, as he smacked the back of Groag's head with a good-sized, more than adequately heavy rock. The guard's mouth was coated with drying blood, and his eyes burned with vengeance. "Teach you to take a shot at me!"

Groag perforce dropped the chain and lost his grip on the log. The force of the water dragged Toede downstream and pulled Groag in as well.

Taywin grabbed for him, but her fingers closed on empty air as the pair of chained hobgoblins disappeared in the torrent.

"Serves them right," muttered the guard, tenderly touching his swelling lower jaw. Taywin's response was most unladylike (and is best not quoted, as the main thrust of the tale had moved suddenly and precipitously downstream).

The low falls below the fallen maple was little more than a bump, and after constricting into a still-smaller chute, passed through a pair of hydraulics and into a wide, fast-moving pool. Groag's head broke the water briefly, sank again, then crested a second time. Dog-paddling madly in his chains, he could barely keep afloat.

Groag felt a tug from the connecting chain. "Toede?" Groag asked, and was rewarded with a mouthful of water as he sank slightly. The small hobgoblin sputtered and dog-paddled harder. He heard nothing in response, though whether that was because of the thunder of the river or an aftereffect of Miles's well-aimed rock was unclear.

Highmaster Toede surfaced three feet away, water streaming from his nostrils in a fine spray. He looked angry, and a little afraid.

"You all right?" sputtered Groag, gaining another mouthful of cold river water.

Toede raised an iron-shod wrist and pointed at one of the banks, slightly upstream.

Groag tried to shake his head. "Upstream? Better try to make land a little downstream."

Toede pointed again, frantically.

"If we go downstream, then we have the river going with . . ." Groag's voice died out once he realized that he could not hear his own words over the increasing thunder—the sound of water falling from a very high place to a very low place.

Then it suddenly became obvious why Toede wanted to swim against the current. Groag began dog-paddling madly alongside him. Both were extremely aware that the surrounding banks of the river were slipping past them, and the thunder was growing louder, until it reverberated in their very bones.

The river erupted over a high barrier of hard shale, through a narrow passage no more than five arm-spans across. The force of the water was such that it flung itself out ten feet into the air before gravity finally got its due and pulled it into a cascading plume of white tinged with rainbow drops reflecting the afternoon sun. Also spewed out this distance were two humanoid figures connected by a length of metal chain. One of them, the smaller one, was screaming at the top of his little lungs.

The falls thundered into a quiet, wide pool of deep green. The sound of the two figures striking the water was lost, and the ripple of their splash erased by the time those ripples reached the shore.

Some time later, the two hobgoblins crawled onshore, still chained together and making small motions with their arms and legs. Both were bloody and battered, but still breathing. Water streamed from Toede's nostrils as Groag panted and cursed between openmouthed gulps of air.

"We're bloody doomed," Groag panted. "We can't run. We can barely walk. Every kender in the countryside is going to want our backsides for breakfast, and I can't say I blame them. That was the kender leader's daughter you attacked, and she's going to see us put up on spikes once the guard tells her it wasn't our intent to rescue her, and we can't move with all this iron, and why are you smiling that damned smile?"

Indeed, throughout Groag's tirade, the hobgoblin highmaster had been smiling beatifically, a canary-digesting feline sort of look. After Groag shouted at him, he paused a beat, then stuck out his tongue.

Resting on that pale pink expanse was an iron key, until recently worn around the neck of Taywin Kroninsdau.

Toede held the key up to the sun and laughed wearily. "I hope you don't feel like resting," he said. "I want to be in Flotsam by nightfall."

Chapter 4

In which Our Protagonist discovers that time has not stood still for him in his hometown, and fully realizes his own mortality, the fickle nature of those who are ruled, and the nature of his opposition.

In actuality, it took three days to reach Flotsam, caused first by a miscalculation on Groag's part as to direction, and second by a necessary evasion of a kender hunting party. The latter was seen at a distance, armed with spears and accompanied by their golden and black hunting hounds. Toede recognized neither kender nor dogs, but thought it the better part of valor to evade them.

The fact of the matter was, had the hobgoblins headed in the right direction at the outset, the kender, who set out for Flotsam immediately, would have caught up with their quarry. But since Toede and Groag got slightly mislaid, the kender patrols made it to Flotsam and back before Toede and Groag even neared the vicinity.

The second night was spent in an abandoned cottage that had not seen human habitation since before the War of the Lance. There was no food other than the lizards that Groag rousted from beneath the collapsed bed. There were a few long human-sized cloaks, easily altered by the rusted but serviceable knives abandoned in a stuck drawer. Toede had seen, lived through, and dealt out worse during the war.

But Toede could not sleep, for Groag snored a saw-touched rhapsody across from him. He considered smothering him with a pillow, but Groag's likely uses in the future stayed his hand.

Also, there were no pillows in the cottage.

The long hike had given him a chance to think about what Groag had said. For six months Toede had been gone. His armor and clothing, while beaten and singed, neither wore nor smelled like he had been wearing them for six months. Perhaps he had been dead. Or put into cold storage for six months, which was one and the same for all intents and purposes. But how—and to what end?

To return and live like a noble. Clouds passed over the wafer-thin sliver of Lunitari, and Toede thought of the shadowy giants and the promise they had made to him in his dreams. He *would* be treated like a noble. Well, obviously not at the moment, in the tumbledown cottage, but once they reached civilization. Once they reached Flotsam.

After they reached Flotsam, then what? Obviously, when confronted with a highmaster in the flesh, Gildentongue would have to step down. Although since Toede wasn't truly a high *lord*, officially recognized as such, there might be question of his right to rule. The perils that a lack of nobility caused were obvious to the hobgoblin.

Perhaps he would have to call in his favors with the true highlords, and the dragonarmy itself, still billeted in the northern half of the city.

Ah, but Gildentongue always had a way with the great reptiles, being draconian himself. There might have to be a few bloody discussions in the barracks, but in the end, Toede had a dragon (of sorts) in Hopsloth, and Gildentongue would be vanquished.

Perhaps after all this, the highlords would grant him a real, permanent title, and award him Flotsam as his enfiefment. His own duchy. Perhaps that's what the dream meant.

Duchy of Flotsam. Duke of Flotsam. Had a nice ring to it, he thought, leaning against the windowsill.

He was still writing his acceptance speech and ordering his first series of retributive executions when Groag shook him awake. Dawn had broken, and far in the distance, there were dogs baying.

Now was the time to move on, Toede thought, to claim his rightful throne.

The land broadened quickly into the low rolling hills that surrounded Flotsam, ending finally in the bay upon which the city was built. It was, at last, territory familiar to Toede. They approached from the southeast, trundling over the low hills that flanked the city on that side. The hills had mostly been denuded, noted Toede, and rich fields of barley and wheat and plots of vegetables had replaced the wildlife and underbrush. The fields were brown earth sprinkled with the first tufts of green from the spring. When he had last ridden through the land, the grain had been a rich harvest gold, and the trees were heavy with fruit. It seemed a lifetime ago. As they topped the last low rise overlooking the city, Toede wondered what else had changed.

The pair of footsore travelers stopped and regarded Flotsam, sprawled out before them like a drunkard curled on the pavement. A low miasma hung over the city—the sum of collected exhalations, smokes, fumes, and fires of the inhabitants that even the steady breeze off Blood Bay could do nothing to diminish. The subtle stench of pirates, merchants, craftsmen, middlemen, travelers, adventurers, soldiers, entertainers, barbarians, and priests tickled his nostrils even at this distance.

Toede let out a contented sigh. Nothing had changed after all. Except . . .

"Groag," said the highmaster with a frown, "who decided to repair the wall?"

Indeed, the city wall, more of a ten-foot-high apology to

advancing armies than any real impediment to a concentrated attack, had been restored. The wall ran along on its original foundation, forming a long, looping enclosure that cradled the harbor from southern edge to northern tip. The Southwest Gate was before them, framed by thirty-foot towers. A small trickle of wagons lined up as they passed by the guards. Toede squinted and could see similar traffic snags at the Southeast Gate on his right and the North Gate across the way.

"Uh, Gildentongue," mewled his companion, figuring (correctly) that this was a proper answer for any mischief committed in Toede's absence.

"*Hmpf*," snorted the highmaster. "If Gildentongue is really in charge, it shows what he knows. Why bother with walls when you have a wing of dragons camped out within your city? Typical Draconian overkill. No sense of subtlety in the least."

"Well, now that you mention it . . ." ventured Groag in his meekest voice.

Toede flexed an eyebrow, his time-honored method of recognizing a flunky about to deliver bad news. Groag kept his eyes focused on a spot two inches in front of Toede's boots.

"I had heard from Miss Taywin—Kronin's daughter—that the dragonarmy had . . . uh . . . relocated. Up the Rugged Coast and closer to the ogre territories. Better recruits and all was what they said, but the kender laughed and elbowed each other in the ribs, and I guessed it was too difficult to maintain the army inside the city walls. Rebels and sabotage and desertion and . . . all that."

The highmaster grumbled deeply, and Groag fell back two spaces.

The growl broke into discernible words. "Then what you're saying is that there is no dragonarmy in Flotsam?"

Groag nodded, then he gave a most irritating, almost kenderish shrug of his shoulders, and added, "That's what I heard, at least."

"So much for Plan A," muttered Toede. Louder, to Groag, he said, "Is there anything else that you should tell me about my domain that I don't already know?"

Again the shrug. "I have been held by the kender for some time now, Highmaster," said Groag. "I only heard about the dragonarmy changing its base because the kender themselves threw a great party when it happened. Seems they felt responsible for the move. I remember the feast—there were twelve geese to be stuffed, and two full stags . . ."

Toede waved the rendition of the menu aside. "The barracks are empty, then?"

"Well, they're probably used for warehouses and things like that."

"But the rest of the city is still as it was. No temples to Habbakuk or Mishakal? No gods or kindly-but-powerful wizards taking up residence within earshot of the gates?"

Groag looked up, hurt. "Other than some new cult-thingie the kender mentioned Gildentongue is wrapped up in, no. I mean, I don't *think* so," he said, stressing the word 'think' as if it implied true cogitation and analysis.

"And my own luxurious manor house still stands?"

"I suppose so," muttered Groag.

"And the rock upon which it rests has not been washed out to sea?"

Groag shot back, "I do not know, O Wise Highmaster. Perhaps the next time I get captured, I'll arrange in advance for a bard to visit with the current claque?" Groag's face tensed for a moment, then returned to its normal befuddled state. "I mean . . . Milord, you must understand if I am not fully up to date."

Toede smiled, and for once it was not a wicked smile. It was the first indication of spine Groag had shown since Toede encountered him in the kender encampment. Toede was afraid his companion had been swept away by a world of goose-cooking and poetry. Groag seemed to be regaining his old manner, now that he was restored to basking in Toede's illustrious presence.

Well enough. If Gildentongue proved unwilling to step aside, Toede might need someone with the fortitude to jam a knife between the draconian's ribs. At the moment, until he could gauge his own popular support, Toede had an army of one, and that one—Groag—had to suit.

Groag returned the smile uneasily, as if he were unsure whether the highmaster was laughing with him or at him. When no immediate rebuff came from his superior, Groag relaxed.

Toede looked out at his city, still stench-ridden but wrapped behind a new cloak of stone. Even so, he was home.

"Well, there's nothing for it, then," he said. "Let's go tell Gildentongue that his master has returned."

* * * * *

Wrapped about a deep-water harbor on the western shore of Blood Bay, Flotsam was so named for its red-tinged beaches and proximity to the larger (and more crimson-tinged) Blood Sea. The original city was built from the ruins of Istar (and other pre-Cataclysm sites now covered by the scarlet ocean) that had washed up on the new shoreline. The city's name reflected both the original junk used to make the houses and the nature of its population: a collection of drifters, refugees, would-be warriors, fleeing fighters, leaderless mercenaries, merchants, corsairs, and all manner of middlemen.

The great majority of the city evinced a hodgepodge of styles slapped together with whatever construction supplies were available at the moment. The most noticeable exception was the eastern part of the town, where a rugged headland jutted into the sea, forming the safe barrier of Flotsam Harbor. Here on "The Rock" were the most beautiful homes, the finest inns, the best taverns, and of course, raised just a little above all the others, the resplendent manor of Highmaster Toede himself.

During the war Flotsam had proved a haven for rebels and dragon highlords alike, under the supposedly ever-watchful eye of Highmaster Toede. Until the day of his disastrous hunt, Toede had ruled with a combination of carrot and stick, offering benefits to those who abided by his rule of law, and punishment to those who did not. All the players quickly learned what could and could not be done within Toede's city. Trade caravans from the inland territories made Flotsam their terminus for Blood Sea cities, and the city attracted those men and women looking for easy coins. Toede's court was full of them: sycophants and inventors and adventurers with all manner of honeyed words and magical maps and wonderful ideas.

In short, individuals who made Groag look like a pillar of wisdom and strength.

Except Gildentongue. He had always been a tricky one, Toede reflected, even then. Always dealing with the dragonarmies and the highlords. Always playing politics. And subtle, always subtle, such that Toede could never pin anything underhanded or treacherous on him. Toede mused about how Gildentongue ought to resign—on bended knee or with a flurry of blades.

The surrender approach would be much preferred, he reflected. He pictured himself striding into his reception hall, with Gildentongue sitting there, signing some meaningless proclamation. The pen would fall like a lead weight from Gildentongue's hand, and the draconian's scaled face would react first with shock, then anger as the consequences of his misrule sank into his reptilian brain. Reaching for a handy halberd and uttering a great curse, Toede's unworthy successor might try to charge him. Gildentongue would take all of three steps before he was cut down by the loyal guardsmen, who would then drop as one on bended knee before their master: Toede, Earl of Flotsam.

No, that's not right, thought Toede. Gildentongue

should by rights be kept alive—if barely. Gildentongue was of the Aurak race, and dying draconians had a nasty habit of exploding. Yes, Gildentongue would be allowed to survive, and Toede would order the manor guards to perform a few experiments on the traitorous and false-hearted courtier. And chefs. Let's not forget the manor chefs.

Toede giggled at the thought. Groag shot him a sharp look, but seeing that the highmaster's eyes were not entirely focused, decided he was not the subject of Toede's musing. The highmaster sighed with relief as they passed the short line of caravan wagons awaiting inspection and entry to the city of Flotsam.

Or tried to, at least. The guards were letting foot traffic pass unimpeded through a smaller door alongside the main gate. When the two hobgoblins tried to enter, however, each of the flanking guards dropped his spear low, barring their path.

"And where are you going, Frog-face?" said the one on the right.

Toede looked up, surprised by this mode of address. The guard was human, of course, and had that gritty, unwashed nature that seemed an unwritten requisite for those humans in the service of Takhisis. Both the speaker and his companion were totally unfamiliar to Toede. Nothing unusual, since turnover was always high in the highmaster's service, but this one Toede would have remembered. The guard had a scar running down the front of his face, from above the right temple across the nose. The puckered line ended in an explosion of infected acne and scars on his left cheek. It looked as if someone had tried to carve a comet on his face. His eyes were cold and lusterless.

Toede returned the glare, feeling his own face flush with irritation. "I have business within," he said flatly, trying to brush aside the spears. The obstructing weapons held steady in front of him.

"Not here you don't, Hob-gob," snarled Comet-face.

"Since when is Flotsam a closed city?" Toede pulled himself up to his full height and tried to stare down the guard. In his full regalia, mounted on Hopsloth-back, and backed by a unit of handpicked warriors, he was usually effective. Backed only by Groag, and the pair of them dressed in ragged, badly cut cloaks, the effect was severely lessened.

"Only closed to your kind," snapped the guard. "Unless you got special permission, by the regent and the will of the Water Prophet." Toede noticed that the other guard, the silent one, touched a small disk hanging from his neck at the mention of the Water Prophet's name. "So sod off, Shorty."

"Excuse me a moment," said Toede to Comet-face. He wheeled about, looking for Groag. His companion had already fallen back a few paces. "Water Prophet? What *is* all this about?" hissed the highmaster.

"I don't know," said Groag, looking honestly confused. "I've been out of the swim for a few months, remember? Likely this Water Prophet is the cult-thingie the kender mentioned."

Toede turned back to the guard and saw that the spears had moved from blocking their entrance to pointing directly at his chest. Toede's eyes went to small slits, and he touched the tip of the spear, showing little fear of the weapon. "It has been a long journey for me, human, and I'll be the first to admit I don't look my best at the moment, but do you have the slightest inkling in your crenelated brain whom you are speaking with?" He attempted to push the spear aside, but the weapon did not budge even a fraction of an inch.

Toede now scowled and locked eyes with Comet-face. "I am Highmaster Toede, Ruler of Flotsam and Master of the great Amphidragon Hopsloth! Let me pass, or I'll have you keelhauled beneath the docks!"

At last he got a reaction. The silent guard gave a sharp

intake of breath and grabbed the little disk. Comet-face, on the other hand, brightened visibly at this revelation.

"Is that so," he replied, smiling. "Well, ain't that coincidental, since I'm really Sturm Brightblade. I just sent my armor out to be cleaned. Now get back to your lairs, Hobgobs!"

Comet-face punctuated his sentence with a sharp jab of his spear. Toede backpedaled a few paces. Comet-face advanced again, spear lowered and shouting epithets. Toede heard faint footfalls behind him, growing softer by the second, and knew that his army of one was retreating. Summoning what dignity he could manage, Toede wheeled about, shouting, "I will remember you, when I drag you out for judgment!"

The only answer was laughter aimed at Toede's back.

Groag was waiting for him behind the last wagon, out of sight of the guards. "Some help you were," grumbled Toede.

"What now?" muttered Groag.

"We wait for nightfall, then you chew through the closed gates with your teeth," answered Toede. Groag looked pale, and Toede added, "That is a joke. We both know your head would be a much more efficient battering ram. Let's try another entrance."

It was about a half mile to the Southeast Gate, and the pair took a wide swing that cut across a number of fields. To the north, the wall continued in an unbroken line, and even Toede had to admit that Gildentongue had done a fair job mobilizing the local population to repair the old structure.

When they at last came within sight of the Southeast Gate, Toede turned to Groag and said, "Right, then. You try to walk in. Don't mention me or your own name. If they give you any trouble, come right back.

"But what are you . . . ?" asked Groag.

"I'll be making a contingency plan," said Toede sweetly, and walked off toward the end of the caravan line, where an ox-drawn wain laden heavily with wheat waited its turn. The farmer, a thin whipping pole in hand, was standing by the oxen's yoke. He was already staring at the pair. The rest of the wagon crews were scrupulously ignoring the hobgoblins.

Toede bowed low, at the waist, to the farmer. The farmer smiled, the sun catching the few remaining teeth in his mouth. Groag shrugged and padded off toward the main gate.

If anything, the second attempt went more poorly than the first, no doubt because Groag lacked even Toede's skills of bluff and bluster. Specific mention was made of what body parts Groag would lose if he ever darkened the gate again. A duly chastened and threatened Groag quickly beetled to the back of the caravan line, only to find Toede waiting there, in pleasant conversation with the human farmer.

Toede looked over at Groag and said brightly, "In you go." He patted the side of the hay-laden cart.

Groag stared at Toede until the highmaster had to motion jerkily with his head. Groag climbed uneasily into the wagon. Toede looked around to see if they were being observed, then followed. Both hobgoblins burrowed into the wheat, and the farmer took his position up next to the oxen.

The wain smelled slightly of rot. The wheat was obviously the last of the winter crop. There was a rustle of hay and a low whisper from Groag. "What next?"

Toede hushed him. There was a sharp crack of the whip on oxen backs, and the wagon began to creak forward, the noise nearly drowning out conversation.

"The farmer recognized us, at least as being part of the previous administration. More brains than teeth, that one."

"What?" said Groag

Toede snarled as quietly as possible. "I told the farmer you were a former "hob-gob" notable, seeking to visit your poor, sainted mother. That sob story, and the promise of a pouch of coins, bought us this passage."

The cart stopped, and both hobgoblins fell silent. Then it rumbled forward again, and Toede resumed. "Actually, I think it was the promise of the coins that got us this far. It's nice to know some things in Flotsam haven't changed. I was also gathering information. Apparently our regent, Gildentongue, *has* set up some kind of church. What do you know of the Water Prophet?"

"Only the name," came the answer. Another stop. This time they heard an official voice loudly questioning the farmer. The words were indistinct, but Toede and Groag both felt the hay shift around them. Toede felt something definitely long and spearlike slide against his leg. The guards were no fools. They were poking spears into the hay to look for riders. The only question was if the guards were thinking in terms of human or hobgoblin size.

It appeared to be the former, since the wagon soon lurched onward. After about twenty seconds or so, Toede said again, "We should be clear, let's drop away."

Groag whined quietly, "My bones ache. Can't we just ride a while?"

Toede whispered back, "Of course. Just remember that we promised the farmer a pouch of coins. Why don't you pay the man? I seem to be fresh out."

There was a silence, then. "I see your point. We should be off."

The pair scrabbled their way to the back of the hay pile, dropping as carefully as possible from the wagon, so as not to alert the drover. They were aided by the murkiness that was part and parcel of Flotsam's existence, at least in the lower city. There could be an army of dragon high-lords forty feet away, and no one would notice. If anyone saw them (and there were several on the street who might have noticed a hay wain extruding a pair of hobgoblins), they decided to keep it to themselves. That, too, was the nature of Flotsam.

As the pair scurried into the lengthening shadows of an

alleyway, Toede was laying out his makeshift plan.

"Right, from here on in, it should be easy. We find Gildentongue and demand he hand the city back over to me. Threaten popular revolt. Threaten to bring the dragon-armies back if we have to. You may have to take a message to the highlord, but they should remember you. First we find Gildentongue."

He looked up and saw that Groag was staring down the alley. There was a crowd of people standing there, their backs to the hobgoblins, watching something in the street beyond. They were shouting, like fans at a cockfight.

Toede frowned, and the pair stalked carefully down the alley, picking their way among the debris and waste. Toede found a few crates near the entrance, and climbing them raised the pair slightly above the human heads, but close enough to the walls to remain unnoticed.

The crowd lined both sides of one of Flotsam's market streets, where normally there would be vendors' stalls and merchants hawking their wares. Some sort of pageant or parade? thought Toede. The crowd was in good voice, at least. Perhaps a public execution?

Peering around the corner they saw the cause of the excitement. A great, wagonlike bier thundered along on heavy, solid wood wheels. Twenty strong men and ogres, naked to the waist, sweated and strained against anchor-cable-sized ropes to lug it forward. Atop the bier was a whip-master and some gent in priest garb that Toede had never seen before.

And Hopsloth and Gildentongue.

"Somehow I don't think finding Gildentongue is going to be the problem," said Groag quietly.

The draconian caught Toede's eyes first, his scales glittering like ancient coins in the westering sun. His head was like that of a human-sized dragon, all spikes and whiskers and teeth, with red, cunning eyes. Most of his body was wrapped in garb similar to that worn by the priest, but of obviously finer cut and fabric: a brocaded undergarment covered by a crimson apron running from neck to ankles, bound by a sash of woven gold. Gildentongue's thin, clawlike arms were free, and he was motioning to the crowd, acknowledging their adoration, and touching the medallion around his own neck.

Hopsloth occupied the bulk of the bier and accounted for the majority of the weight. He was a huge, hulking abomination, more frog than dragon, save for thin wings situated a third of the way down his back. And his eyes. Hopsloth had dragon eyes, the type of eyes in which was revealed a malicious, independent intelligence.

Hopsloth looked miserable, Toede thought. He hated anything dry, and those sea breezes that reached this far inland couldn't be enough to comfort his brooding hulk.

They were within earshot now, and the voice of the gent in priest's garb could be heard—ragged and ravaged from trying to outshout a multitude.

"Cheer, O Flotsam!" he bellowed. "Cheer in honor of the great Regent Gildentongue, First Minion and High Priest of the Faith of the Water Prophet Holy Hopsloth. All hail to their wise and wondrous rule!"

The words all ran together in a chanted litany.

"Hopsloth?" said Groag, a chuckle catching in his voice. "Hopsloth is this Water Prophet?"

"A front for Gildentongue's takeover." Toede nodded sagely. "More than I expected from a draconian. And I'm disappointed in Hopsloth. But let's see how they react when the *real* Lord of Flotsam appears!"

Toede would have jumped down from his perch and pushed his way through the crowd, were it not for a sudden cobblestone sailing through the air, striking the chanting human priest full in the face. The human dropped to his knees, his face a mask of blood, spitting teeth.

"False prophet!" came the shout with the rock. "False god!"

Toede froze. "Trouble in paradise," he noted quietly.

Gildentongue was not taken aback by this in the least.

"Let the accuser step forward and show himself."

The rock-thrower did nothing of the kind, but the other Flotsam citizens gladly stepped back to reveal him. He was a tall, beet-faced man, and Toede wondered how much of the bravery in his blood had been fueled by grog.

Groag gurgled next to Toede, "I know that one. Used to be your cook."

Toede nodded as if he had recognized the human as well." His eyes darted from the human attacker to Gildentongue and back again.

"Step forward," said the draconian, his voice cold and level.

The human remained immobile, his eyes staring at the stones before the bier. "False prophet," he said, more quietly this time.

"Step forward," repeated Gildentongue. "Look at the face of the true prophets."

The human remained in place, eyes down.

"Look at us!" Gildentongue bellowed, and raised his hands. Twin balls of greenish flame erupted from his clawed paws and exploded, one to either side of the human.

The human looked up suddenly, staring the draconian full in the face, and froze again, like an insect caught in ice or amber.

"Step forward," said Gildentongue.

The human began a slow, lurching walk forward, as if his legs were newly made and as yet untried. His face, still locked with Gildentongue's gaze, contorted in pain.

"Kneel," said Gildentongue calmly.

The human swayed, then dropped to his knees on the pavement, hard.

"Bow," said Gildentongue. "Touch your head to the pavement in honor of the Water Prophet."

The human dipped forward and rapped his head, hard, against the pavement before the bier. Next to Toede, Groag winced.

"Again," said Gildentongue.

The human dipped again, and a sharper rap resounded along the parade route. No one shouted now; no one breathed.

"Again," said Gildentongue "Faster."

This time the human bobbed forward, and there was the sound of something breaking as he slammed his head against the pavement. Then back, and forward again, bashing his face into the blood-colored spot forming before him. By the sixth repetition, the human's face was a bleeding smear. By the twelfth, it was an unrecognizable slab of red meat.

After the twenty-first repetition, the man slammed his head against the pavement and lifted it only a few inches above the street before striking the ground again as his entire body collapsed.

"Such is the fate of those who doubt the Water Prophet," proclaimed Gildentongue.

He nodded to the whip master, who snapped his instrument over the backs of the slaves. With a grunting groan, they resumed their tugging. The bier rolled over the bloody human, one wheel crunching a leg in the process.

The crowd shouted, though to Toede's ears their enthusiasm sounded a little more strained than before. Then they surged forward after Hopsloth's passing, the first ones thinking of looting the body, the ones farther back of looting the looters.

Toede leaned against the wall. Gildentongue was flashier than the highmaster had remembered him, and crueler as well. But just as short-tempered, it seems.

Toede looked over at his companion. Groag was paler than normal, almost a greenish shade, and his hands shook slightly as he brushed the hair out of his face.

"Any thoughts?" asked Toede.

"I think," said Groag in a wavering voice, "that this is not going to be as easy as you think."

"I think," said Toede with a scowl, "you may be right."

Chapter 5

In which Our Protagonist real-
izes that his reputation and
social status has slipped down-
ward, considers the nature of
life, and demands to be taken
seriously.

By the time dusk claimed
Flotsam fully, and the small
lamp urchins scurried from
light post to light post with
their long-handled wicks,
Toede and Groag had re-
treated to the common room of a rundown inn near the
south wall.

The inn was called the Jetties and had seen better days,
none of them, Toede wagered, during *his* lifetime. The
exterior stairs and porch were rotting away, and the walls
were dirty stone, the grit of the city only barely covering
scrawled graffiti. The interior was little better, the lathe
and plaster walls pitted from numerous brawls. The graffiti artists had moved inside as well, and switched from
paint to knives, incising new designs on the dusty wood-
work.

Still, the owner, a wide, battle-scarred gentleman, had
not spit at them when they asked about rooms. That alone
put this dive leagues ahead of the last three places they
had stopped. Apparently Gildentongue had issued some
decree that this was an acceptable mode of treating nonhumans, at least when addressing anyone who looked
like Toede.

It was abundantly clear that Gildentongue held the city in the grip of fear. If the protester at the parade was any indication, the choices were death or belief in Holy Hopsloth, the Water Prophet.

The Water Prophet. Toede rolled the name around in his mouth as if it were a wafer made of hard salt. He had pieced together the entire story from a few people on the street—at least those who would talk to them.

There were three types of humans in Flotsam nowadays. First and foremost were those who would flee when Toede approached, as if he carried a blood-drenched dagger and wore nothing more than a lunatic grin. From these he got nothing. Several seemed to recognize him, and fled all the faster, clutching their small medallions as they scurried off.

The second group of humans were even more insulting. They treated both Toede and Groag as if the two had been recipients of a sudden spell of invisibility cast by a slightly demented wizard. Their eyes seemed to lock on something slightly to the right or left of the hobgoblins, and they breezed past, oblivious to their existence. Toede tried to commit their faces to memory for eventual revenge, but had to abandon this idea after the dozenth such incident. Not to mention, to a hobgoblin all humans look alike.

But there were a few in the city who would dare being seen talking to a hobgoblin. These were beggars, sailors, layabouts, and similar dredges, along with a handful of nonhuman servants who were working toting bales and sweeping streets. They would talk to anyone. Indeed, a few seemed to be talking to themselves when Toede joined their conversations.

A one-eyed goblin servant with a straw broom told him that the story of Lord Toede's death had swept through the city like a smoldering fire in dead, wet brush—slowly jumping from bard to bard, and from bar to bar, met with toasts and small smiles.

An ogre that was carrying rusted metal to the dock told

him that at first the tale was disbelieved. People thought it part of some plot of the highmaster's to draw out dissent. When a week passed without Toede's reappearance, all assumed that, whatever the cause, Toede was gone.

A woman who looked half sea elf told him about the carnival that followed, a week-long celebration that ended in a series of bloody confrontations between the townies and the local detachment of the dragonarmy. It was then that Gildentongue, Toede's "faithful" liaison with the highlord armies, stepped forward to calm the troubled waters and announce his own revelations.

A street preacher said Gildentongue revealed that Hopsloth, a unique and divine creature, had been sent by the True Gods to lead Flotsam to greatness. Toede had been Hopsloth's first student and minion but grew greedy, and sought to keep that power and wisdom for himself. Gildentongue, being sensitive to the true nature of Hopsloth the Water Prophet, shared this revelation with all, and had proved to work wonders for the city in the few months of his reign.

Gildentongue had made good his promise, acting as the Second Minion (the late, unlamented Toede being the first) of the Holy Hopsloth. The city wall was rebuilt, said one beggar. The nonhuman trash of hobgoblins and kender that roamed the streets was exiled, said another. The green dragons and their riders were sent inland to a new base, and Gildentongue's Flotsam was granted a degree of autonomy, said another. About this time the medallions appeared. Holy Hopsloth had cured the sick. Holy Hopsloth drove the sharks from Flotsam Harbor. Holy Hopsloth was an agent of the were-insects from Nuitari.

Toede took it all in, discounting the bulk of it. Hopsloth was about as bright as a bag of lampreys and incapable of communicating any advanced theology beyond a desire for his next meal. The former highmaster originally thought he had been given the beast as a joke, a satire of the highlords' own elegant dragon mounts. For Hopsloth was no more a servant of the greater gods than Toede was king of the kender.

No, Toede thought, Gildentongue has proved himself as politically astute and slime-ridden as ever. Gildentongue would have had a hard time following Toede's illustrious (if apparently misunderstood) reign. So the draconian borrowed a page from before the war and set up his own church, of which he was the mere spokesman.

Give the people a few bones and musty miracles, and you're set for life.

The pair of hobgoblins had shuffled from inn to inn looking for quarters, or at least recognition, until they had reached the Jetties.

Now Toede surveyed the room. A drunken barbarian sprawled on a nearby bench, snoring softly. A trio of domino players lazily laid down their tiles with occasional clicks. An old man with a pipe was immersed in a musty tome. A few sailors chatted and lied over drinks. A hooded priest in a voluminous, ragged robe, worshiper of some abandoned god, was propped against a far wall. The serving girl had vanished soon after the hobgoblins' arrival, and had not reappeared since.

And lastly Toede and Groag, a pair of ragged, ratty-looking hobgoblins with no appearance of nobility, or even adequacy.

Toede sighed. The good news was that it was unlikely to get any worse. The bad news was it was at the moment unlikely to get any better.

The smaller hobgoblin had vanished fifteen minutes earlier, abandoning Toede to the cold stares of the other patrons and his own dark thoughts. Toede had wrapped himself up in his tattered cloak and sulked. If sulking had a sound, it could be said that he was sulking loudly, but as it was a (mostly) silent practice, the only noise being the crinkling of his forehead skin, that dry flesh crinkled more tightly. Groag brought a pair of ales to the table, smiling.

"Where did you get those?" said Toede sharply.

"Comes with the room," said Groag, clambering up onto the bench across from the former highmaster. Neither hobgoblin's legs touched the floor, but Groag swung his back and forth, while Toede's limbs hung motionless like pieces of dead meat.

"Ah, so we caught the tavernmaster on 'leave-your-brains-at-the-door day,' " sneered Toede, "or have you forgotten that we have no money?"

Groag gave that kenderish shrug again. Toede wished his companion would lose that habit and lose it quickly.

"I . . . ah . . . have taken care of that, Highmaster," said Groag. "I showed the master of this house that I was not at a total loss in the kitchen, and he offered a trade of services for quarters."

"What you're saying," said Toede, "is that you got a job."

Groag looked hurt. "Well, if you're going to get technical about it . . ."

Toede took a pull on the ale, which slid down his throat like hot grease. His last meal (lizard tartare) had been before they had entered the city, and the liquid splashed on an empty stomach. He ran a pointed finger over the puddle left by the mug's sweat. Groag sighed, bracing himself for another hobgoblinish blowup.

Instead Toede sighed and said, "Do you remember the old days, Groag? Before the coming of the dragon highlords?"

"I remember them being cold and unpleasant," said Groag flatly.

"Bracing," corrected Toede, "and challenging."

"Violent," said Groag, "and primitive."

"Exciting," replied Toede, the ale warming him now, "and dynamic."

"Deadly," said Groag. "Nasty. Bloody."

"Untamed," said Toede. "Primal. Challenging."

"You already said challenging."

"It deserves to be said again," said Toede, slamming the now-empty mug down on the table with a hollow metallic clang. "It was a challenge. What happened to us as a people, that we have been reduced to serving as lackeys for other races, used as dragon-fodder for battles, banned even from proper cities now? What happened, I ask you?"

Groag was silent for a moment and swirled the ale in his mug without drinking it. At length he said, "Perhaps what happened was . . . you."

Toede looked long and hard at Groag. The smaller hobgoblin continued to surprise him at every turn. Meekly accepting kender masters, learning to cook, getting a job, and now this. It seemed to Toede that at any moment Groag would grow wings and fly away.

As it was, all he could grunt out was a surprised, "Eh?"

Groag leaned forward, as if to tell Toede a mighty secret. "Not *you* in particular. You in general. A lot of chiefs, shamans, petty ogre lords, and the rest joined up with the dragonarmies, coming out of the cold wilderness and discovering that fireplaces and cooked meat had a lot to recommend them."

"Of course, the thinkers, that would be you," Groag went on, "and me, kept themselves from the battlefield and let the warriors go out and fight. And die. Those that survived would have been great warriors indeed, but the masters we served used our forces as soak-offs. Throwaway troops. Units to keep the opponents' wizards busy while the real troops mopped up *their* throwaway troops."

Groag sighed and continued. "So our best, most savage warriors were thrown into a meat grinder. Those of us who talked them into it got soft, and those that went the furthest—you, me, your honor guard—got soft faster than the rest."

Groag, with a small smile, sat back. "Then we found out that the same bloody backstabbing rules applied in the cities as in our own corner of the world. But we found it out *after* everything fell apart on us." He took a long, satisfied pull on the mug. "Another?"

Toede grunted as his companion pushed himself off the bench, weaving his way to the back. Toede thought of asking for something more filling, but let the thought slip away.

He scanned the room again, a habit ingrained in him back in the "dark old times" Groag talked of. The common room remained the sleepy paragon of an inn that had seen better times. The old sage had fallen asleep; his pipe had gone out, sliding into the front of his robes.

When Groag returned with another pair of foaming mugs, Toede took a long pull on his drink and felt the warmth flow into his fingers and toes. He looked at Groag and asked, "Since when did you get so smart?"

"Not smart, Highmaster," said Groag with a small smile. "A-dap-tive. When I was in the old tribe, I worked with the old ways. When I joined up with you in your court, I adapted to the new ways. When I was caught by the kender, I picked up their ways. Now I'm back with you." Again the shrug. "The good news is that while we were out playing human games, our wilder, more savage cousins were breeding hardier warriors, so at least there's hope for the race, if not for us."

Toede was silent for a moment, feeling the blood rush through his temples like rampaging dragons. "That's the answer, of course."

"Eh?" Groag looked confused.

"Our wild brothers," said Toede. "We go back into the wild and gather a horde of them and lead them back here. Take the town by force. Gildentongue will never give it up. Abyss and Takhisis, he won't even find out that I'm in the city. Nobody recognizes me, and his guards won't even let me get close!"

"Easy, milord, you're shouting," cautioned Groag.

"And I *should* shout!" bellowed Toede, standing up on his bench. "I expect people to pay attention, to realize who they're dealing with! I am not some 'minion' of a fake god, in whose name one should paw one's collarbone in reverence!"

All heads in the common room turned to watch the commotion. The sage snorted and blinked up from his book. The dominos stopped, and the hooded priest rose from his seat, stopping briefly by the sleeping barbarian.

The innkeeper poked his head into the room and frowned. Groag smiled weakly at his new employer and grabbed at Toede's robe. It was like trying to close the door on a hurricane, and about as effectual.

"Citizens of Flotsam!" cried Toede, stepping onto the table itself and elevating himself to human level. "I have returned to my city to find it laboring under delusions of my death! Delusions that have been put in place by a false prophet and his draconian manipulator! Tell the world that Lord Toede is back, and demands that someone pay attention!"

There was a silence in the room as all froze. Then one of the domino players nudged his companion, and the companion laid down another tile. The sage fished his pipe out of his shirt front and returned to his book. The others returned to their aforementioned drinks.

Toede's face flushed an almost-human shade of pink. "Do you not hear me?" he shouted. "I am Toede, your rightful ruler! Let us storm the gates and bring down the false lord Gildentongue! Spread the word that Toede has returned!"

Again silence. Then the reprise of clacking dominos and normal conversations.

"Toede's complexion darkened to a still-redder shade, "Doesn't anyone care? Isn't anyone listening?" he bellowed.

The silence following Toede's shout was broken by a sharp twang, then Toede's left shoulder exploded in pain. The highmaster clutched his arm and found that a smooth, feathered cylinder protruded from midway in the upper arm. From where the cylinder met his flesh, a growing smear of blood stained his ragged robe.

A crossbow bolt, said one part of his mind.

You've fallen to your knees, said another part.

Someone is talking to you, said a third; you'd best pay attention.

"Hobgoblin," said the hooded priest, dropping the spent crossbow and pulling a sword, "I hereby arrest you in the name of Lord Gildentongue and Holy Hopsloth the Water Prophet, blessed be their names. You are charged with insurrection, heresy, blasphemy, and"—the human smiled at this—"imitating the First Minion, the departed Lord Toede. You are guilty of all these crimes. The sentence is death."

Toede heard Groag say, in a voice that seemed to be at the far end of a tunnel, "Of all the times for someone to listen to you."

Chapter 6

In which Our Protagonist is set upon by an agent of his opposition without benefit of a proper introduction, and decides to bring the war home to his enemy.

A blackness rose within Toede and threatened to overwhelm him. But something else rose as well, a feeling of rage, a bright red blossom against that black. He had not come so far just to die in some pigsty of a bar, like a common, a common . . . commoner.

Toede forced open his eyes and saw the human "priest."

Part of his mind made the mental correction—everyone knows priests don't as a rule use swords—so he must be an assassin or warrior or whatever. Some agent of Gildentongue's. Stars danced and glittered around the approaching figure.

The other figures in the bar had evaporated. The barbarian was still asleep on his bench, but as for the rest, they vanished within moments of the crossbow bolt striking flesh.

Toede's mind was working faster than his body. He's going to kill you, noted one part. Find a weapon, said another. Run, said a third. Do *something*, reiterated the first.

Toede's left arm had stopped sending panic signals, or at least Toede had become immune to them, for the limb now hung like a dead weight. He dropped his right hand back to his side, his knuckles grazing something metallic that rolled slightly as he jostled it: his empty ale mug.

As he fumbled for the mug, his fingers felt like they were wrapped in bandages. The human figure now towering over him raised an arm. Laughing, said one part of Toede's mind. The swing of the blade will pass right through my neck, said the second. I think we all agree that I should do something, said the third, and relatively quickly at that.

Have to find time to collect my wits, responded Toede (or at least one part of Toede's brain). His fingers closed at last over the mug's handle, and all the disparate parts of his mind united to shout, "Swing it!"

Toede brought the mug around, hard as he could. His aim was bad, and if he had been standing toe-to-toe with his assailant, he would have smashed it against the front of the other's calves, square in the protective armor shin guards.

However, Toede was not toe-to-toe with his opponent. He was kneeling on a tabletop, so the wild swing connected with the human a short distance below his belt line, which is a position not protected by buckle, armor, or anything else beyond normal cloth.

The human attacker howled. Toede could not gloat from his well-placed strike, however; he was carried by the force of his own blow off the table. His wounded shoulder screamed with pain as he hit the flagstone floor. Colors never seen in nature swam and danced before his eyes.

Toede tried to rise, but had to settle for a three-limbed crawl to put some distance between him and the howling human. At ten feet (or ten miles, he was unsure about the exact distance), he ventured a look backward.

Groag (*Groag!* shouted his mind) was fighting with their human assailant. Well, not so much fighting as dancing, trying to keep a large serving platter between himself and the assassin.

But to Toede's pain-overloaded mind, Groag did have the grace of a dancer, nimbly parrying an overhand blow with the platter, jabbing the platter's edge at his assailant, then stepping aside sprightly as a side-arm slash went wide and carved a new divot in the plaster.

To a more objective (and less damaged) observer, Groag was little more than a flurry of motion, trying everything at once to keep the assailant at bay, while scurrying for cover between the tables and benches. The small hobgoblin's face was sheet-white, but he seemed as yet unmarked.

The human's face was knotted in pain and flushed red with anger, but otherwise their assailant was none the worse for wear.

The various parts of Toede's mind held a quick confab. Run, said one part of his brain. No, the human would finish Groag off in a matter of moments, then Toede would be on his own. Then fight, said another part. No, Toede was in no shape to do anything more than bite his attacker in the shins. Get help, said that third part.

The sleeping barbarian.

Toede smiled painfully and started to pull himself slowly toward the inert form still reclining on a bench, an empty mason jar overturned nearby.

Barbarians were easy targets, thought Toede, especially if drunk or sleepy. Or breathing. A quick story about how an evil spirit had transformed itself to look like the queen's brother, and one of these shaggy-headed warriors would charge any old castle, leaving destruction in his or her path. One such as this, bare-chested, animal-skinned, bedecked with daggers and sleeping atop a scabbard with a great sword, would be a perfect rescuer. The fact that Toede was already bleeding and helpless would just further underscore his peril.

Toede reached the sleeping form and realized that Gildentongue's agent had apparently had the same thought—but much earlier. A second smile bloomed underneath the barbarian's chin, and the blood was starting to drip onto the floor in heavy clots.

Panic now seized Toede, and he looked back in time to see Groag's impromptu shield being batted from his hands and sent clanging against the far wall. Half a minute tops, thought Toede, and I will lose my army of one. And then, it will be my turn.

The barbarian was lying on his scabbard, so Toede grabbed one of the daggers hanging from the dead man's belt. He held it by the blade, as he always did for throwing.

The knives that Toede had practiced with, a lifetime ago, were weighted such that an expert toss would cause the weapon to spin in a half-circle, end-over-end, so that the business end of the blade would bury itself in the target upon impact. It was a stylish way of driving one's point home in any semantic argument, but required a dagger specially intended for such use—lean and thin, finely balanced, with just enough weight to punch through a leather jerkin.

This was a barbarian's blade, and as such crafted more for close infighting than stylish tossing. A thick hunk of ragged metal chipped to something close to an edge, then jammed into a makeshift hilt made of horn and wrapped with leather strips.

The mason jar would likely be easier to throw, but at the moment Toede did not have time to shop around. He muttered a short curse to any dark gods that may have been listening and flung the knife in the general direction of the human. Perhaps it would at least distract the human long enough for Groag to gain some new cover.

The blade left Toede's hand and flew with all the grace and delicate deadliness of a brick. It spun, as he'd hoped it would, but when it straightened it traveled with the hilt first and blade trailing. Oops.

But it was enough. The human assassin turned toward

it, either with an instinct for its approach or just looking around for Toede. The heavy hilt struck him just above the right temple like the aforementioned brick. The human's head snapped suddenly away from the impact, and the blade bonked to the ground.

The human swayed for a moment, his eyes trying to focus on Toede. Then he slowly collapsed, as if all the air had been let out of him.

Toede staggered to his feet uneasily. Groag lost no time in capitalizing on Toede's throw, and could be found beating on the human's head and shoulder with his serving platter shield-weapon. The human twitched a few times, held his hands up to ward off the attack, then dropped fully into unconsciousness.

Toede looked around. The regulars and sailors had vanished into the night, along with the old man and the domino players. The scar-faced innkeep reappeared once the noise subsided, his face trapped between the horror of what had happened and fear about what might happen next.

"Get me a healer," hissed Toede to the man.

The innkeep motioned toward his collarbone, and Toede guessed there was a coin-shaped medallion beneath his shirt.

"That was an agent of Gildentongue, minion to the Water Prophet," said the innkeep.

Toede had had enough. He snarled, "Gildentongue is the *second* minion. I am the first, and I have returned to bring my vengeance upon those who use Holy Hopsloth as a puppet. Bring me a healer. Potion. Poultice. Something to stem the bleeding and close the wound. Whatever you have, but bring it *now*."

Toede said a few other things at this point, but they are unprintable, and most were said to the innkeeper's back as the scar-faced human scurried out of the room. Toede staggered over to Groag, who was leaning against the wall, serving platter still gripped in his paws, breathing heavily, his tiny piglike eyes bulging from their sockets in exertion.

"Has anyone," said Groag, gulping for air, "has anyone said you were a dangerous person to hang around with?"

"None that lived," muttered Toede. "Good to see you haven't lost your 'savage' nature after all. He alive?"

"Uh-huh," gasped Groag. "You think I have the strength to kill a human with a dinner platter? Go ahead, you try. I'll be glad to watch."

Toede rolled the human over on his back. Thick, curly black hair and beard around an otherwise nondescript face. Another stranger. Was that because Gildentongue had brought in his own band of agents, or just that Toede never paid attention to the humans in the good old days? Toede grimaced half in embarrassment and half in pain. He unbuttoned the assassin's shirt and found a large coin-shaped locket, this one as big as a hill giant's thumbnail.

It was the first one he'd seen at close range, and he pulled it from the human's neck. The chain was good quality gold, as was the clasp. The disk was some bronze or brass alloy, apparently stamped for production in mass quantities. One side was flat, the other showing the beaming features of Holy Hopsloth. From the beatific glow of the amphidragon's face, the creature had just eaten a team of oxen. He looked fatter than ever. Toede doubted that Gildentongue even took the beast out for rides.

Toede grunted, pocketing the symbol. Groag wiped the sweat from his brow and said, "He was a fanatic for Hopsloth and Gildentongue."

"Fanatic?"

"Didn't you hear him during the fight?" asked Groag.

"I was busy bleeding." Toede realized that his fingers were growing stickier by the moment.

Groag nodded at the unconscious man. "He was shouting about how he was the messenger of the Water Prophet and all, and that he had been commanded to strike down the imposter of the minion (that would be you), and so on and so forth."

"A soak-off," grumbled Toede.

"Pardon?" said Groag.

Toede scowled. "Gildentongue must have got reports of me, or someone claiming to be me, in the city. Probably from one of the guards this afternoon. So he sent an assassin—not his best, likely, or else he would be seen as paranoid. Just a soak-off. A throwaway warrior."

Groag saw Toede's face curl into a tight ball, and was suddenly unwilling to ask his lord to share his thoughts. The innkeep returned with a pair of small vials and a short strip of cured leather.

As the scar-faced innkeeper worked the bolt loose from Toede's arm, the highmaster sat down and bit hard on the leather. Flashes of pain, like sudden, silent lightning, flickered inside his tightly shut eyes. Toede half hoped for the blackness to return and claim him, but was spared that luxury.

Then a glass vial was pressed against his lips, and a sickeningly sweet syrup oozed down his throat. The colors faded, and the blackness retreated. A second vial-load of curative potion dripped into his esophagus. The pungent aroma gagged Toede, making him think involuntarily of death by pancake syrup.

He opened his eyes and touched his wounded arm. The cloth was still sticky with his blood, but the pain had subsided. Rubbing it, he could still feel the small crater where the bolt had entered his body.

The innkeep rose. "You should go now," he said solemnly.

"We'll need some supplies," said Toede.

"You should go now," repeated the innkeep.

"You have served the minion well," intoned Toede, knowing that this seemed to command attention. "But let us consider the deviousness of my enemy, the false minion of Hopsloth, the anti-minion. His own servants will be here soon, brought by your fleeing patrons. Upon discovering you aided us, they will torture and perhaps kill you, and most definitely burn your inn to the ground. You have shown kindness to us, and I cannot allow you to come to harm. Therefore, I tell you to quickly gather a few items for us. Then we will lock you in your own cellar, if you wish, and leave, so that the agents of the false minion will find you a victim as well."

Toede did not say that, were he in charge of Flotsam once again, he would burn the entire inn to the ground just as a safety precaution, regardless of the innkeep's guilt or innocence. No sense in making the poor human worry.

As it was, the human readily nodded, and Toede rattled off a list of supplies he would need. The human said he had them available and would go fetch them.

This readiness surprised Toede, who thought that some of his requests were for items that might take some time to collect, or might cause the innkeep to leave the building, allowing Toede and Groag to rifle his remaining stocks. It occurred to Toede that the innkeep might have his own reasons for sticking to the premises and keeping his building from burning to the ground. He filed that away for future reference.

Groag had recovered his breath and was kneeling over the body of their human assailant, who was still breathing shallowly, but steadily now. "He'll be coming around soon. You want me to kill him?"

"No," said Toede. "I have a better idea."

He retrieved the heavy dagger of the dead barbarian and thumbed the point. Razor sharp, as he had hoped.

Toede then kneeled over the prostrate form of the human and opened his shirt the rest of the way, baring both chest and belly. He used the knife to inscribe two lines in the flesh of the man's chest, not cutting deep enough to severe muscle or puncture organs, but sufficient enough to break and open the skin. The first line ran from nipple to nipple, while the second ran from the center of where this line crossed the sternum to the belly button (an "outtie," he noted).

He stepped back to admire his handiwork and heard the heavy tread of the supply-laden innkeeper. The innkeep whistled low at the hobgoblin's artistry.

The assailant had a crimson *T* carved into his chest.

"He said he was a messenger, eh?" Toede said to Groag. "Let this be the message he carries back to his master."

To the innkeep he said, "You can make sure he doesn't bleed to death with one of your potions. That way he will be indebted to you for rescue instead of suspecting you of aiding us.

The innkeep nodded and said in a strained voice, "You should."

"I know," said Toede. "Now, what's the quickest way to the docks?"

Chapter 7

In which Our Protagonist demonstrates his skills in not making waves, reassuring his allies, and influencing those he encounters, and in which he benefits from the nature of Evil to hire from the shallow end of the genetic pool.

Flotsam Harbor was a wavy, smoked mirror reflecting a moonless sky. Looking into it, one could see the inverted images of Kiri-Jolith and the other constellations, small diamonds glittering against its black luster. There was a light breeze coming off the bay, smelling slightly fetid from the wastes dumped into it earlier in the day by the city's denizens. The sour wind drove small ridgeline waves ahead of it. A half dozen ships rocked slowly at the docks. The bay was otherwise empty.

The water closest to the headland sent out different ripples as a pair of small bumps broke the water and dragged themselves onto the beach. They looked like sea lions, for they were cloaked in tight, dark coverings that enveloped their entire bodies.

Almost. The lead sea lion turned to his companion and hissed for him to bring the stuff along and not dawdle. The leader's most un-sea-lionish face hovered like a pale ghost against the blackness of his shiny clothes, and had there been any moon, would have reflected it back full-force. His companion sea lion grumbled and pulled a large, black satchel behind him.

"Come on, Groag, move it," said Toede.

Groag grunted and dragged the satchel fully onto the beach. The parcel, and the two hobgoblins for that matter, were wrapped in waterproof leathers. Each hobgoblin's outfit consisted of ankle-high slippers, leggings, mittens, and long-sleeved jackets with hoods. The jackets and leggings were for larger individuals, and the sleeves and legs bunched up on the hobgoblins' short limbs. The leathers came from the hide of seals and thanoi, and were said (by the innkeeper) to have been specially treated to retain their suppleness. The entire ensemble closed around the wrists, legs, and face with drawstrings made of cured leather. The manner of dress was something a gnome might think up, but actually came from a tribe of isolated fishermen far to the south, in Ice Mountain Bay. Toede had been hoping only for a waterproof bag made of the material, but was delighted that the innkeep (for reasons all his own) had the full suits available.

Toede filed away his temptation to have the Jetties burned to the ground at the first possible chance after regaining his throne. This innkeeper was too ingenious to leave without proper governmental supervision.

Groag sat on the parcel, breathing heavily as Toede began stripping off his oilskin to reveal somber clothes—undershorts and a dark shirt—underneath.

"Shake a leg," implored Toede, hopping on one foot as he shed a thanoi-flippered slipper. Groag nodded, but moved slowly, puffing as he pulled the oilskin tunic over his head. By that time, Toede was already unwrapping the parcel, his stubby fingers flying over the cords.

First he pulled out a burlap bag, dry despite its recent submergence, and pulled from it a brocaded vest and a set of proper ankle-length pants. Sturdily made for dwarven miners, the pants were a bit snug in the crotch but were otherwise suitable for a pair of hobgoblin invaders. A pair of boots transformed Toede the seal into Toede the . . .

Well, he looked like a miner or a merchant more than anything else. Nondescript, aside from being a hobgoblin.

But, unless there were a shapechange spell available, or perhaps an improve looks cantrip, it was the best Toede could do. As Groag was grunting into his own dry clothes, Toede draped the pendant and chain taken from his would-be assassin around his neck, allowing it to hang in front of his shirt.

Toede pulled a pair of short swords, four daggers (of the proper throwing variety), and a crossbow with a small bolt case from the oilskin parcel, then two small backpacks. One clinked ominously as he hefted it. This one he set carefully down on the beach. The other billowed a small cloud of black dust as he tossed it on the sand. Toede breathed through his mouth as he swatted at the cloud, dispersing it.

Groag was not paying sufficient attention and as a result sneezed and gasped. "How did you know about this way around the Rock Gate?"

Toede began stuffing the sealskin clothing, the parcel wrapping, the cords, and the long reeds they had used to breathe underwater into the burlap sack. "When I was highmaster of Flotsam," said Toede in a sharp whisper, "I thought about how one would best sneak in and murder me in my sleep. This was the most appealing route." He followed the sealskin garb with a couple good-sized rocks.

"You figured this out?" said Groag, handing over the last of his own oilskin clothing. "And you didn't do anything?"

"Of course I did something. I told everyone that I had stocked sharks in Flotsam Bay."

Groag's eyes went wide for a moment. "But if there are sharks . . ." Groag paused as Toede stared at him, waiting for him to catch on.

"Oh, you *told* everyone you had stocked sharks in the bay," Groag said, nodding.

Toede smiled, and if Solinari had been present in the sky, it would have reflected his sharp, lupine teeth. "Head up the embankment; I'll take care of this."

Groag started to climb the headland to the upper, inhabited reaches, while Toede hefted the sack. His shoulder was a little stiff, but otherwise none the worse from its earlier piercing. He swung the bag overhand once over his head and flung it twenty feet out into the bay.

The burlap bag filled with sealskin and stones disappeared immediately, leaving a concentric bull's-eye of ripples as the only marking of its passage. Toede smiled again.

That smile died on his thin lips as a large triangular dorsal fin, as tall as Toede himself, broke water, knifing a sharp wake behind it. It moved to the impact point of the burlap bag, then dove beneath the surface.

Toede rubbed his neck. "Hope you choke on it," he said, and quickly followed Groag up the slope.

* * * * *

The headland of Flotsam, known in those days as the "Rock," jutted from the southern shore like a poorly mounted incisor erupting from a dragon's jaw. Cliffs on the seaward side protected the land from the bulk of the Blood Sea storms. The peninsula was about five hundred feet across at the widest, and was the home of the wealthier merchants, more moneyed travelers, and, of course, the city rulers. The Rock was cut off from the rest of the city—the Lower City, more of a financial demarcation than true elevation—by a heavily garrisoned fortification across the neck of the peninsula. This barrier was known (imaginatively) as the Rock Wall, and broken only by the (equally imaginative) Rock Gate.

The first thing Toede noticed upon reaching the top of the cliff was that many of the original larger buildings had been converted to barracks. Brackets that once held tavern signs were now empty, flower boxes were absent, and lower windows were barred or boarded over. The wrought-iron furniture of outdoor cafes had disappeared. Instead, there was the emptiness of a parade ground at midnight, when all the soldiers are either at their posts or asleep.

Toede smiled. Obviously, once Gildentongue had convinced the local dragon highlords to leave the city in his care, he had to bring his own people in to keep the peace. New troops were to the hobgoblin's advantage, since none of them would likely remember the late, departed Lord Toede, either by face or deed.

The second thing the dearly-departed Toede noted was that things had been allowed to run down a little, to a degree surprising even by Toede's slovenly standards. Perhaps it was only memory, but it seemed that in bygone days, the Rock had been a cheerier place.

Toede puzzled a moment before he hit upon the reason. Yes, that was it. There were street lamps, large iron constructs into which bundles of tarred hay could be fitted and set alight. Yet most now stood empty, and only one in three had been lit. The lamps in the Lower City were all lit. Money troubles at the top, perhaps?

Beneath these sputtering iron-held fires, small groupings of men clustered and talked in low voices.

Toede smiled. The thing about humans was that they feared the dark because it hampered their vision. One more reason that human kingdoms would never stand in the face of determined hobgoblin assaults.

"*Hsst*," whispered Groag from a nearby shadow. "Guards!"

"I can see that," said Toede, in a perfectly normal voice. "Now come out of there."

A pause from the shadows.

Toede, trying to be patient, shoved his hands deep in his pockets and rocked slightly back on his heels. He did not look directly at Groag's shadows. "If they see you hiding, then they'll know you're up to something. If we walk right up to them, then their first thought is 'What do they want?' as opposed to 'What are they doing here?' " With that, Toede, affecting the quick, irritated stride of a man (or hobgoblin) with important business on his mind, approached the two guards.

Groag pulled himself from the alleyway and carefully followed, noting that Toede had not offered to lug either of the backpacks. Groag's nose was already running from the dusty contents of one, and he cursed as he toted them toward the retreating backside of the former highmaster of Flotsam.

The guards, three of them, were gathered around the base of the sputtering street lamp. No trouble was expected on the Rock, and Toede timed it so that he addressed them only at the last moment, when one of them finally noticed him.

"You men! Why are you shirking about like this?" He put iron into his voice, and two of the guards immediately pulled themselves upright in an automatic response before it was clear to them who, or rather what, they were being addressed by.

The one who looked up started to say, "See here, what do you—" But Toede was already ahead of him.

"It's very important that I meet with Lord Gildentongue immediately!"

The guard started to say again, "What do you—"

Toede interrupted again. "I haven't time for this foolishness. Haven't you heard the news? Toede is back!"

The three looked at him as the information sunk in. The first one shook his head and said, "Toede? You mean Highmaster Toede? But he's dead."

"Would that it were so," said Toede, reverently touching the disk of Holy Hopsloth that he wore. "I fear the menace was playing a cunning stratagem. And now he's come back, and Lord Gildentongue, indeed, all of Flotsam, is in grave danger."

"Mehbeh we should get the sargant," said one human, with a northern accent thick enough to be cut and sold in slices.

"Mehbeh we should," Toede shot back, aping the human's tone and accent. "Come on, now, let's shake a leg. Every moment lost is a moment of danger."

The first guard held his hands out. "Now hold a moment . . ." he began.

Toede crossed his arms, tapping his foot. By this time, Groag had come up alongside him. "Yes?"

"Who are you?" asked the guard, regaining his verbal footing.

"Who do I *look* like?" snarled Toede.

Silence, then, "Well, you look like a hobgoblin." The voice held just the first trace of suspicion.

"Ex-act-ly!" shouted Toede, pointing a finger at the guard. "And who better to track another hobgoblin? I've been following him for months, ever since Lord Gildentongue first suspected Toede survived his apparent—and obviously staged—death.

"It was brilliant, I'll admit," continued Toede, "particularly tricking the kender into thinking the dragon was their idea. Turns out the dragon was in on it from the start, and Toede drove the kender in its direction so as to appear roasted and broasted, going out in a blaze of glory and not leaving much in the way of evidence."

The three guards nodded sagely at the explanation, as if that were exactly the way they would have handled the situation.

"Now," said Toede, "where is Lord Gildentongue?"

Another silence. "He's in the city," the guard with the northern accent finally replied. "Went dahn earlier t'night. He's not back yet, I dawn't think."

Toede stifled a smile behind his knitted brow and stern jaw. "And this 'sargant' you mentioned is the highest ranking officer on the Rock?" Head nods all around. "Then take me to him at once. Unless . . . you'd rather explain your delay to Lord Gildentongue later."

That got them moving. The trio, more than happy to dump responsibility on someone of higher rank for the loud, obnoxious and apparently important creature, formed an official escort for Toede and Groag to the sergeant's office.

As they crossed the streets, walking past darkened windows and a few other guard posts, Toede whispered to Groag, who was lumbering along beside him. "Were my guards this twitchy?"

"Twitchy?" came the nervous response.

"Scared," said Toede. "I almost expected them to faint when I alluded to Gildentongue's orders. Were my guards this frightened of me when I wasn't present?"

A pause for three steps. "In general," said Groag in his delivering-bad-news voice, "no, they weren't." Only because they thought you a fool and a horse's behind of the first water, the small hobgoblin added silently to himself.

"Good," said Toede. "That means the guards won't question orders, and maybe the sergeant won't either."

As it turned out, the sergeant-at-arms was another low-level hack outside the circle of influence of the local rulership. This much was obvious at first glance, for he was a nondescript functionary in chain mail of little better quality than that worn by the guards, and was seated in a dingy office that had once been the entry of a feasting hall. He had a stack of paper gathered on his desk, next to a candle guttering in its holder.

He was ideal for Toede's purposes.

As soon as the guards opened the doors, Toede stepped in front of them, positioning himself opposite this worthy local authority.

"Your report on the Toede situation, Sergeant," snapped Toede, in a manner that suggested he had seen the officer only moments before.

The sergeant, rising from his desk, blinked twice. Then

the cogs of his human brain finally found purchase, and he asked, "Who are you?"

Toede stared at him the way one human stares at another before imparting a great secret. Then he said in a stern voice, "The dragon flies at midnight."

The sergeant again blinked twice. "What?"

"I said, 'The dragon flies at midnight.' " Toede seated himself across from the sergeant, elbows resting on his knees. He held his hands out, palms upward, and motioned with his fingers. A response was expected. Groag hung as close to the door as possible between two of the guards.

"Is this some sort of game?" asked the sergeant,

Toede slapped his knees, hard. "If only it were!" he shouted, jumping to his feet. "I have information to give, and they seem to have left an idiot—sorry, I'm sorry, it's not really your fault—behind who doesn't know the password."

"Password?"

"Password. The response to 'The dragon flies at midnight.' Quickly now, where is Gildentongue?"

"He left for the city, er, the Lower City, an hour or so ago. Took the captain with him. There was some sort of disturbance. . . ."

"At the Jetties, yes, what do you know of it?"

"Only that there seemed to be some sort of trouble," said the sergeant.

"Trouble?" howled Toede. "Istar finding itself the bull's-eye for a cosmic game of darts is trouble. Waking up to find a medusa in your bed is trouble! Toede is back, and more dangerous than ever! That is not trouble, that spells disaster!"

"Toede?" said the sergeant, wondering just when he lost complete and utter control of the conversation. "Wasn't he the bumbler Lord Gildentongue replaced?"

Toede almost tripped over his tongue in his desire to defend his good name, but restrained himself. "A careful ruse he manifested. He is a being of great and subtle power. That's why he was made highmaster in the first place. He is most displeased with the fact that Gildentongue has apparently seized power from Hopsloth the Water Prophet." Toede again touched the disk hanging around his neck. "He destroyed an entire unit of city guards in the common room of the Jetties this very evening.

"Toede has great wizard's skills! He transforms himself at will into a fiend from the pits, with great bloody spurs on his elbows and knees. He chewed through those men like . . . like . . ." A brief silence fell on the room as all (even Groag) imagined the battle-frenzied Toede-fiend tossing men around like rag dolls. Then Toede looked up from his reverie, adding, "Tell me that at least you've sealed the city."

"Well, I have not received . . ." began the sergeant.

"Dark Lady in a festhall!" bellowed Toede. "Do you *want* to die in your sleep tonight? No, sorry, it's not your fault Gildentongue doesn't trust anyone. Auraks are typically paranoid, but this is not a time for caution. Is Lord Gildentongue living at my . . . er . . . the large manor house?"

"Aye, with the Holy Hopsloth." The sergeant touched his own disk at this point.

"Good, I'll wait for him there. I want you to alert the full complement. Get as many men as you can to the main gates and posted on the perimeter wall. Toede may have an army out there, for all we know. Triple the guard on the gates to the Rock and the docks. Send a runner to the Jetties to fetch Lord Gildentongue. Am I clear?"

The sergeant shook his head. "By what authority do you . . ."

Toede stomped his foot. "By Lord Gildentongue's authority! If my actions are inappropriate, I will take full responsibility."

Toede saw by the way the human's face relaxed that he

had struck the correct chord. Denying personal responsibility was almost as attractive to humans as it was to hobgoblins.

The sergeant nodded, motioning to two of the guards. "Escort these two to the Manor." He pointed at the guard who spoke with the northern accent. "You go down to the inn called the Jetties," he barked. "Tell Lord Gildentongue . . . what?" He turned to Toede.

"Tell him"—and Toede could not help but suppress a smile at this—"tell him an old friend wishes to discuss an old enemy. At his home and at a time of his convenience."

The sergeant nodded, and the guard vaporized into the darkness.

Toede chuckled inwardly. That should bring the damned lizard running, he thought.

Chapter 8

In which Our Protagonist returns home, discovers the nature of what has been sleeping in his bed, and lays his trap. As a bonus to the devoted reader, we are treated to a glimpse inside Gildentongue's head before his final battle.

"What do you know about auraks?" said Toede to Groag, once they had been left alone in the manor's front hall.

Toede had instructed the two guards to stand watch outside the front door until Gildentongue's return. The windows were shuttered, and light was entirely lacking. This did not bother the hobgoblins, as the red shadows made everything visible to their sensitive eyes. The more visually limited humans were uncomfortable, however, expecting some monster to leap out at any moment. The guards gladly retreated to their newly assigned posts.

Maison Toede was a lumpish brute of a building. With its imposing walls, it was more apt to be mistaken for a stone giant's mausoleum than a viable structure for the living.

The central building was two stories high, with stubby wings to the right and left of the main hall. To the right was the treasury (once inside, Toede noted that Gildentongue at least had the good sense to put a new lock on the heavy brass door). To the left were the kitchen and the servants' quarters. Opposite the entrance were the great iron-shod doors that led to the audience room. On either side of the doors, a pair of staircases wound up to a balcony and an upper hallway. Private rooms were located on the upper levels, and in its heyday the building had been alive with hobgoblin feasts, revels and mayhem.

Such was not the case in the warm, fetid darkness of the present administration. Gildentongue had definitely let the place go downhill.

Groag looked around, letting his eyes grow accustomed to the dark, thinking about Toede's question. "I know auraks are ugly creatures," he said at last.

"Aye," said Toede. "Heads of dragons, bodies of men, souls of fiends. Short tails and long claws. Skin the color of ancient coins. And Gildentongue's among the ugliest of the lot. See if you can find some torches in this tomb."

Toede took the two satchels (finally) from Groag and scaled the right-hand stairs two at a time, talking as he did so. "We'd best hurry. I think Gildentongue will be running back as soon as he gets the message."

"He can't fly?" asked Groag, shouting up from the first floor. The acoustics were perfect in the hall, such that Groag's voice seemed to come from everywhere at once. It was a very good building for long pronouncements and speeches, which was one reason Toede had requisitioned it in the first place.

"Thank the Dark Lady, no," replied Toede. "Auraks can run pretty fast and pop around a bit, vanish from one place and appear in another. They can render themselves invisible to human sight and change their shape. They can throw fireballs off from their hands, or at least something that looks like fireballs. They spit acid, use magic, and are unaffected by most spells. And they can control minds, but you probably figured that out from his effect on that parade-goer this afternoon. So don't look him in the eyes, okay?"

As he spoke, Toede reached the top of the landing directly above the iron doors to his old audience room. He unslung and opened both packs, holding his breath as the black dust wafted up from one. Most of the paper containers of the dust had been broken open, but Toede made sure the rest were ruptured as well.

Then he turned to the other satchel, the one that clinked solidly with glass. It was filled with a rack of light wood, and each slot in the rack was filled with a small glass bottle. Toede set the rack upright in its satchel, and unstoppered about half the vials. A rich, musky odor surrounded him as he did so.

"I heard the highlords make draconians out of good dragon eggs," shouted Groag, accompanied by the backbeat of cabinets being opened and closed.

"Kender lies and propaganda," replied Toede. "Discount that. It's not as if we don't have enough to be concerned about."

"Fireballs, acid, magic, mind control. Right," shouted Groag. "Anything else I should worry about?"

"Don't stand too close to him when he dies. They *really* get mad when they're killed."

"Good joke," Groag replied. "Hey, I found some torches and a lit brazier in the kitchen."

"Not joking," said Toede quietly, finishing his preparations. Louder, he shouted, "Put the torches in the main hall and the audience room. I want him to know where I am, so he doesn't go wandering about."

There was silence down below.

"Groag?"

"I think you better come down here," said Groag in a voice cracking with fear.

Toede descended the staircase, though not before loading the crossbow with one of the special bolts he kept, floating in an ichorous, oily substance, in the separate box. He was careful enough to don gloves before loading the weapon. But downstairs, instead of a battle, he found Groag, torch in hand, standing in front of the open iron doors leading to the main audience chamber.

"What's so bloody . . ." Toede walked up and stopped next to him.

Bloody was the correct term. The entire room had become a charnel house, filled with torn and dismembered bodies. Some had been reduced to a few gnawed bones, others were bags of dripping flesh, and there were a few semi-whole corpses, missing only some minor portion of anatomy. The stench was enough to send anyone but a hobgoblin reeling.

"Can't say I care for his decorator," muttered Toede.

"It sure explains why the guards are afraid of him," said Groag quietly.

"And why there seem to be few servants in evidence," added Toede. "Living ones at least. Let's see what other changes Gildentongue's made."

Toede took a torch and entered, stepping as gingerly as possible over the fresher-looking corpses. There were a large number of humans, but also kender, elves, and not a few hobgoblins. Toede could guess the fate of his loyal supporters and now understood why the populace seemed so supportive of Gildentongue. Just the rumor of such a place would inspire either fearful praise or revolution.

"It looks like a battlefield," said Groag.

"Battlefields are seldom this bountiful," replied Toede. "Hi-ho. This is different."

He stood over a wide, square hole punched into the flagstone floor. It was about fifteen feet square and opened into darkness. There was the slosh of water below.

"It's the chute to Hopsloth's lair," said Toede, who then canted his head and let his voice go chirpy. "Hopppppp-sloth! You there, boy?" He clicked his tongue a few times.

Something dark and malodorous broke the water like a dead kraken bobbing in an ebony sea. Twin orbs opened, throwing back the torchlight like accesses to the very Abyss.

"Miss me, Hopsloth?" asked Toede.

The response was a deep, enthusiastic belch.

"We'll be ri-ight back after we deal with that na-asty old Gildentongue, okay, Hopsey?"

There was another slosh of water, and the twin fires closed.

Groag looked at his lord and said, "Hopsey?"

Toede cleared his throat. "Well, it's obvious the aurak's been treating him poorly. Probably just takes him out for show. And smell this place."

Groag nodded at the hole. "Gildentongue . . . he bored the chute in the floor to dispose of . . ."—he waved at the carnage in the abattoir around them—". . . all this?"

Toede shook his head. "Does 'all this' look disposed of to you? Auraks like to kill things. You saw it this afternoon. It's one of those personal habits that endears them to the dragon highlords. They just aren't all that hot on cleaning up after they're done playing with their food. Poor Hopsloth. Trapped down there, a religious icon, with all this food up here." He sighed and tossed what may have been a leg down into the water. There was a splash of impact and the larger splash of something submerging beneath the surface.

"See that. Starving," noted Toede. "But Gildentongue didn't bore the hole as much as remove the trapdoors that I had already installed. It was a great trick for retainers who met my disfavor." He did not notice Groag's pained reaction. "You call them into a private audience, throw the lever, and catch the look on their faces as the floor drops out beneath them."

Groag, the favor-currying retainer, looked around. "I guess it's too late to recommend we go someplace else for the rest of our lives."

Toede grabbed his companion by the shoulders. "You have nothing to fear, Groag," he lied calmly. "Gildentongue will be after me first, and that's the way we both want it. All you have to do is hide up on the balcony. When I shout 'now' you throw the first satchel. When I shout 'again' you throw the one with glass in it. Got that?"

Groag nodded his head.

"Then you run," said Toede. If his plan didn't work, it would be better to have two hobgoblins running around the city as opposed to one. Not that Groag would live that long, but his dead body might throw off the search for Toede's live one.

Groag nodded again. "Right. Now what?"

"We get a mirror from the upstairs hall. Then we throw the dead bolt on the front door. And we wait."

* * * * *

Gildentongue returned from the Lower City alone, as he could make better time on his own than with a retinue of mewling humans. The captain would make a sufficiently tasty meal, he decided, for dragging him out at ten bells for the wild goose chase to the Jetties. Now it was nearly midnight. The messenger, the soldier from the north, he would die first, then the captain. No, the toadying innkeep of the Jetties, the messenger, and then the captain.

Or all three at once, he thought, smiling, as he waved his way past the guards at the Rock Gate. The guards saluted and stepped aside, as it was obvious even to them that Lord Gildentongue was not in the best of moods. Indeed, steam seemed to puff from the creature's dragon-like muzzle, and energies already were radiating from his balled fists.

It had to be Toede, Gildentongue realized. No one else would care to imitate the old highmaster. And since most of his old court was now part of Gildentongue's "collection" there were few left who knew the city well enough to get around. The old wart probably had a secret passage burrowed into the Rock for just this purpose. The Jetties was just a diversion.

Only Toede would have the stones to commandeer his

own manor house and send for Gildentongue to meet him there. "Old friend," indeed.

If Toede was in the manor house, the outside chance existed that the hobgoblin would enlist Hopsloth as an ally. Gildentongue had never liked the amphidragon much, though it had obvious uses. Perhaps it was time to add a few poisonous spices to the beast's next meal. It wasn't as if anyone needed to see the smelly frog-dragon anymore in order to venerate "the Water Prophet." Probably be better for the faith if the faithful had to use their imaginations a little more.

There were a pair of guards at the front door of the manor, who quickly and quietly melted away on his approach. The shutters were closed, but he could see that someone had lit torches or lamps within. He pulled on the double doors, one handle tightly gripped in each hand.

The doors pulled a half inch forward, then stopped. Gildentongue could see the dead bolt in place.

Someone. Toede. He had been assured the little beast was dead, but somehow, like an unlucky coin, he had resurfaced.

Gildentongue considered ripping open the doors with raw strength, but held himself in check. Such rages were typical, and there was no point in destroying his own lair. There were subtler ways.

Gildentongue wrapped himself in his cloak and muttered a few words, moving quickly from *here* on one side of the door to *there* on the other side. He did it within the course of a single breath and poised ready for attack in the main hallway.

He looked around. Torches had been lit in the hall, casting scarlet shadows on the bloodstained floor. He nosed the air for a moment—no, no alien magics were present—nothing illusionary or invisible at work here, either.

The iron doors to his private room were ajar. Fewer lights there, a pair of braziers set before the chute down to Hopsloth's muck-pit. On the far side of the pit the old throne still stood on a low dais, and standing on the seat of that throne . . .

. . . Toede, looking quite contented with himself.

"Come on in," shouted the squat little creature. "Mind the chute. And thanks for keeping my place warm."

Gildentongue snarled as Toede's words echoed through the hall. The idea of gripping Toede's face like an overripe melon, driving his thumb-claws into the tatters of the hobgoblin's eye sockets, appealed to him. But all things have their time and place, and first he would have to trick and trap his prey.

Gildentongue wrapped himself in his cloak and muttered a few more words, moving quickly from here by the doorway to there on the other side of the pit, directly in front of the dais. He did it within the course of a single breath, and upon emerging on the other side, immediately lashed out, driving his clawed talon into Toede's heart.

Chapter 9

In which the battle is joined between Our Protagonist and his hated foe, a final resolution of sorts is reached, a final revelation of sorts is made, and a final meal, of sorts, is served.

Or rather, Gildentongue drove his taloned claw into the space where Toede should have been, had the hobgoblin truly been standing on the throne. Instead, Gildentongue drove his hand into the hallway mirror Toede and Groag had positioned on the seat.

The glass surface of the mirror spider-webbed and shattered, raining shards of glass in all directions. The mirror's metal backing ruptured under his claws, and three of his talons pierced the steel entirely. Gildentongue cursed and tried to shake the metal from his hand. Small wounds laced across his scaled skin, but they were minor scratches that welled with blood and would swiftly heal.

There was a low, mocking whistle behind him. Toede stepped out of his hiding place among the dead bodies, crossbow tucked under his arm. Toede looked as if he were one of the landed gentry out shooting coneys. Tilting the mirror on the throne, to create the illusion of his presence there, was an old trick, more suitable for a traveling show than anything else, but it had proved effective.

Toede laughed as Gildentongue attempted to disengage himself from the shards of the mirror. This infuriated the draconian further, such that steam was leaking upward from each nostril. Toede raised the crossbow and . . .

Gildentongue disappeared with the soft popping of a soap bubble.

Toede hesitated for a second. Had Gildentongue magically moved, or . . .

The frame of the mirror, still on the throne, moved slightly, as if an unseen hand was trying to extricate itself. Which was exactly what was happening.

Toede aimed at the wobbling frame and shot.

Gildentongue reappeared as the arrow struck him and bounced off his scaly hide.

It was Gildentongue's turn to laugh. "Arrows, little goblin? You'll need better to pierce my skin."

He reached down to pick up the arrow, noticing that it ended in a broad-headed, inverted cone, with the wide end striking first. A fowling arrow, used by hunters to knock down birds relatively unharmed. The head was smeared with some gummy substance that had left a mark the size of a steelpiece on his chest. Without thinking, Gildentongue touched it. It felt like resin.

"Not arrows alone," came the shout from beyond the iron doors, where Toede had now retreated. "I took the liberty to coat them with a very potent contact poison. Should work even through your hide. Especially if you have any cuts . . ." The voice broke up in mocking laughter.

Gildentongue looked at his clawed hand, radiating with a fine tracery of blood from the broken mirror. He felt the room close in on him, then shook off the effect. Suggestion was as deadly as reality when it came to combat. Tell a warrior he is poisoned, and he acts as such. Mentally Gildentongue cataloged the poisons in the house and figured there would be more than enough time to seek the proper healing magics.

More than enough time, once he had twisted Toede's head from his shoulders and given it to the city's lamp-urchins to use as a kick-ball.

Still, Gildentongue felt woozy and resolved to take no more chances. He wrapped himself in his cloak and muttered a few words, moving from there, near the throne, back to here on the near side of the pit, by the doorway. He hesitated and stepped slowly into view.

And stepped back quickly as a bolt winged through the opening, clattering behind him in the darkness. Gildentongue stepped forward again, but by the time he had entered the main hall, Toede already had another bolt drawn. The broad head of the fowling arrow dripped with some ichorous, spongy substance.

The draconian held up his hands. "Talk?" he suggested, smiling, his sharp teeth glowing scarlet in the flickering torchlight.

Toede kept the bolt leveled on Gildentongue's chest, about fifteen feet away. "So talk."

"To what do I owe the pleasure of your visit?" Gildentongue asked smoothly. The back of his mind was curling like a snake, ready to strike.

"This *is* my house, and you have taken *my* position," said Toede. "What else needs to be said?"

"Is that all this is," queried the draconian, "a question of hierarchy? Why, my friend, I was just holding the seat for you. A regency, as it were. Check the records, you'll see. I never thought you truly dead." The back of the draconian's brain reached out to the hobgoblin, whispering hypnotically. "I'm a friend. Put down the weapon and let me come closer."

"I *was* dead," said Toede, looking the draconian full in the face. "But I'm back to . . . to . . ." His voice seemed to lose some of its coherence as the effects of Gildentongue's mental abilities began to infiltrate his brain. "To be made a nobleman," he said, shaking off the sudden drowsiness.

"Then let me help," said the draconian, taking one step ahead, then another, into the center of the room, closer to the little highmaster. Gildentongue could feel the energies tingling through his palms. He would blast the flesh from this creature's body and make a chair of the bones. "I can put a good word in, set things up with the highlords. We can finalize that brevet promotion. First thing in the morning."

The crossbow began to dip, and Gildentongue took another half-step forward. Toede shook his head like a drunkard, trying to shake off the bees that seemed to have lodged in the back of his head. "Not in the morning," he slurred. "Now."

Whether the command was intentional, accidental, or some part of Toede's subconscious straining to escape Gildentongue's mental control, it worked. Groag had been watching the entire proceedings from above with the interest of a youth watching a snake hypnotize a bird, but when Toede said 'now' his companion reacted immediately, as he had been ordered.

Groag shoved the first parcel, the dusty one, off the balcony, onto the draconian below.

It fell like a gray comet, a tail of black dust streaming behind it. The draconian was not hit by it, for it landed at his feet and erupted in a huge ball of small granules that danced in the air and stuck to living flesh.

It was a burning, acrid cloud of strong spice, pepper to be exact.

Gildentongue was trapped in a huge cloud of the harsh, abrasive grindings. The draconian sneezed, if the act of trying to expel one's own lungs out one's nostrils could be considered mere sneezing. He waved at the pepper cloud and doubled over in pain as the dust caught in his eyes and nostrils.

Toede was far enough away to avoid the bulk of the explosion, but his eyes began watering as well, bringing him briskly back to the real world. Cursing himself for letting his guard down, Toede fired a shot at the weaving lizard-man form. At this range hitting anything was easy, and Toede caught the draconian in the face with the fowling arrow. There were two arrows left in the case, and Toede retreated to the right, edging up the grand staircase.

As the cloud began to subside, Toede could see that Gildentongue was already gathering his wits about him. Lights pulsed and danced on the creature's fingertips, and Abyss-born eyes now regarded him. "You die now," Gildentongue gagged.

Toede looked directly above Gildentongue's head and shouted, "Again!"

Groag threw the second package, the one with the vials, off the balcony.

Gildentongue spun and shouted, "Not again!" He probably meant to say, "You'll not catch me by the same trick twice," but there was only so much time between when a satchel is tossed and when it strikes the ground. In that brief time Gildentongue managed to lash out with balls of greenish energy from each palm, an attack originally intended for Lord Toede but easily pressed into service to handle a falling package of noxious spices.

Except there were no spices in the second package, but rather bottles of oil. Fine lamp oil.

The satchel caught fire, and the oil streaming out from behind it formed a red tail to match the black one of the pepper comet. The entire parcel hit slightly behind and to the right of the draconian, but as with the pepper, accuracy was not a major concern. Upon impact, the remaining vials ruptured, and burning oil splattered in all directions.

Most of the oil fell on the dirty, bloodstained stones of the hallway and did little damage. A wave of flaming oil engulfed the gagging, poisoned draconian, and was much more effective.

Gildentongue shouted something in a tongue that Toede did not recognize, but that the hobgoblin assumed was a curse. The draconian dropped to his knees, attempting to roll the fires out, but instead succeeded only in picking up more oil to feed the flames and pepper to be rubbed into his wounds. Toede vaulted up the stairs to the balcony, where Groag was enjoying the proceedings.

"It's almost beautiful," said Groag, watching the aurak's agony.

"Beautiful like a dagger in the dark," said Toede, grabbing his companion. "Now we have to get out of here before . . ."

Groag was transfixed. "Ooooh, the fires are turning green now."

Toede shot a look at the first floor and saw that the red flames had subsided and were replaced by ones shot with green, like a coppersmith's hearth. Toede cursed loudly and said, "That means Gildentongue just died."

Groag smiled. "So he's dead."

Toede nodded. "So now he's really steamed.

Groag looked down and saw that the burning form of Gildentongue was rising from the ground in a parody of its former self. Its head had already been charred to a blackened skull, wrapped in pale tongues of green fire. The beast began shambling up the right-hand stairs, leaving a blackened scorch mark in its passing.

It croaked a single word from its useless throat: "Toede."

It ascended swiftly. Toede grabbed Groag by the collar and dragged him down the opposite stairs. Or halfway down, since the fabric of the collar tore loose and the pair of them tumbled the rest of the way to the floor. The remains of Gildentongue had reached the top step and now descended the other staircase after them. The hallway was a smoking, scorched ruin, and small fires still flickered in pools of oil.

Toede was up and running to the double iron-shod doors of the audience room. He reached them and began to swing them shut when he saw Groag, still at the bottom of the steps, lying on the ground and not moving. Gildentongue's eldritch remains were descending the stairs directly above the fallen hobgoblin, glowing more intensely than before. Groag's clothes were already smoking from their proximity to the intense heat.

Toede bid a fond mental farewell to his loyal retainer. But still, he could not resist one last taunt of his enemy.

"Gildentongue," shouted Toede, "you're frying the wrong goblin! Remember to tell your masters in the next life how you screwed up to the very end!"

With that he slammed the door, sliding the metal latch home as he did so. A final glimpse told him that the draconian had either flown or jumped over Groag's body and was charging toward the doors, aiming to burst them by sheer force.

The doors buckled five inches, and the latch cracked from the force of the blow. The thunderous noise sounded like a bell throughout Flotsam, rousing more than a few people from their sleep and summoning the guards who had not already been alerted by the strange display of lights inside the manor house. Now many stood outside, holding their symbols and wondering what manner of beast the Holy Hopsloth and his faithful minion were battling. The guards who did know were of course attempting to book passage on the next boat out of port.

Inside the manor, the door rocked again with a hollow boom, and the hinges on each side began to pull from the frame. At any moment, Toede knew, the draconian would reach the end of his unliving tether and explode in a burst of eldritch fire. And it did not look like the door would hold long enough to shield Toede from the humongous blast.

Toede looked around the abattoir of Gildentongue's lair. Nothing presented itself as a tool, a weapon, or a way out. The windows were tightly shuttered, and there was no egress other than . . .

The pit that yawned at his feet. Hopsloth's pool. Toede knew that it would be the equivalent of jumping into a giant spittoon.

The door boomed a third time, bursting off its hinges,

with pieces flying to the far corners of the room. Gildentongue's animated corpse strode, like a hot green bonfire, into the audience hall, blistering the paint from the walls. Toede jumped a foot into the air and felt the wave of heat push him backward and down into the foul blackness of Hopsloth's lair.

He was halfway to the water when Gildentongue detonated in a flash of light, like a faulty skyrocket. Toede saw his own shadow framed against the water, then he was slammed into the pool with the force of the explosion.

The soupy, almost solid water of Hopsloth's pool forced itself into Toede's eyes, mouth, and nostrils, and for a moment the highmaster feared he was covered with burning oil. No, he was merely immersed in the sludge. A great shape moved beneath him and nosed him to the surface. Gasping, Toede broke the surface of the water, multicolored sparks dancing in front of his eyes.

Above him, the manor house was burning. The pool was lit with a red glow. Bits of bodies and other, less pleasant material floated in the water.

Toede struggled to paddle a few yards, then felt firm earth beneath him. He pulled himself up on the shore, the air already excruciatingly hot from the billowing flames above.

Gagging for breath, Toede saw he was being watched from the water. A great hillock of a frog, its vestigial wings hanging uselessly at its sides, sat, its lower body submerged in the pool. The light from the flames danced over its sickly yellow flesh, giving it a macabre appearance.

"Hopsloth," said Toede with a weary smile, "I knew you wouldn't let me drown. Let's get out of here."

But the amphidragon just sat there, regarding its longlost hobgoblin master.

"Come on, you misbegotten dragon-spawn, we have to leave before the roof caves in on us." Toede tried to rise, but found that his arms no longer bent in the proper direction. He was sore, weary, barely alive.

The amphidragon remained inert, then belched out a single word. "Why?"

Toede shook his head. "You talk?" he said, wondering if the force of the aurak-blast had driven him to delusions.

"Sometimes," came the belch. "Why?"

"I was . . ." gasped Toede. "I was told I would be made a noble. After I died. The first time. Gildentongue didn't agree."

"So you . . . killed him," the amphidragon croaked. "Burning . . . my . . . house."

"Our house! And he tried to kill me!" shouted Toede, his voice ragged from the heat. "He sent an assassin after me."

"Not him," croaked Hopsloth. "I . . . sent one . . . to kill . . . you."

Toede blinked the filth from his eyes. "Hopsloth?" he said. "But you're my friend."

"No friend. You live. I'm a . . . mount," croaked Hopsloth in an almost-sneer, his mouth opening between the grunting bellows, showing a slimy line of teeth. "You die . . . I'm a god." Hopsloth gave a creaking laugh. "Which . . . would . . . you . . . choose?"

Toede tried to scuttle backward, but his legs did not seem to be functioning well either. "I was supposed to be a noble!" he whined, almost as a plea.

"I knight you . . . Lord Toede," boomed Hopsloth, his tongue snaking out and striking Toede in the chest. Before the hobgoblin could protest or even scream, the amphidragon had pulled the highmaster fully into his gullet. Toede felt the darkness enfold him in a single, sharp, exquisite pain as his head bent backward off his neck.

"Misbegotten . . . *indeed*," muttered Hopsloth, sinking slowly into his pool, seeking the coolest, deepest spot while the fire raged over his head.

Interlude

In which we take advantage of Our Protagonist's current deceased status to check in with those who made a wager in lands far from our own.

Meanwhile (if that word has meaning in a place of eternal torment), a pair of winged, lizardlike figures discussed Toede's situation. They lounged comfortably on the Castellan's stairs of smoking coal, leading downward to the crypts. The owner of said crypts sat on those steps and growled in disapproval, and if there were betting slips in the Abyss, they would have been shredded and discarded in front of him. His taller companion smiled broadly over a steaming gold cup of reddish ichor.

"Not much of an experiment," sniffed the Castellan of the Condemned after a time.

"A failure, I'll grant you that," replied the Abbot of Misrule, draining the last of his saint's blood. "And not even a noble failure, if you'll excuse the pun."

The tall one motioned to the sky with the cup, as if offering the heavens to a toast. "Look. She's back."

A crimson blur streaked across the stygian blackness above them. The Castellan shrunk back slightly against the wall, but the Abbot just squinted at the quickly moving form of the hell-maiden. She cut through the stagnant air like a knife, leaving twin tornadoes of black fog in her wake. Her armor still gleamed and looked newly polished, and her ebony blade rested sheathed in her belt.

"It's Judith, all right," confirmed the Abbot, "and she's caught her prey."

Indeed, the enforcer of justice in the Abyss carried the inert form of a warrior in her sinewy arms. Shards of the warrior's armor fell away from his body like strips of torn paper, revealing a blood-crossed, pulpy mass of ripped flesh.

Head dangling at an odd angle, the paladin (for it had to be he) made no move to resist Judith's handling.

"Is he dead?" ventured the Castellan.

"Care to bet that he's not?" replied the taller abishai, smiling.

"How would you prove it one way or another?" said the shorter one, warily.

The Abbot of Misrule nodded aloft. "By how she disposes of the prize. If she just dumps it, or consumes it in flight, it's dead. If she slams it into the ground, that's a coup de grace, a killing blow."

"Another cup of saint's blood?" asked the Castellan.

"Agreed. And prepare to pay off," warned the Abbot. "Look."

Judith swept in low over the ground, and both abishai got a good look at her face—a face locked in intense fury. She passed within a hundred paces of them, but would not have noticed the malingering fiends even if they had feathery wings and aureoles.

Then she arced upward, sharply, at a right angle to the ground. The Castellan groaned as the Abbot chuckled. Both knew what was to come next.

At a height of about a hundred feet, Judith flipped over and raised the paladin's body over her head. At the apex of her upward arc, she flung him down, overhand, onto the blasted terrain below.

There was time for a long, very human scream, then the ground shook.

"Well, that was nice," said the Abbot, tapping his now empty goblet. "Care to make it double or nothing on how big of a crater he made?"

The Castellan's grumbling reply was below the level of even his companion's sensitive ears. He stomped down to the crypt; the Abbot sauntered down after him.

"And speaking of wagers . . ." The taller creature grinned. "I believe we need to settle that previous one as well. Toede could not prove his nobility, as you had hoped, so I win that as well. Just leave your keys to the crypt on your way out.

The Castellan paused from rattling his soul-bottles and held up a taloned paw. "Hold, now. If we don't learn anything definite from an experiment, then we might as well call it a draw."

"Experiment?" The Abbot smiled. "And here I thought this was simply a bet."

The Castellan ignored his companion. "We could make a case that, by calling the draconian's attention to himself, Toede saved his companion Groag from certain death."

The Abbot snorted rudely. "Or that he was hoping the draconian's fiery form would explode upon striking the cold iron door. Objection overruled. Leave the keys by the door."

"He did save his companion a few other times," added the Castellan.

"Usually for his own self-interest. Besides, that's loyalty, not nobility," replied the taller abishai, "and is beyond the purview of this discussion. At no point did anyone, even his erstwhile companion, recognize the slightest inherent spark of nobility within the subject's breast. And before you mention Hopsloth, you know he was being ironic, or as close to ironic as something like that creature can be. Indeed, if anything, Toede further enhanced his evil reputation by this, er, second coming."

The Castellan frowned and moved to another case, shoving aside, in his quest for the correct bottle, containers filled with last essences of sinners, murderers, and government bureaucrats.

"I would be lying," smiled the Abbot of Misrule, "if the results of Toede's failure were not pleasing to me. Yet another small metropolis spun into disorder through the greed of a few. But you should be pleased as well." He motioned to the shelf, where a new bottle, shining like ancient coins, glistened, its draconian captive howling in eternal green flames. "One more addition to the collection." He smirked.

The Castellan of the Condemned just harrumphed. "The problem . . ." he began and stopped. "The problem is we were unclear about the initial edict. 'Live nobly' we instructed. Apparently that was too vague for our subject. Note that he quickly transposed it from an order or directive to a promise or assurance, that if he returned to his old sinecure, all would be set aright and he would be granted all that he desired. He expected to be treated as a noble soul, and as such did nothing to help make that happen."

"I sense you are trying to weasel out of your bet," said the Abbot.

"This isn't about the bet," lied his portly companion. "It's about an interesting experiment. We gave flawed instructions and in turn gained flawed results. What do mortals do when confronted with a failure?"

"Retire to the local inn and get blotto," said the taller one. "Speaking of which, have you found that saint's blood yet?"

"No," said the Castellan, correcting his companion's response (though not his request, for he produced a small flask carved from a single ruby). "Humans pick themselves up and try again."

"You're dinking of domes," muttered the Abbot, with the stopper in his teeth. He spat it out and repeated. "You're *thinking* of *gnomes*. Humans prefer to get blotto after a failure, whether it's a lost battle or a dead calf."

The Castellan would not be swayed. "Similarly," he said, "we can assume that our mortal agent would learn from previous experience, and, with more precise orders, demonstrate whether nobility is possible in his hardened little heart."

"I don't think I care for where this discussion is leading," muttered the Abbot, leaning back against a red-hot wall.

"I'd like to run this experiment one more time," said the Castellan.

"I have no interest in risking my earnings against some additional scheme," interjected the taller abishai.

"Double or nothing on the bet," said the Castellan quickly.

The taller abishai licked his lips at the prospect, and at length lifted his goblet in a toast to the smaller creature. "Perhaps your argument has merit after all, particularly at double or nothing. When do we start?"

Chapter 10

In which Our Protagonist is returned again to the land of the living and is made to realize he has a higher calling whether he likes it or not. Further, he learns that no act of kindness is without both vested interest and inherent punishment.

Toede awoke with a queasy feeling, a sour ache in the pit of his stomach. Digestive problems, something going down the wrong way.

No. The something going down the wrong way was him, going down the gullet of Hopsloth. Had it all been a dream, or . . . ?

He looked at himself, still dressed in the sturdy gray trousers, shirt, and brocaded vest that he had battled Gildentongue in. A little combat-scarred, but none the worse for wear. Certainly his clothes did not look like he had taken a trip through the digestive system of a dragon-spawned abomination.

The battle with Gildentongue was not a dream, however, nor was the confrontation with Hopsloth. They were slices of reality, carved off and sent spinning into the void. He had died, *again*, Toede mused, and scowled at the thought, in the hopes it would retreat meekly from his mind. He had died twice now, with dragons and their kin responsible for both deaths. And something or someone had brought him back each time.

Something throbbed red and painful in his mind, and he closed his eyes to think about it. Something that happened after he had been pulled into the maw of the holy Water Prophet, but before waking up here. It was like catching the tattered remnants of a dream, but all at once it came into sharp and singular focus.

He had been on some otherworldly, metaphysical plane. Those godly figures were back, towering brutes of great power, the same who told him earlier that he was to be granted nobility. The figures seemed displeased with his actions, particularly the wider figure who seemed wider than the widest ocean. Their voices boomed like thunder, rattling him from forehead to heels.

This time they had not promised anything. They had told Toede only to "live nobly," not that he would become a nobleman. His mission was to live in as noble a manner as possible, said the other one, who was taller than the tallest mountain.

Then he awoke, the metaphysical door hitting his backside on the way out. Toede wondered if this was what it was like to be a priest, with one's deity always nosing about and making damnable orders.

Also, he wondered how one was to live nobly if one was not a noble already—unless one acted as a do-gooder like the Solamnic Knights and that breed? Toede assumed that people like that were born with silver short swords in their mouths.

Toede opened his eyes. He was back on the banks of the stream, the same stream where he had awakened earlier, beneath the same maple as before. Spring and high summer had passed in his absence, and now the scenery was a brilliant shade of yellow. The first leaves were drifting down in the breeze and settling on his prostrate form.

Toede squinted, looking at the brilliantly garbed tree and wondering if it had been created specifically to bother him. Perhaps next time they would send him back with an axe to take care of such beauteous offenses.

No. He almost forgot. Noble people did not threaten trees just because they did not care for their looks. He reached out and patted the trunk. "Nice tree," he said aloud, feeling immediately foolish. For all he knew, noble-acting people felt foolish all the time.

There was an excited chittering overhead, and Toede looked up to see a squirrel, bushy-tailed and red-gray, taunting him from an upper branch. Again, his first thought was to grab a stone and put the little rural rodent out its misery, but he caught himself. "Hello, Master Squirrel. Sorry to disturb you," he said, pointing at the squirrel with two fingers, imagining them in his mind to be a crossbow aimed at the creature's heart.

The squirrel chattered for a few more moments, then fled, obviously perplexed. Anyone who might have been able to talk to this squirrel in the next two months would have heard a story about how the squirrel saw a drunken hobgoblin appear out of nowhere and speak sweetly to the trees and flowers. Fortunately for Toede's reputation, no one did query the squirrel in this manner, and after two months the squirrel's memory had returned to more important facts, like remembering where all its nut-caches had been stored.

Toede stood, rocked on his unsteady heels, and stumbled to the shore. He splashed water on his face. Again his stomach rebelled. He knelt over the stream but could manage nothing more than dry heaves. Just as well. There was no way (at least no way that Toede knew of) to vomit in a noble fashion.

Toede sat on the shore for the longest time, trying to determine his next move. He was probably a wanted man in Flotsam by whatever government had replaced Gilden-tongue's bogus faith. And he couldn't stay where he was. There were kender in the hills.

He toyed with the idea of retreating from it all, much like Groag, being nothing more than a servile slave to a beneficent master. Groag seemed to have matured in the process. Adaptive, that's what he had said. On reflection, Toede would have called it imitative. Aping the mannerisms of his superiors. Still, it had proven a sure survival trait.

Toede shook his head. Poor Groag, nothing but smoked hobgoblin on a stick, now.

Toede took stock. Whatever had returned him to life had not thought to send any food, supplies, or weapons along with him. A most inconvenient oversight on their part, particularly with kender stalking the woods.

The thought of kender made Toede uneasy. True, they'd taken in Groag as a slave and tried to rehabilitate him, but Groag didn't smash a kender guard in the face and try to drown Kronin's dippy daughter. They might not be very happy to see Toede, and after all, he was weaponless.

The lack of weapons also mitigated against an immediate return to Flotsam. Without knowing who was running things, it would be a safe bet that the new powers-that-be would be as unwilling to hand the throne to Toede as Gildentongue. Without a small army backing him up, Toede was unlikely to get past the gates.

In the end the wisest choice was to put distance between himself and Flotsam and stay away from the kender as well. Move somewhere else, somewhere near Balifor, where one's past could be safely forgotten, or even back to Solace. Surely, no one was left alive there who might remember him. If, in the course of his travels, he happened to encounter a band of hobgoblins of the old-style, whom he could razzle-dazzle and convince to capture a city, well, then, what harm would there be? It would even be a noble thing, almost, bringing his people out of savagery and into a better world.

More cheerfully, Toede started on a trail along the creek, careful to keep his thoughts sufficiently intact to avoid any spills and watching for the beginning of the swamp.

Move far away, that was the right idea, reflected Toede. Perhaps even enter into some holy order or another, like the Solamnic Knights or the Tower of High Sorcery. Learn, relax, gather one's strength, then take over some small town or hamlet in the name of goodness. That would give him a chance to flaunt his nobility, or at least enough nobility to keep his shadowy masters happy.

Perhaps a lordship would come in time, he mused, for humans were always singling out those of their number who acted in a noble or selfless fashion, and providing all manner of rewards to them. Perhaps individuals would come from miles around to listen to Toede's wisdom and to seek his advice, for a noble being would undoubtedly be considered wise.

Lord Toede the Wise. Saint Toede the Protector. Toede, Master of All Noble—*Splash*!

Toede had found the edge of the swamp again, in his customary fashion. Unmiring himself, he noted that the cattails began in earnest another hundred feet away. To the left, the rising hills led to the kender encampment—not the best group of people to be around at the moment.

So Toede, finding a spot to cross the stream, turned right this time. The land was flatter on the far side of the creek and rose only slightly to a low series of hillocks and ridges, dotted by russet maples and divided by other small streams feeding the swamp. A couple times Toede had to double back as the ground ahead became marshy and impassible.

The journey was harder than Toede had expected, and the exertion began to wear on him. His thighs complained brutally. Add to that the regular complaints his empty stomach now made, and Lord Toede was soon thinking less of a sainted position in the annals of men than of a soft bed and hot gooseflesh suspended over a fire. Indeed, his last rest had been in the cottage before reaching Flotsam, and his last "meal" that foul-tasting concoction that cured his shattered shoulder.

Reflexively he touched the once-wounded shoulder. While the flesh was still puckered in a small scar where the bolt had struck him, he was otherwise uninjured. Indeed, it was the only part of his body that was not complaining of the unjust strain being placed on it.

Toede could scavenge as well as the best of his kind, but the bogs seemed to be notably free of any edible wildlife beyond a few worms and squidge-beetles that scurried away from overturned rocks. He considered them for a few moments, then moved on. He recognized some raspberry bushes, but they had already turned a grayish tan and were festooned with dead leaves. So much for previous experience coming in handy.

Finally, after the third small hillock and the third marsh directly behind it, Toede flung himself on a relatively dry patch of ground and surrendered to exhaustion. The squidge-beetles were starting to look good. He toyed for a moment with the idea of starving himself to death, imagining himself appearing before the two spirits as big as seas and mountains and (rightfully) claiming that he had done no harm to anyone during his last sojourn on Ansalon, so what could be more noble than that?

Toede's stomach replied with a low whine. The hobgoblin patted it with a fleshy hand. "Beetles it is, then," he muttered.

Then he heard another whine, one that did not come from any part of his own pain-wracked anatomy.

Toede cocked his head. It was there to his right, down the hillock's slope, issuing from a particularly brushy-looking patch of marsh. It was a sharp repetition of high-pitched squeals. Some sort of animal in pain.

Toede's mind immediately leaped to the thought of some giant suckling pig whose entire purpose in life was to wander into this dismal swamp and into some dire predicament. Say, perhaps, into the jaws of a trap laid several months ago by a forgetful kender poacher, a trap baited with pig-attracting turnips. And now, on its last legs, said hog was crying for someone, anyone, to put it out of its misery.

Toede set off in the direction of the whining, ignoring the reflection that if he always expected the best, he would without a doubt always be disappointed. As it was, Toede was bound to be disappointed, first because it took a short while to locate the source of the sound, and second by the nature of the sound itself.

It was a dog, or something that looked like a dog, mired in the bog. The poor creature was trapped in the viscous and unavoidable draw of an oily patch of quickmud. The swamp was full of such patches, Toede imagined, where the water contained enough dirt and other debris to look like solid ground, yet was slippery enough to become a mini-quagmire.

The dog-thing was trapped, its gold-yellow head and muzzle straining to remain above the water line. Mud caked its fur up to the jawline, and Toede could see that it was in the last throes of its struggle. The dog looked like one of the kender's mastiffs, with a few exceptions accountable to differences in breed. The nose was more pointed, like that of a weasel. The ears, set farther back on the head, were triangular and upright. The neck (what was showing) was significantly muscular and hunched.

And the look in its eyes was the dumbest-dog-look Toede had ever seen, exceeding even the stupidest of his hunting hounds. The eyes regarded Toede with a look halfway between pleading (please get me out), unadulterated hatred (how dare you not drown with me), and mild pleasure (did you bring any food?). Even as it regarded him, the pathetic dog-thing ceased to struggle, and sank a half inch farther into the muck.

Toede cursed. Not because of the cruelty of fate that apparently led the animal to its near demise. And not because Toede expected better food on the hoof.

Toede cursed because the creature was about fifteen feet out in a nearly circular pond of mud. Here was dinner, almost dead and ready to be served up, and it was out of his reach!

The mud-hole was surrounded by willows and other bushy trees, a few of which had sufficient overhang for a normal male hobgoblin to reach the animal. Unfortunately, Toede was much less than a normal male (in the height department, at least) and would still be unable to reach and grasp, much less haul up, a struggling animal.

Toede wracked his brains while the dog whined at him. "I'm thinking," he snarled, as if the dog would immediately understand and die quietly rather than disturb him. The dog whined again.

"Simple. Got it," said Toede. "Don't go away," he told the dog, "I'll be right back." And Toede set off for higher, drier ground, returning a minute later with two pieces of wood, one a long, misshapened pole about five feet in length, the other a truncated club. He put the club next to the base of one of the younger willows and, holding the pole in one stubby mitt, began to shimmy up the sapling.

The willow bent as he ascended, a little at first, then more and more until its trunk was running parallel to the surface of the mud. Toede was prepared to abandon his plan at the first sound of the tree cracking, but he had chosen well, for the sapling was supple enough to bend, but strong enough to hold his weight easily.

As he climbed, Toede talked to the dog in the same manner as he talked to his own hounds when coaxing them out of their dens for another hunt. "Okay, boy"—all dogs were "boy" to Toede, unless proved otherwise by bearing puppies—"I'm going to climb up here and steady myself. Then I'm going to take the pole, and you're going to take it with your mouth. Bite it. Then I'm going to drag you back to shore. Okay?" Toede silently added: And then I'm going to bash your skull in before you regain your strength. Part of his brain was already thinking of dog carcass roasting on an open fire.

Throughout all this the dog remained inert, no longer struggling and sinking. The creature's lower muzzle was only an inch above the muddy water, and it no longer whined, or for that matter, growled. It continued to regard Toede pathetically with its dumb-dog looks.

"Okay, I'm steady now," said Toede, locking his legs around the bending bole of the tree. "Now you're going to bite the stick. Bite the stick, boy. Come on, bite it." He whistled at the creature and clicked his tongue.

It was then that the dog did a very undoglike thing. A huge, muscular arm, its fur caked in muck, rose from the water by the creature's head and grasped firmly on Toede's stick, pulling hard on the makeshift pole Toede had lowered.

Toede panicked and immediately dropped the pole, trying to shimmy back down the willow sapling without unlocking his legs. But even as he dropped the pole, the giant undoglike creature reached out and grabbed a nearby branch of the Toede-bent willow, and slowly began hauling itself out of the water, moving hand-over-hand toward the shore.

Toede shimmied backward even faster, in the process reducing the weight on the willow and helping the creature emerge that much faster. The doglike head and huge neck were mounted on a great humanoid body, with a broad, muscular chest. Its arms were each the diameter of Toede's paunch and another half-Toede for good measure. Toede's mind raced to think of creatures that matched its unusual appearance.

Gnoll. The undoglike dog was not a dog but a gnoll. Toede's mind reviewed what he knew of the hyena-headed humanoids, noted for their low intelligence, nasty dispositions, and voracious appetites. Toede's mind wondered, How could anyone be so stupid as to think this was a dog? Toede's mind looked shamefully at his feet.

Of course Toede was not listening to his mind at the moment, or his stomach or any other organ that was not directly involved with getting him far from this snarling beast (and it was snarling now, unrecognizable gnoll-curses as it half pulled, half waded its way to shore).

Toede slipped back a few more feet, then leaped for solid ground.

Or at least what he thought was solid ground, only a few feet from where he had stashed the club. And the ground was solid, as far as the weight of a small being walking around on it was concerned. Leaping from a tree four feet up in the air was another matter entirely.

The soil crumbled away, back into the mudhole, taking the highmaster with it. Toede bellowed as he fell forward. He felt his entire lower body slide into the dirty water.

It's only worse if you panic, his mind said, and was rewarded with a lively string of curses from the rest of Toede's body, which was flailing, reaching, and twisting in all directions at once to pull itself out of the muck, while only succeeding in driving more of itself deeper into the mire.

I don't know why I even try, sniped Toede's mind.

Toede reached out with one muddy arm for a handful of long grass attached to the (presumably) solid bank, only to be rewarded with the entire plant being pulled out by its roots. Toede cursed one more time as he felt the muck touch his lower lip.

Then a strong arm, its biceps as wide as a Toede-and-a-half, wrapped itself around him and lifted him bodily from the mire. The ebony mud clung to him for a moment, stretched, then abandoned the contest and returned to its sludge state.

As Toede felt himself lifted off the ground, his legs dangling uselessly below him, the world whirled around. Dirt stung his eyes, but when he blinked back the mud he realized he was firmly in the grip of an equally filthy gnoll.

He was spun around again, face-to-muzzle with the mongrel monster. Saliva was dripping down in long, ropey strands from its fang-ladened maw. Toede's arms were pinioned against his sides, and he could see the creature's chest heave as it breathed hard. Or laughed. The gnoll could very well be saying grace and Toede wouldn't be the wiser. Or saying grace.

The maw opened in a mighty yawn, and Toede closed his eyes, ready for the next life, if there was one. At least it was quick, his mind noted astutely as the rest of his body told it to just shut up.

Chapter 11

In which Our Protagonist learns not to judge a book by its cover, which is all for the best since he will soon be in the company of individuals more scholarly than his present companion.

And then the gnoll licked Toede's forehead.

Toede squirmed, not only because the gnoll smelled of wet dog, but because its breath smelled of *dead* wet dog. In addition, Toede's face was one of the few areas that was not covered with slime. Until the gnoll licked it, that is.

It's either thanking me, thought Toede, or tasting me, deciding if I need a little salt.

Then the large humanoid set Toede on the ground and smiled at the small hobgoblin.

"Charka," it said, pounding its chest to indicate its identity, sending flecks of mud in all directions.

"Oh, you're very welcome," said Toede, angry and disappointed that his expected meal not only could talk, but had waded out of the mire with plenty of energy.

The two stood there for a moment, regarding one another. Then the gnoll struck its hairy chest again. "Charka!" it said.

"Right," snarled Toede. "It's not like this hasn't been riveting, but there are beetles out there I have to root around for."

The gnoll repeated the motion a third time. *"Charka!"* it nearly shouted, pointing at the hobgoblin.

Toede sighed, and pointed at himself. "Toede," he said, then added, "Lord Toede."

The gnoll snapped its head back and howled in what Toede took to be a paroxysm of amusement. "Name means 'King of Little Dry Frogs,' " the creature said, smiling a wolfish grin (or close enough, from one with the head of hyena). Then, still chuckling, it sat down to unbind its feet.

It was only then that Toede noticed the lower extremities of the creature had been chained and weighted. A thick metal chain had been wrapped twice around the gnoll's ankles, and three suitably heavy morning stars had been threaded into the links.

The gnoll did not seem to be sufficiently depressed to be a suicide attempt, so Toede asked, "How did your predicament come about?"

The gnoll looked up at him with the look animals give humans when they are asked to explain gravity. "Hur?" said the gnoll.

"I was admiring your footwear," said Toede, "How were you fitted with such stylish fashion statements?"

The gnoll waved its massive hands. "Speak humanjabber too fast. Talk real."

Toede frowned, pointing at the chains. "How?" he asked in a loud voice.

"Ah," said the gnoll, pulling one of the morning stars free and tossing it on the dried ground. "Bartha. Chief Bartha. Hate Charka. Beat Charka. Chain Charka. Leave Charka in mud to die."

"And what could possess anyone to do this to such a charming and genteel creature?" asked Toede.

"Hur?"

"I said why?" repeated Toede.

"Bartha hate Charka," said the gnoll, pulling another morning star out from the tangled mass at his feet, and starting to work on the third.

Toede waited for a moment. Nothing else seemed forthcoming, so he prompted. "And this was because . . . ?"

"Hur?"

"Why Bartha hate Charka?" Toede said, feeling his higher brain functions shutting down like street vendors in the path of a city patrol crackdown.

"Bartha hate Charka," said the gnoll.

"Well, *that* makes sense," added Toede.

"And Charka kill Bartha's brother," said the gnoll.

"Ah," encouraged Toede.

"And Charka kill Bartha's other brother," added the gnoll. "And Charka kill Bartha's mother."

"There's a pattern forming here," said Toede.

"And Charka kill Bartha's mother's brother," recounted the gnoll. "And Charka kill Bartha's mother's other brother," finished the gnoll, as the chains slipped away from its ankles. The gnoll stood and stretched. "So Bartha hate Charka. No good reason."

"Let me guess your next course of action," said Toede, smiling.

Puzzled, the gnoll looked at the hobgoblin.

"What Charka do next?" asked Toede.

The gnoll bared its teeth. "Charka kill Bartha."

"Never would have guessed," said Toede. Before the gnoll could add anything, Toede said, "Toede help Charka kill Bartha."

The gnoll looked at Toede for a moment, then tilted its head upward and howled. Toede waited for it to subside, but it did not, at least not immediately. Charka dropped to its knees and howled again, panting hard, clutching its sides as if to keep its lungs from exploding.

"It's not that funny," muttered Toede.

"King of Little Dry Frogs help Charka kill Bartha?" said the gnoll, then howled again. "Maybe King of Little Dry Frogs bite Bartha's feet? Or King of Little Dry Frogs run up and punch Bartha in knee? Maybe King of Little Dry

Frogs yell at Bartha and Bartha curl up and die?" More howling.

"That's enough," said Toede and pointed a pudgy finger at the gnoll's chest (possible only now that the gnoll had dropped to its knees in amusement). "I saved Charka's carcass, remember?" he said. "Nice and noble thing to do, saving your life. What you do when someone saves your life?"

The gnoll looked puzzled, then a dawning light broke on its features. "Ah! Gratitude!"

"Something like that," asserted Toede, feeling his brain cells dying in droves with every passing moment.

The gnoll rose to its feet. It towered over the hobgoblin, holding out one beefy paw. "Thank you!" it said.

Toede reached out and took the gnoll's hand, which reached halfway up his own arm. The gnoll shook it sternly, once, then let go.

"Bye now," said Charka. The gnoll turned to go, picking up one of the morning stars as it lumbered to the edge of the swamp.

"Wait a minute," bellowed the hobgoblin. "That's it?"

Charka looked back. "What *it?*"

Toede fumed. "That's all? I save your smelly hide and all you say is 'thank you'?"

The gnoll pursed its brow. " 'Thank you' not right humanjabber?"

Toede waved his hands. "Right humanjabber. But I help you, you help me." He spoke as slowly as he could bear, motioning with his hands.

"Help me how?" The gnoll's forehead furrowed more.

"Well, you could guide me out of the swamp," said Toede slowly.

The gnoll shook its head like a wet dog. "Bartha live in swamp. Charka go kill Bartha. Not go out of swamp. Bye now."

"Right," said Toede. "Well then, is Charka hungry?"

That stopped the gnoll again. "Charka hungry." It nodded.

"So Charka go get food, no longer hungry," prompted Toede. "*Then* Charka kill Bartha."

The gnoll scratched itself again, then brightened and slapped its forehead. "Charka go hunting!" With that the creature started lumbering deeper into the swamp.

"Hey, wait for me!" said Toede, charging forward, but brought up short by the edge of the swamp itself. Gnolls seemed to know where the deep and muddy parts were, but that talent did not extend to hobgoblins. "Charka, I can't follow you! You have to come back!"

The gnoll was about fifty paces away, with the murky waters now rising to its hips, well above Toede's height. The massive gnoll turned and shouted back at Lord Toede, "Thank you!" then continued to wade deeper into the swamp. "Bye now!"

Toede waved weakly. "Hurry back!" he muttered. Perhaps the gnoll knew what it was doing and would return with food. He wondered how long it would take something that big to flush out a boar or a brace of geese, and how much it would demand for itself. Toede sat down and waited.

And waited. The shadows grew long as the sun set over the western hillocks, lighting up the sky with long strands of crimson and magenta. Mosquitoes and biting flies came up in small hordes and buzzed about Toede, still encased in mud, sitting, with his knees drawn up, beneath one of the willows.

Lunitari rose, bathing the land in a more subtle, reddish hue. Nocturnal creatures began to stir, answering their own internal clockworks.

A ferret poked its thin, narrow nose out of its burrow beneath a large willow tree, sniffing the air for small insects, birds, or tiny, furry prey. It took only half a sniff before a set of pudgy hands closed around its neck and throttled the life out of it, then pummeled its form against the base of the tree until it was little more than a mess of bloody fur.

Toede popped the raw bits of ferret into his mouth, rolled the meat around his tongue, and spit out a thigh-bone. " 'Thank you,' " he mimicked in a mock-deep voice. " 'Bye now!' "

Toede swallowed and took another bite. "Nobility be damned," he muttered.

* * * * *

It took two more days of backtracking and weaving to get past the swamp. Finally the land began to rise steadily and larger birches appeared, their paper-thin white bark peeled away. The land was still wet but no longer sloppy-wet, and ferns were spread through the underbrush.

All of this was lost on Toede, who kept scanning the underbrush for the sight of anything that might be edible, or close enough to edible so as not to matter much. He had brought one of Charka's morning stars with him, and dragged it behind him, letting the hollow metal ball on the end clang musically against the occasional stone.

Toward the end of the second day, Toede began wondering why they put cities and towns so far apart, or if it was just a cruel twist of fate that sent him in the one direction where no civilization lay. The sun was setting and the bare trees were alight with a glorious evening radiance that was totally lost on the depressed highmaster.

It was then that Toede noticed another light, nearer to the ground and in front of a larger hill. Someone or some-thing was in the area.

Toede's mood brightened as he moved cautiously toward the light that flickered and danced ahead of him. A campfire. The hobgoblin hoisted his oversized morning star at the ready, in case the owners of the fire were gnolls or kender. Though at this point, he would have been glad to see either, and was even beginning to understand Groag's embrace of enslavement.

As Toede approached, he noticed that the land changed

visibly, with younger trees and clear patches open to the sky. In the gathering dusk, he nearly slammed into a great stone pillar that had been moored securely in his path. In the dying light he could see that it was deeply carved with faces, snakes, and tongues of fire. A declaration of ownership, perhaps, or a warning?

The campsite was centered in one of the larger open clearings, surrounded by a number of these carved stone plinths. Toede now saw that they were sprinkled throughout the forest, and that many had been toppled and partially buried in woods, while others were canted at odd angles. About twelve of the objects still stood within the glow of the campfire. They ranged from ten to fifteen feet in height, all set toward the perimeter of the clearing.

Other than these stony vigils, there were no outriders or other guards that Toede could see, which meant that the inhabitants of the camp were either very powerful or very stupid. Also Toede noted that the tents were made of new, bleached canvas, and threw off the light of the fire in all directions in brilliant white reflections

Looks like a paladin's circus, thought Toede.

Human figures moved around the tents, gathering things, talking, and sitting on fallen monuments, writing in the growing dark.

The dusk had now reduced visibility, and Toede was so busy with his surveillance that he nearly stumbled over the guard. Actually, guard is not the correct word, since the human was hunkered down on one of the stone plinths like a priest in fervent prayer.

As Toede's knees struck the human form, the hobgoblin rolled forward, coming up with the morning star in hand, ready for attack. The human remained hunched over, facing the pillar, scribbling furiously.

Toede furrowed his brow. "Hello?"

"I'll come back to camp in a moment. Just let me finish this inscription."

"Oh. Right," said the hobgoblin, nodding uncertainly.

"Take your time." At least, Toede thought, I've found a place where prepositions are commonly used. He looked at the campsite, then at the scribbling human. In his best officious tone of voice, Toede said, "And where is the man in charge?"

The scribbler did not look up, nor did he halt his writing. He did raise his (non-writing) hand and wave in the general direction of the camp.

Heartened, Toede hoisted his weapon over his shoulder and sauntered in. A human passed him, clutching a heavy volume of velum notes, totally ignoring him. Another pair approached him, deep in conversation, parted around him and continued on, without even breaking their discussion to notice him. There were about twenty humans in the encampment, he guessed, and not one of them paid the least attention to a weapon-carrying, muck-encrusted, bad-tempered hobgoblin in their midst.

The scales tipped heavily toward the "very stupid" end of the spectrum.

Toede waddled up to the largest tent in the collection, which was actually a pavilion of the type used in street fairs and rainy wedding receptions. The entire front was open, and a number of large cooking pots were set on metal grills. No one was tending them at the moment, and Toede looked over the edge of one. A boiling gruel of what looked like wild carrots and tubers churned within the water, which smelled decidedly swampish (though that might have been just the smell of Toede himself).

There was a low table in the pavilion, and several humans were seated around it, addressing a small, hobgoblin figure. The humans were strangers, but the hobgoblin highmaster couldn't help an astonished smile as he recognized the smaller being's voice.

"I can't believe you failed to pack enough food," said Groag, in his very high, grumpy voice.

"And we can't believe you would let so obvious an omission escape your notice," said a voice, nasal, nasty and decidedly human.

"Ah. We did hire you, and, ah," said another of the humans, in a droning, sonorous, almost bored tone, "we thought you'd know best. Double-check our plans and all that."

"You hired me as a cook," said Groag, stomping a foot on the hard-packed dirt floor. "I cook the food. That doesn't mean I catch the food. For that you should have brought along a . . . a . . ."

"Foodcatcher," said Toede, walking into the tent.

"Right, a foo—" and Groag wheeled to look at the grimy, mud-spattered, torn and worn form of Highmaster Toede. "Ooooo," he said, his piggy little eyes rolling up in his head.

A few seconds later, the older, sonorous human said, "Ah. Does he always, ah, faint like that?"

"Only at reunions," Toede responded, smiling.

Chapter 12

In which the nature of scholarly research in Ansalon is examined, Our Protagonist and his former servant compare notes and rate the merits of an early departure, and Charka returns, which the reader undoubtedly suspected would happen.

Groag awoke, his head spinning, in his small expedition tent. The pressure had finally got to him, he thought, the stress, the responsibility for feeding this lot of human apes. He had heard of such things, individuals seeing voices or spirits or . . .

Toede looked up from his seat across the tent and locked eyes with his former lackey.

To his credit, Groag did not faint again, but his throat tightened. "You're alive," he choked out.

"That should no longer be such a great surprise at this point," said Toede, lacing his fingers and leaning back on Groag's bedroll. "Paradise does not want me, and the Abyss is afraid I'll take over. The amazing thing is that you're alive. The last time I saw you, you were sprawled and smoking at Gildentongue's feet, if his flambéed form had feet, that is. What happened?"

Groag sighed and tried to explain, his voice slow at first, but picking up speed and surety as he went. "It was a near thing. About the time Gildentongue was smashing down your door, a mob from the Rock was smashing down the main entrance. This mob consisted of guards, concerned natives, the sergeant-at-arms, the captain, and some visitors who had audiences scheduled with Gildentongue the next day. They found me, burned pretty badly, inside the charnel house that had been Gildentongue's lair."

"I'm surprised that anyone in that town would care to aid an ignited hobgoblin," growled Toede.

"Well, to be exact, they didn't," said Groag, raising his eyebrows in an expression of sad bewilderment. "It was the visitors—a group of scholars from the west, looking for permits and collecting supplies for their investigation of folklore and legends in the area. A group of lesser sages, and librarians under private sponsorship."

"That wouldn't be this lot?" said Toede, motioning to the entrance of the tent at the greater world beyond, where the scribblers and scriveners had finally abandoned their work to the darkness.

Groag nodded. "They were quite decent. They rescued me and took care of me, using their own potions and poultices to bring me around. Of course, by this time, most of the seaward side of your manor had burned and collapsed, and they found Hopsloth."

"Parboiled, I hope," muttered Toede.

Again the eyebrows raised, pinched in the center. "Happy and healthy. By the time I regained consciousness, his story was on everybody's lips. You never said the creature could talk."

It was Toede's turn to shrug. "I, myself, learn new things each and every day."

"Well, he talks," added Groag. "And spins a mean tale through his own spokeshumans. Gildentongue had kept him in squalor, he said, intending to tyrannize Flotsam. He had prayed to the Dark Gods for your return, and you were sent by Takhisis herself to restore rightful order. Unfortunately, you died locked in mortal combat with Gildentongue, and the pair of you were immolated by the draconian's final destruction. Freed of such traitorous minions, Hopsloth could now take rightful control of the city. It all sounded like something you might have dreamed up, had you lived, but the idea of Hopsloth in charge made me very nervous, so I promised these scholars my assistance in the field for a while."

"The question is," asked Toede, "what are you and (by connection) they doing here? You undoubtedly realize you are on the borders of a gnoll-inhabited marsh accompanying a group with the common sense of a troop of kender?"

Again the pinched eyebrows. Toede decided that this (new) trademark gesture was Groag's alternative to the kenderish shrug he had adopted the last time Toede was alive. Toede thought to change his line of questioning. "This time, how long was I . . ."

"Dead or missing?" said Groag. "Again, about six months, give or take a couple days. As to what the scholars are doing, well, how much do you know about ogres?"

"Ogres?" asked Toede, mildly surprised by the sudden change of subject. "Nasty, filthy brutes. Make gnolls look positively angelic. At least the gnolls wash their muzzles after biting the heads off kobolds."

"Right," replied Groag. "Well, the idea these scholars have is that the ogres weren't always like that. That they were once a more noble, gentle, and good race that was twisted by some foul magic or catastrophe. They believe that this area was once the home of these proto-ogres, and these stone markers were their handiwork. Work's been slow, since only Bunniswot has a handle on the proto-ogre language. Everyone else has been copying carvings, making rubbings of the stones, and minor excavations, but Bunniswot is the mastermind of the operation."

"Ogres serving the cause of good," sniffed Toede. "What a load of gorgon patties! This Bunnysnot is the older gentlemen with the sonorous voice?"

"No, that's the chief scholar, Renders," corrected Groag.

"Bunniswot is the other one, the one with the fiery red hair."

"Talks through his nostrils," said Toede. "Seems fairly unpleasant. Since he's the only one irreplaceable here, have you thought of gutting him in his sleep and just going home?"

"That would be unkind," said Groag, and Toede was surprised to see that he was sincere. "As well as unnecessary. Renders keeps Bunniswot on a short leash. Besides, I don't think the human ever sleeps. He's in the field all day, and works on translations all night. He keeps a magical stone in a box, which gives off sufficient light for his work."

At this point the front flap of the tent vibrated, and Renders poked his head in. "I heard voices. Are you awake, Groag?" Such stating the obvious was a peculiarly human trait, Toede observed silently. For all he knew, that would be the next ugly habit that Groag would pick up.

Renders entered carrying two trays heaped with the boiled vegetables in gravy that Toede had seen cooking in pots earlier. The food looked fairly gray and unappetizing, even to someone whose last real meal was raw weasel. Toede took a sniff, wondering once again if the humans were drawing their water directly from the swamp. Still, it promised to be filling (after a fashion), so he dug in.

Groag picked at his food, as Renders squatted between the two hobgoblins, his bony knees jutting up like mountains on an old map. "I hope you're feeling better. I had a few of the boys finish the cooking, but I'm afraid they haven't the hang of it." He gave a patriarchal smile that reminded Toede of Gildentongue.

"It's . . . pt . . . very good . . . pt . . ." said Groag, trying to spit out little bits of grit. "Though next time tell the lads they should skin the vegetables, since it . . . pt . . . gets rid of most of the dirt."

Renders nodded as if sage wisdom had been imparted

to him. "I'll tell them it was a good first attempt. But they were a bit . . . ah . . . lavish with our remaining stock. I'm afraid that someone will have to return to Flotsam to purchase some supplies sooner than, ah, expected."

The hairs on the back of Toede's neck immediately went up.

Renders continued, addressing Groag. "You can take the horses, and, ah, be there and back in four days. We should be able to hold out that long. You can take your, ah, your friend along." Renders motioned toward Toede, who rose to his feet.

"*Advisor*, actually," said Toede, smiling broadly. "We haven't had proper introductions yet. You can call me Underhill." He held out a hand.

Renders admired Toede's outstretched paw with the caution usually reserved for investigating locks for poison mechanisms. Then he shook it once, quickly, and turned back to Groag as if Toede had suddenly vanished in a puff of smoke.

"You and, ah, Underhill, can leave tomorrow morning. We'll give you sufficient moneys for the supplies." With that, Renders turned and left the tent, without even saying good-bye to Toede.

"Who does he think he's talking to?" huffed Toede.

"The cook . . . *pt* . . ." said Groag, spitting out a particularly large stone, then added, "and the cook's advisor." He pursed his eyebrows together, and Toede suddenly realized he had seen the same expression on Renders's face when talking about "the boys'" attempt at cooking dinner.

It was almost enough to make Toede miss that irritating kender-shrug.

Groag, now fed, drifted off in a light, muttering sleep, but Toede remained up, sitting in the entrance to the tent, watching the humans. They were less feverish than in the last hours of daylight, but no less insane in their actions: involved in deep discussion with each other, examining scrolls and old books in the light of the dying campfire, pawing over bits and pieces of what they had discovered during the day. Even from this distance Toede could see that they were pawing over veritable garbage: shattered pot shards and pieces of aged leather.

There was one unusually bright light in the camp, coming from what Toede assumed was Bunniswot's private tent. He could see the silhouette of a human crouched over a camp table piled with scrolls, books, and paper. The figure seemed to be working hastily, checking one tome, leafing through another, getting up, pacing, writing a few words, then repeating the cycle.

Garbage and maniacs, thought Toede. It's a wonder any humans at all were made highlords. And he too pursed his eyebrows in the center—in bewilderment.

* * * * *

Actually, they could not leave the next morning as Renders had proposed. This was chiefly because Groag had some duties to tend to that included rationing out the remaining supplies for five days of meals, leaving rough instruction to "the boys" (actually two full-grown men who looked more capable of eating than cooking) on how to avoid poisoning the campers in his absence, and cleaning out the cooking pots that said "boys" had left on the fire last night until the bottoms consisted of over-baked gravy soufflé.

As a result, Toede had sufficient time to explore the encampment. Not out of any human or kender form of curiosity, but for defensive reasons. If anything larger than a wild hamster attacked this group, the camp would fold up like a piece of origami. He wanted to know where the best bolt holes were, and the quickest route to escape.

He found Bunniswot sitting cross-legged on the moss in front of a tilted plinth, writing in a notebook bound with two great slabs of wood. The red-haired scholar must have noticed Toede's approach, for he snapped his book shut quickly as Toede drew near.

"What?" said Bunniswot, in his high nasal tone. It was a short, dismissive, "go away" what.

"Just watching you work," said Toede innocently.

"Don't," snapped Bunniswot, ending the conversation. However, Toede did not budge and neither did the scholar reopen his notebook. Silence reigned in their part of the universe.

"What?" repeated Bunniswot.

"I was just wondering what you were looking for out here," said Toede. "I mean, is it treasure, or magic, or something else entirely?"

"I really don't see that it's any of your business," said the scholar. "Good-bye."

"Hmmm," said Toede, wandering up to the tilted plinth and cocking his head. "Interesting. Very interesting."

"You can read Proto-Ogre 1?" said Bunniswot, and Toede noted that his voice cracked.

"Hmmm?" said Toede, cocking an eye sideways at the scholar. "No, no, I was just noting that the carving sequence is similar to the song cadences among my own people. Dah-dah-dee, dah-dah-dee." He pointed at a collection of glyphs. "Is this a song?"

"Not a song," said Bunniswot quickly. "A . . . memorial. A memorial to a fallen ur-ogre hero. Look, what do you want?" Not waiting for Toede to reply, he added, "If I tell you what we're here for, will you go away and let me finish?"

Toede nodded. The red-haired scholar summarized, moving his hands rapidly as he did. "Before there were ogres, back in the time of legend, there had to be something that would become ogres, correct? Now, old legends speak of a tall, beautiful, noble race. Enlightened, wealthy, powerful in magic, and artistic in expression. Suddenly this race disappears from the legends, with only a few scattered references to a great fall. Just as suddenly, the ogres appear and start doing ogrish things. What does this suggest to you?"

"That the ogres killed all your beautiful artists and took their lands," said Toede. "If I go to sleep with a bird in my room and wake up with a cat there, I don't assume that one became the other."

Bunniswot gave Toede a pained, withering look, and not for the first time in this discussion the hobgoblin wished he had not left his morning star behind in the tent. "It *means*"—Bunniswot stressed the second word—"that the ur-ogres became the ogres that we know about today. And I believe we can learn from their example."

"We can learn how to become ogres?" suggested Toede.

Bunniswot ignored him. "Their culture, their arts, the high level of their existence that exceeded that of the elves. And these are all that's left of their fabled civilization." He gestured toward the plinths.

When Toede made no further crass remarks, Bunniswot continued, softening his tone a little. "This is the closest possible location of a surviving ur-ogre encampment. It took five months of scouting to find it. Renders handled most of that. He's the chief scholar, and the one who dealt with that toad-monster in Flotsam."

Toede opened his mouth to say something, but realized that the scholar was speaking of Hopsloth. "And have you learned to read this?"

Bunniswot's voice tightened slightly. "Parts of it," he said at last. "A lot of the grammar and sentence-parsing is lost to me. But I may yet succeed, and if I do, my reputation will be made. Even the Towers of High Sorcery will sponsor me. Then I will be able to find the great lost ogre cities, and teach others about what I found, and publish a work of lasting value. . . ."

Toede was spared Bunniswot's continued dreams of scholarly achievement by a shout from Groag, who had already saddled up the small, shaggy horses and was ready to ride.

The hobgoblin excused himself and backed away from

the scholar. As soon as Toede was a sufficient distance away, Bunniswot's wood-clad notebook sprang open again, and the scholar went back to examining and writing, as if Toede had never interrupted him.

One thing is certain, thought Toede as he walked back to Groag, there is more here than meets the eye—human, ogre, or otherwise. Toede could smell the sweaty fear on the human when Bunniswot suspected, briefly, that Toede could decipher the glyphs.

* * * * *

It was two days' ride back to Flotsam, and Toede figured that gave him two days to convince Groag to head somewhere else, with the money and horses. One day, actually, since if Groag could not be convinced, Toede would sneak off in the dead of night without him. If Flotsam was under the control of Hopsloth, it was among the last places he wanted to go without a small army. Living nobly is one thing, but dying nobly is quite another.

The path was wide enough for the pair to ride two-abreast on their short, sturdy horses. For most of the afternoon they rode in silence. The shadows grew long as they rode in the shade of the western hills. Toede felt the farther the distance from the camp, the likelier that Groag would throw in with him. It wasn't as though they were kender slaves, after all.

It was Groag who broke the silence. "I suppose I should thank you."

Toede scowled, thinking of Charka. "Thank me?"

"You kept the draconian from killing me," said Groag. "I heard that. You called to it."

"A moment of weakness," said Toede, speaking the truth as far as it went.

"And you died in combat with it, in a burning pyre," sighed the smaller hobgoblin. "Sacrificed yourself so I might live."

"Ah," said Toede, playing with the idea of letting Groag think of him more heroically, but reluctantly abandoning it. It seemed more noble to be honest, particularly if it would help him scare Groag into going along with him. "To be truthful, I didn't die fighting Gildentongue."

"Then you've been alive all this—" Groag started, but Toede interrupted.

"I *died*," said he, "but not from Gildentongue. I was . . . digested, for lack of a better word." Groag looked at him blankly. "Hopsloth ate me," Toede added flatly.

"Oh, my," said Groag, his voice a mixture of concern and amusement.

"It seems," continued Toede levelly, "that the assassin we fought at the Jetties had been sent by Hopsloth, not Gildentongue. My mount was . . . less than pleased with the idea of my glorious return, and when the devoted gate guards reported that someone claiming to be me had reappeared in the city, he took what he thought was appropriate action."

"Dumber than a bag of lampreys, you said?" chided Groag.

"You learn new things each and every day," responded Toede.

"That might explain what happened later," said Groag. Toede shot him a questioning look, and Groag continued. "After my recovery, I told my story to the scholars, or what I *thought* had happened. About your return from the dead, and our misadventures, and what we discovered in your manor. But I didn't know that Hopsloth had . . . ah . . . eaten you." Again the mix of bemusement and interest. "I thought you died in combat with the aurak.

"Anyway," Groag said, "with Hopsloth in charge, there have been more disappearances. Like with Gildentongue, but more important people. The priests serving Hopsloth would denounce one person or another, and a few days later, they'd be gone."

"That sounds stupid enough to be Hopsloth's doing,"

agreed Toede. "He might as well hang a sign out in front of the city saying: Tyrant begging to be iced by adventurers— Heroes of the Lance preferred."

By now the darkness was almost complete, and while the hobgoblins were not totally inconvenienced by the gathering gloom, the horses were becoming less sure in their steps. The pair stopped beneath a particularly large oak with a modicum of clear terrain at its base. Neither one sought to make a fire, since that was a human custom, and they had slept in worse conditions without benefit of bedrolls.

As the pair bedded down, Toede said, "Groag, do you think we're doing the right thing? Going back to Flotsam, I mean. It doesn't sound particularly healthy."

Groag was already bunched up in a small coil. "As right as anything. I mean, if you don't go in announcing who you are, we can likely get in and out without any problem."

"We could just take the horses and the pouch of coins and head west," said Toede, as if the idea had just occurred to him. "Have you ever been in the Solace area? Nice land, and the humans are easy to control."

There was a silence, then, "If we did that, then the scholars would probably starve."

No great loss to the world, thought Toede. He weighed his options, trying to berate Groag into joining him versus just slipping away in the dead of night. At length he said, "You're probably right," and stretched out, lacing his fingers behind his head. "Goodnight, Groag."

"Goodnight, Toede," said his companion. No title. Not lord, not highmaster, but just Toede. Toede scowled.

Toede stared above his head at the dark tracery of the bare oak branches against the night sky. He waited until Groag's breathing was regular and deep, then quietly rolled out of his own bedding.

He checked Groag and frowned, for the smaller hobgoblin had the pouch of coins clutched in his hands and resting under his chin. He'd have to abandon the money, unless he killed his companion. That was a tempting idea, but probably unnecessary under the circumstances. Groag was snoring loudly, and was deeply asleep. At length, Toede decided to take both horses and equipment, since he could sell or eat one if need be.

Besides, thought Toede, this way Groag could still get the supplies for his precious scholars. It would just take a few more days. Not that they couldn't stand to lose a few pounds.

Toede quietly untied the horses and led them a short way from the oak. One of them whickered softly but followed without further complaint. Toede was about to saddle up and ride off when all the hellish Abyss seemed to rip open and dump its contents into his life.

The first thing he was aware of was the scream, or screams, that came from all sides. Blood-curdling howls that would have frozen the blood of a lycanthrope. Then they were all around him, huge creatures swarming over him.

Had Toede mounted up and tried to ride away, he would have gotten fifteen, maybe twenty feet before a dozen spears pierced him. He didn't have the chance anyway; he was immediately swept up by a huge set of furry arms, then thrown roughly on the ground. He heard the horses neigh in panic as the wind was knocked out of him.

Then three spear points pushed roughly on his chest.

Toede looked up into the faces of three large gnolls, their faces caked with reddish mud in lines and swirls. A larger gnoll stood behind them, bellowing.

"King of Little Dead Frogs!" shouted Charka. "Charka thought you starve by now!"

Kill me now, thought Toede, careful not to voice his desire.

Chapter 13

*In which Our Protagonist makes
threats he cannot carry out and
promises he does not intend to
keep, and also places his fate in
the hands of greater powers, and
is not surprised as to their per-
formance.*

The other gnolls looked at
Charka, and the large gnoll
barked something at them in
some swamp-tongue that
Toede could not follow.
Charka, draped in a broad swath of quilted armor that
could have been used to make blankets for fifty kender,
with a wide belt and sword hanging on the side, was
more impressive now than before. A steel skullcap ornamented with a single blood-red gem was fitted between
the gnoll's hyenalike ears.

Whatever Charka had said had its effect, for Toede was
pulled up and frog-marched back to the oak. Other gnolls
were holding Groag under spear-point guard. Toede
noted the tatters of the bedrolls and decided that Charka's
goons had cut his companion out, probably after Groag
wrapped them tightly around himself in hopes that their
attackers would ignore him.

There were about thirty gnolls, all told, dressed in
quilted armor that was significantly more faded and less
flashy than that worn by Charka. Charka got the best and
the newest material, which indicated a stature not evident
when they had first met.

The gnolls tossed Toede against the tree trunk next to Groag and leveled their spears on the pair of them.

"Friends of yours?" muttered Groag.

"We've met," said Toede quietly, then added, "I heard a noise and went to investigate."

"So you took the horses with you so they wouldn't get lonely," suggested Groag. Without looking at him, Toede could imagine the arch of his eyebrows.

Charka squatted in front of the two hobgoblins. "Charka wonder one question," he said. "Where get horses?"

Toede managed the broadest smile he could manage with a dozen well-armed gnolls around him, and asked, "Charka kill Bartha?"

Charka's smile widened in a happy grin that made Toede think of a duck-sated hunting dog. "Charka kill Bartha!" The gnoll's face immediately dropped back into a somber mode. "Where get horses?"

Toede hesitated as the gnoll spears lunged a few inches closer. Groag made a gurgling noise. The spears drew back slightly.

"They belong to some humans," said Toede in as neutral a fashion as possible. "They're loaners."

"They're the property of Chief Scholar Renders," Groag interjected. "We are under the humans' protection, and you'll be in great trouble if any harm falls to . . . *Aurk!*"

Charka started frowning the moment Groag started speaking, the furrow in his forehead growing craggier by the instant. He gave a hand signal, as one of the gnolls drove his spear into the wood by Groag's head, accounting for the "*Aurk.*"

"I think they want me to do the explaining," said Toede quietly.

"I think you're right," gasped Groag, trying to force the blood back into his face by sheer mental effort. "Carry on."

"Human horses," said Toede, motioning at the two

mounts for effect. When none of the gnolls proceeded to stab him for his actions, Toede tried rising to his feet. "Powerful humans," he added.

A few of the gnolls growled, but Charka gave them a dismissive chop of the hand. They silenced at once. Impressive. "Powerful humans?" asked Charka. "Muscles and swords?"

Groag made a rude snort despite himself, and Toede inwardly cursed for not having left the area five minutes sooner. Apparently Charka did not notice the snort. He asked, "Humans in forest of stone?"

Toede tilted his head to one side. "Hur?" he said, trying not to smile.

"Forest of stone!" said Charka loudly, then motioned with sharp-taloned, furry hands, vertically, to indicate trees. "Forest of tall rocks. Carvings. Forest of stone!"

"Ah," said Toede. "Forest of *stone*. Yes, humans in forest of stone."

Charka snarled. "Forest of stone taboo. All who see must die. Humans. Horses. You."

"I knew that was coming," muttered Groag. "Call it a premonition, but I just knew it."

"If you don't mind, I'm bargaining for our lives," Toede shot back.

"Go right ahead. You're doing a good job so far."

Toede moved his wish of departure up to ten minutes before the gnolls had arrived and said to Charka, "Charka not want to kill humans. Humans powerful wizards."

"Hur?"

"Wizards," said Toede, grasping for synonyms. "Magic-users. Magicians. Thaumaturges. Juju priests. Charlatans. Shamani . . ."

Something sunk into the gnoll's skull. "Juju? Humans have great juju?"

"Moby juju," nodded Toede. "Humans seek more juju in forest of stone. Angry if gnolls disturb them."

Charka rocked back on his heels for a moment, deep in

thought. Toede could almost see the steam leaking out of his pointed ears from the stress the thought process was placing on his brain.

"Human in forest of stone . . . humans must die. Humans have great juju . . . humans kill gnolls." Toede saw the coin mentally flip. Charka smiled. "Charka think you lie, King of Little Dry Frogs. If humans have big juju, humans attack gnolls first."

"Incredible logic," noted Toede for Groag's benefit. To Charka he said, "Humans not care about gnolls. Humans care about forest of stone. Gnolls attack humans, humans care about gnolls. Humans kill gnolls."

There was another pause as Charka digested this last bit of information, pondering for a good two minutes. Toede imagined the two parts of that gnollish brain swatting the concept between them: sacred tradition versus a palpable fear of possible death. Then Charka leaned close to Toede and snarled. "Prove."

"Prove?" said Toede, surprised.

"Prove humans have great juju. Prove humans worthy to be in forest of stone." Charka shot a glance at the other gnolls. Toede saw they were nodding back, stern-faced.

Toede held his hands out, empty palms upward, "Well, gee, guys, I didn't pack anything *with* me. . . ."

Several of the gnolls brought their spears around, but when Charka chopped the air they lowered them. They kept the spears pegged on Groag, however, Toede noted. Charka gave his "confused-dog" look, and Toede didn't wait for the "Hur."

Toede stepped forward a half pace and thumped himself on the chest. "King of Little Dry Frogs get proof. Get moby juju from human chief." As an afterthought, he put in, "From human chief Renders."

Charka was impressed by the name, at least. "Human chief name is Boils Flesh?"

"Great chief of juju, Boils Flesh." Toede nodded. "King of Little Dry Frogs go to Great Chief Boils Flesh, bring moby juju for Charka."

"When did we stop speaking a common language in this conversation?" muttered Groag, earning himself another mild poke with a spear.

Charka thought for a moment. Toede sighed deeply and added, "Or . . ." He paused for effect. "Charka kill King of Little Dry Frogs, and Great Chief Boils Flesh turn Charka to chutney." Toede was unsure if "chutney" was part of gnoll cuisine, but Charka got the point.

"What if King of Little Dry Frogs go warn Great Chief Boils Flesh, so humans attack Charka here, eh?" asked Charka. "What if, "the gnoll added, "King of Little Dry Frogs just fly away?"

Toede smiled. "Charka keep friend of King of Little Dry Frogs as hostage. Kill hostage if King of Little Dry Frogs not bring moby juju back."

"No, you don't, damn you!" shouted Groag, rising to his feet in one motion and trying to charge Toede. "You're going run off on me . . . *oof!*" One of the gnolls had grabbed Groag around the waist and flung him full-force into the oak trunk. Groag hit the tree and slumped to the ground, silent.

Charka turned to Toede and said "Hur?"

Toede smiled reassuringly. "King of Little Dry Frogs' friend thinks he should go to Forest of Stone, talk to Great Chief Boils Flesh, risk anger of Boils Flesh instead."

Charka was impressed. "King of Little Dry Frogs' friend loyal."

"That he is," said Toede, smiling. "That he is." Then he added, "And by the way, my friend is carrying all my money. Could you fetch that pouch of coins for me?"

* * * * *

In the end, the gnolls gave Toede the pouch and one of the horses. Charka told him (in his unique, preposition-less way) to return by dawn or else Groag would be killed. Charka went into some detail over the nature of gnoll ritual slayings, which impressed even Toede. It was surprising what a culture could come up with without the benefit of fire, cold steel, lead weights, or kender poetry.

Toede rode out from the gnoll encampment like a flying mammal escaping the Abyss, though as soon as he knew the flying hooves of his mount to be out of earshot, he slowed to a comfortable canter. Of course, dawn would come, he would be nowhere to be found, and Groag would regrettably perish. Regrettably, after a great deal of suffering and torture. Then the gnolls would move on to the human encampment in the gnolls' sacred rock garden, and, regrettably, rampage through them with a minimum amount of mercy.

All of this was regrettable in that Toede couldn't hang about to watch.

There was an off chance that Groag could convince Charka of Toede's escape earlier than dawn, but it was an off-off chance. Toede chuckled as he played out the possible conversation aloud.

"But I tell you he won't be coming back!" Toede imitated his subaltern's whiny voice.

"Too bad," replied Toede-as-Charka. "Charka start skinning you now. Hold hostage down, boys. Charka get rusty knife."

All in all, a win/win situation. Transportation, money, and elimination of all witnesses, without so much as bloodying his own hands. Earlier, Toede had spotted a western path that broke from the main route, not as well traveled, but still serviceable. That western path promised relief from gnolls, scholars, kender, assassins, Hopsloth, and Groag. All in all, a good day.

Except for a grumbling in his stomach, but that was brought on more by Groag's cooking than anything else. There was still some jerky in the saddlebags. He could probably find some farmstead or army post long before he hit Balifor, someplace where a few coins would wangle a hot meal and a decent bath.

These assurances did nothing for the present state of his stomach however. Toede leaned back and rummaged through the left saddlebag, looking for the jerky.

Instead, his fingers closed around a disk hanging from a chain.

He hauled it out to examine it, even though in the pit of his stomach he knew what it was the moment he touched it, and a sympathetic pain shot up from his belly, stabbing at his heart.

The disk had an engraved picture of Hopsloth on one side. On the other was a deep, crudely etched *T*, some lighter, spidery writing, and numbers.

It was the holy symbol he had pulled from the assassin in the Jetties back during his first reincarnation.

When, exactly, Toede had lost the device was unknown to the highmaster. Probably when we were jumping around trying to avoid being toasted by Gildentongue, he thought. But how would Groag have found it? Either in the heat of the battle, or perhaps in the burned debris afterward. More likely one of the scholars had found it near his smoking body.

Then why did the device have the hand-drawn *T*?

Toede held it up to the russet moonlight, tilting it to catch the faint illumination. To the lower left-hand side of the *T* was the date, about six months ago, give or take. And in the right-hand corner, more faintly inscribed in Groag's spidery hand, were the words: DIED NOBLY.

Live nobly, the shadowy figures had said, the mountain-high being and sea-wide creature. Well, if he needed proof when they came calling, perhaps this was it. Somebody had certainly mourned his passing this time, unlike the previous occasion with its festivals and general relief. He pictured Groag laid up in a cot with the scholars bustling around him, turning the disk over and over in his hands, finally inscribing it as a small memento to crystalize his feelings of regret and loss.

Groag would probably be telling the shadowy beings about these very feelings firsthand by the end of the day tomorrow, tops, after the flesh had been scoured away from his quivering form (Charka had been very explicit, and though gnollish vocabulary was limited, on the matter of death it was quite expansive). Of course, between now and then Groag might quite possibly change his opinion of Toede.

The pain in Toede's stomach flared, and he dropped the disk back into the saddlebag, finding a chunk of smoked beef in the process. He chewed it as he rode. The meat was the best thing that had landed in Toede's stomach for six months, but did little to abate the vast hunger there.

"Only a fool," Toede said aloud, presumably to the horse, "would fail to take advantage of this situation. To escape and start a new life, where one can 'live nobly' without danger of one's past biting one on one's backside."

The horse, respectful of its place in the scheme of things, said nothing.

"And," said Toede, "and . . . it's not as though Groag didn't have a chance to join me. No, we could have both been gone, have taken the western fork, and never have met the gnolls. He made his choice. I cannot deny the right of any creature to determine its own destiny, and verily, he determined his."

The horse remained silent, but it seemed an accusing silence, pregnant in its damning hush.

"Not to discount the influence of the gods," added Toede quickly. "Gods are important." That he said loudly enough so that, if any were resting in the trees among the slumbering squirrels, they would hear his affirmation. "But gods are subtle and show their works best in signs and portents. I mean, dropping a mountain on Istar was a definite message, if you follow my meaning."

The horse continued to impugn Toede silently.

"So indeed, if the gods did want me to hang about here,

they would have given me an obvious sign, right?" Toede asked.

The horse refused to be drawn into Toede's line of argument. The branch to the western path appeared up ahead.

"So if the gods are paying attention," said Toede, "then it wouldn't be out of line to ask them for guidance. Correct? I mean, the words were "live nobly" not "prove your faith in us, whoever we are."

The fork was upon them. To the west lay freedom, to the south more problems than Toede wanted to think about.

He pulled back on the reins, and the horse halted. "So we have a decision to make, and need guidance, and are willing to leave it up to the will of greater powers. Should the mount turn west, we shall go west. Should it turn south, we will follow the trail to wherever it leads us." Toede eased his grip on the reins.

The horse did not move. Toede dug his heels in its sides to spur it forward, but still the horse did not move. Toede slapped its flanks with the ends of the reins, and even then horse did not move.

Toede pulled lightly on the right rein, the one that would lead the horse west, but the horse remained immobile. He pulled again, harder, then gave a firm tug. Nothing. Toede gave the slightest tug on the left rein, the one that would lead south to the scholars. The horse swung, as if it had been fixed on a pivot, immediately in that direction.

"Stupid horse," said Toede, realizing at once that the animal would rather travel a well-worn route than one never trod before. Not a fair test, all in all, he reasoned. Toede pulled the defaced symbol of the Water Prophet out of his saddlebags again and held it up in the moonlight. "Right then. Toede-side up, we go south. Hopsloth-side up, we go west."

He flipped the disk as best as he was able from horseback, the symbol spinning and dragging along its chain in a loose elliptical orbit. The flip carried it out of Toede's reach, where it landed among the debris of fallen leaves and dead ferns by the side of the path.

Toede squinted into the dark to see on which side the amulet had landed. Then, seeing the result, he snarled, and thought for a moment of just riding on anyway, of defying the coin-tossed decision influenced by the gods.

"Dark Lady in ribbons and bows," he muttered. "Probably a rock slide would fall on top of me if I went west anyway," and with that, he turned the horse south.

In the forest debris, the abandoned holy symbol shone in the crimson moonlight, the etching of the faceup *T* deep and visible from a surprising distance away.

Chapter 14

In which Our Protagonist heralds a warning, learns that some discoveries are best left undiscovered, and resolves to trust in his own instincts and abilities as opposed to those of greater powers.

They can make me come back, but they can't make me stay, thought Toede, guiding the horse back toward the forest of stone. By "they" he meant the gods, or the shadowing, shadowy beings, or whatever perverse creations were responsible for acts of fate and luck. A short mental list of true gods failed to reveal any whose personal province might be making his life miserable, but Toede felt there had to be one or two who were gripping their sides, trying to keep their intestines from bursting loose from the elation they felt at his ordeal.

It was nearly midnight. More than enough time to alert the camp and convince them to start running and running hard in the face of an imminent gnollish invasion. Unless the gnolls were willing to engage the scholars in a penmanship contest, there was little chance the humans would last more than fifteen minutes.

He had ridden this far, Toede thought, it would be a shame not to inspire just a little panic and fear among them. Toede dismounted and sighed, trying to decide who he would most like to shock into apoplexy first. The magical light source that Bunniswot kept for his all-night sessions shone brightly and steadily, and Toede spotted a solitary shadow moving against the tent wall. "Might as well discomfort the awake first," said Toede. Of course, awake or asleep, Bunniswot likely would have been one of the first people Toede would have brought the bad news to, anyway, just to enjoy the human's reaction.

Toede rapped on the tent wall, and the figure started. Toede was disappointed only in that he had hoped the young scholar would plaster himself against the opposite tent wall in shock.

The shadow moved quickly around the tent. "What?" shouted Bunniswot.

"No time for that," snarled Toede, pushing aside the tent flap and entering. "We have to evacuate the area at . . . once." Toede, smirking, strode into the scholar's small tent. Every flat surface and several tilted ones were piled high with paper, rubbings, scrolls, books, and thin metal plates. A strong, steady light was provided by a glowing metal ball set into an iron holder, the entire assemblage mounted on a small cherrywood box.

The cause for the smirk was the scholar's appearance. Bunniswot had a random collage of paper clutched to his bare, hairless chest. He was dressed in pajama trousers with a drawstring top and a long, open-fronted robe. The robe was hand-made, with patches in the shapes of holy symbols and magical formula crudely stitched to it. But the real source of amusement was the scholar's footwear. Each close-fitting slipper had a pair of protruding eyes jutting from the front, as if the scholar had slipped a pair of rabid beavers over his feet.

"What is the meaning of this intrusion?" shouted Bunniswot softly, in the tone and volume of a man in the mood for arguing but unwilling to wake the neighbors. He stomped his foot for emphasis. Toede noticed the eyes on his slippers were clear little half-shells, with black marbles set inside, and they wiggled as he stomped.

Toede tried unsuccessfully to stifle the image of Bunni-swot running from the gnolls, his little foot-eyeballs spinning. Instead he said, "Scholar, you and your party are on grounds that are sacred to a tribe of gnolls. They are massing for a major attack shortly after sunrise." Unless they get bored and kill Groag early, he added silently. "Your cook and I were ambushed, and I barely escaped with my life. It is imperative that you and the others leave this place as soon as is humanly possible."

Bunniswot grimaced and collapsed onto his folding chair, much like a man who had just had his shin tendons severed. The papers fell from his hands, cascading onto the ground. He raised a delicate hand and pinched the bridge of his nose, squinting his eyes tightly.

"But our scouts said that there were no gnolls around here," the scholar said weakly. "Kender, yes, a necromancer, yes, but no gnolls."

"Next time make sure to check the swamp," said Toede, walking up to a pile of papers lying on top of a leather trunk. "I'll go wake the others, then I'll ride to Flotsam for help. You probably won't be able to load up this mess, and it would slow you down, anyway. If you want to save your work, you should put the most important material in a trunk and bury it, then come back later." And if you're like most scholars, thought Toede with a malicious grin, you'll still be organizing your piles of notes when the gnolls come crashing down on the last few moments of your life.

Instead, Bunniswot responded, "Perhaps it's better this way. Everything here will be trampled if we're attacked. If we're lucky, they'll burn the entire lot of it." Then he gave out a brittle cry, put his head in his hands, and began to sob.

Toede did not fancy himself an expert on human behavior beyond the standard buttons he could push to get his way: fear, terror, greed, threats, greed, fear, and greed. But it struck him that this was odd behavior for a man whose life's work was in the direct path of a gnoll invasion.

Perhaps the ogres had dark secrets that no living mortal should know. That was worth investigating. Toede glanced at the papers he had been clearing. The scholar's handwriting was crabbed but readable in the pale light of the tent.

"*I didst come unto her skyclad and unshorn, seeking the teachings of the flesh, wearing nought but my finger cymbals and the night air,*" Toede intoned. Eyebrow raised, he looked at Bunniswot. The scholar just shook his head and returned to sobbing.

Toede picked up another piece of foolscap. "*We danced among the water lilies that evening, Angelhair and I, and dined upon each other's fleshly pleasures.*"

A third. "*. . . and we were joined in our revels in the pavilions by two others, fair of face and unmarred of beauty, their eyes as bright and comely as the pale full moon . . .*"

Bunniswot sighed deeply. "Stop," he pleaded. "I'm so ashamed."

"This is your secret?" smirked Toede. "That you toil through the night writing naughty poetry? A minor sin at best, punishable by brief immersion in white-hot magma. Nothing to lose your grip over. The gnolls can't even read."

"You don't understand." Bunniswot, tears in his eyes, looked up. "It's *all* like that. All of it." He gestured around the tent walls.

Toede realized that the scholar meant the forest of stone beyond. "You mean the pillars," he said, now smiling broadly.

"Yes, the bloody pillars," cursed Bunniswot. "I've deciphered forty of them now."

"And they're all . . ." prompted Toede.

"This!" He picked up a packet and threw it against the far wall. The pages fluttered like pigeons landing in the square. "Love poems! Trysts! Revels! Rendezvous! Smut!"

"That's really, *really* interesting," said Toede, edging

toward the tent entrance. "And perhaps we can discuss it later, say, after you hurry up and save your life."

Bunniswot ignored him. "I put Renders up for this exploration, did you know that? I found references to this place in preCataclysmic texts, stressing its age, its beauty, its mysterious origins. There was supposed to have been a great battle here, where the local inhabitants, my ur-ogres, battled and caged a creature of the Abyss. I expected a lost city, a temple, or at least a monument. Something to justify the time and effort. Something worth publishing."

Toede thought for a moment, then said, "Perhaps later you could spruce it up a bit, clean up the smut. Sort of a vulgate version, for the masses."

"This is the cleaned up version," said the scholar, seeming ready to collapse again. "Even the vulgate is vulgar," he sighed.

"And you haven't told Renders because . . ."

"Oh, Gilean's book and bladder, I can't. He showed so much faith in this project, and all I have to show for it is . . ."

"Ogre pornography," said Toede, shaking his head. "Not that this should depress you any further, but there are bloodthirsty gnolls to worry about now."

"What shall I do? What can I do?" moaned Bunniswot, staring at the debris in his tent.

"What you would do anyway?" said Toede, realizing that Bunniswot in his present condition was not high on the list of prospective survivors of the upcoming massacre. "Pack as much as you can, particularly your . . . er, translations, while I wake the others. Then have them bury the chest, but not so deep that water can't get to it. Then you wait several years before coming back and discover your notes have been destroyed. You reconstruct as much as possible, but of course, the gist of it is lost. Your reputation is saved, not to mention your life."

Bunniswot shook his head for a moment, then said quietly, "That *could* work."

"Goood," purred Toede, edging to the opening of the tent. "I'll wake Renders and get everyone else."

Once outside in the cool autumn darkness, Toede fought the urge to double over in laughter. It was unbelievable what humans would worry about when faced with extinction. This experience made his third life worth living, regardless of whatever happened next. Maybe it would be worth saving these humans after all, just to watch Bunniswot go crazy trying to hide his little off-color secret from the others.

"Ogre love poems," he chuckled, heading for Renders's tent.

* * * * *

"Ah. Quite impossible, you realize," said Renders, stroking his beard. "We couldn't pack sufficiently in darkness, even given a, ah, day or so. There is too much left to be done."

It was ten minutes and one quick explanation after Toede left Bunniswot to his fate of "publish and/or perish." Renders was being more difficult than the hobgoblin had deemed possible. Once more, the hobgoblin was on the verge of abandoning the thick-headed humans to their fate.

Instead Toede argued, "Let's recapitulate. A huge horde of hundreds of gnolls is about to attack at dawn, maybe . . ." He made some mental calculations about Groag's ability to hold out. "Thirty minutes afterward, tops. They will be screaming for blood since you're on land they think is sacred. They will kill first, ask monosyllabic questions later. I'm leaving now and strongly recommend you do the same."

"Hmm," said Renders, continuing to stroke his beard meditatively. "No. No. We'd lose too much data, too many samples, too many pot shards. Why, ah, Bunniswot's material alone would take days to properly sort and pack."

"Bunniswot is already packing the best of his material," said Toede, imagining the fire-haired young scholar stuffing as much ogre erotica as possible into the leather trunk.

"Oh, dear," said Renders. "If he's rushed, something may be accidentally destroyed."

He should be so lucky, thought Toede, while continuing aloud, "I've done my duty. I've brought the warning, and if you're smart you'll withdraw to Flotsam."

"Wait a tic," said Renders. "You said the gnolls were coming from the, ah, the north, down the path we've been using. Correct?"

"Right," nodded Toede, rolling his eyes.

"And the marshes are to our south and east, and are also gnoll-inhabited, eh?"

"I have had a limited exposure to the extent of the gnolls' influence, but I think it's a given that they could find us easily there," said Toede.

"So, *ergo*, you are trapped here with us," finished Renders, as calmly as a merchant explaining the difference between a chicken egg and a goose egg.

"Beg to differ," said Toede, already halfway to the opening of the tent. "For there's a path from the road north that leads west. Good-bye."

"Ah," said Renders. "Ah. So you don't know, then?"

At the tent opening, Toede turned again. I'm going to regret this, he thought. "Don't know what, then?"

"About the necromancer," said Renders as calmly as if he had said "about the flower shop" or "about the new maid."

I was right, Toede thought, I'm already regretting it. He raised his eyebrows and asked, "Necromancer?"

"Nasty sort," said Renders. "The first scouts we sent were returned as . . . ah . . . zombies, carrying a message that he didn't care what we did with the pillars, as long as we stayed out of his territory." Renders thought a moment. "Interesting chap—it seems he can speak through the zombies he creates, like puppets. Or marionettes. Or something like that. In any event, he rules the west."

Toede came back in, leaving the tent flap open to the cool night air. He could feel time slipping away like a handful of mud. He sat down opposite the elder scholar. "My horse wouldn't go that way," he said dully.

"Your horse is, ah, smarter than you," said Renders, not presuming to understand why Toede would have wanted to go in that direction in the first place.

"What you're saying is that we're trapped here," said Toede, mentally cursing himself for not fleeing to Flotsam earlier, not coming up with a better story, not learning about the necromancer, not leaving Charka to die in the first place, not killing himself as soon as he realized he was alive again. Pretty much everything that had occurred in the past few days of his life, he cursed.

"Well," said Renders, counting off the cardinal directions. "Marshes. Marshes. Gnoll army. Necromancer." He nodded. "Seems you are right. Trapped, that is."

A long silence fell between the two as Toede felt the mud of time in his fingers turn to water, and then to vapor. Finally, Renders said, "Perhaps you could *talk* to them." He ignored the cold look the highmaster gave him, which could have frozen water.

Renders continued. "After all, they are a murderous nonhuman bunch of savages, and you, well . . ." He motioned toward the empty air as if to say the point was obvious.

"I've learned to chew with my mouth closed, thank you," said Toede, keeping his voice in check and wondering if the gnolls would thank him if he started in on braining a few scholars now. Judging from Charka's earlier attitude toward gratitude, probably not.

"You could at least try. To talk to them," added Renders.

Or talk my way *through* them, thought Toede, mentally adding another notch to Charka's intelligence for advancing toward the camp along their only real line of retreat. "The problem is," said Toede, leaning back and stroking his chin. "The problem is, we need some superiority, some dominance that they might fear. Say, for example"—Toede looked at the lamplit roof of the tent—"magic. Do you have any wizards of any ability in your group?"

Renders chuckled. "In my experience, wizards aren't very willing to share their knowledge. And they're always looking for this magical item or that artifact. No, we never bring them along on a dig if we can help it."

Bloody wonderful, thought Toede. "What about warriors, someone good with a sword?"

"We had some scouts," said the older sage, "but we let them go soon after we started. Cheaper that way, with the necromancer not bothering anyone, and we didn't know about the gnolls, of course. There's always . . . you."

"It would be difficult for all of you to hide behind even my muscular, battle-hardened frame," said Toede, confident by this point that Renders was immune to sarcasm. "And besides, I'm not for hire, and I don't think that Groag's cooking would be reason enough for me to want to die at your side."

"Ah," said Renders, jerking himself upright. "Of course. How foolish. I was so used to dealing with the other one, the cook, that I just assumed. Hmmm, where did I put it? Ah!" The elder scholar pulled a large box out from his trunk and rummaged through it. He removed a large gem, about the size of Toede's thumbnail, and set it on the table before the hobgoblin.

"Will that do?" he asked.

Toede picked up the gem and turned it over a few times. If it were a fake, it was one that could pass his critical eye (and by connotation anyone else's, short of a dwarf's). Toede nodded, pocketing the gem. At least I'll die rich, he thought.

Toede looked out at the still-sleeping camp, thinking of recommending that the scholars just take their chances with the swamp or the necromancer. Across the dying embers of the campfire, he could see the clear light of

Bunniswot's magical stone, showing the dancing shadow of the young scholar trying to re-cover that which he had so recently uncovered.

Toede smiled. "Actually, Renders, I *can* talk to them, but first I'll need some things from Bunniswot."

* * * * *

It was a few hours before dawn. Groag was still seated beneath the oak, watching his fingers. He flexed them, wiggled them, and in the likely event that Toede would not reappear, bid them a fond farewell.

Such pleasant hands, he thought, pity they're going to be gone soon, and all because of that rat-bastard Toede. At least he (Groag) had thought better than to tell his captors outright that Toede was likely going to head for the high country as soon as inhumanly possible. There could still be a chance for a miracle rescue, up to the point of the first hatchet-fall on his digits.

He was being watched over by a pair of Charka's guards. Charka didn't seem as interested in him as the gnoll chieftain had been in Toede. Groag idly wondered what the link between the two was. When he wasn't saying mental good-byes to his extremities, that is. If their positions had been reversed, would he have fled? Probably not, but then he (Groag) thought that he (Toede) had sacrificed his (Toede's) life for his (Groag's) own. If that was true, then why was the former highmaster acting untrustworthy this time around?

Groag's gloomy reverie was broken by the sound of approaching hooves. His heart leaped for a moment, but his brain turned surly and sour. Whatever it was, he thought, it couldn't be good.

The horse carrying Toede stopped at the edge of the clearing. At first thought Groag thought it wasn't the highmaster at all, that it was one of the scholars disguised as Toede. Then he realized that it *was* Toede, and that

Toede was wearing Bunniswot's ridiculous dressing gown, the one his mother made for him. The gown hung long and loose on the sides, with the sleeves rolled back and tied off at his elbows. The patches of alchemic symbols were dark blotches in the red moonlight.

Toede did not dismount, such that he remained only a little shorter than the surrounding gnolls. The former highmaster intoned in his deepest, darkest pronouncement-style voice: "I bring greetings to Charka from Chief Boils Flesh. Boils Flesh is most displeased with Charka for doubting power of Boils Flesh. Most displeased."

By this time most of the gnolls were staring at the mounted hobgoblin. Toede raised a hand, revealing a small, dark wooden box.

"Boils Flesh gives challenge to Charka," continued Toede.

"Box hold weakest juju of Boils Flesh. If Charka can defeat juju, Boils Flesh and other wizards become dinner. If Charka cannot"—and here Toede smiled his most evil smile—"Boils Flesh will curse Charka and Charka's people."

Toede tossed the box at the gnoll chief's feet. Charka picked it up with all the care usually reserved for a live skunk. The gnoll turned it over in his hands a few times, then carefully lifted the lid.

The bright rays of the light-stone struck the chieftain full in the face. Charka squinted, snarled, and dropped the box. The box hit the ground and flew fully open, bathing the entire region beneath the oak in near daylight.

Gnolls, though unharmed by something as simple as light (unlike vampires, goblins, or other mythological creatures) were by nature nocturnal, so the entire company took two steps backward from the unusual radiance.

Weakest juju indeed, thought Groag bitterly. That was Bunniswot's piece of magical light, purchasable from any hedge wizard passing through Flotsam. Was Toede so stupid as to imagine that Charka had never met a wizard, and had never witnessed a light spell?

Actually Toede was hoping exactly that, but additionally hoped that the wizards Charka and his people had encountered were all of the necromancer class: powerful figures best seen at a distance, and not meddled with unless one was tired of living. Toede certainly looked pleased by the result so far; he was fighting to keep the smile from his sallow face.

"Defeat juju and live," said Toede. "Fail and be cursed. You have until dawn."

Charka blinked the sparks out of his eyes and picked up the small ball, apparently curious that something so bright could be so heavy. He closed his fist around it. The light seeped between his taloned fingers and gave his fur a soft glow. He tightened his grip, and the light was extinguished.

Charka smiled and relaxed. As soon as he opened his fist, the light resumed, leaking out through the gaps between his fingers. Charka growled and gripped the stone harder. Again, the light was extinguished, only to return as bright as before. A third time Charka tried to crush the stone, but to no effect.

Charka barked something in swamp-talk to the other gnolls. Two of them bustled away. He tried to squeeze the stone into submission with both hands, but with the same result. Toede was obviously enjoying himself. "King of Little Dry Frogs explain curse to Charka."

Toede did so, as Charka strained with the magically lit stone and the other gnolls watched. Toede's description was detailed, graphic, and delivered entirely in the pidgin language Charka could understand.

As could a few of the other gnolls, for Groag could see their faces blanch in the cursed light. As for Groag, he had no problem with the flesh melted off the bones part, but the threat of live boring beetles being shoved under the fingernails was a bit much even for him.

The two gnolls who left earlier returned with a bucket

made of lashed leather, filled with swamp water. Charka plunged the lighted stone into the water and was rewarded for his trouble with wet fur along both arms and a pleasant light-show across the bare trees as the light shone through the ripples of the water's surface.

Charka cursed, or at least Groag thought it a curse, for it was long and bitter in nature. One of the other gnolls strode up to Charka, babbling something else in swamp-talk. Charka snarled back. An argument ensued that was ended only by Charka backhanding the babbling gnoll. The other gnoll retreated, his ears flat and head slunk low. Charka snarled, an apparent challenge. None of the other gnolls responded. Charka set the magically lit stone on the ground and began pounding it with a rock.

At first all Charka did was pound the sphere into the ground. Then the chieftain placed it on another rock and tried crushing it between two stones. Then another attempt, hammering at it with his morning star, bringing the heavy iron head down on the rock.

As Charka hammered, light danced beneath the denuded oak, highlighting the surrounding trees; the gnolls, looking more uncomfortable by the moment; Toede, as motionless as a carved figure on his horse; and an increasingly beaten and dejected Charka. Long ropes of saliva were dripping from the gnoll's wolflike mouth, and the muscles of his face and neck were tight with strain.

Groag stood up then. Neither of his guardian gnolls were paying attention. He began edging around the tree, ready to bolt any moment. He was ignored. The sky was already beginning to lighten, turning that slate-gray shade that preceded the dawn.

Charka pounded until he dropped his morning star in disgust, panting heavily. The sphere was now more of an ellipsoid, but all the gnoll's activity had not diminished the radiance of it in the least.

Toede shifted atop his horse. "I see Charka has failed.

Nice knowing you, Charka. Good-bye!"

With that, Toede began to swing his mount around. Groag thought Toede was bluffing, but faded deeper into the brushy shadows anyway, just in case.

Charka turned to Toede. "Wait!" panted the large gnoll.

Toede stopped, turned halfway on his horse. "Yes?" Toede smiled.

Charka fumed for a moment. "Charka kill Boils Flesh anyway. Kill many wizards."

Toede leaned back and laughed, as Groag pulled himself deeper into the brush. "Charka cannot defeat wizard's toy? What chance has Charka to defeat wizard?"

Charka bit on the air for a moment, and Toede turned back to leave. "Wait!"

Toede smiled again. "Yes?"

Charka said, "Charka still has hostage."

Toede said pleasantly, "Charka has no hostage."

At that moment Groag's heart skipped a beat, as the collected gnolls suddenly realized there was an empty spot where Groag had been. There was consternation among the gnolls, as none had noticed his disappearance.

Several of them moved toward the brush, looking for Groag. Toede held up a pudgy hand. "Don't bother," he said. "Powerful juju chief."

"Wait!" said Charka, even though Toede had not turned to go again. The gnoll chief shook as though he were about to explode into pieces. Then quietly he reminded Toede, "Charka save King of Little Dry Frogs. Save life. King of Little Dry Frogs owes Charka."

"Ah," said Toede. "Gratitude." He paused a beat and smiled. "Thank you, Charka. Good-bye now." He turned to leave.

Charka strode around to the front of the horse, about four gnoll-strides. The gnoll chieftain stepped forward, hands spread wide. "Charka take people back to swamp."

Toede shrugged. "Charka still cursed."

Charka fumed. Finally he said, "How Charka appease

Great Juju Chief Boils Flesh?"

"Charka sorry?" said Toede.

There was a mutter from the massive gnoll. Groag thought the creature responded, "Charka sorry."

The two talked for a moment. Then Charka ran to retrieve the magically lit stone and the box and handed them back to the hobgoblin. Then the two talked for another moment. Charka began bellowing orders. The gnolls, all thirty of them, faded into the trees on all sides. Toede then rode southward, Groag's horse tied to his, Charka at his side.

Groag was abandoned. Not an abnormal situation, all in all, he thought, pulling himself from the briars. Toede regularly abandoned people, though usually through the means of one or the other dying.

Groag thought of heading north, back to Flotsam, but two things stood in his way. First, he wanted to make sure the scholars were safe, and that Toede had not betrayed them. And second, he had not expected Toede to return at all. Honoring any obligation was most unToedelike. It should have made Groag feel relieved, that his faith in the former highmaster was somehow justified.

Instead, it just increased the feeling of dread in his stomach, that when the end came, it would be all the worse.

Sighing, Groag set out southward toward the camp as the first rays of dawn set the surviving autumn leaves on fire.

Chapter 15

In which Our Protagonist reaps the fruits of his labor, considers his lot in life, and receives a vision of greater things to come.

By midmorning the scholars' camp was a flurry of activity, none of which was directly connected to imminent escape. Various librarians were leaping around the fallen pillars, making last-minute notes. A few of "the boys" were digging trenches, into which Bunniswot would dump badly wrapped satchels of notes (and in one case, an overloaded leather trunk in one grave-deep trench) for "later recovery." (Of course, Bunniswot made a nasty giggle when he said this). Renders scurried around, trying to make a map of where everything was buried. No one had taken down any of the tents, nor packed any personal effects. And of course, breakfast had been skipped by mutual agreement considering the cook had already been presumably eaten by the gnolls.

So it was a surprise when, about three hours after dawn, the gnolls finally appeared. A surprise not in that their arrival came later than expected, but in that they did not arrive screaming and seeking to use their spears for impromptu exploratory surgery. Instead, only one gnoll appeared, accompanying Toede, who was still mounted on one of the horses and dressed in Bunniswot's dressing gown. The gnoll was large even by gnoll standards, and dressed in a manner that Renders could immediately trace to preCataclysm humanoid war cults.

The two stood there, hobgoblin and gnoll, immobile, until one by one the scholars became aware of their presence. Those involved in arguments left in midword, those making stone rubbings in midrub, and those making maps in midcartographical flourish. Bunniswot was patting down the last of his buried treasure and notes with a shovel. When he looked up, saw everyone else gazing elsewhere, he joined the silent tableaux of scholars staring at the strange pair of humanoids.

Renders set his bone pen aside and walked toward the pair. The old scholar was dressed in white and cream, as was his personal preference, and the sun bounced beams off his shining form. He stopped all of five paces away from the gnoll and hobgoblin, noting that the gnoll chieftain looked even taller close up.

The gnoll chieftain gestured imperiously. Two large gnolls strode out of the brush, each carrying the carcass of a freshly slain boar. Then two more, carrying baskets of tubers, currants, and wild grapes. Then another pair, carrying wooden platters made of sassafras bark, and heavily laden with chestnuts, walnuts, and hickory nuts. Then another pair, one with a clutch of catfish strung through the gills on a leather thong, the other with a similar string of mountain trout. Then a gnoll with a basket of freshwater eels, and lastly one with a hemp basket of live crawfish, still skittering slowly over each other.

The tall gnoll slapped his chest and cried, "Charka!"

Toede translated. "Charka begs forgiveness of the mighty wizards and offers these gifts in apology."

Renders made to hold out his hand, but Toede shot him a quick, nasty look. Instead, the scholar placed it over his heart and proclaimed solemnly, "Renders."

The gnolls bowed. "Great Chief Boils Flesh."

Renders arched an eyebrow at Toede. "Ah. Ah. Boils flesh?"

"He believes you and yours to excel in culinary abilities," Toede put in.

Renders looked cross for the first time. "Whatever gave him that accursed idea?"

"Hur?" said Charka.

"Great Chief pleased for now. Accepts gifts. Warns Charka's people to behave or curse returns." To Renders, Toede added quickly, "Fine language is not their forté. Just leave out anything that sounds as if it would stump a gully dwarf, and you'll be fine."

"But I think we should inform him that I am not such a great cook." Renders shook his head, then smiled pleasantly at the curious look he received from the gnoll.

"Some things get misunderstood in translation." Toede shrugged. "And note that this one can break you up into small pieces if he ever believes you *not* to be a great wizard and chef."

"Ah," said Renders. "Ah. Well then." To the gnoll Renders spread his hands out, imitating Toede. "Great Chief Boils Flesh thanks Charka for gifts. Build fire, have mighty feast!"

Then he turned to the collected scholars, who were observing the entire business. "Let's get with the program, gentlemen," Renders hissed, clapping his hands.

* * * * *

Fortunately for all, by the time the fire had been sufficiently banked to a good bed of coals, and the pots (still dirty from the previous day) sufficiently graveled and washed, Groag made his return, footsore and cranky. He found Charka, Toede, and Renders engaged in lively debate with a few of the gnolls in the main pavilion, Bunniswot cursing and excavating a trench furiously, and the remaining gnolls seated at the southern perimeter of the camp. A couple of Renders's "boys" were arguing about how to best boil a boar.

Groag waded in to save the "boys" from culinary disaster. In short order, the boars were properly skinned, the nuts shucked, the fish deboned, and the grapes and currants properly rinsed. A pot bubbled as the crawfish boiled, turning a brilliant shade of blue.

After about an hour, Toede broke away from the pavilion group and padded down to the cooking fire, where Groag was still puffing and shouting. From what Toede had learned of swamp-gnoll rituals, as long as dinner wasn't burned too badly, the visitors would be happy. Cooked food was still a novelty, apparently, in the swamp.

"Nice of you to show up at last," said Toede.

Groag wheeled and shot a nasty look at the former highmaster. "I've nothing to say to you," he said, turning back to tending the impromptu boar-spit that had been rigged up for the occasion.

Toede rocked back on his heels slightly. "That's no attitude to take," he sputtered, "after all I've done for you!'

"All you've done?" Groag hissed. The "boys" looked up from their tasks, but none of the gnolls seemed to notice, or care. "Every time . . ." Groag continued, "every time I hook up with you, something horribly unpleasant happens. Dragons. Assassins. Exploding draconians. And this time, you left me hostage and ran off."

"I came back," Toede hissed, "and saved Bunniswot and Renders and all the rest of the mentally impaired."

"And that worries me even more," said Groag. "Why? You always have a scheme, some angle on things. What is it? Are you after Renders for money, or what?"

Toede shoved a hand in his pocket, stroking the large gem that Renders had given him in payment. He flinched from its warmth, as if the stone had been recently pulled from the fire. "I told you," he said firmly, "I'm trying to live in a noble manner. I'm surprised that you of all people have trouble believing that."

"I have trouble believing it because I know you," grumbled Groag. "I'll be watching you, just keep that in mind.

Now sod off, I'm cooking dinner." With that, Groag turned his back on Toede.

Toede fumed, briefly considering hobgoblicide. However, they did need Groag to cook. And the fact was that Groag was probably right. He did know Toede too well, and he probably ought to be worried.

So instead of braining his companion, Toede stomped back to the white fabric pavilion, where Renders was translating the War of the Lance into short, pidgin common. "Then Great Flower-Warrior Heavy-Rain Shining-Sword swung Dragonlance, and kill dragon! But dragon kill Heavy-Rain, too!" said Renders. Charka and the gnolls present nodded.

Toede had discovered that the common ground between scholar and gnoll was extremely limited, primarily to war stories and alcohol, and not having much of the latter, he had steered the socializing toward the chronicles. As long as Renders was holding their attention, there seemed little danger of flare-ups between the two groups.

Toede himself had been mentioned in passing, early on, though not by name (thank the Dark Lady) as an "Evil Slave-keeper, Master of Few."

"Master of Few caught the Companions and did not know who they were," Renders had explained, "so Master of Few put them in a cage-wagon. Master of Few was to take them to his master, Worm-Guts"—or at least that was how Verminaard was translated, to Toede's amusement—"but the great wizard Doesn't-Bubble and the elves helped them escape. The cage-wagon was burned, and Master of Few fled into the night."

He had met these "Heroes of the Lance" early on, before anyone knew anything about them. And they had proceeded to escape from under his very nose—not once, but repeatedly. Not the brightest spot on his resumé, Toede thought, reflecting on how far he had advanced since those days.

If he had advanced at all, he fumed. Groag didn't seem

to think so, but then that was the problem with longtime acquaintances. They seemed to only see the part of you that they knew from *before*, and ignored the fact that you might have developed into a better being over time.

In the old days, back when Toede ruled Flotsam, he could have had Groag killed. It seemed that Groag was developing a spine. He, too, was changing. Adapting.

Well, Toede could change just as much. He was quite proud of his newfound nobility. True, he had been doubtful, even challenging the fates, but once he made up his mind, he had stuck to his choices. He saved Groag, saved the scholars, and saved himself. And had got a ready supply of good food in the process.

So why did he feel displeased with the entire turn of events? Not just Groag, but the fact that both Renders and Charka failed to recognize his heroic efforts. The gem Renders had given him was a nice touch, but instead of making him feel as though he had been rewarded, he felt as though he had been cheapened, almost insulted.

Apparently there was more to this nobility thing than just acting in a self-destructive manner.

Was all nobility just a scam, then, an excuse to advance one's own case and position, and then have people thank you for it? That didn't seem right, from what he knew of the noble heroes Renders was babbling on about. If anything, the Dragonlance heroes seemed to settle for far less than their actions had earned them, but perhaps that was only to gain some greater advantage later on. His reward for doing the "right and noble" thing was more tangible: the feast.

It was finally ready by midafternoon, and turned out to rival the best of the halls of the Silvanesti, though served on cruder dishware than elves would ever tolerate. Groag proved to be an expert chef once given proper ingredients, and the boar had been roasted to the point where the meat fell off at a touch and melted on the tongue. It had been seasoned in a gravy with herbs and nuts. Scholar, gnoll, and hobgoblin ate until they could eat no more, and afterward Groag threw spiced potatoes wrapped in wet burlap onto the coals to cook for dessert, while Renders continued the tales from the War of Lance for the entire assemblage.

"And so our heroes passed through this very land, on the way to the town of Floating Junk. And there the Master of Few reigned, but he was so afraid of the heroes that he hid from them, and let the Dragon Highlord Small-Cat-Crown seek them out. . . ."

"I wasn't hiding," muttered Toede, "I was busy." He wandered a little way off from the main group, sated but far from satisfied. The boar was the first good meal in how many months? Over a year, really, unless he counted the goose sandwiches the kender girl had packed. And that had been six months ago.

The former Evil Slaver, former Master of Few, former Highmaster of Flotsam, perhaps future Lord of some place unknown and unrevealed, sat at the base of a tilted pillar and tried to sort out the various conflicting feelings that jousted in his head and heart. Or at least tried to, for the combination of a full belly and over a day without sleep finally caught up with him, and within moments he was snoring softly.

* * * * *

Toede dreamed, and it was more than a standard dream of hobgoblins. His dreams (at least the ones he remembered) were usually monochromatic nightmares, the color blood red or deathly gray. Old fears rising, old enemies returned, old battles fought or fled.

But this dream was different. It had the soft texture of a well-rendered oil painting, a glow that seemed to diffuse in all directions. The color of ghosts walking in the evening light.

He awoke in the dream and knew in a moment that it was a dream, for reality did not possess this fairyland beauty. He was still in the forest of stone, but things had changed.

The inscribed plinths were there, but the birch trees around them were gone, and the tilted and overturned pillars had been righted. Now they glowed with an eldritch power all their own. There was laughter in the air, from voices unseen in the darkness, and lithe ghosts moving and dancing at the edges of his vision. Toede could not look directly at them, for they reveled just beyond his conscious grasp and melted into darkness as soon as he focused on them. Yet what little he saw of them, from the corners of his eyes, told him they were fair of form. Toede knew he was dreaming, for this beauty did not immediately turn his well-fed stomach.

Where earlier the cooking fire had been, there was now a tall, glowing woman, who did not fade when Toede stared at her. She was clad in shades of blue and white, and her hair was the color of yellow stained glass. She lit the pillars around her with the power of her aura.

She smiled at Toede, and when she did Toede felt the bottom fall out of his world. She motioned; he followed her.

The blue woman and Toede traveled through the forest of stone as dreamers travel, ignoring the briars, brambles, and bumps in the path, but instead gliding smoothly over the surface, ignoring everything in their way. Occasionally the blue woman would point at a particular landform—such as cleaved rock, or a boulder that looked particularly like a hawk—as they ascended to the west into hillier country that was (would be?) the necromancer's territory.

At length the travelers reached a low hillock that was not a hillock at all, but a great stone temple. The ghost-ogres were burying the temple in a great mound of dirt, and Toede saw that the lower reaches were already covered in grass and small trees.

The blue woman led Toede to the entrance of the temple. The ghost-ogres ignored the pair entirely. Then she motioned, and the great iron doors parted at the top of the temple stairs, and both she and Toede were bathed in a great golden radiance.

Toede awakened with a start to find that it was much later in the evening. The campfire had been broken down to little more than embers, and the gnolls were scattered around the ground, where they had drifted off to sleep among the remains of the burlap potato wrappers. There was no sign of Groag, Renders, or any of the humans.

Someone had left a cloak draped halfway on Toede, so the hobgoblin drifted back off to sleep. Now he slept more soundly, without dreams, for the shadow-gods had judged him, and now he knew what the rewards for his noble actions truly were to be.

Chapter 16

In which Our Protagonist follows his dreams, provides his own version of history, and even though the feast with the gnolls is now over, discovers the concoction "Toede in the Hole."

"I don't feel comfortable about this," said Bunniswot, stopping and rubbing his left shin again. He had injured said limb after the first rock slide, and had been carrying on and limping ever since, seeking sympathy just because he was the one carrying the pack and shovels. "Let's go back and get a few more people."

Toede shook his head and turned to look at the human, amazed to find someone in worse physical shape than himself. Sweat was running down Bunniswot's face, and from his higher elevation, Toede for the first time noted that the human had a small bald patch on the back of his head.

"We could go back," said the former highmaster, "and get some help from Renders, and explain to him why following a hunch was more important than your ogrish erotica."

Bunniswot winced at the suggestion.

"Or," Toede added slyly, "we could count on Charka to send a few of his boys into territory that is not only taboo, but under the control of a known, dangerous necromancer. Risk two of his tribe to me and a man called—now what did he name you?"

"Whacks-the-Rabbit," said Bunniswot in a mild voice. His encounters with the gnolls had not been as positive as those enjoyed by Renders.

Toede nodded, continuing, "If I'm right, and by the powers I believe in I think I am, you'll have something really important to take back to Renders." And with that he resumed climbing, not bothering to add that, if Groag had been on speaking terms with Toede, he'd much rather have taken the smaller hobgoblin as opposed to a hapless human.

"Seems like a lot to stake on a dream," said the young scholar, scrambling after him. "It's not very professional."

"Don't discount dreams, child," said Toede. "Raistlin dreamed of sunken Istar before setting sail on the *Perechon*."

"Where did you hear that?" said Bunniswot sharply. Panting, but sharply nonetheless.

"From Raistlin himself," lied Toede, turning halfway around to look down on the sweaty human. "We talked that morning before he boarded the ship out of Flotsam. Last I ever saw of him, but I still get the occasional letter, magical sending, and whatnot."

"So you knew him?" Bunniswot's voice broke as he said it. "You knew Raistlin, and Caramon, and the Heroes of the Lance?"

"About as well as anyone," said Toede, warming to the subject and wondering how far he should go with his dissembling. "You might even say I gave them their start, but that would be bragging." Toede turned his face to the upward slope, both to handle the difficulty of the climb and make sure his face did not betray the truth in his statement.

"Have you told Renders?" asked Bunniswot, his voice suddenly less haughty, less nasal, and more human.

"Should I?" asked Toede, turning to shoot a practiced blank look at the scholar.

"*Should* you?" said Bunniswot, catching up with Toede, "You heard Renders tell the story of the War of the Lance to the gnolls last night. Even cut down into language they could understand, it is a moving and epic tale."

"Well, I guess it is," said Toede, shrugging. "I mean, if you like that sort of thing."

"Renders would sell his own grandmother to interview the old Heroes, to talk to people who knew them," chuckled Bunniswot. "When we were in Flotsam, he talked to anyone who might have known them: bartenders, sailors, all sorts of riffraff."

Toede thought idly of the innkeep at the Jetties. Yes, he could imagine that one spinning out wild tales in exchange for a few coins.

"And to think that someone who was there—who *knew* Raistlin—just wandered into camp." Bunniswot laughed. It was an easy laugh, a laugh of comrades who had shared secrets. "So what were they like? Like they're portrayed in the tales?"

"Well, it would be immodest to speak as if I were a close confidante," Toede said, bowing his head in apparent modesty.

Bunniswot took the bait like a trout rising to a salmon egg. "What about Raistlin? He was my favorite of the group—brooding, dominant, so sure of himself."

"Raistlin, yes," said Toede. "He was a friend, and you don't speak ill of friends who go beyond." The hobgoblin sighed. "I still remember that last night. We both had gotten very, very drunk, and he tore into one of his long crying jags."

The hobgoblin heard the footsteps following him stop. "Crying jag? Raistlin?" said the voice behind him, astonished.

"Afraid so." Toede hunched his shoulders. "Caramon had been . . . well, you know that Caramon had always been bad tempered, and sometimes took it out on Raistlin. Simple jealousy, really. Raistlin was afraid of him, but couldn't abandon his brother. I offered for him to stay at my place, but . . ." He let his voice trail off.

"I can't believe that!" said Bunniswot. "It goes against

what the tales said. Caramon loved his brother!"

"Well, he did," said Toede. "That's why Raistlin stayed. Of course, he would get into these moods, and Raistlin would try to help and . . . oh, my, it was awful. Simply awful." Toede stopped by a large boulder that looked like a falcon or some other bird of prey, and stole a glance at Bunniswot.

The look on the young scholar's face was priceless. His eyes were the color, shape, and size of newly minted steel groats. His eyebrows had nearly vanished beneath his ragged hairline. His jaw was hanging loose, as if on a single thread.

Toede continued, as if embarrassed. "You see why I don't mention it. Here these people were heroes to you, and just people to me."

"I just find it hard to believe," said Bunniswot, obviously finding it incredibly easy to believe. "But what about the others? What about Tanis?"

"Tanis? Oh, he was the stalwart of the party. Brave, loyal, noble, honest. Of course, sometimes . . ." Toede made the motion of tipping a flask to his lips.

Bunniswot's eyebrows shot into his hairline. "He *drank*?"

"Like a fish," sighed Toede. "But he has had a lot of help and counseling since then, and I understand it's under control nowadays. Still, I remember Riverwind and Goldmoon pouring him into the ship that morning. Sad, just sad. Maybe it's better to not mention this to Renders. Rested? Let's get on."

"One more: Tika," said Bunniswot.

Toede feigned an embarrassed blush. "I really don't feel comfortable talking about Tika," said Toede. "I mean she was pleasant enough, but she never liked nonhumans, not even kender. And me being a hobgoblin, well, that just sparked all kinds of fireworks. One reason I never joined them."—sigh—"The stories I could tell of their time in Flotsam . . . No, no, the world needs heroes, and once you start showing them to be ordinary men and women, everything falls apart. They earned their status, and let's only recall the good times."

Toede started up the hill past the falcon-shaped rock, remembering how easy the journey had been in his dream. His knees were complaining.

Despite the pain Toede smirked to himself, sincerely hoping that his newfound nobility did not preclude him feeling so good about lying to the officious little scrivener.

"Toede?" the scrivener in question asked.

Toede replied testily, "Yes? I mean, what about him?"

"Highmaster Toede," said Bunniswot. "You're a hobgoblin, and Toede was in charge of Flotsam at the time. You had to have met him. Were you one of his bodyguards? Maybe a servant?"

Toede huffed menacingly. "The human assumption is that all nonhumans know each other. Do I assume you knew Astinus of Palanthas, just because you are both scholarly humans?"

Bunniswot looked hurt. "Well, I knew *of* him."

"Exactly," said Toede. "And I knew of the highmaster. And I also knew what people said about him after he disappeared. In my experience, limited though it might be, I thought of Highmaster Toede as a fair, reasonable, rational being, thoroughly misunderstood by later human bards and scholars who were engaged in a desperate scramble to create 'good guys' and 'bad guys' for their epics."

"Sorry," said Bunniswot. "Didn't mean to upset you."

Toede huffed. "I'm not upset as much as disappointed. You're a bright young human, but you swallow all the lies and half-truths your elders dig up, tainted by blatant pro-human rhetoric."

"Sorry," repeated Bunniswot. "If it is any consolation, in retrospect the highmaster didn't nearly seem the bumbler he was made out to be."

"How's that?" said Toede.

"Well, his successor was a draconian," said Bunniswot,

"who apparently murdered small children in their beds, as it turns out. And *his* successor is Toede's old mount, this Hopsloth abomination, who's dressed out in finery and has his own corrupt priesthood. So in comparison, Toede seems almost enlightened."

"My point exactly," said Toede. "You never know how good you have it until it's gone."

"Groag knew him, I think," added the young scholar. "He said that Toede had died, but was sent back to fight Gildentongue, then both Toede and the draconian died in battle. Groag was there, and said Toede was a hero. So you're right, he was sadly misunderstood."

Toede turned and smiled. "Groag said that?"

Bunniswot nodded. "For a while, right after he recovered from his burns. Then he stopped talking about Toede. I think . . ." Bunniswot paused, puffing for breath, "I think that Hopsloth's cultists got to him and convinced him to hush up."

"You're very observant," said Toede, and the pair continued the climb in silence.

The top of the low plateau they had been scaling was not especially high, but just high enough to discourage Saturday-afternoon adventurers. As they reached the summit, Toede turned to look out over the land below. Most of it was covered in a low autumn haze that appeared most dense over the marshlands. The birches were golden, and Toede could see the smoke rising from the scholars' campfire. Farther off, hidden by several ridges, was another wisp of smoke. Toede fancied that one to be kender in origin. To his left was a deep valley, and on the opposite side of the vale was a citadel, dark and misty against the white haze. Its general shape was that of a skull, and Toede surmised that was the intended effect of its construction.

"So there is a necromancer," he said to the panting Bunniswot.

Trees had grown up on the plateau, atop the low hillocks that had been in Toede's dream buildings of amber and glowing jade. What was once the main thoroughfare was now a bracken-filled mass of shrubbery. In the back, vaguely definable through the dead, brown brush, the leafless and lifeless trees, and the withered vines of wild grapes, was a hillock somewhat higher than the rest.

"That's where we're heading," said Toede. "Come along." He plunged into the brush, unaware of, and totally ignoring the scholar's moans and complaints trailing behind him.

* * * * *

The two explorers did not have much to say as they pressed their way across the plateau's cluttered debris and waste. Their conversation was limited to warning each other about branches or loose rocks beneath their feet. Sometimes the original flagstone pavement would appear, taunting them for feet, sometimes yards, before diving beneath another tangle of briars.

In time they reached the hill that, according to Toede's dream, would cradle the buried temple. The hill in question was relatively free of brush, and nothing more healthy than a sickly, yellowing moss grew on its flanks.

Toede scaled the hill about halfway, pointed to an otherwise unremarkable depression in the dirt, and ordered, "Dig here."

Bunniswot muttered a few vague curses, but pitched in with the larger of the two shovels. The dirt was not packed solid, however, and after breaking through the sod, the scholar quickly uncovered a low carved stone, wider from side to side than bottom to top.

"A step!" said Bunniswot, delighted. Toede just shrugged as the scholar dropped to his knees to examine it. "No writing on it, but the carving technique is identical to the forest of stones. But this city is so far removed from the plinths. The question is why?"

Toede frowned. "Far for your legs or mine. Perhaps your

proto-ogres had longer limbs, or more endurance. Also, the neighborhood has changed a great deal since these areas were last used. What say we keep looking, eh?"

Bunniswot's enthusiasm lasted for a second step and most of the third. He started to tire significantly by the fourth, and if there had been a fifth step, he would have insisted that Toede take a turn at the shovel.

Instead, metal hit metal. Bunniswot beamed at the hobgoblin. "Pay dirt," he said, and began clearing the area around the door, until a two-foot-square area of rusted iron was revealed.

Toede smiled, noting, "You're going to have to clear a lot more. The door swings outward."

Bunniswot reversed his shovel and pressed the handle firmly against the iron barrier. It fell away at his touch, and the sound of it striking the flagstones rang through the darkness beyond. A strong breeze smelling of wet rot and decay billowed out, and both human and hobgoblin stood there for a moment, gagging on the fumes.

"First time you're wrong," smiled Bunniswot. Toede just furrowed his brow and peered deeper into the hole. It yawned like the Abyss. No far wall was visible from their entrance.

"Awful dark in there," said Bunniswot, then added, "We didn't bring torches."

"I don't need them," said the hobgoblin. "My people were hunting by night while yours were still trying to invent socks. But here . . ."

Toede fished through his pocket, pulled out Renders's gem, placed it in another pocket, and produced the small box containing the magically lit stone.

"My stone," said Bunniswot. "You never returned it," he added sharply.

"You never asked for it," said Toede absentmindedly, looking into the temple's new entrance. "But that's all right—you've been busy."

While it was true that hobgoblins such as Toede did not

particularly need light to see, the presence of light did help him discern colors, and now revealed to him a checkerboard of purple and bright yellow stretching out into the darkness.

"Guess we better go in," said Toede.

"After you," said Bunniswot. "You are smaller than I."

"The history should say that Sir Bunniswot was the first to enter the greatest temple discovery since the War of the Lance," said Toede. "Please, I'm feeling noble about it," he added for anyone or anything that might be listening.

The scholar could not dispute that last point, and so, taking the light-stone, he poked his head through the small opening and slowly wormed his body through the doorway. When there were no immediate screams of pain or sounds of flying axe blades whirring through the air, Toede tossed in the large shovel and followed.

Bunniswot had not wandered too far from the door, and indeed was inspecting the frame and tiles that the falling iron door had smashed.

"You were right," he said, the scholarly part of his mind running at full tilt. "This door should have opened outward. The pins had rusted almost clear through, and that push knocked it off its hinges."

The air was thick with humidity, and in the darkness Toede could hear the distant sound of water dripping. Seepage from farther up the hill, or perhaps some natural spring.

Toede picked up the shattered tiles. They were square, about a foot across and the thickness of a fingernail. The purple ones were lapis lazuli, sliced to a thinness that would make a dwarven craftsman salivate. The yellowish ones were beaten gold, sliced even thinner. Toede held one of the purple ones up against the doorway. The light reflected through its thinness, casting smokey purple shadows on his face.

The tilework stretched farther into the darkness. Bunniswot shouted and was rewarded with a crisp, clear echo.

So there *was* a solid wall on the far side, far out of reach.

The human and the hobgoblin exchanged glances as they started down the hallway.

The entranceway was lined with statues and inscriptions. The statues were humanoid and bilaterally symmetrical—that is, the left side of each blobby figure matched the right side. Some had definite heads or arms, but others seemed to be nothing more than fire or water caught at an opportune moment and transformed to stone.

"Are these your proto-ogres?" asked Toede.

"Yes and no," said Bunniswot. "I think their sculpture, aside from the carvings down in the camp, is supposed to represent the 'true form' of an individual. In the temple's prime, there would have been colorful pigments smeared on the stones, or even magically illuminated ones."

Toede grunted, wondering about the sanity of these creatures, if they truly were the ancestors of the ogres. He had heard worse tales, but he definitely did not want to meet the original models of some of the statuary—particularly the ones represented clutching spikes.

The hallway opened into a large room, its side walls falling away in the darkness on the right and left. The tilework continued, ending in a great edifice carved into the living rock at the center of the hill. This carving was over thirty feet high and tilted forward at the top, so as to loom over those below.

There was no abstract nature to this carving. It was the leering head of a jackal or coyote, its eyes not circular, but hexagonal hollows that once held lights or flames. The jackal head only had an upper jaw, its ivory spears of teeth set into stone. What would have been the lower jaw was instead a wide horizontal roller, like that used for children's toys or a baker's rolling pin.

Both explorers stopped and looked up at the monstrosity. It towered over them so that the ceiling itself was lost to view.

At length, Bunniswot said, "The legends I told you

about, the ones that brought us here?" His voice carried a thrill of wonderment.

"Uh-huh," said Toede, suddenly aware of a chill in the air.

"In those legends, the ur-ogres had fought an Abyss-spawned fiend, defeated it, and trapped it."

Toede thought of his own dream, of the ogres burying the temple. "You think this is commemorating the battle?"

"Uh-huh," said Bunniswot. "Or warning people that here is where the fiend is trapped."

Bunniswot, with the light, took two steps backward, just in case. Toede took two steps forward, to examine the carvings closer.

Several hundred years before, the timbers supporting portions of the floor had rotted away, such that little was holding up the panels of the ancient floor. Stone and gold made thinner than a sheaf of paper were now spanning deep pits and hidden underground passages.

Toede stepped onto one such location, where four unsupported tiles met. They cracked immediately beneath his modest weight.

The hobgoblin pitched forward, his arms pinwheeling to grab on to something concrete. He shouted what might have been a cry for help, a curse, or both.

The scholar shouted something back and stepped forward, but Toede was already gone. Bunniswot counted to three before he heard the impact, a loud splash. The sound echoed and rebounded off the walls, booming in the scholar's ears like a castle falling into the sea.

The booming diminished, until finally Bunniswot was left with the silence.

He dropped flat on the floor and crawled to the edge, testing every move before placing any weight on the fragile surface. He edged up to the rim of the void below.

"Hello?" he asked meekly, afraid there would be no reply.

Chapter 17

In which rescue is sent for, and once it arrives, Our Protagonist must argue in his defense from a decidedly inferior position, yet despite this almost succeeds. Almost.

The reply came, not in any words that Bunniswot would wish to repeat in mixed company. Mixed, in the terms of containing men and women, adults and children, or the living and dead.

The long colorful string of loud curses bounced off the walls of the upper temple.

"Are you in pain?" shouted the scholar when the verbal onslaught finally wound down.

"Yes," shouted Toede. "My feelings are hurt that I'm down here and you're up there."

"What do you see?"

"Darkness and water," said Toede. "I'm in some kind of flooded hallway or aqueduct. It's neither deep nor swift."

"Thank goodness for the water," shouted Bunniswot.

Another string of curses, followed by a pause. "Why do you say that?"

"You fell about fifty feet," replied Bunniswot, estimating by his count. "If you had hit something hard, you wouldn't be alive to be cursing now."

Toede refused to be comforted by this news. Above him, a bright light revealed Bunniswot's position. To the right and left everything faded into darkness.

"I can try this passage that heads toward the south," said Toede. "I think I hear rushing water in that direction."

"Not a good idea," said Bunniswot. "We had to dig our way in here, remember? It's unlikely that there's another exit. You notice any vermin? Any rats?"

The sound of someone turning around swiftly to look in all directions at once, while standing in water, then a quiet, concerned, "No."

"That's too bad," said Bunniswot with the manner of man who was not at the bottom of a watery hole. "If there were, that would mean I might be wrong—there is another way out."

"I'm out of options," said Toede crossly.

"I'll go get help," said Bunniswot.

"What an original idea. Throw down some food, will you? It may be a while before you get back."

"Right." Something shadowy splashed into the stream near the hobgoblin. Toede waded over to it and pulled it out. "Got it? You want the light?" Bunniswot shouted.

"You'll need it," said Toede, adding to himself, if there are any nasty creatures left, I'd rather Bunniswot's light attract them to him as opposed to me. "I'll find a dry niche and wait."

"Right-oh," said the scholar. "I hate to leave you like this."

Toede considered yet another string of curses, but instead said, "I'll be fine. I've hosted dinner parties in worse neighborhoods than this. Now go, before I catch the cobbiewobbles or something worse."

"Right-oh," Bunniswot repeated. Toede heard footsteps retreating in long strides. There was another shout about a minute later. Bunniswot, letting him know that he had reached the door unharmed, was indeed heading for help.

Toede sloshed through the water and found an uncomfortable pile of damp, rotted timbers that had cascaded from the ceiling a few millennia earlier. He clambered up on them, shucked off his boots, emptied them of water, and unwrapped the package Bunniswot had tossed to him. Strips of cooked boar, still fresh from the previous evening. Toede chewed on the meat, reflecting on his situation.

His dream had been a sending, of that he was certain. An opportunity to further enhance his noble status by helping the young scholar.

And to enhance his own name and line his pockets with any ancient coins that were lying about.

Again, the idea of noble actions and self-advancement seemed to go hand in hand. He helped the scholars and got a gem and a fine meal. He discovered the lost temple of the proto-ogres, and was meant to find great treasure. It wasn't his dream's fault that the floorboards were weak, was it?

The noble heroes always followed their dreams. So Toede followed his, and now it left him seated on some moldering wood awash in fetid, lifeless water.

Of course, the dream didn't mention the big edifice above, the jackal-faced fiend with the rolling-pin lower jaw. Was that more than just an oversight?

Toede shuddered and cast a glance around. It looked as though nothing had passed this way, fiendish or otherwise, for the past five hundred years or so. So either the creature from the carving was very lackadaisical about its housecleaning habits, or the temple was empty.

Except for him.

Toede leaned back, staring into the darkness above him. He closed his eyes and listened, but heard nothing except for the rush of a distant waterfall. He was unaware of the passage of time and fell asleep without intending to. His dreams were monochromatic, unenlightening, and unremarkable. No shining women showed him the way out.

Then was the sound of boots on tiles above, and Toede bolted awake. The sound of rushing water in the distance had stopped, but Toede could discern the sounds of a careful, heavy tread, as if each footfall were being tested and retested before proceeding.

There was no light from the hole far above, only the same murky grayness.

"Hello?" said Toede, his voice echoing in the darkness. Louder, he shouted, "Bunniswot? Anyone there?"

From above came a quiet, level voice. "Hello, Toede."

"Groag, is that you?" Toede could just make out the smaller hobgoblin's silhouette, black against darker black.

A pause, as if the shadow were thinking it over. "Yes," came the response.

"Did Bunniswot send you?" Toede said, growing concerned. It sounded like Groag, and looked (as far as he could tell) like Groag, and since Toede could not imagine much of a market for Groag-imitators, it must be Groag. But something was amiss here.

Another pause. "Yes," came the answer, "and Renders, before he left."

"Did you bring a rope?" said Toede.

"Typical," came the response. "Yes, I brought a rope."

"Well, nice of you to drop by and all, but do you think you could hurry up and get me out of here?"

Another pause, and when the answer came at last, it was all choked. "Why?"

"Well, because it's wet and cold and I'm in a temple dedicated to a creature who might not be entirely dead," said Toede.

Another pause. "And?"

"And I'm asking you nicely," said Toede, smiling in the dark. "Very nicely."

"Oh." Another pause. "That makes it all better, then, doesn't it?"

Toede frowned and said to the figure above, "I sense that something is wrong here."

"You might say that," said Groag's voice.

"Something in the temple?" His voice caught. Something ugly and fiendish and heading his way?

"No," said Groag's voice.

"Something at camp, then. With Bunniswot and the others?" Toede felt a chill creeping up his spine.

"Yes," said the voice from above.

"Groag," said Toede, "I really enjoy playing 'ask-me-another' with you. Just tell me what happened."

Another silence, and Toede was just about to launch into a string of invectives aimed at his hobgoblin partner, when Groag said in a strangled voice, "You happened, Toede."

"Pardon?"

"You happened." The voice grew stronger, sounding more like Groag every moment. The extremely irritated Groag Toede had left by the fireside the previous evening. "I survived your last little encounter among the living, just barely, and pulled my life back together. Yet every time you show up, everything falls apart again." It sounded as though he were on the verge of weeping.

"Groag, I did come back for you. Didn't I? It's not as if I were going to leave you among the gnolls." Toede tried to give his voice the consistency of buttermilk. If Groag cracked up, he'd never get out of here.

"You came back," came the accusation, "to make matters worse."

"Worse?" shouted Toede. "I foxed Charka into helping us. I got hot food in everyone's bellies. I found this old temple for Bunniswot, and you say I've made matters worse. How?"

A very long silence this time. "By being you. Just by being Toede."

Toede waited for Groag to pick up the thread and explain himself, and after half an eternity the hobgoblin did. "You left Renders and the rest of us behind when you went off haring with Bunniswot. While you were gone, Renders told more stories about the Heroes of the Lance. He also told the story of your death. The first one, with the kender and the dragon."

Again silence, another eternity. Then Groag picked up

the story again. "Renders told about the kender and the dragon and your disastrous hunt. And Charka said that Renders was talking about you, King of Little Dry Frogs." Groag chuckled, not a pleasant sound.

"Listen, Groag," said Toede, "Whatever Charka says . . ."

"Don't interrupt," said Groag, loudly and surprisingly sharply. "Renders said that Charka had to be mistaken. He said it in a way that made Charka feel stupid about it. Charka argued, and soon the two were going at it heatedly. You've seen Charka's style of argument."

A sinking feeling gripped Toede in the stomach and would not let go.

"Then Bunniswot arrived with news of your discovery. . . ." said Groag.

The sinking feeling became sunken.

"Charka was angered that you two had gone into the necromancer's territory. Renders said that Charka had mistaken you for Toede. Bunniswot launched into a loud tirade about how misunderstood Toede had been and anyway no hairy dog-man was going to tell him and you where to go. And then . . ."

"Charka hit Bunniswot?" Toede suggested.

There was a sigh above. "Square in the face. Bunniswot hit the ground like a sack of dung." Then sobbing. Toede was surprised, as he did not think that Groag and the scholar were that close.

When Groag continued, his voice had regained its steely tone. "So Bunniswot was lying on the ground, bleeding from the nose and mouth, and Renders got angry and pushed Charka. And Charka pushed back, and Renders fell over backward.

"Then Charka stopped, and realized what he had done—pushing a powerful wizard around. Remember, you told him Renders was this great, flesh-boiling wizard? Except the wizard didn't react as a wizard would, throwing fireballs, with lightning dancing off his beard.

He reacted like an old man who'd been pushed down."

Toede finished the thought. "And Charka realized he'd been fooled . . ."

Groag continued, and Toede imagined him now sitting at the edge of the hole, staring into the darkness. "Charka ordered the gnolls who were still in camp to go out and gather the ones who had gone hunting. Renders went after them, to 'set things right' in his words."

"Charka will decorate a stick with his head," said Toede to himself.

"Yes," said Groag, and Toede was surprised he had heard him. "And then he will return and beat the rest of the scholars to death with it. Bunniswot was in no shape to travel, so he gave me the rope and told me how to find you." A pause. "When I last saw him he was digging up his papers. Said he was going to throw them on the fire. His shirt was drenched in his own blood."

Groag's voice had become softer as his tale wound down. "They're all going to die, you know, and it's all your fault," he said at last.

Toede frowned in the darkness. "Now wait a moment, that can't be right. I wasn't even there!"

"Exactly!" shouted Groag. "You weren't there! You were out getting in trouble elsewhere! Were you there, you would have come up with some glib lie and forced it down their gullible throats, and they would have thanked you for it, and they would keep believing you until you betrayed them sometime later on."

"Groag, I . . ."

"You're always abandoning people, either leaving them to fend for themselves—or dying—and you don't even have the decency to stay dead!" Groag was bellowing now, and with all the echoes and reverberation Toede had a hard time making out his words. "It's not a question of if you will betray someone. It's a question of when!"

Groag was bubbling with rage. "You think this new nobility scam will bring you back into power, but I won't let anyone else die because of your venal stupidity!"

Groag said a few other things that were lost in the echoes. His tirade ran out of gas finally. All Toede could hear was heavy breathing.

"Finished?" asked Toede.

"I suppose I am," said Groag in the darkness.

"Then throw the rope down," said Toede.

A long pause, broken only by gurgling noises. "Have you heard even one word I've said?"

"I've heard every word you said, and they're well-said words." Toede took a deep breath, feeling his tongue physically rebel at the next words. "I want you to know . . . I'm sorry. I was"—he felt his stomach coil—"wrong. I was *wrong*."

There was no response from Groag, so Toede pressed on. "I've been wrong in the past. I'll admit it. So full of myself and sure of everything that I led you into disaster, and paid for it with my life. Twice now. I'm sorry. I was wrong. Now throw the rope down."

A silence continued at the top. Toede was reminded of his nonconversation with a horse the day before. That at least had a resolution.

"You mention the scholars," continued Toede, shifting tone slightly. "We both know that the only thing that can save them is me. Only I am smart enough, and cagey enough, and yes, greedy and venal enough to pull it off. Only I can deal with Charka and the gnolls. Otherwise they'll die, Groag, unless you toss down the rope."

"I . . . I . . ." Then silence.

Toede wished he could command, could yell, could scream Groag into obedience. No, this was the only way.

Toede took another deep breath, and the next lie came more freely. "I wish I were more like you, sometimes. A-dap-tive. I want to make things better now. For you and for me. Throw the rope down, Groag," said Toede, the tiniest bit of steel creeping into his voice.

"I suppose you're right," said the small voice at the top.

"It's just been so confusing—you, the kender, the humans. I mean, who knows what's right anymore?"

"I understand," said Toede carefully. "Just throw the rope down."

"Oh," said the voice above.

Toede missed the 'kay' that should have followed it. After a moment, he ventured, "Groag?"

Groag's voice was now a whisper, "There's someone here."

Toede felt the return of a glacial fear. "Get out of there, Groag! Come back for me later. Can you hear me? Get out of there." Images of some Abyss-spawned fiend bearing down on his former courtier (rescuing rope in hand) coursed through his hobgoblin mind.

"You don't understand," said Groag, his voice lightening. "She's all blue and beautiful."

She? Blue? thought Toede. Suddenly he recalled his vision. "Groag, it's a trap!" he shouted. "Some sort of magic! Don't look at her! Don't listen!"

He paused for a reply. All he heard was Groag saying, "Me? Chosen by destiny, really?"

"Abyss-fire, Groag," bellowed Toede. "Get out of there! Throw the rope down. Do something!"

"I never thought . . ." said Groag. "Me, Lord of Flotsam?"

"Groag!" screamed Toede. "Throw the rope down!"

There was the sound of something falling, and a loud splash echoed about four feet from Toede's position. The hobgoblin waded to where it floated and picked up one end of the line.

And then the other end of the line.

"Groag!" shouted Toede.

"Yes, I suppose we should be going," said Groag to his beautiful blue vision. "Good-bye, Toede. Wish we could stay and chat, but I've got things to do. I know that, now."

Groag gave an off-key whistle that faded into the darkness, ending only with the sound of a busy shovel and then a few rushes of dirt. The gray spot where the hole had been became solid black as the main entrance was resealed.

Toede stood in the darkness, holding both ends of the rope. Despair rose in his heart, only to be shoved aside by another emotion.

Anger.

Anger at Groag, at Hopsloth, at the dark gods, at Charka and the gnolls, and at anyone else who crossed his path. He had believed. Nobility had played him for the sap. And now he was paying the price.

"That's fine then," he muttered. "No more 'live nobly' for you, Master Toede. See if I help out again."

And then Toede heard the waterfall start up once more.

Chapter 18

In which Our Protagonist finds someone who has been worse off than him for a lot longer, forms a fiendish alliance, and makes a breakthrough.

Toede headed south in the darkness, toward the sound of rushing water. One part of his mind was still reeling from Groag's abandonment. One part was concerned that some evil undead creature would at any moment leap out and attack him. One part was planning various forms of tortuous revenge against Groag, who had overtaken Hopsloth on Toede's list of individuals most-likely-to-be-found-someday-soon-as-the-mystery-filling-of-a-meat-pie.

And one part was very curious about how a waterfall could turn itself on and off. Particularly since the passage rose slightly as he moved south, toward firm and (relatively) dry ground.

The most logical supposition was that the waterfall was the result of some ancient device, still in operation after all this time, that had allowed water to fill to a certain point, then tipped and emptied. That indicated the possibility of an access hatch, or even a lower exit, perhaps at the base of the plateau.

Also to be considered a dread possibility was the fact that there was something (or several somethings) alive down here after all this time, and that the waterfall was a result of its (their) actions, perhaps as a transportation device, like locks or canals.

Least logical but most likely was that the waterfall would turn out to be something that Toede had never seen before. The idea that it was something novel kept one of the parts of Toede's mind occupied while the other parts were sulking, worrying, or plotting foul revenge.

Actually, the cause of the waterfall sound proved to be all three. The passageway opened and spilled into a large, dimly lit, dome-shaped room. The interior of the dome had been tiled in silver and blue, but many of the individual tiles had fallen away. The room was lit by a large pale stone overhead. Once it had undoubtedly shone with the full radiance of Bunniswot's light-stone, but over time diminished to no more than a dull amber luster.

The room was circular, its curved wall broken by what Toede assumed were reliefs and more of the odd statuary he had observed above-ground. The floor was also bowl-shaped, mimicking the ceiling, and filled with soft, black mud.

In the center of that mud was Bunniswot's fiend, the creature the pair had seen carved into the interior wall of the temple above. It was mounted not on one but two rollers, the front held in place by what would otherwise be the creature's arms, the rear by its legs. Its head overhung the front roller and consisted of a wolflike muzzle with its lower jaw removed. Its eyes were hexagonal orbs cut from garnet or some other blood-colored stone.

The fiend was about twenty feet long with the front roller fifteen feet end-to-end. It was bright red against the darker mud, and shone with the rich luster of newly cast iron. It was spinning both rollers frantically but making no forward progress in the thick mire. Instead, it was rotating counterclockwise slowly, spraying a new layer of mud on the statues.

The sound of that spray was what Toede had mistaken for a waterfall.

His path entered slightly above the level of the mud, which had a staircase leading down into it. Everything below the top step was covered with a crust. Toede scanned the room. There could be a hundred and forty doors in here, but if so, they were hidden beneath the grime.

He turned to leave.

"Yo! You alive?" came a deep voice behind him.

Toede winced at the deepness of the voice. The part of his mind that was wondering about the waterfall earlier now was wondering how fast he could check out the other end of the tunnel. The other parts of Toede's brain, those that had fallen into squabbling over whether Hopsloth or Groag was more deserving of defenestration, was made aware that something unpleasant was happening out in the real world.

"Pard—" His voice cracked. "Pardon?"

"You alive?" repeated the creature. Toede realized it had a mouth of sorts, situated under the overhang of the jaw, above the main roller. "Ya know, like breathing?"

"Yes, I'm alive," said Toede.

He meant to add, "Are you?" but the answer set the creature off. With a mighty roar it spun its rollers faster and more furiously, with the result that it rotated faster in the dome. Toede stepped back into the passage as the rooster-tail of grime swept past.

The creature stopped its struggling and drifted to a stop, almost facing Toede.

"Damnation," said the native of the Abyss. "Damnation and crudbunnies."

Crudbunnies? thought Toede, but instead he asked, "What was that all about?"

"Sorry, natural reaction," said the metal beast. "You're alive, and the first thing I always do when confronted with the living is try to run them down."

"Must make you real popular at formal dances," said Toede, in a tone drier than anything else in the place.

The fiend regarded Toede for a long moment, then let out a low, appreciative whistle. "I'd heard that you ogres had taken a fall," it said. "I just wasn't aware you guys fell so hard!"

"I'm not an ogre," said Toede, crossing his arms.

"Don't tell me you're a human. Even they don't get *that* ugly."

"Hobgoblin," said Toede, defensively.

"Never heard of 'em," said the fiend. "Must be new. Lot of new stuff going around. I'm a juggernaut. You can call me Jug or Jugger if you want."

"Is that a real name?" asked Toede.

"As real as most folk can make it," replied the creature. "The real name is Crystityckol'k'kq'q." The clash of consonants grated on Toede's ears. The juggernaut's name sounded like a wheelbarrow of crowbars going down some stairs.

"Stick with Jugger," said the Abyss-spawned abomination. "The old guys, the real pros, they have names that would shatter glass at fifty paces. That was in the old days before the Abyss was overrun with wanna-bes. Cute little fiends with user-friendly names: Castlebaum, Bloodripper, Muranitlar, and that new kid, Judith. What kind of names are those, I would ask, and they would say, 'Ones that can be pronounced—nobody wants to deal with a fiend whose name they can't pronounce.' Smug little varmints."

"Excuse me for interrupting," said Toede, "but I take it this is your temple?"

Toede felt as if the creature's eyes had gone misty and then suddenly refocused on him. "Temple?" it shouted. "This is my tomb!" And began laughing.

Toede felt the vibrations beneath him and had to wait three minutes until the laughter of the fiend called Jugger subsided.

"Whew," said the creature. "That felt good. I haven't laughed like that in an elf's age. Is this my temple! Ha ha!"

Toede stepped in before Jugger set off on another round of mirth and memories. "You are the creature from the legends? The one the ogres, the original ogres, defeated?"

"Trapped, but not defeated!" boomed Jugger. "I'm still here, waiting to make my quota." It paused for a moment, then added, "Six hundred fifty-one."

"Okay," said Toede, with the caution one usually uses to approach such conversational booby traps. "Why six-fifty-one?"

"That's how many I've gotten so far!" said the juggernaut, beaming in pride. "My quota's an even thousand. Can't go back without my quota. You'da been six-fifty-two if I could just get loose. Then three-forty-eight more after that."

"So you can't get loose?" said Toede.

"Mired to the axles," grumbled the creature. "Can't get any traction worth a squat."

"Well," said Toede, thinking of how to turn the conversation toward the prospect of his own escape, "they did a good job on the temple. Built it up, decorated it, then buried it."

"By the five-headed bitch-dragon, little living buddy, they couldn't help themselves," said the juggernaut. "They were *ogres*. Everything they did was beautiful and fancy. They didn't even have ugly garbage. That's one reason I was called in." Another chuckle, as it added, "I got six hundred and fifty of them, you know, before they pinned me like this."

Toede was scanning the perimeter of the room for the barest hint of another opening. The juggernaut put in, "You'd better abandon all hope at finding another exit. There ain't one. The passage behind you leads up to a solid stone plug. And there ain't nothin' else lives down here, not even little blind cave fish. Unless you bore yourself a new opening, you're stuck. It's just the two of us."

"Just wonderful," said Toede, sitting down on the top muddy step and setting the rope and food satchel down next to him. "I take it you think I should just wade in and sacrifice myself to you, since I can't get out."

"Save you some time and trouble, little breathing pal," said the juggernaut. "I mean, I like the company as much as the next denizen of the Dark Lady's pit, and I want to know what's going on topside, but more than anything, I want my six-fifty-two."

Toede sat on the step, looking pensive.

"I mean, starvation is an ugly, ugly thing. You get so you're just begging for death." Jugger sighed. "Whereas, I'm quick! You'll never feel it. Death is like that, you know."

"I know," said Toede. "I've died before." He toyed with the idea of throwing himself under the juggernaut's roller, and maybe returning somewhere else in his third life. But *with my luck I'd come right back here*, he thought, *three hundred and forty-eight more times.*

"You died before?" asked the juggernaut with curiosity.

"Couple of times, so far," replied Toede. "And you're right, while there's a lot of pain leading up to it, the exact crossing over into death is a relatively painless thing."

The juggernaut let out a low whistle that sounded much the way steam escaping from a kettle would, if the kettle were the size of a hay wain. "Boy, I don't know. If you kill someone who has already died before, does that mess up the bookkeeping? I don't know if I can count you or not." The fiend was silent for a while.

"You've been down here since before the ogres were . . . ogres?" asked Toede.

"Yep," responded Jugger. "I was real peeved the first couple hundred years after they lured me into this pit. First I think, Okay, I'll sink to the bottom and slowly wheel my way out, but the mud's just thick and heavy enough to keep me afloat. So, then I think, Okay, I can empty the mud by splashing it around a lot. So I do that for a couple hundred years. The mud gets nice and thick around the edges, and then dries up and falls right back in, so guess what? I'm still hosed."

"You've tried waiting for the mud to dry out?" asked Toede.

"For a thousand years or so," answered Jugger. "A coupla times, actually. First I waited a century, not moving, until a thin crust formed on the mud. Then I shifted into low, and it all broke up. Then I waited two centuries, three, and each time it broke up as soon as I set the wheels spinning. So I waited a real long time, and then the bump came along and knocked everything back to the muddy state."

"The bump?" said Toede.

"Bump," repeated the juggernaut. "Just one, but it was a loop of one. Gave the whole room a shake, and all the crust just caved in. That's when the other feller was here."

"Other fellow," said Toede dully.

"Some human spellcaster from Istar," said the juggernaut. "Seems the gods got PO'd at Istar and dropped a mountain on the place. He teleported out randomly and ended up here. That's how come I know your modern language, and also how I learned that starvation is such a horrible way to kill yourself."

"He was number six-fifty-one," surmised Toede.

"Right, and ever since then, I've gone back to spinning my wheels, hoping to generate enough heat and traction to get out."

"So you've been running your rollers for over three hundred fifty years?"

"I guess," said the juggernaut, adding defensively, "I don't get out much, you know."

Toede was silent, weighing his options. He had rescued Charka out of his own hunger, and lived to regret it. If he helped Jugger, then he would surely die, and over three hundred others with him.

But if among those three hundred were Groag, Charka, or Hopsloth . . .

"I'm going to help you," said Toede.

"Wha' the?" said the juggernaut.

"I'm going to get you out of there," said Toede. "I can't get out on my own, and neither can you." He picked up the rope and walked to one side of the passage, where he chose something that might have been a statue and started pounding on the mud. It flaked away in thick clumps to reveal what looked like an egg rendered in pale brown stone. Toede tied one end of the rope around it.

"I should tell ya, little live one," said Jugger, "that if you wade in here and get close, I may just try and run you down. It's what I'm supposed to do. Can't help it."

"I'll take that chance," said Toede, taking the trailing end of the rope. He tested the muddy steps with a toe. Slippery but solid enough. He started to wade in.

"Three things should stop you from grinding me into the mud," Toede continued, slowly moving down into the mire. It supported his weight easily, as he guessed it would. After all, it supported an Abyss-spawned killing machine made of cast iron.

"First, if I die, you get one kill, whereas if you escape you can make your quota and go back to where you belong. Second, figure it out. If you get one visitor every three hundred fifty years, it'll be over a hundred thousand years before you see the Abyss again."

"One hundred and eighteen thousand years and three centuries," noted the juggernaut, and Toede could hear the faintest touch of wistfulness in its voice.

"Right. And third, you don't know if I count for your tally or not."

The hobgoblin was swimming through the mire at this point, dragging the rope behind him and moving to the side of the great crimson monster, near the front roller.

Once a whale had washed up on the beach near Flotsam, and Toede and a delegation of merchants went down to investigate it. It was a huge, black monster and towered over them, stinking in the sun. The gulls pecked at it, and it smelled horrible, and at length Toede had dispatched a crew of prisoners to bury it then and there. Something that large made Toede feel extremely vulnerable and small.

Touching the huge front roller, still smooth and shiny after millennia, made him feel the same way.

"I'm going to dive down," he told the juggernaut, "and slip the rope under one end of your roller. Don't move."

Toede took a deep breath and submerged in the mire, feeling his way alongside the creature. The mud grew thicker and harder to move through as he plunged downward, but at last he touched the underside of the roller. He shoved the line underneath it and ran it up the interior curve of the creature's body.

The juggernaut remained inert, but Toede could feel a vibration that seemed to rise in intensity as he worked.

Finally, he surfaced, sputtering mud and wiping the thick grime from his eyes.

"What now?" asked Jugger, and Toede detected a sense of impatience in its voice.

"I'm getting on board," said Toede. He took the leading edge of the line that ran under the front roller, in his teeth, and climbed up the side of the creature. As he climbed, the mud slid off him in clumps. Toede looped the rope beneath the rocker arm holding the front roller, and now stood directly above the creature's face.

"Okay, give me a little power," said Toede.

He almost hurtled from his perch as the juggernaut lunged forward, but managed to grab hold of a cast iron eyebrow. Even so, he fell flat on his face and could taste blood.

"Enough!" he bellowed almost immediately. Jugger subsided.

The rope was looped around the front roller for two revolutions. Toede grabbed the leading end and pulled it to the back, dropping it in front of the rear roller. In the process, he noted a human skull jammed between the body and the roller cavity. Six-fifty-one, no doubt.

"Again!" shouted Toede, then immediately, "Stop!" Jugger's drive gave him about ten more yards of slack. "I have to get down to do your rear wheels. Do you move in reverse?"

He slipped back into the warm mud and repeated the process on the rear roller, tying it off so that the line would gather on the roller like a spindle or a winch. Toede pulled himself, grimy and exhausted, to the top of the creature again.

"You done?" grunted the juggernaut, sounding like metal under strain, raring to go.

"Yes," said Toede, tugging on the lines to make sure they were taut. "Okay," he said, "I want you to start your rollers slowly."

Jugger let loose with a mighty bellow and threw both rollers into "high." The hobgoblin almost went tumbling backward off the beast as it leapt forward.

The line grew taut and held. The column that it was attached to did not, however. It began to bow severely, pulling away from the wall in a staccato of stone.

The juggernaut edged forward as the front and rear rollers acted as winches, pulling it out. Toede was bellowing for the juggernaut to slow down before it hurt something. Like Toede.

If Jugger could hear, it wasn't listening. It only redoubled its effort. The column bulged farther outward, and the rope started to unravel in twangs of sundered strands.

It was only a question of which would go first.

The winner (such as it was) was the column, which erupted from the wall in a shower of granite shards and mortar.

Toede uttered a curse, thinking they would have to start all over. However, the toppling column fell forward, directly into the path of the moving juggernaut. Toede heard the granite boulders grate and crunch beneath the front wheels, and realized Jugger was really moving now, erupting from the cesspool.

That was when the business end of a whip cracked above Toede's head. The end of the rope had spun through the front roller and nearly severed the hobgoblin's head in its race to reach the back wheel. The juggernaut had climbed out of the mud and was crushing the millennia-old stairs to a fine powder, heading for the entrance. Toede ducked behind the large, flanged forehead of the beast.

"Y'okay, little breathing buddy?" asked the juggernaut, and Toede nodded. Then, unsure if the creature could see him, he said, "Fine. Watch out, the corridor ahead is flooded—*urgh!*"

Water exploded before him as they hit the water-filled tunnel full tilt. Had the juggernaut had a sufficient running start, it possibly could have hydroplaned through, but as it was the water came up to its axles and was no impediment to its progress.

Thoroughly soaked, Toede peeked up from behind the rill of the creature's forehead. They had cleared the flooded section and were almost at the opposite end that Jugger had said the ogres . . .

Had sealed with stone.

Toede dove for cover as the juggernaut hit the stone plug faster than a diving dragon, and with greater effect. The impact slammed Toede toward the front as the rock before them opened up like soft mud. The sharply-angled features of the juggernaut's lupine "face" acted formidably as a plough. There was more grinding, and then the pair burst into bright afternoon sunlight.

"Hooowee!" shouted Jugger, and spun around the hill a few times, taking a gander at the outside world. "Things have gone downhill! Thanks, little living buddy, for springing us. You know, I really wanted to jellify you, back in there."

Toede patted the top of the creature's head. "Maybe that's one of the signs of nobility—the willingness to do damn-fool things that aren't in your best interest, in exchange for longer-term goals."

"Whatever," said the juggernaut, already crashing through the low underbrush. "Now, the question is, where are some other living sparks so I can make my quota, little living buddy?"

"I can take you there," Toede offered, smiling. "And if we're lucky there's one person in particular who will still be there. And do stop calling me 'little living buddy.' I'm tired of people giving me long names. The name is Toede, and no jokes about it. Now head for the town to the east and watch out for the hiiiillllllll!"

Chapter 19

In which the combination of hobgoblin brains and Abyss-spawned machine prove to be more than anyone bargained for, and Our Protagonist is allowed some say in the separation of the quick and the dead, before joining one of those aforementioned groups himself.

Bunniswot passed a filthy rag over his forehead and leaned into the shovel. After the argument, the stupid argument that unfortunately demonstrated to the gnolls that Renders and the rest of them were not powerful wizards, the gnolls had melted into the swamp, presumably to debate what to do next. The idea that they would be back with blood on their minds had set everyone into an honest, full-fledged panic. It was one thing to hear a rumor of attacking humanoids, another to see them up close, and then learn they are *still* murderous, flesh-eating fiends.

Renders had gone out "to talk some sense into them," and taken two of the "boys" with him. The rest of the group had drifted off in groups of two and three, some fading into the swamp, some heading west to take their chances with the necromancer, and others trying to reach the main road before the gnolls closed it off. The horses had vaporized quickly in the first moments after the argument.

Bunniswot tried to organize some kind of defense, but

to no avail. The only person who even listened was the other hobgoblin, the cook, when the young scholar told him to go fetch his friend, the dreamer called Underhill.

Now the cook was overdue; perhaps he had abandoned them as well.

Bunniswot decided that the best thing to do would be to dig up the old manuscripts, save the original rubbings, feed his notes into the fire, and see if he could smuggle the rubbings back to civilization. Even if they could not be published now, there might be a time for it in the future. To that end he had half the trench reexcavated—so that it was only about three feet deep and ten feet wide—and started a modest fire that was burning merrily. Bunniswot threw a small log on the blaze.

He was sweating more than he ever had in his life, and wondered if it was heat or fear that drove him. The late autumn sun was merciless. He passed the rag over his face, wincing as it touched the bloated, bruised side of his body where Charka had struck him. The bleeding from his nose had stopped, but the swelling in his face pounded with every beat of his heart.

That was when he saw them, emerging from the forest into the now-deserted camp. There seemed to be about twice as many gnolls as before, and Bunniswot thought perhaps they had gathered reinforcements, just in case these humans were powerful wizards.

The returned attackers fell upon the empty tents, tearing them down with their bare claws and howling dark curses.

Then they noticed Bunniswot, and suddenly it didn't seem to have been such a smart idea to have lingered behind.

Bunniswot took a step backward, then a second step, and he would have taken a third were it not for the fact that he had already reached the edge of his own trench on the first step. The second sent him hurtling backward into the soft earth, as dirt-covered papers erupted skyward.

Bunniswot looked up, seeing the gnolls silhouetted against the sun. The largest one present wore Charka's metal skull-piece, but it was not Charka, he noticed. That was a scant solace as the flint-headed spear this one carried was pointed at his chest.

Bunniswot shouted what he thought were some well-prepared last words, but the spear-chucking gnoll was not paying attention.

Suddenly, nearby, there was the sound of something crashing through the birch trees at high velocity, and an object with an impressively huge shadow passed directly over the trench and the prostrate scholar.

The spear-threatening gnoll barely had time to look up and twist his face into something that resembled alarm before the shadow passed and the gnoll's spear bounced into the trench, the flint head crushed and the wood splintered.

"Six-fifty-two!" came a deep, rumbling voice that could be heard over the sound of crashing wood and screaming gnolls. There was another, high-pitched voice mixed in that was lost in the deeper, deadly counting. *Whump!* "Six-fifty-three!" *Whump!* "Six-fifty-four." *Whump!* "Six-fifty-hang on, we just winged him!" *Whump!* "There we go! Six-fifty-five!"

Bunniswot cautiously peered over the edge of the trench to witness the ongoing devastation. The agent of destruction, mowing down gnolls right, left, and center, looked like a siege engine, the type that was normally lugged up by invading armies to storm the local castle. Except that this particular engine lacked the units of troops that were normally used to ferry it, and was moving about on its own.

No, not completely on its own. Perched on its back was Underhill, and his was the higher voice that Bunniswot had heard amidst the rampage. Underhill would beckon and shout, and the great runaway siege engine would spin around and roll through enemy gnolls, toppling trees, flattening tents, and crushing everything in its path.

Whenever it struck another gnoll, a great shout would go up, as if the True Gods were keeping tally of the battle.

The engine was effective, but nondiscriminating in its targets. The device struck an ogre plinth dead on, and the aeon-old carving vaporized in a puff of stone dust. Some gnolls had chosen to hide behind the plinths for protection, while their wiser brethren had dashed for the swamp at the first sight of the flame-red creature. The siege engine plowed through stone columns and gnolls as if they were one being, and with double the glee.

"Six-sixty!" It bellowed as it caught a gnoll cowering behind a plinth and decimated both.

Bunniswot was delighted to see that Underhill had not only rescued himself from the temple, but had brought aid. Still, the destruction of the plinths was too high a price to pay, and the gnolls seemed in full flight already. The red-haired scholar struggled to his feet and waved, using both arms, and shouting for Underhill to direct the behemoth elsewhere.

As Underhill saw him, the hobgoblin's face lit up, if the combination of shock and fear could be considered "lit up" in humanoid terms. The hobgoblin said nothing, but motioned, fingers splayed, palms downward, raising and lowering his hands frantically.

There are times when, under stress, an individual cannot understand a common sentence or a particular written word, or is confounded by such simple matters as whether a door opens inward or outward. This was one such time for Bunniswot, and he stared dumbly at the mounted hobgoblin, trying to piece together what he meant by . . . ah! He must be signaling Bunniswot to get down.

By that time the device had turned to face the entrenched scholar, and Bunniswot realized that the horrible visage at the front of the siege engine was also the horrible visage in the temple.

So it was not a siege engine at all. The creature spun its huge rollers and snapped off two more pillars while closing the distance between itself and the terrified scholar.

Bunniswot swooned, and in the swooning saved his own life, for he toppled backward. Had he tried to dive sideways, or even engage his brain in the question of what to do, he would have been too late, and the Abyss-engine would have crushed him.

As it was, he came to, alert, as soon as the heavy shadow passed over him again. A deep voice vibrated through the soil. "Missed that one. Hang on while I hit 'im again."

Bunniswot thought about rising and running, but caught himself. Instead he flattened himself further, trying to burrow his body into the deep, twice-turned soil of the trench.

The shadow passed a second time, very quickly, and then a third, this time from the side. Each time the scholar was convinced the entire trench was going to collapse on him, but each time the trench held, and the shadow passed.

Finally the great engine rolled over the trench and parked, leaving Bunniswot directly underneath in its inky black shadow. The scholar willed himself immobile.

"What now?" said Underhill's voice.

"I can grade down to him," said the engine, in a voice so low that it made Bunniswot's teeth ache.

"And that would take?" asked Underhill.

"Hmmmm." The engine made a sound like a gnomish device. "Figuring soft soil, about a week. Less if it rains, little . . . ah, Toede."

Toede? thought Bunniswot. As in Highmaster Toede?

"Sounds boring," said Underhill/Toede, sounding more pensive and worried than bored. Bunniswot wondered which one of the two was trying to crush him to death.

"And you have a better idea?" grumbled the engine.

"Uh-huh," said the hobgoblin. "A place where you can make your quota in a day's work."

"I'm game," said the engine.

"The only thing," added the hobgoblin, "is that there is a special individual I want you to make number one thousand. A particularly large and nasty frog."

Again the rumbling. "Don't know if it counts. Frogs don't talk, and that's a basic rule to counting."

"Oh, this one talks, and plots, and schemes," said the hobgoblin. "Promise me you'll go after this one and I'll guide you to Flotsam."

The engine grumbled a little, something about a "sure thing" right here versus a "maybe" tomorrow. The hobgoblin explained, patted, and cajoled, and suddenly Bunniswot knew that this *was* Toede—the legendary, venomous, dangerous, twice-dead Toede.

The engine rolled off the trench, and there was more crashing as birch trees and plinths snapped in its path.

Bunniswot sat up carefully, ready to fling himself to the ground in case the great engine reversed itself. But no, it was pounding its northerly way up the path, trampling a wide swath with it. And on its back was the hobgoblin Toede, who turned and waved as they disappeared into the brush.

Bunniswot's knees failed him. He had to try several times to organize himself in a sitting position on the edge of the trench. He was surrounded by the remnants of the camp. Everything the scholars had abandoned was now smashed, along with a dozen extremely two-dimensional and soil-impacted gnoll corpses. The engine had been thorough in its devastation, in that not a single plinth seemed to have survived unscathed.

I could have died, he said to himself.

And you were spared, he answered himself.

By Highmaster Toede, he added.

Bunniswot looked around at the wreckage, and then rose, walking to the fire. He kicked at it until all the larger sticks had been scattered, and stomped on the hot ashes until they were dying embers.

Then he returned to the trench, grasping his shovel and

shoving the rag in his pocket. He began to uncover the last surviving words of the ogres, his unwanted life's work that almost had become his death's work.

* * * * *

There was not a great deal of opportunity for chat during the journey from the camp to Flotsam. This was due both to a limited range of discussion, and to the fact that the juggernaut had been designed without any idea that anyone would ever care to ride it. As a result, it lacked such modern amenities as seats, windows, springs, or intentional handholds.

Toede found that he could manage by a tactic he called "hanging on for dear life," which worked fairly well. He shouted directions whenever he could, bellowing over the noise of Jugger's passage. Once or twice Jugger had to slow to reasonable speeds to learn which way to proceed, but as soon as Toede said anything, or even motioned, the infernal device was off with a commotion.

It was early dusk when they hit Flotsam. Jugger's total had reached the six-nineties by that point, aided by a handful of farmers, a pair of elves, one or two stragglers who could have been among Renders's fleeing scholars, a few gnolls, and two creatures that Toede thought counted but Jugger said were undead zombies and as such were "gimmies."

As they topped the last rise, Toede noted that the low-slung sun had set the golden fields alight with a crimson hue. Ahead, the city hugged the coast, as if seeking consolation from the blood-red bay.

Jugger only growled and muttered, "Walls." Then the front of the creature bucked upward as the rear roller bit into the road, and they lurched forward in a blur of red-hued speed and hobgoblin curses.

Two hay wains and a traveler's pushcart later, they burst through the Southwest Gate, sending splinters of both the heavy oak doors and the two guards raining in all directions. It was late in the day, and those street merchants who had stayed late to make one more sale, or those townsfolk who tarried behind to eke out one last bargain had just enough time to look up, startled, as the runaway siege engine hurtled down on them, leaving a wake of smashed bodies, broken ironwork, and crushed cobblestones. Jugger's body count put his take in the low seven hundreds.

"Gate!" bellowed Toede. "Gate to the east!"

Toede meant the Rock Gate leading to the headland, but the juggernaut swung a hard right (through several not-abandoned buildings), and toward the Southeast Gate. Given that Jugger was a stranger in town, it was an understandable mistake.

As a result, Toede and his infernal device went slashing along the inner perimeter of the wall Gildentongue had erected almost a year earlier, taking out interior buttresses and supports, then weaving into the city again as the wall crashed behind them. Toede wondered if the creature would get full credit for those killed indirectly by collapsing buildings and crushing walls, or only partial. Figuring the politics of the Abyss, it was probably all or nothing.

The two guards at the Southeast Gate had enough time to hear the disaster approaching. One fled his position, the other, the one with a comet-shaped scar on his face, turned to gape and became number seven-six-three as the juggernaut crashed back through the gate and found itself outside the city.

Toede beat on the unyielding surface of Jugger's body and screamed. "No, we're heading the wrong direction!"

Jugger rumbled, "You said the eastern gate."

"North and east," screamed Toede, his face turning pink. "The gate to the upper city, to the headland!"

"Right, hang on," roared Jugger. "I'll take care of it and pick up the spare as well. . . ."

The guard who ran was paralleling the southern edge

of the wall, and shortly was made one with the city wall he was charged with protecting. The wall itself bulged inward and flew apart in a cascade of mortar and loose stone.

Poor workmanship, thought Toede, as the first measly arrows of defense started peppering Jugger's hide.

Resistance had appeared, finally, in the form of a unit of crossbowmen, who took up position beneath a statue of Lord Hopsloth. The crossbowmen were trying to pick off the "driver" of the device and were protected by some (very nervous) spearmen in the front line.

Toede flung himself down on the top of the juggernaut, and shouted, "Take out the statue, too!"

Toede did not see the statue explode, but he certainly heard it, combined with a rain of spears, and Jugger's declaration, "Eight-zero-five!"

Toede grabbed one of the spears and started using it to steer, banging on one side of the juggernaut, then the other. He soon learned that Jugger took notice of buildings in the same manner as humans noticed wildflowers when charging across a field, and if he tapped too early (or late), the corner of a building would disappear in a shower of masonry.

Another unit of crossbows and spears in front of the Rock Gate raised the total to eight-fifty-something, and Toede began worrying that Jugger would hit its quota long before Toede reached his own quarry. Then he would be left alone in the middle of the destruction, with some very angry and organized citizens surrounding him.

The Rock Gate was made of sterner and older stuff than the new walls, and Jugger almost slowed as it crumbled into fragments. Now the troops were mobilizing, but morale evaporated as quickly as mobilization when the humans in the rear echelons saw the humans in front reduced to red, splotchy pulps in the cobblestone.

Toede banged the right side of the device, and they swung toward Toede's old manor. They charged up the front steps (reducing them to a gravel slope in the process). Then, all of a sudden, a powerful explosion rocked Jugger and sent Toede sprawling to the pavement. He felt something give in his ankle, but skittered clear, so when Jugger tipped and fell, thankfully, Toede was not underneath.

Thunder echoed in Toede's ears. He raised himself on the spear to see what happened. Jugger was on its side, swaying back and forth, its great wheels spinning helplessly in the air. A small collection of humans in vestments, gathered by the north wing of the manor house, had been the source of the effective attack.

Wizards. Hopsloth had no true priestly powers, so like the old frauds and charlatans of the prewar days, he had hired spellcasters who drew their powers from impure sources. Pity, too, because real priests were unlikely to have the ability to summon and fling magical lightning bolts.

The wizards walked slowly toward the tipped, rocking juggernaut, behind a wall of spearmen who showed uncommon sense by not scattering in fear. Several were congratulating each other as they neared, as if the surrounding carnage were nothing more than an everyday field exercise. Toede thought again of the dead, beached whale, and the pygmies who came out to watch it bake in the sun.

None of the wizards or spearmen noticed Toede yet.

Toede saw that Jugger's rocking had become more pronounced, not less. The infernal device was starting to move in wider arcs. Leaning on the spear as a staff, Toede hobbled up the stairs of the manor, knowing what would come next.

The mages didn't notice that the juggernaut was figuring out how to right itself until they were about twenty paces away. Actually, the mages regarded the rocking as one more interesting phenomenon, and it was the spearmen who realized what the rocking truly meant. They started to fall away in panic as the last great swing of the machine's body brought the rollers back in contact with pavement. A jet of cobblestones shot backward as Jugger stood up and charged the astonished crowd.

Half the spearmen fell instantly under the massive wheels, as well as some of the more powerful (and incautious) wizards. One spread his arms and began to rise in the air, but Jugger's sharpened top jaw caught him, and only the upper torso continued to float upward, raining blood beneath. A few of the mages in the rear ran, as Jugger pursued.

It's in the nine hundreds now, thought Toede. He shouted to Jugger, but to no avail. Eventually, Jugger would realize no one was pounding on its back, but likely not before several more buildings were leveled. And if it hit a barracks, well, that would spell the end of his cursed presence on this plane of existence.

Toede limped up the steps to the double doors of his manor, picking up a discarded and uncrushed dagger from the smashed body of its previous owner. He jammed the dagger into his belt. He estimated the length of the spear and the width of the door, and pried open one of the door's twin panels.

"I'm home, dear," he bellowed into the manor.

With the door forced open, he could see the renovations made by Lord Hopsloth. The entire rear section of the building and his sacred throne had been lost in the flames and/or removed entirely.

All that could be seen was a stone scaffolding lined with plates of rare sheet glass. The front hallway was now a balcony, with a long staircase leading down into a pool, surrounded by fronds and other plants. The sun had set behind Toede, so the pool was as dark and inky as a sleeping octopus.

"Hope you have supper ready," continued Toede. He saw ripples in the water and remained in the doorway, holding the spear.

"I don't know about you, but I feel like eating frogs'

legs tonight," he shouted with a grin. At that, the shadowy hulk of Hopsloth emerged from the depths, at the edge of where the stairs vanished into the water.

"You're . . . back," grunted the amphidragon.

"Can't say I like what you've done with the place," said Toede, ignoring what sounded like an explosion behind him and to the left.

"You did . . . this," came the grunt.

"So I got peeved," smiled Toede. "I'll call it off if you agree to surrender. Now," he added, hoping that Jugger wouldn't vanish for at least the next five minutes.

"Killed you . . . once. Kill you . . . again," murmured Hopsloth. His tongue lashed outward and upward, striking Toede full in the chest.

Toede had only a second's warning, but was ready for Hopsloth this time, and used the second to full advantage. He turned the spear so it would form a bar across the outer door, a foot overlapping the frame on either side. Even so, Toede's arm was nearly ripped from its socket as the tongue-tip lassoed him and tried to suck him back into the amphidragon's maw.

Toede bit down on the pain he felt. With his free hand, he pulled the dagger.

"Doe!" shouted Hopsloth, which was "No!" with your tongue moored fifteen feet away.

"Sorry, Hopsey," muttered Toede, "but you had your chance." And he drove the dagger into the creature's outstretched tongue.

Hopsloth arced in a spasm of pain. He tried to lunge (slowly) up the stairs, toward his tormentor. Toede drove the blade in up to the hilt and started to make a sawing motion. Greenish blood coated his torso and lower limbs, while the arm anchoring the spear grew numb.

Toede knew that Hopsloth could not immediately disengage his tongue. Everything depended on Hopsloth losing more blood on the way up the stairs than in the end he would need to bite Toede in two.

Hopsloth closed the distance in slow motion, or at least it seemed so from Toede's standpoint as he jammed the dagger into the flexing, writhing muscle that held him aloft, anchored only by the spear across the door frame. Ten feet between them. Then five. And then Hopsloth was close enough to leap forward and swallow Toede in one bite. Again.

"Nine-nine-seven" came a powerful bellow that Toede felt more than heard, and he swiveled his head to see Jugger charging up the stairs. One last foolish mage was aiming a wand at the juggernaut, and was rewarded with a shriek and the solemn declaration, "Nine-nine-eight!"

Toede saw what was going to happen and closed his eyes. Hopsloth realized a moment later. His eyes grew wide and wild, exactly like those of a frog's caught in a sudden flash of light.

Jugger struck Toede and Hopsloth, and all three pitched off the balcony, over the pool. The far wall shattered like a dry crust of sugar, and Hopsloth's body was left twitching on the remaining spurs of stone.

"Nine-nine-nine!" bellowed Jugger. "And a thousand!"

Jugger and Toede's remains flew over the deep red waters. Jugger began to fade, and only Toede's body reached the hungry jaws of the sharks circling below.

Interlude

We return again to the Abyss, surrounded by the spirits of the damned, for analysis, color commentary, and accusations.

"Well, it was entertaining," said the Abbot of Misrule, lining up his next shot carefully. "Much better the second time around. Or third in his case. See you in a few years, my friend. I'll keep your charges safe."

He stepped up to the chalk-marked line and let go of the paladin's skull in a smooth, underhanded motion. The skull bounced erratically down the hallway of the crypt, striking a triangularly-arranged set of soul-bottles. The skull struck the most forward of these bottles, sending all but two hurtling in various directions. All but two.

The Abbot harrumphed and contorted his face into a mask of disappointment. "Seven-ten split. This must be the plane of punishment."

The Castellan of the Condemned held an angry silence as his companion recovered the tossed skull. Then he said with a low threat in his voice, "You cheated."

"Cheated?" said the taller abishai, trying to transform his lizardlike features into a semblance of honesty. "Me?" he touched the spot where his heart would be—if he had one—just for effect.

"You . . ." said the Castellan, slamming a fist down. "You sent that vision to Toede, led him down the Abyss-intended path to that anachronistic creature Jugger. *And* appeared to his companion when he was just about to be rescued. A heavenly figure in blue and white, indeed! That had your greasy clawprints all over it."

"Oh, I see," said the Abbot, drawing himself up to full height. "And I am supposed to abandon my own appointed tasks just because of some silly bet," he said crossly.

"It's not a bet," snarled the Castellan. "It's an experiment, one that was going swimmingly. The test subject was starting to put things together for us. Then you decided to pitch him in over his head!"

"I won't argue with you about terms," said the Abbot, who was of course arguing about terms. "But it is in my portfolio to make sure bad advice is heeded, correct?"

The Castellan was silent for a moment, then muttered, "Right."

"And through my bad advice, an ancient evil was freed, a city was wrecked and left leaderless, and a great repository of early ogre erotic epics destroyed," said the Abbot, leaning against a counter made of obsidian, polished with the ashes of fallen heroes. "I am just doing my job. In fact, I might even get a promotion out of this."

"If Judith doesn't sack you for goofing off in the first place," muttered the Castellan. The Abbot winced but let that comment slide.

Instead the taller fiend gave a snarl. "And it's not as if I were the first to influence our little pet noble-to-be."

"I had nothing to do with that coin flip," said the Castellan hotly.

"Coin flip?" said the Abbot, looking innocent as the driven sleet. "I wouldn't even suggest that you would have meddled so blatantly in your valuable experiment, to interfere with an affair of chance. I always thought you had more style than that. It never even entered my mind." He let his voice trail off, as if the idea were entering his mind.

"So?" prompted the Castellan.

The abishai nibbled on a problem nail, then admired his handiwork. "There was a little matter of the first assassination attempt, back at that little bar—the Jetties, was it?"

The Castellan was silent, but nodded.

"Think of it," said the Abbot, "A crowded room emptying of its patrons. Pandemonium erupting on all sides. The assassin wounds our subject in the shoulder with a crossbow bolt, then engages in mortal combat with his companion. Our subject limps across the room during this fray to a deceased barbarian prince, pulls a dagger,"—the abishai mimed the action—"and lets fly."

The Abbot flung the imaginary dagger at the Castellan, who continued to regard his fellow abishai in stony silence. "Wounded thrower, off-balance, tossing a weapon that is not designed to be thrown at a target engaged in melee," summarized the Abbot. "And yet it not only hits the intended target but strikes in such a way that it renders said target insensate immediately. And through it all no one present regarded this circumstance as odd." The taller abishai finished with a flourish. "If there was an area where I would have acted, where I would have influenced the normal course of events, that would have been it."

The silence hung in the air like a convicted criminal at the end of his last rope. The Castellan bit his words off. "You never mentioned that before."

The Abbot made a broad sweep of his arms, at least as broad as he could manage without scraping some soul-bottles to the floor. "I was not accused of impropriety, before."

Another silence. Then the Castellan sighed and said, "Well, we'll have to do it again."

The taller abishai rose, palms outward. "We have wasted enough time away from our official duties. If Judith found out . . ."

"Triple or nothing," put in the Castellan.

"We'll be missed from our posts for sure," said the

Abbot, smiling as if being caught missing were not truly a problem.

"Quadruple or nothing," added the Castellan.

"And all for some little bet," put in the Abbot.

"It's not a bet!" shouted the Castellan, then added more softly, "Quintuple or nothing. Five years on the line."

"But then, what is life without risk?" said the Abbot of Misrule, hefting the pickle jar with Toede's name on it. He smiled. "Shall we proceed?"

Chapter 20

In which Our Protagonist decides to defy convention and not go anywhere or get involved with anything. Not that this does him any good, but it's the thought that counts.

Toede awoke feeling flat, or at least a little smashed. Was there a party the previous evening? No, that was with the gnolls a few evenings back, and was followed by all sorts of unpleasantness. His last clear memory was of a tremendous force behind him, thrusting him through the windows of the manor and giving him a very brief look at the Blood Sea from a very high altitude.

Toede looked around and saw that he was once again on the bank of the same creek as before, beneath the same maple, several days' journey south of Flotsam. The trees were fresh with new leaves that caught the sun, shading the water in myriad hues of green and amber. A few lazy flies buzzed, and far to his left, a wood thrush began its throaty call.

"I understand now," said Toede. "It's all a plot to make me pay for my sins. The rest of eternity I'll be sent back here to suffer and die again and again."

He shuddered, but in the darkest corners of his hobgoblin heart, he had to stand back in awe and wonder at the fiendish genius who could come up with so elegant and cruel a punishment. Would that he someday might have an opportunity to use it on someone else!

Toede scanned the horizon and realized he was holding his breath, waiting for something to leap out of the bushes and throttle him. Or an army of gnolls on the horizon. Something. Anything.

The wood thrush continued, then petered out. A stiff breeze came up and shook the willows and maples. The sound of leaves rustling was akin to the crashing of the surf. Still nothing.

Toede pulled his legs up and wrapped his arms tightly around them, rocking slightly, thinking mightily. He was back, and it was a good guess that six months had elapsed since his last sojourn in the world. The question was, what to do with his restored life this time?

"Live nobly," the voices—sea-wide and mountain-tall—had said again, leaving it at that. Thank you very much. Perhaps this time, Toede reflected, he would concentrate on the first word, and let the second word come along at its own speed.

The first time, he had gone downstream and turned left at the swamp, found kender and trouble, and died soon afterward.

The second time, he had gone downstream and turned right at the swamp, found gnolls and scholars and trouble, and died soon afterward.

So this time, perhaps he should head upstream, into the hills, find some cave and hide there for a few years until he was certain that no one was left to capture, lure, or ambush him.

Or he could remain where he was, which had the added benefit of not having to travel far, and in the likely event he died and was restored again, he wouldn't have to go to much effort.

Toede looked at his surroundings with the eye of an amateur camper sizing up a potential resting spot for the night. The willows by the creek were supple enough to form a rude frame, like those the kender used. And the maples could be easily stripped of their bark for cross supports. He could lash bundles of grass to it, at least until he got good enough to catch and skin a beaver or moose or other suitable furbearer (He had never skinned a wild animal skin before, but how different could they be from a human?). He'd have to locate berry bushes and other edibles. Perhaps even launch a small raid on the kender encampment, if it was still there. . . .

There was a sharp snap of a breaking branch, and the brush behind him and to his right gave a brief, animated shake. Toede saw it from the corner of his eye, and instantly was alert and on his feet. Subconsciously he reached for the dagger jammed in his belt. When his fingers closed on empty air, he made a mental note to die with a scabbard on, next time, so he would be reborn with a weapon handy.

The brush continued to shake. Toede saw that someone or something was trying to force its way through the brambles. He could see an arm wielding a sword that glinted in the sunlight as it came down, hard, on the underbrush ahead of it.

Toede cursed. Bending halfway over to conceal himself as best he could, he made for the sidelines. Somehow, he just knew he should not hang around and hope no one would bother him. He dived into some brush about the same time the figure worked itself into the open.

Toede held himself very still in the tall grass and weeds, crouched under a particularly large bush. From his vantage point he could see little, but the thrashing to his left indicated that the intruder was now strolling the bank where previously Toede had been.

Toede saw a pair of boots—calf-high and made of some dusty gray leather—pass by. A set of trouser legs, once blue but faded into a sea-gray shade, was stuffed into them. Nothing else was visible, and the human (or elf, Toede allowed) was facing the opposite direction.

The boots went past his hiding spot and stopped, then

turned around and went past again. Again, three paces past him they stopped, and turned around yet a third time. This time they stopped in front of Toede's lair.

Then they turned directly toward where Toede was hiding.

Toede exploded from the brush, head down, arms together and ahead of him, hands clenched in pudgy fists, literally diving upward at his pursuer. He hoped to catch his visitor in the stomach (or perhaps a little lower) and to knock him senseless enough to either affect an escape or grab his foe's weapon and turn the tables.

He was not expecting his adversary to explode at first touch into a cloud of fluffy gray tomb dust. Nor for the upper torso of said adversary to pitch backward from the force of the blow, leaving the legs standing there for a moment, then to collapse slowly onto themselves, twisting slightly as they did so.

Toede the victor stood over his conquest, coughing and sneezing on the dust that danced and sparkled in the spring sun. The battle had all the excitement, and the precise results, of kicking a puffball mushroom.

His vanquished foe lay face-up in two separate pieces on the river bank. Toede looked in the face (what remained of it) of his opponent, and saw why the creature put up so little fight.

The face of his would-be stalker was nothing more than a gray mask of dried skin, pulled tightly over the yellowed remnants of skull. The lips were slightly parted, the creature's teeth like pegs knocked out of their peg-holes, all askew.

A zombie. He was in the middle of the wilderness, caught between gnolls and kender and gods-knew what else, and here he encounters an armed and armored zombie in the first five minutes of his new life. What, he thought bitterly, had he done to deserve this?

And more importantly, he added to himself, who had he done it to?

One suspect rose immediately in Toede's mind. The

fabled necromancer could call up a single zombie, or a dozen, in his free time between tea and supper, without even breaking a sweat. However, said necromancer would not know exactly where Toede's location was when he reappeared, nor would the death-mage have any particular reason to want Toede dead.

Toede went through a mental list of individuals who might want to see him restricted to shambling on undead feet through some unlit passageway for all eternity and was distressed to find that it was so long.

Or it could be someone else entirely.

It could be a chance encounter; maybe this zombie got bored doing his mundane tasks and decided to go for a spring stroll.

Toede smiled, but his a smile was without mirth. He took the long sword and the dagger from the undead creature's deathlike grip, snapping a few finger bones in the process. The dagger he shoved in his belt, and the scabbard he slung over his shoulder, since if he wore it on his belt the tip would leave a faint furrow in the soft ground.

Then he headed north, upstream along the creek, wondering where he could find some kind of defensible place to call home.

* * * * *

The climb was relatively easy, as the stream divided into two smaller creeks, and the rightmost creek into two smaller brooks, and the rightmost brook in a series of rock-strewn trickles and tributaries.

As the creek bed rose above the vale below, Toede turned and regarded his world. He was facing south and could see a landscape dotted with the light greens and cyans of new buds, and a sprinkling of wildflowers. Far toward the horizon was the accursed swamp, a thick miasma of haze blurring its outlines.

Toede resumed climbing, congratulating himself on his

cunning. Were someone like the necromancer pursuing him, he would assume Toede took the easiest route: downstream.

The tributary Toede had been following finally ended in a natural spring bubbling up from the rock. The brush had surrendered utterly to rocky ground, dotted by a few gnarled, ancient trees. Not the best territory to eke out an existence, but sufficient for protection, Toede noted.

Whatever fates there existed were with him when he spotted an old, half-tumbled hovel halfway up the hill above the spring. It was little more than an entrance hall, and ran about fifteen feet back into the hill, with a low ceiling that sloped downward in the back to join the floor.

The cabin had been abandoned. The rotted remains of a musty bedroll, tarnished platterware, and termite-infested wood littered the small one-room interior. The dry smell of food that had spoiled, rotted, or evaporated hung heavy on the air. An open sack of flour stood on one low shelf. Toede tested it with his dagger point; it had solidified into a powdery white brick.

Toede imagined that this had been the home of some dwarven miner, guessing from the low ceilings and amount of rusted iron present. Probably there was an excavation somewhere nearby, or a shaft back into the hills. Probably, said shaft ended with a cave-in and a pair of dwarven boots sticking out of the rubble.

Toede cleared out the garbage (that is to say in general, emptied the cabin), but declared the bedroll serviceable after removing it, thwopping it against a boulder a few dozen times, and standing back as enough dust billowed from its insides to gag a mummy.

By the time he had finished reintroducing the concept of livability to the hovel, the sun was already nuzzling the horizon, and Toede's stomach was grumbling. He sat on his front porch (a patch of dusty ground, actually) and nibbled on dinner (the last bit of smoked meat that looked semi-edible). In the morning he would have to look for some berry bushes, maybe set a few traps (a deadfall was a deadfall, regardless of what it was falling on), and scout for neighbors.

The last of the sun retreated, leaving a band of reddish fire along the horizon. In the distance there was the howl of a wolf or wild dog. The air was cooling, and Toede thought briefly of building a fire, but he had no idea what else was living in the neighborhood, and there was no need to advertise his presence just yet.

Toede rose, sighed, and leaned against the frame of the doorless entrance to the hovel (that creaked alarmingly). The reddish hue along the horizon was ebbing, and the stars were coming out overhead.

"Perhaps," he said to no one in particular, "this is the answer. No Flotsam. No Balifor. No kender or gnolls or scholars. Perhaps."

So he retired to bed, lying face-up, his fingers threaded behind his head, considering his options. Maybe this was what the shadowy figures were saying: travel and die or remain in place and build your own little lordship. Not a bad concept, and maybe it would do for a while. Even if a week passed, and he became bored beyond belief, that would be three days longer than he had survived before.

There was the wolf howl again, and Toede's last thought was that he would have to fix up a decent door. That resolution belonged on the upper end of his "things-yet-to-be-done" list.

* * * * *

Toede awoke to a deep growling. He opened his eyes to see a large, shaggy black hound sniffing his face. The idea of a decent door moved even higher into the top ten of his "to-do" list. The creature was as black as soot, with pale green eyes. It would have been considered huge even if Toede were not lying on his back looking up into its slavering jaws. The hound sniffed at Toede and growled again.

Toede's eyes never left the hound, but his hand spidered along the bedroll until it closed on the hilt of the zombie's short blade.

Still in silence, he swiftly brought the dagger up between himself and the dog. The creature had some experience with weapons, because it backed up a few paces. Toede rose, snaking his other hand out to grab the zombie's sword from its scabbard. Now with two weapons, he advanced on the creature.

The creature backed up a few more steps. From his position Toede could see no more animals, and assumed that this one was a stray or loner. Toede moved forward another couple of paces, as the creature backed fully out of the cabin, into the moonlight beyond.

In the moonlight, the creature seemed to shrink in size and menace. Indeed it was a dog, a large mastiff, inky dark and mud-spattered. It stretched its back out, pushed forward on its paws, and wagged its tail, its tongue hanging out the left side of its mouth. It whined at him.

Toede smiled, thinking of when he had first met Charka, and assumed the gnoll was a dog. Perhaps this dog *was* a dog, and would prove some help in hunting. Either that or make for a good meal in a tight spot.

Toede tucked the dagger in his belt (keeping a firm hand on his long sword) and stepped through the doorway, reaching out to pet the animal, making small, affectionate clicking noises with his tongue.

"Gotcha, you rat!" said a vaguely familiar voice as the back of Toede's neck exploded in a spasm of pain. The ground came up very fast (the dog leaping out of the way), and he was swallowed by blackness.

But not before another, more familiar voice said, "Oh, pooh, I think you hurt him."

Chapter 21

In which Our Protagonist is lured away from his pastoral setting and his final reward, and becomes involved with a situation of his own making, but not quite exactly as he would have expected it.

Toede awoke with a ringing that started at the base of his neck and radiated throughout his entire form, ending in (what he imagined were) vibrating fingertips.

He expected to be back on the stream bank, having set a new record for dying. Instead, he was inside a suspiciously familiar dwelling, made of hooped wood and brush in the kender style. He blinked his eyes, trying to focus.

"Hello, Toede," said a small figure across the room. "You really *are* Toede, aren't you? The one and true Toede."

Toede squinted, normal vision returning. The figure was familiar, child-sized, and dressed in fringed leather. Her face was more tightly drawn and serious than before, and the soft russet ringlets of her hair had been replaced by a short, rust-colored down that snugly wrapped her skull.

"Taywin," he muttered. "Kronin's daughter. The berry picker. The kender poet. You've changed your look." He couldn't help but frown in disapproval, though to his hobgoblin sensibilities anything was an improvement over her previous appearance.

Taywin Kroninsdau passed a hand over her scalp. "It *is* you," she hissed, then in a more normal voice added, "You saved my life, a year ago."

"I was . . ." Toede paused. If she had wanted simple vengeance, she would have had him killed immediately. Try honesty, he thought, but temper it with wisdom.

"I was just trying to escape," said Toede, raising his eyebrows to indicate his sincerity. "Saving you was a happy by-product."

"Yes," said Taywin, her face furrowing. "It was that awful Groag's idea, wasn't it?"

Now comes the wisdom part. Toede nodded as if in agreement, but added, "Groag's involvement is immaterial to my own actions. One must take responsibility for one's own deeds."

"Ah yes," nodded Taywin. "*Be truthful in thy trysts and reap the bounty of thy trust*," she said, smiling at him.

Toede wondered if her poetry had taken a turn for the worse. That would explain the haircut. He shook his head, waved his hand, and said, "Whatever. Where am I?"

"In our camp," said Taywin, ignoring his confusion. "We're having a major moot this evening, and Daddy's going to have to decide if we're going to join the Allied Rebellion or not. You'll be there, of course."

"Of course," said Toede, already checking the exits and wondering how many guards must be posted outside. They hadn't chained him up, which was a good sign, but this talk of a rebellion was bad. Perhaps he could learn more, then head for the hills until he ascertained whoever it was they were rebelling against.

"This revel alliance . . ." began Toede.

"Rebel," corrected Taywin. "It's the *Allied* Rebellion."

". . . is a new thing," finished Toede. "Assume I'm unaware of what has transpired since we last met. Pretend I'm ignorant in all this."

"I come to you skyclad and unshorn, seeking the teachings of the flesh." She was quoting again, and something tickled the back of Toede's mind. "The rebellion got its start about five months ago, after the destruction of most of Flotsam by a magical creature of great power," she said.

"His name was Jugger," muttered Toede. "At least that was the name you or I could pronounce."

Taywin's eye lit up in childlike glee. "So you were there! Both sides have claimed so!"

Toede shrugged and said, "For a little while I was. But what . . ." Toede's question was interrupted by a knock at the door, and a tall, flame-haired human who was kneeling down to peer inside.

"Is our guest awake?" said Bunniswot, looking tanner and (if possible) thinner than he did at his last meeting with Toede.

"I was just telling him the tale of the rebellion," Taywin said brightly. "He was there, as you said, at the helm of the mighty hammer-creature . . . What did you say its name was?"

"Jugger," said Toede, regarding Bunniswot as if the scholar had just popped out of a cake. "I was unaware you two knew each other," he said, eyes wide, adding to himself, *But not horribly surprised, given that you're both a few boulders short of an avalanche.*

Taywin shot a concerned look at Bunniswot. "And our other guest, is he . . . ?"

Bunniswot sighed. "Out spreading the good word, again. I last saw him trying to win over your father's guards."

Taywin rose and stomped her small feet. "I asked him to stop doing that. Daddy will get the wrong idea about the movement, and he'll never help us. I'll go get him."

Bunniswot nodded. "Good idea, but take Miles with you." At the sound of his name, a vaguely familiar kender guard popped his head in the hut. He nodded at Taywin, then stared at Toede and smiled. It was a creepy smile, made all the more so by the fact that every second tooth, top and bottom, was missing.

The berry-picking guard, Toede realized, and he suddenly understood the force of the blow on the back of his own head. Toede touched the lump there and smiled back venomously. Whatever else, this matter was far from over.

They locked glares for a moment, then Taywin breezed between them. She curtsied before Bunniswot, and said, *"Dance upon the water lilies,* Scholar Bunniswot."

Bunniswot returned the benediction. *"Dance upon the water lilies,* Taywin Kroninsdau."

The two kender disappeared, and Bunniswot, still hunched over, shuffled over to where Taywin had been seated and sat down, stretching his long legs.

Bunniswot managed a tired smile. "So, how are you feeling? When Miles and Taywin dragged you in, I was afraid they were too rough on you."

Toede shrugged off the concern and said levelly. *"I come to you skyclad and unshorn, seeking the teachings of the flesh,* eh?"

Bunniswot reddened and coughed. "Ah, that," he said, gulping. "You know, I'm glad to have this time alone with you, so we can sort this out."

"It took me a quote or two to make the connection," said Toede with a smile. "That's what all this lily-dancing and trusting trysts is all about, isn't it? The ogre pornography."

"Well, yes and no," said Bunniswot. "And it's *ur-ogre,* and *erotica.*"

"What does 'yes and no' mean?" said Toede.

Bunniswot spelled it out. "After Renders disappeared and the gnolls were defeated, I had trouble getting my . . . er, findings, published. There was neither funding nor support, and frankly, the material did have a . . . risqué . . . nature to it."

"So . . . ?"

"So I had it published myself," said Bunniswot. "Initial

release of twenty handwritten copies. Second release of a hundred. Working on a third now."

"I know there's something coming that I won't like," said Toede, reducing his eyes to slits. "Why not tell me now and get it over with?"

"I didn't publish it as historical documentation. No one in academia would take something like this seriously." Bunniswot smiled weakly.

"And instead . . . ?" continued Toede.

Bunniswot looked at the floor, speaking very fast. "I said it was the political and scholarly advice of one of the most misunderstood warrior-leaders of our time. The not-so-late Highmaster Toede."

"*What?*"

"It's gotten very good reviews," put the scholar in quickly. "The Tower of High Sorcery alone has asked for three copies. We're talking about reprinting it for the libraries of Sancrist."

"You signed *my* name to your ogre pornography?" hissed Toede, keeping his volume down as best he could.

"Well, I didn't *call* it pornography," replied Bunniswot with a 'what-kind-of-idiot-do-you-take-me-for' tone to his voice.

Toede felt his face grow red. "What. Did. You. Call. It?" He bit off each word.

"Political and social allegory, concentrating on both the relationship between the ruler and the ruled, and the relationships between rulers and other rulers," said Bunniswot.

"So all the talk about sex is . . . ?" Toede felt a mounting pressure building behind his eyes.

"Not about sex at all," Bunniswot said, nodding, "unless you have a filthy mind. And since no one admits to having a filthy mind, it's okay."

"Wonderful," muttered Toede. "And I take it our kender poetess has read the book."

"She can quote it chapter and verse," said Bunniswot.

"It's the text book for the Allied Rebellion."

Toede did not know if he was supposed to laugh or cry. "So I'm credited with a book I didn't write, that is about sex although it isn't, and that is being used by a rebellion that has yet to rebel?"

Bunniswot tilted his head slightly, as if considering Toede's argument. "Good summary," he said at length.

Toede pressed his hands to his temples. "Just bloody wonderful. Okay, what else can go wrong?"

"We're back!" said Taywin, bouncing into the hut.

She was followed by a large, angry-looking human dressed in black. Toede's eyes widened. His shirt was open to reveal a large *T* that had been carved into his chest.

* * * * *

The assassin from the Jetties towered over Toede. Even hunched over, his shoulders grazed the ceiling of the hut. The assassin's eyes glowed like hot embers with barely contained emotion. At his hip was a great sword in a rune-carved scabbard.

Toede felt his throat go dry, his tongue turn to sandpaper. Toede choked out, *"Dance on the lilies*, warrior."

The assassin let out a great cry, and Toede backed up. As it was, he was pressed flat against the wall of the hut when the human drew his sword and collapsed to his knees, presenting it, hilt-first, to the hobgoblin.

"My life is yours, O sage leader!" said the warrior, his eyes focused on Toede's toes.

Toede pried himself from the side of the wall with as much decorum as he could muster. He took the sword (the same one, he noted, that had previously been used in combat against Groag) from the warrior's hands, and strongly considered ramming it right back into the human's *T*-inscribed chest. However, as this might lead to further complications with the kender, (particularly the guard with the club), he instead gently touched the warrior with it on the shoulder, his mind scrambling for something suitable to say for the occasion.

"Your life is yours to live," mumbled Toede. "Arise, good Sir . . . In all the previous excitement I never learned your name?"

"Rogate, most sage leader," muttered the warrior, eyes bent to the floor.

"Arise, Sir Rogate," said Toede. "You have pledged your quest with my own." Whatever the heck that might be, he added to himself.

Rogate tottered to his feet, swaying slightly, and declaimed to the others, "I serve the mighty Toede, and have been accepted and forgiven! Behold, the first of the Toedaic Knights!"

Bunniswot and Taywin applauded politely. Miles, the kender guard, grimaced and left to return to his post.

"Now, if everyone will please sit down," said Toede. "Perhaps someone would like to tell me exactly what is going on."

Rogate drew himself up to his full height, or at least as much height as the hut permitted. "But you know all, most puissant and sage of wonders!"

Toede motioned for Rogate to sit, saying softly, "*I come to you skyclad and unshorn, seeking the teachings of the flesh.*" He made a mental note to get a few more quotes under his belt.

Rogate's face brightened, then he quietly sat down. "Perhaps, then, it is best that I begin, my wondrous leader, for I have been in Flotsam for most of the past year, and have seen what has transpired."

Toede nodded. Rogate continued, "I awoke in the Jetties with my wounds healed, the innkeep declaring that you had considered taking my life, but spared me instead. In that moment I realized your true mercy and felt ashamed.

"I did not return to my post that night, or ever again. I

know now that I was a dupe of the false creatures known as the Water Prophet and Gildentongue. When Gildentongue's dining habits were revealed to the masses I was angered, but more concerned when it turned out that Hopsloth's own priests chose to rule in the same highhanded fashion.

"I sought out one who I believed would tell me what had happened to you, and found that unworthy creature, Groag." Rogate looked as though he was about to spit. "He helped me not, and soon afterward he left the city himself, to further his own ambitions."

Toede slid a look in Bunniswot's direction, but the scholar declined to mention his tenure of eating Groag's cooking. Instead, he stared blankly out the hut door.

Rogate continued. "I knew that retribution most divine was upon us, and began to preach, to warn others of your next return. The priests of Hopsloth crushed all dissent, and many early martyrs disappeared without trace." Rogate lowered his eyes in silence.

"I was correct, and you did return, on the back of a great metal elephant that spoke in a mathematical tongue!

"You were magnificent, my sage leader!" beamed Rogate.

"You cut down the followers and guards of Hopsloth right and left, charged his fortress-lair, and dispatched him forthwith. Some say you died in the struggle, but I believed that you passed only after you had removed that foul stench from our land. It was then I founded my simple Faith-of-Toede-Returned.

"And yet," added Rogate quickly, "the foulness reappeared. In the turmoil following your triumph against Hopsloth, a dark being returned to Flotsam, the obscenity known as Groag."

Another silence hung in the air for a brief ice age. Toede prompted, "And then . . . ?" But the newly christened Toedaic Knight sat, shaking his head.

"It seems that Groag captured Rogate's audience,"

Bunniswot put in.

"Kidnapped!" roared Rogate. "Stole their minds and souls! Filled then with false fears and threats and had himself declared Lord of Flotsam, chosen by powers beyond our ken! It was then that the darkness truly fell, and I was forced to leave!"

Toede was stunned. "He succeeded? Groag?" he stammered. He looked at Bunniswot. "Short fellow, whines and faints a lot?"

The scholar nodded. "In the confusion following your . . . er . . . death, Groag arrived and usurped Rogate's preachings, but with the added punch line that he controlled your return, and unless all of Flotsam toed *his* line, you'd be back with a vengeance."

"An effective argument," said Toede. "And what happened when the populace laughed in his ugly face?"

"That's just it, they didn't laugh," said Bunniswot. "They'd seen the local ruling class decimated twice in previous months by your apparent actions. They figured things could hardly be worse with Groag on the throne, so he took control by acclamation. After all, he claimed to be acting in your name."

"False pretender," muttered Rogate. "False minion! *And he wore a mask, so none might know his face, though many knew his touch.*"

Toede was silent for a moment, unable to think of a suitable reply. Then he asked, "So how's he doing?"

Rogate snarled. Taywin shook her shorn head. Bunniswot answered, "You know how once I told you about Renders's histories, the ones that called you a fop and fool and a bumbler?" Rogate started to snarl again, so Bunniswot quickly added, "In a moment of light jest."

Toede nodded, an eye cast toward his new knight. "In a moment of light jest, I remember." It might be interesting having a follower with the protective nature of an attack dog.

"Well, Groag makes you look like wise king Lorac of

the Silvanesti," Bunniswot said.

Toede leaned back against the wall and whistled. "That bad?"

"Corruption, despotism, whimsical rulings, oppression," said Bunniswot, ticking off his fingers.

"Nothing new there," said Toede, then added quickly for Rogate's benefit, "That's par for the course in half a dozen cities throughout Ansalon."

"Summary executions," said Bunniswot.

"Part of any ruler's rights," said Toede.

"Without hearing, involving torture, and in public," sighed Bunniswot. "The bodies displayed on the gibbets for crows."

Toede winced. "A little too much of a good thing. And was the population recalcitrant, to earn such heavy-handed responses?"

Bunniswot shook his head. "Not before. They are now."

"I suddenly understand why your . . . ah . . . *my* book on government is so popular," said Toede.

Bunniswot nodded. "Some inhabitants fled, and many merchants avoid the city now. Groag used to threaten the populace in your name, now he just threatens them period. He has hired small armies of mercenaries to protect him and his court. Nonhumans are banned once again. *Other* nonhumans, that is."

Taywin broke in. "We had heard about the new Lord of Flotsam from refugees around the time we found our hunting grounds being patrolled by hired swords. I went to Flotsam to see if it was the same Mister Groag that I had picked berries with." She touched her scalp. "It was. He had me arrested for poaching, my head shaved publicly, and my execution scheduled for the next day."

"Unfortunately, the paperwork was lost," said the scholar innocently. "So we ferreted her out of town in a flour barrel. We hooked up with Rogate here, who had moved in with the kender."

"We thought you'd be returning again," said Taywin.

"In six months, as before. So in between we organized our resources and arranged to keep an eye out for you."

"Now that you have returned," intoned Rogate, "the Allied Rebellion can move forward and crush the spine of the false minion, and spill the blood of his corruption on the sands of history!"

"We arranged for a meeting," Bunniswot added, "with the leader of the kender: Kronin, Taywin's father. With you present we can convince him to join us, and with his approval, the kender raiders will swell our rebellion."

"Uh-huh," said Toede. He looked at the others, then said, "And tell me, exactly, how many people do we currently have in this rebellion I am leading?"

Taywin said brightly, her eyes shining with hope, "Including you, me, Bunniswot, Sir Rogate, and Miles . . . that makes five."

Chapter 22

The moot is met, during which Our Protagonist shows both his mettle and his metal in matters diplomatic and domestic.

The moot that Taywin had mentioned was another name for a big kender party, and the planning for said party had been bubbling and ebbing for days. The last of the winter stores (mostly salted trout and grape preserves) were being plundered, along with the standard complement of goose, boar, and a delicacy that had eluded Toede previously—hedgehogs wrapped in mud and roasted in their own shells.

Toede watched the geese roasting over the fire and thought of Groag, curled up in his manor (meaning Toede's manor), seated at a table heavily laden with culinary treasures and surrounded on all sides by fawning sycophants. He could imagine that, but equally he could imagine the new lord of Flotsam tightly curled up in his bed, eyeing the darkness nervously, unable to sleep, jumping at every noise.

From what the others had described, it sounded as though the city had fallen on hard times indeed under Groag's rule. There was little there to attract Toede, unless he put Groag's death high on his "to-do" list.

Groag's death was on his list, but not in the top ten, to be honest. After all, the drive to claim his vaunted lord-

247

ship had several times resulted in an unpleasant death. Toede might have a learning curve verging on a flat line, but he did connect Flotsam with messy, bloody deaths (usually his). Toede thought of Groag, and his drunken palate wrapped around the word: a-dap-tive.

The problem was that his compatriots—pornographer, poetess, nut-case, and guard—were intent on helping him regain this flawed gem, this dead dog of a city, and did not care to take no for an answer. Particularly the nut-case, who, Toede was sure, would get agitated should the target of his fervor prove less than excited about the prospect of reclaiming his historical throne.

Rogate the nut-case was wrapped up in some kind of fantasy version of justice. Taywin was in it for revenge and retribution. Bunniswot apparently considered this some great adventure, like those accursed Heroes of the Lance. And Miles?

Toede looked at the kender guard, who hovered close by him at all times. Miles beamed back at him with a gap-toothed grin, and Toede smiled weakly. Miles? Well, someone in every revolution has to do the heavy lifting, make the tea, pass out the leaflets, and make sure the hero of the rebellion—in this case, Toede—doesn't head for the hills.

Tomorrow, he would have to face Kronin.

Toede winced to think of the kender leader, and wondered how Kronin felt about him. After all, it was Toede who had ordered Kronin and another kender shackled and chased on that disastrous hunt, on the last day of his first life. And even though the kender elder seemed to have a mind like a steel sieve, the pair of them had run rings around Toede and his hunting party, right up to the point when Toede confronted the fire-breathing end of an angry dragon. And died.

Perhaps Kronin was setting Toede up. Perhaps the kender leader intended to shackle him to a boulder and give him a fifteen-minute head start before setting the hounds loose. Toede rubbed his chin at the thought. The kender were little more than savages, and Kronin could be holding a grudge.

Then again, so could Toede. It wouldn't hurt to pack a little extra precaution.

The present kender camp was located near the spot where Groag and he had plunged into the river almost a year ago. Most of the huts had been erected far from the water, and the intended moot-site was among the taller trees that over-looked the berry patches. Toede wandered back to his hut, his guardian in tow. Miles stopped at the entrance while Toede ducked in and searched through his meager belongings.

Taking the sword was out of the question, unfortunately, but the dagger would be just fine. Nicely weighted, it would suitable both for throwing and for use in tight combat, while the blade was fine enough to slip between the ribs of an opponent, be he human or kender.

Perfect precaution, thought Toede, slipping it into the oversized dwarven boots he had been wearing for a year (Krynn time). Or maybe more than just precaution. Given an opportunity, perhaps he would extract a little ven-geance on his own. Kronin had caused his death, after all. The first of many, and the beginning of all his troubles.

Not that Kronin would be alone on his list of vengeance. Groag had suggested that ill-fated hunt, after all. And Miles had been all too quick to strike him down, earlier.

Toede realized he would have to keep expanding the list as he went along, but Kronin, Groag, and Miles would do for now.

There was a knock, and Taywin stuck her head in, look-ing like a shaved chipmunk. "We're starting! Come on!"

Toede smiled and walked out of the hut to join the oth-ers, limping only slightly from the additional weight in his boot.

* * * * *

A kender moot, or at least *this* kender moot, differed from most regular kender festivals chiefly in that during the moot there were tables set up. They weren't much in the way of tables, in that they were only a foot off the ground, and the kender had to sit or kneel on the hard-packed earth, but at least they kept the food within a set boundary.

Already several of the revelers were using the tables as impromptu dance platforms. Toede identified two polkas and a reel, dancers bouncing between tables and sending dishware and bits of the feast in all directions.

Typical kender behavior, Toede thought.

There were already several makeshift song groups warming up, Toede noted, including not a few rehearsing ribald choruses regarding the social habits of elves. A white-haired kender elder, his hair spun into an elaborate braid that ran to the small of his back, was leading two tables in a call-and-respond contest. The lyrics of this drinking song shot from one table to the other like a shuttlecock. Those at the first table would shout "Oly-Oly-Oly-Ay!" and those at the second table would respond "Oly-Oly-Oly-Ay!". Then the first group would shout "Aley-Aley-Aley-O!" and the second group "Aley-Aley-Aley-O!" The kender at both tables would spend the time between responses drinking as quickly and as much as they could. This continued until both sides passed out.

Toede suddenly understood why Taywin's poetry might be considered sophisticated among these people. Then again, so might limericks about the Dark Queen's consorts.

Miles escorted Toede to the main table, situated on a patch of earth slightly higher than the rest, with a wall of woven grass behind it to frame the utmost important personages at the feast. These personages were Kronin's cronies, and in this case, leaders of the rebellion.

Miles was on the end, then Rogate and Bunniswot (both looking terribly uncomfortable and oversized). Then Toede, seated in the place of honor on Kronin's right. Then Taywin on his left, along with a pack of kender politicos—clan leaders and the like. The entire group was seated on one side of the table looking out over the assembled tribes.

Just what Toede had in mind for a pleasant evening—watching a hundred kender gorge themselves.

As Toede was duly escorted to his place of honor, Kronin rose to greet him. The kender leader always reminded Toede of a white-tufted squirrel, his childlike but ancient face looking as though it had walnuts stored in its cheeks. Toede pulled out his all-purpose let's-be-nice-to-the-local-ruling-class smile and warmly took the kender's extended hand.

"It is good to see you again, Toede," said Kronin.

"And you as well," beamed Toede. "Especially under such pleasant circumstances."

"More pleasant than last time, eh?" joshed Kronin, elbowing Toede in the ribs. The hobgoblin had to fight with all his willpower to avoid pulling the dagger and stabbing the cheery little freak right where he stood.

Instead he said, "At least the food is better."

"It should be," smiled the elder kender. "It came from your forest."

"It's not my forest," smiled Toede, adding, "Anymore." But he added silently, At the moment.

Toede looked for some clue behind Kronin's eyes, some telltale glint that this moot was in fact a ruse, a trap, or a stratagem. Yet if there was revenge in Kronin's heart, it was carefully concealed, for Toede could discern no apparent clue. This worried him further.

Toede remained standing as Kronin motioned for the kender horde to quiet down.

"Welcome to the moot, all the clans of kenderdom!" There was polite applause. Someone yelled "Toast!"

Kronin continued without pause. "I want to thank all and sundry for coming on this festive occasion, in particular our human guests." Rogate and Bunniswot nodded to general clapping. "Especially our honored guest, the

Highmaster-in-Exile of Flotsam, Lord Toede." Toede nodded to decidedly less applause, and there was another shout for "Toast!"

"His highmastership spent a few brief days with us almost a year ago," Kronin added, "and was responsible for saving the life of my lovely daughter." More applause, though this was mostly for Taywin, who waved at the assemblage.

Kronin motioned to Toede that now he was expected to utter a few words. The hobgoblin cleared his voice. "My only regret is that I was not here long enough in days of yore to get to know every one of you wonderful kender." Greater applause to this compliment, and Toede sat back down, thinking, *And I further regret not having a team of talented torturers with me at the time.*

During Toede's small speech, Kronin rescued from the table a wooden goblet that he now held aloft. "I give you the first toast of the evening." There was wild applause, and Kronin looked pensive, as if summoning some ghost of a memory. Then he proclaimed, *"Drink deep the cup of life, for time will sup it if you do not."* It was an appropriate toast, and there were cheers and the clinking of mugs.

Kronin turned to the hobgoblin, clacking goblets with him. Toede nodded politely. "A good toast," he said.

Kronin smiled. "It should be, you wrote it."

Toede's smile froze for an instant. Then he said smoothly, "True, but you seem to have caught the nuance of the passage perfectly. I have never heard it recited better." He added the mental note that, until he himself had read the dratted thing, he had best assume that every smutty or hedonistic statement uttered around him was a quote from his supposed book.

Kronin did not seem to notice Toede's tightened facial muscles. "When I first read the book, I couldn't believe you were responsible for it. It's so . . . deep. Thoughtful. Intelligent."

Toede tried to unclench his teeth. "Surprised?" he

asked.

"Very," responded Kronin, ignoring the color crawling into Toede's face. "I mean, in our limited dealings, you struck me as a bully, a lout, and a simpleton. No offense meant."

"None taken," said Toede, aware of the drag of the dagger in his boot.

"And yet, such clear, precise thinking, masking itself in sensual analogy . . ." Kronin shook his head. "It only makes me wonder why you didn't put such thoughts into action earlier, before you got yourself killed."

"Retirement gives an opportunity for reflection," smiled Toede.

"Exactly my conclusion!" said Kronin. "I would no more think of you saying such things, or even sitting down here with us, than I could imagine a badger singing opera. This only confirms a personal theory I have about your tyrannical rule."

"Oh?" said Toede.

"Your heart wasn't in it," concluded the kender elder, slapping the table. "You could not reconcile your own conscionable beliefs with the dragon highlords who created your position and supported your regime. So as a result, you sought to appear as the bumbling, hedonistic, groveling petty tyrant that everyone thought you were. Whereas, in reality, you were the very opposite."

There was another call for a toast. Kronin rose to address the crowd.

That does it, Toede thought. I'm going to kill him. This time for sure. The only question is when. A true smile blossomed on his sallow face.

Kronin made another suggestive toast involving blossom petals and honey, and sat back down. Toede took a pull from his cup and enjoyed the pleasant cranberry wine, very potent.

"You're going to quote me all night?" chided Toede.

"Your words are honest and brave," said Kronin,

"unlike the public facade you presented to the world. My daughter has always been sympathetic to you, but I fear I could not see behind the mean-spirited boot-spittle lackey image you showed to the outside world. I mean, is it true you once went drinking with Raistlin, and that he was almost left behind by the Companions as a result?"

As the evening continued in a similar vein, Kronin's tongue became looser, his prose more direct and explicit, particularly as to how the new Toede was far superior to that gutless, inbred, despotic little excuse for a sliver-of-worm-larva that he had been when he was in charge of Flotsam. All of these insults were delivered with a glib smile, and an assurance that the kender leader knew that Toede was much better now.

Kronin's opinion of Groag was even worse, but only in the matter of degree. At one point the kender was saying how Groag was more Toedelike than Toede had *ever* been, when the elderly kender's conversation took a turn, and he mentioned the loss of his daughter's lovely locks. It was an off-hand reference to Groag's senseless cruelty, but it halted Kronin in his conversational tracks. The old kender grew quiet, and Toede could almost hear his old kender heart breaking.

Then the moment passed, and Kronin resumed his detailed comparison of Toede and Groag. Toede felt his blood pressure climbing. The worst thing that could happen, thought the hobgoblin as the kender nattered on, would be for him to die again. At the hands of kender it would take a while, because they wouldn't know how to proceed properly and would probably talk him to death.

Five more toasts and an hour of comparative comments later, Toede's head was aching, both from the conversation and the wine. Kronin interrupted his fourth analysis of Toede's first death to stagger to his feet and gesture to the increasingly rambunctious crowd. "You have heard many toasts this evening," he slurred, "all from the mind of this incredible individual known as Toede." There was drunken and thunderous applause at this point, with the by-now-woozy Toede convinced they had forgotten who they were cheering for. The inner rage at pompous Kronin, foolish Taywin, the kender rabble, their stupid songs and their excessive eating habits, had pushed him to the boiling point. It wouldn't take much more to push him over the edge.

"But I do not want to be the only one speaking," Kronin continued, "so I grant the floor to my daughter, Taywin."

Oh, no, thought Toede.

Kronin went on, oblivious. "Taywin will be reading a litany of her best poems. . . ."

"That does it," muttered Toede, as he leaned down to grab the knife out his boot, and then jam it between Kronin's ribs. Then a quick escape into the darkness and freedom.

There was a prickly feeling that passed over Toede's neck when he bent forward, and then, when he looked up, dagger in hand, he saw to his astonishment that there was already a dagger sticking in Kronin's side. The kender elder looked in confusion at the blood fountaining out of his right side, mouthed something incomprehensible, and collapsed onto his daughter.

Toede looked at the unused dagger in his own hand, at the implement jutting out of the kender, and back to the dagger again, as if unable to believe that there were multiple poetry-haters at the moot.

Then Miles gave a shout. "The hobgoblin's stabbed Kronin! Get him!"

Toede felt the entire weight of two-hundred-plus eyes fix on him simultaneously, backed up by two-hundred-plus hands, all armed with knives, forks, and other instruments of potential personal damage.

Toede rose halfway, looked out at the angry faces, and seemed about to speak. Then he wheeled, cut a long, savage rip in the screen behind the main table, and bolted, leaving the charging kender behind, and Taywin screaming for order.

* * * * *

Kronin's assassin moved as silently as possible toward the river bank. He had to make a large loop to avoid the mass of confusion, for an impromptu posse of impassioned and drunken kender had charged in various directions after the incident—to the village and Toede's hut, to the river, to the old campsite. Bands of kender in fours and fives went tumbling in all directions in the dark, intent on fetching the hounds and catching the traitorous criminal.

Twice now, packs of dazed kender had boiled past him, completely unaware that the true murderer was in their sights and providing erroneous information to them.

The assassin smiled as he slipped quietly between the large boles, down to the embankment and toward the lone maple bridge across the stream. The water glowed white in the moonlight.

He was at the near end of the bridge when a small shadow detached itself from a tree about fifteen feet away. The hobgoblin-shaped shadow strode forward into the moonlight, as the assassin stopped dead in his tracks.

"Hello, Miles," said Toede, tapping his dagger against his nails.

"Toede," lisped the kender guard. "Thought I'd find you here."

"No, you didn't," smiled Toede. "You thought nothing of the kind. You thought this was the easiest way to escape. I know because I had the same route planned."

"I don't know what you're talking about," sputtered the kender.

"You threw the dagger that hit Kronin."

"You don't know that!" said the kender. "You were

looking elsewhere, leaning under the table."

"You would notice that," said Toede. "Then you must know that I could *not* have done the deed. Yet you were the first to shout for my head. It was you, Rogate, Bunniswot, Kronin, and I on that side of table. If it had been Rogate, you would have seen it clearly, and maybe even have stopped him. Bunniswot is a scholar who can't even handle a butter knife without causing himself grievous injury. I was leaning forward, you said so yourself. So the only one who could have done it was . . ."

"I didn't mean to hit him," spat the kender.

"No, you meant to hit me," finished the hobgoblin. "But I leaned forward, so you missed and struck Taywin's father."

There was a silence. Finally the kender guard said, "You can't take me back, you know."

"I can't?" said Toede.

"Look. You take me back, and as soon as I get within shouting range, I shout that I've spotted you." Miles chose his words carefully. "There are a hundred crazed kender out there, all of them after your hide. You may know the truth, but by the time anyone listens, you will be garotted."

"I've been dead before," shrugged Toede.

"And you really want to be dead again?" said Miles. When the hobgoblin didn't respond, the kender said, "I'm going now. Best of luck on your own escape." He started across the slippery pole, his footing sure and even.

"Miles?" came Toede's shout behind him. Halfway across the pole, the kender turned, looking over his shoulder at the hobgoblin.

"Yes, Toede?" he said.

"Why?"

Miles turned on the narrow bridge. He spread his hands out to explain that if Toede was supposed to be a *dead* martyr, for he knew about all the lies and half-truths that Bunniswot and Rogate and even Taywin told. He wanted to prove Toede an unworthy being to follow, and the best thing for the hobgoblin was to die under the kender swords.

Miles intended to say all that, really. But as he spread his hands, he felt a harsh, sharp thump in his chest, and looked down to see the hilt of Toede's dagger protruding from his shirt, just to the left of his sternum.

Then he felt the cold rush of the waters hit, and then nothing more at all.

"*Dance upon the water lilies*, Miles," said Toede. "*Dance upon the lilies.*"

* * * * *

It was about a half hour later when Bunniswot found Toede, still at the bridge, listening to the thunder of the rapids.

Toede started for a moment, then nodded as Bunniswot sat down next to him.

"How bad is it?" said the hobgoblin.

"Not as bad as it seemed," said the scholar. "It became apparent soon after the attack that you were not responsible, and would have been realized sooner if Rogate had not gotten into a wrestling match with a dozen kender, defending your good name."

"Kronin alive?"

"They have a few good healers," Bunniswot said, nodding, "and they anticipate injuries at a moot, so he's fine. He thinks you're out finding the assassin."

"Already found him," said Toede. "Miles."

Another nod from the scholar. "They figured that, too. He alive?"

"No," said Toede, not adding anything else.

"Well," said the scholar, "after they sorted out that you didn't try to kill Kronin, but Miles probably did, the entire party shifted into a celebration in your honor—you know, the brave little humanoid, unfairly accused, who seeks out the guilty party."

"That's a new one," grunted Toede.

"And it's now more than ever likely that the kender clans will join the rebellion," added Bunniswot. "You want to head back?"

"In a moment." Toede sighed, then added, "Ever kill anyone, scholar?"

"Me?" A nervous laugh. "Oh, no. Uh . . . and you?"

"More than I care to count," said Toede. "Even more that I have been indirectly responsible for. And yet, this one, felt so . . ."

"Troubling?" suggested Bunniswot. "Painful? Thought-provoking?"

"Satisfying," finished Toede, ignoring Bunniswot's sudden start. "This one was worth it, as though I had accomplished something. You know?"

"Uh," said Bunniswot, "I don't, I'm afraid."

Toede sighed again. "Must be a deficiency in your species. I guess we should go back. What's on tap now?"

Bunniswot brightened. "You missed several more toasts to your glory, and now Taywin is reading her poetry."

Toede made a face. "Perhaps we ought not to hurry back," he said. "Maybe we should get our story straight about my epic battle with the assassin. It would help if I had a scholarly witness to the culmination."

Toede looked at the scholar for a moment, then added with a smile, "And while we're at it, you can remind me of some of 'my' quotes."

Chapter 23

In which Our Protagonist is swept along by events, and the oft-mentioned necromancer finally makes an appearance, after his own fashion. Also, a council of war is held, havoc is cried, and the gnolls of war are unleashed.

"When are these mysterious allies going to show?" snarled Toede, sitting on the crushed remains of an ogre plinth. They were back at the scholars' old campsite that, except for the rot, looked just as Toede had left it six months earlier. The remains of the birches and stone monuments lay like broken toys around the site.

Bunniswot shrugged, squinting at the sun. "He said about midday. Does it look middayish to you?"

"Remind me to not let you draw up the battle plan," muttered Toede. He looked over to Taywin and Rogate. Rogate had sketched out a map of Flotsam and was drawing arrows from outside the walls to inside the walls. With Miles's death, Rogate had become the "honor guard" for Highmaster-in-Exile Toede.

Toede watched Rogate draw a long, sweeping arrow that started in the west, looped entirely around the city, and attacked the Rock from a seaborne invasion. "Or him, either," added Toede.

Bunniswot sniffed "Taywin says the best mode of attack would be from the south, where the walls are still in disrepair. I tend to agree."

Toede nodded. "The problem is not the condition of those walls. The problem is the wall between the Lower City and the Rock. In case of invasion, the public plan was always to mobilize the populace and meet the enemy at the outer walls. The secret plan was for the upper classes to pull back into the Rock and leave the rest to fight and die in the streets."

"Do you think Groag would continue that policy?" said Bunniswot.

"If it works, don't mess with it," responded Toede. "Besides, you said that Groag's first order of business was rebuilding the Rock Wall, then the manor, and is only now starting to rebuild the outer wall."

"And quickly," added Bunniswot. "There are a lot of cheap materials and cut corners in that particular project. I wish we could find another siege machine like your friend Jugger."

"Jugger is . . . was . . . unique." Toede shuddered, thinking of that long, lazy arc over the Blood Sea. "At least I hope so. I never want to meet another denizen of the Abyss. . . ." Toede stopped for a moment, then asked, "Do you hear that?"

"What?" said Bunniswot.

"Sounded like someone laughing in the distance," said Toede. Another pause. "It's gone now."

Bunniswot shrugged, shaking his head. "Groag has hired a number of mercenaries, including ogres from the Balifor area and some minotaurs from across the Blood Sea, all for personal protection. Most of the rest of the armed forces have survived two of your 'visits' to Flotsam already. As a result, they are battle-hardened, but they have no desire to face an army with you at the helm."

Toede grunted. Nor did he have any desire to lead an army with himself at the helm or any other position, but he had not been able to come up with an easy way out for the past two days.

"Most of Groag's courtiers are loyal," continued Bunni-swot. "But it is a loyalty built more out of fear than trust. Groag is even more mercurial than . . . you were, and if the going gets tough, they will probably fold and surrender."

"You seem to know a lot about how Groag's court works," noted Toede.

"I should," said Bunniswot, "since I am the official court historian."

Toede stared at the scholar. "You're the what?"

Bunniswot shrugged. "I returned to Flotsam with my notes, without a sponsor and needing a job. Groag was just setting himself up, and knew that I was not part of the 'old mob' that followed Hopsloth or the priests. So I got the posting." He paused a moment, then added, "How do you think I got your book copied?"

"You mean . . ."

"Groag's scribes," said Bunniswot, "who were also Hopsloth's scribes, and Gildentongue's scribes, and now that I think of it, *your* scribes. The bureaucracy remains intact, I've discovered, regardless of changes in the leadership."

"I remember the scribes," said Toede. "I wouldn't trust them with a lead groat."

"Nor I," said Bunniswot, "which is why the initial manuscript came to them on official order from Groag. They leapt on the chance to prove their worth and loyalty to the new master. That was the first print run. Then Groag found out about the book (though not the copying), and screamed bloody murder about Toede traitors lurking in Flotsam. After which, the scribes, afraid for their jobs as well as their lives, produced another hundred copies in exchange for my silence in the matter."

"And the third printing?" said Toede.

"We're working on a profit-sharing plan," said Bunniswot.

Both hobgoblin and human heads spun around as Taywin cursed at Rogate, "We can't use an airborne assault.

We don't have anything that flies!"

"A minor point," countered Rogate, "easily surmounted by a brilliant commander and tactician such as our high-master!"

"*Children*," admonished Toede.

"Even a brilliant commander can't build ships out of nothing!" said Taywin, looking more worn and tired than usual.

Rogate nodded intensely, then looked at the kender, his eyes not quite focusing. "Moles!" he shouted. "What if we get some really large moles, and tunnel under the walls?"

Taywin buried her head in her hands and screamed, also in a ladylike fashion.

"Badgers would do as well," said Rogate in a compromising tone.

"Scholar," sighed Toede, "do you want to separate them until they cool down?" Bunniswot did not respond. "Scholar?"

Toede looked up to see Bunniswot staring at the borders of the clearing, his face a white mask of fear. Toede followed his terror-stricken gaze to the edge, where a great gnoll stood. As Toede watched, more gnolls stepped from the underbrush, in a ring that spread around the entire campsite.

Toede, reaching for the sword slung across his back, rose slowly from his position. He said out of the corner of his mouth, "Friends of yours?"

Bunniswot shook his head slowly.

"Thought not," muttered Toede as he pulled his sword from its back-scabbard. Rogate and Taywin were also on their feet, weapons drawn.

The gnolls regarded them in silence, seeming as tense as the rebellion members. Two of the largest gnolls approached Bunniswot and Toede. The two gnolls parted, to reveal an equally massive gnoll behind them, dressed in the armor and metal skullcap of a chieftain.

"Charka!" cried Toede. Bunniswot let out a groan, and

Toede heard a dull thump behind him and to his right. He did not need to look back to know the young scholar was sprawled out in a dead faint.

At least he'll be quiet, thought the hobgoblin.

"Charka offers greetings to Toede, King of Little Dry Frogs!" Charka saluted.

"Is this a social call," snarled Toede, puffing himself up as much as he could, "or are you here to finish the job you attempted six months ago?"

Toede expected Charka to respond with a typical "Hur?" but instead the gnoll said, "Neither. We come to offer what aid we can."

Toede's eyebrows shot up. "That was almost a complete sentence, Charka."

Behind him, Taywin was bringing Bunniswot out of his swoon, and convinced him that they were not all going to die. At least not just yet.

"Charka has been practicing," the gnoll chief said, smiling. "Charka has had help!"

A smaller, human figure, dressed in the quilted leathers of gnollish garb, stepped out from behind the gnoll, bowed slightly, and waved.

"Ah," said Renders. "Hello, everyone."

Bunniswot groaned and almost passed out again. Pity, thought Toede, the old boy was doing so well. "Greetings, Chief Boils Flesh," said Toede.

"Renders. Ah. Just Renders," said the scholar. "Charka and I worked on homonyms and multiple definitions early on."

"Charka speak good now," bellowed the gnoll.

"Well," put in Renders.

"A hole in the ground that provides water," defined Charka. "Sort of a little bitty swamp."

Renders gave Toede a shrug. "Ah. There are still some rough spots."

Toede still had his sword pointed at the gnolls and the human. He lowered it but did not sheathe the weapon.

"Forgive my confusion," he said, "but the last time I saw your people, Charka, they were being rolled over by a large, heavy object."

"Yes." Charka nodded. "Night of the Flat Brothers, Charka remember it well. We had returned to our swamp to discuss your trick. Many said you fooled us, cheated us into believing scholars were powerful wizards. Some said we should attack scholars. Charka angry, too. Agreed with them. Then Renders arrived."

"Ah," put in Renders, "I'm afraid I was very disappointed in Charka's behavior, and was going to give the gnoll a piece of my mind."

"You're fortunate that Charka didn't leave pieces of your mind scattered throughout the swamp," muttered Toede.

Charka frowned. "Renders talk. Charka agree with Renders," he said. "Think that Toede told truth, that scholars were powerful. Not great in juju, but great in knowledge."

"Ah," added Renders, "after all, Charka did like my stories."

"Charka argue that scholars should stay," said the gnoll. "Brother gnolls disagreed, said Charka not fit for chiefdom. Throw-over Charka."

"Overthrow," corrected Renders.

"Over . . . throw," said Charka carefully. "Brother gnolls attacked and were crushed to putty by great machine. Taboo-area pillars destroyed, magic broken, no longer taboo. Other gnolls apologize to Charka, make Charka chief, Renders shaman."

"Ah," said Renders. "They thought we summoned the Abyss-spawned creature that flattened the gnolls' attack. After a while, of course, we let it be known it was likely, ah, your doing, Toede." The old scholar paused and added, "It is Toede, isn't it?"

"The 'real Toede,' as people keep saying," said Toede.

"I've been meaning to read your book," said Renders.

"Perhaps another day," said Toede. "But Bunniswot didn't even know you two were alive, and you aren't the mysterious allies he was talking about. So why are you here?"

"Ah," said Renders. "Ah, well, we were also told to meet here."

"By whom?" said Toede.

"By me," said a sepulchral voice at the perimeter of the camp. A lone figure limped into the encampment.

It was humanoid and might once have been a man, for it had the required number of arms and legs and what would pass in most societies as a torso. However, the torso was lopsided, as if a large chunk of it had been removed under the left arm and then everything had been resewn back together. The skin of its hands was tightly pulled over a skeletal form, and its tightly drawn face was the color of water-stained parchment. The shadow of a skull could be glimpsed under the skin. As for its manner of dress, it was decked in once-resplendent robes and finery, now reduced to gray tatters dotted with fragmented gems. And it smelled like new earth disturbed by an open grave.

"Now that we are all here," said the far-off necromancer, regarding the others through the zombie's empty eyes and forcing the words through the zombie's weak throat, "we can begin this council of war."

* * * * *

Contrary to what the necromancer stated, they were not "all there," even discounting the several participants in general (and Rogate in particular) who would never be "all there." The figure that appeared before members of the rebellion was a dead form, animated by the spells of the dark wizard. The necromancer moved its limbs like a puppeteer, drew only sufficient breath to strum the vocal cords, and saw the surrounding world through the zombie's now-rotted eyes. The necromancer himself was present only "in spirit," as it were. His body, mind, and soul were safely locked away in his distant tower, and only his "mouthpiece" was seated among them in the garden of ruined ogre plinths.

Charka's gnoll followers were spooked by the living dead and removed themselves to the perimeter of the camp. This left Renders, Charka, the necromancer's zombie, Rogate, Taywin, Toede, and Bunniswot seated in a loose circle on overturned and partially crushed plinths. Bunniswot had recovered nicely and was now engaged in pleasant small talk with Renders.

"I must apologize for the mysterious nature of my manifestation," wheezed the zombie, "for I feared there would be . . ." The necromancer paused to choose his words carefully. "Repercussions . . . if I had used one of my more obvious agents."

"I must admit," said Bunniswot, "the individual who contacted me seemed more . . . lively."

"Newly dead, he was," said the necromancer, "and the . . . victim . . . of a twisted neck. He would not have been necessary had I located the anomaly through my own efforts."

"Animally?" asked Charka.

"Strangeness," defined Renders. "Something, ah, out of step with the rest of the universe."

"Gee," grumbled Toede to the assembled gnoll, kender, scholars, fanatic assassin, and zombie, "what could be considered strange and out of step in *this* universe?"

Six sets of eyes (including the zombie's unfocused orbs) turned toward Toede.

"Thrice you have been slain, Highmaster," said the zombie to Toede, "each time in a drastic and irreconcilable way. Yet thrice you have been restored, unmarked and unscarred, and returned to life—through no earthly agency, nor, so far as I may divine, the will of the True Gods themselves. Do you have any explanation for your return each time?"

"Unfinished business," said Toede.

"That is a matter that usually concerns ghosts," said the necromancer.

"Then blame clean living." Toede threw up his hands and ticked off options. "Or the gods lied to you. Or other forces are at work. Or there's a hole in the natural order. Or overdue library books. Sheer perversity of the keepers of the universe. All of the above. Frankly, I don't care."

"I know you do not," said the zombie, controlled by the far-off mage. "But I do. If you have a secret, and you must, I would like to learn it." The zombie coughed, sounding to Toede like a flurry of scalpels.

"And if you had found me before the kender . . ." began Toede.

"I would not have to be here now," finished the necromancer, "and your Allied Rebellion would have had to carry on with you only as a figurehead and a memory."

Toede decided to change the subject, before the necromancer's honeyed words seeped into his compatriots' brains. "So you called us to meet you here, and Charka's gnolls as well. You could just as easily have ambushed us, killed the others, and captured or killed me."

"A possibility," said the zombie, "but one that might be explored later on. However, I believe in omens, signs, and warnings. Last fall, I found this item on the border of my lands."

The zombie reached inside its chest (not just inside its tattered jacket, Toede noticed, but into the cavity where a beating heart would normally reside), and pulled out a medallion. He held it aloft, and it spun and glittered at the end of its chain.

The others craned to read the medallion's faces. Toede did not have to.

"One side has a picture of Hopsloth the late Water Prophet," said the zombie. "The other a crudely inscribed *T*, a dedication, and a date, all in the same hand. The dedication goes back to a year ago."

Toede kept his voice level. "And?" he said.

"Within a day of finding it, two of my zombies were crushed flat, and Hopsloth was found dead, and the people of Flotsam ascribed the occurrence to the actions of an individual whose name begins with a *T*," said the zombie. "I believe in omens and signs, Highmaster. I believe that it is better to deal with you here and now. Those who encounter you as an enemy seem to end up in a bad way."

"Instead of a charmed life," said Toede, dryly, "I lead a charmed death."

"If you say so," responded the zombie. "I am willing to facilitate the achievement of your ends."

"Which are?" said Toede, looking innocent of any ends.

The zombie's face crinkled in what Toede assumed was an attempt at a smile. "Why, taking Flotsam back as your own domain, what else?"

What else indeed, thought Toede. Five people attempting to conquer a city was foolhardy, even if—especially if—backed up by an army of kender. He had been scanning for an escape for the past two days, with little luck. But that same assault, aided by gnolls and a powerful sorcerer skilled in the nature of undeath, and perhaps, just perhaps . . .

"You assume I still desire Flotsam," Toede said. "I've heard it's gotten a bit run-down in the past six months."

"You want Flotsam," said the zombie flatly. "Otherwise you never would have joined this foolish rebellion. And the other members are willing to give it back to you, since they believe they can get what they want better from you than from Groag."

"And what do they want?"

"Have you asked them?" said the zombie, with the same face-crinkling smile. "They probably talk of rights and grievances and vengeances, but they all want something. What do you think it is?"

Toede looked at the others, who seemed lost in somber

thought. Then Taywin said, "Permission."

"Excuse me?" said Toede.

"Permission," repeated Taywin, her brow furrowed. "The kender are hunted as poachers and thieves, not only by Groag but by his predecessors. Including you. The kender want to hunt and fish in the lands claimed by Flotsam, should we win."

Toede was silent for a moment. "Done," he said at length, "provided that merchants and agents of the local lord are not harassed." Taywin nodded, and Toede thought immediately of five ways to frame the kender and be done with them in the long run.

Charka put in his two coins' worth next. "Charka want to go to Flotsam. Not just Charka, but Charka's people. Not just Charka's people, but other people who are not Charka's."

"You mean lift the ban on humanoids?" said Toede.

"Yes," Charka replied. "Books are in Flotsam, and Charka cannot get to them. Lift ban, and Charka's people fight for Toede."

Toede nodded. "Done." Renders patted Charka on the arm.

"Who's next?" asked the zombie.

Rogate spoke up. "I live only to serve Lord Toede, and accept whatever role he chooses for me."

The necromancer made a wheezing (if rude) noise. "No one honestly believes such."

Toede stepped in. "Rogate does. That's enough for me. He has already been knighted for his efforts and loyalty. Bunniswot?"

"I live only to serve," said the young scholar, spreading his hands.

"I'd buy that from Rogate," said Toede, "but not you. You already have a position of some minor importance in Groag's court. Why risk helping us?"

Bunniswot was silent. "Maybe I want to be a part of history. A part of change," he said at last.

"Maybe you want to play at being the lord's advisor, moving the pieces around the board at your own whims?" suggested Toede.

"I'm insulted," said Bunniswot (bingo, thought Toede). "At most I want your input into the history I will write about your life and career."

"Done," said Toede. Having gone through the list, the hobgoblin returned the conversation to its starting place. "And you, Necromancer, what do you want?"

"There are casualties in every conflict," said the zombie. "Their deaths will swell my ranks. I will not dissemble to inferiors, so I tell you that I foresee many deaths in this conflict. I demand all the bodies of the dead after the battle is over."

Toede shot a look at the other members of the rebellion. Charka was scowling, but both Rogate and Taywin were nodding—the hard, cold-faced agreement of soldiers to whom death was no stranger. Renders looked as though he had swallowed part of his ear, and Bunniswot was going pale once again.

The zombie ignored all this. "Also, I want *your* body."

"You're not my idea of a suitable mate," said Toede.

"You jest," said the necromancer, not jesting. "If you perish in the assault, I want your physical remains. Among other things, I am curious whether you are able to return with or without your body, or to the same location in your next life. Purely scientific interest."

"Purely," said Toede, thinking that the necromancer could build an army of hobgoblin bodies should Toede kick off every six months. Then another image crossed his brain, of an undead Toede sitting on the throne of Flotsam, controlled by the necromancer.

"Only if I perish in battle," Toede qualified. Even through the mask of undead flesh Toede could detect the flicker of greed.

"Done," said the necromancer. "How soon before the kender can mass at the edge of Flotsam's fields?"

Taywin looked at the zombie. "Three days, maybe four."

"Make it three," said the necromancer. "The auguries are right for three days hence. In the morning, south of the city, where the walls are still ruined. Will the gnolls be ready for a fight?"

"Charka always ready!"

"Meet the kender there the night before," said the zombie. "My forces will be ready the next morning. Are there any questions?" There was only silence from the other members of the rebellion.

"Good." The zombie pitched forward, dissolving into dust as it fell. Its bones landed and shook apart where it struck the ground.

Rogate fished the amulet from the now-truly-dead creature's stiff fingers.

"What an odd and unpleasant individual," sniffed Renders.

"Aye," said Toede. "But at least he is one I can understand."

Chapter 24

In which Our Protagonist receives much advice from many visitors on the night before the battle, and we witness the Last Temptation of Toede.

The next two days passed quickly, what with the preparations for war. In the case of the kender this consisted of a number of parties and rallies, and several long explanations as to why they could not take everything that might be useful into battle. There were a surprising number of cast-iron frying pans that had been pressed into temporary service as maces and cudgels that now needed to be returned to their original owners. Sometimes Toede felt he was leading a grade-school outing as opposed to a military operation.

The others were little help. Bunniswot returned to Flotsam (over Toede's objections, but with the approval of the others) to keep an eye on Groag and report any major troop movements. With her father, Taywin handled the daily routine of drilling the kender troops (making sure they all charged in the same direction). Rogate was good for pep talks but still lousy for tactics. Charka and Renders were gathering their forces, while the necromancer remained decidedly aloof.

Toede threw himself into the preparations with half-hearted zeal, spending his evenings studying "his" text on the philosophy of government. Bunniswot had given him the magically lighted stone, but even with that advantage, he made slow progress. The margins were filled with Bunniswot-inspired gloss, explaining, for example, what Toede truly meant by the story of the shepherdess and the three priests of Hiddukel. His explanations were almost as dense and detailed as the text itself, though not nearly as amusing.

Throughout it all, the back of Toede's mind struggled with the nagging question: What happens when it goes wrong *this* time? Not if. When. Even with a dragon highlord's army under his command, there was always a chance that something would go wrong. That the third enemy warrior on the left wasn't just some peasant, but the grandson of a wizard, and in the middle of the battle would start flinging fireballs. Or that the enemy standard was really a gold dragon. Or that one's own troops would have a sudden case of the chills, the gout, the mange, or dropsy.

And that was with trained troops, such as the professionals Groag would have at his beck and hire. With *this* lot—well, Toede planned on using gnolls as shock troops, the kender as skirmishers and streetfighters, and the necromancer's unnamed and unnumbered forces as the cavalry, if the others got repulsed, to cover their retreat.

Toede supposed it could be worse. They could be gnomes.

The highmaster explained the general outline of the attack to Rogate, Taywin, Kronin, Charka, and Renders. They nodded and agreed, since it met with their own racial tendencies. The gnolls would have smashed themselves against the walls if they thought it would work, and the kender liked the idea of fighting from a lot of cover. Rogate liked the idea of anything smacking of holy vengeance, and left with Kronin to inspect the troops (again). Renders just nodded and pretended as if he understood.

None of the five other leaders noted what Toede considered to be the hallmark of his plan—namely, that it put the bulk of his army between him and Groag's forces in Flotsam. If Groag's mercenaries and guards folded as precipitously as Bunniswot seemed to think they would, then the city would be seized without his presence on the front line.

If, as Toede suspected, Groag gave a last-minute pep-talk in the form of emptying the treasury's coffers for the troops, and the attack failed, then he wanted to be as far away from the scene as possible.

The assault would take place along the south, at the ruined sections of the wall that Jugger had created and Groag had insufficiently repaired. The western half of the city would be ignored; the idea was to charge the Rock and taken out the existing government (meaning Groag and his flunkies) with minimum losses.

And minimum meant Toede intended to stay alive. He flirted with the idea of just sneaking out of camp now, heading for the dwarven cabin in the hills, and finding out later from some passing skald who won. After all, a live coward is better than a dead hero.

No, he decided, if he did that, then probably they *would* win, and it would be Kronin who would rule Flotsam and Toede who would be caught for poaching. That was the way his life (or lives) was working out of late.

As it turned out, Toede was not the only one concerned about the survival of a rebellion member. He was talking with Taywin over the remains of the evening meal when Charka dropped to their eye-level with a squatting thud, interrupting their discourse.

"Charka lead troops," said the gnoll chieftain, "but want Renders to be safe in rear."

"Actually, I'd rather be with you and your entourage," said the human scholar, but Charka would not be swayed.

"Renders no has magic," went the gnoll's argument. "Renders no has muscle. Renders going to tell enemy stories? Maybe hit them with brain? No, Renders stays behind at camp."

"Leave Renders with me," said Toede, "behind the main

body, but in a position to come up fast if the attack breaks down." He'll be a big help then, he added privately.

Charka agreed to the plan, if grudgingly. Taywin rocked back on her perch. "You know, I'm amazed," she said, looking at the two figures sitting across the fire. "Humans and gnolls usually fight, yet the two of you seem to have formed a fast friendship."

Charka looked at the kender. "Is it not obvious?"

"Ah," said Renders. "Ah. I think you are thinking in terms of human and gnoll. You should instead think in terms of male"—he placed an affectionate hand on the gnoll's shoulder—"and female."

Taywin stopped rocking, and her eyes grew wide, such that her eyebrows would have disappeared beneath her hairline (if she currently had one).

Toede grunted, rising to his feet. "And on that note," he said, abandoning the kender to press on through what promised to be a conversational mine field, "I have to get back to my own studies." He padded off to his command tent.

The tent was made of motley pieces of stained, formerly white canvas that had once graced the scholar's camp, and had been presented (with as much pomp and dignity as the kender could manage) to Toede by the parents and children of the warriors Toede was sending off to die in Flotsam. Toede hated it because it was a reminder of the faith they had (or at least seemed to have) in him, and because it was such an inexpert job. The evening wind curled and howled through the hastily sewn, jagged patchwork.

Toede stomped into his tent, pulled out the camp chair in the gathering dark, and opened the box containing the light-stone. He fitted it into its holder, bathing the interior of the tent in a soft, warm light. Toede opened the book of his wit and wisdom to where he had last marked it, a passage that Bunniswot noted as being a frank discussion of free-market ethics. Toede was glad for the explanation, for otherwise he would have assumed it was about a noble and street duchess arguing about various prices and services.

Toede leaned back in his chair, balancing on the rear legs, and propped his feet up on a makeshift table of boards and stones. There was a small movement near his bunk, and a small, kender-sized figure appeared.

"Greetings, Toede," said Miles.

Toede would have jumped in surprise at the familiar intonation of the voice, but unfortunately, his current position was not made for jumping, so instead he merely pitched over backward in his chair.

Toede grunted as he hit the soft earthen floor and looked up to see a distinctly waterlogged Miles. His face was partially ruined by days of immersion in water and the tender bashing of the cascades, but it was still recognizable. If nothing else, the ornate dagger sticking out of his chest was a dead (pardoning the pun) giveaway.

Miles grinned, long-drowned muscles pulled almost entirely away from the skull. "I think I surprised you."

"You have a nasty sense of humor, Necromancer," said Toede, pulling himself to his feet.

"Everything about me is nasty," said the mage who was manipulating Miles's body and voice. "But I rarely have a chance to . . . display it."

"Lucky me," murmured Toede. More loudly he said, "Are your troops in position?"

"The bulk of them are," said Miles's corpse.

"Oh, they're platoons of invisible stalkers," said Toede, "with a wing of aerial servants, and a division of unseen avengers?"

Miles made a clucking noise that Toede assumed was laughter. "The bulk of my army has always been here, Toede, even during your reign. Lumber, stone, and trash were not the only things washed up on shore when Istar sank those many centuries ago."

"That's your army?" mocked Toede. "Those skeletons that haven't been turned up by the plow?"

The necromancer gave a kenderish shrug. "I have a small force that will make a . . . diversionary attack on the North Gate at dawn."

"They will be cut to ribbons," said Toede.

"It won't bother them," said the necromancer.

"Our assault will ideally come a half hour after yours."

"Your mind is sharp," said the undead kender. "I look forward to examining it." Before Toede could put in a retort, the necromancer added, "You are throwing your troops in in large numbers to create maximum chaos?"

"As if I have a choice," said Toede. "Subtlety is not in the gnoll playbook. They're going to catch the brunt of it."

"Good," hissed the necromancer. "Any on your side I should . . . spare?"

"You are only to take the dead," cautioned Toede, "not help borderline cases along."

"We agreed to that," said the necromancer. "What I mean is, are there any you wish to give a proper burial to? The scholars, perhaps, or the shaved kender?"

Toede thought a moment, then said, "No. A deal is a deal, and we all agreed to it. Should they fall, they fall into your hands."

"Easy for you to say," said the necromancer. "I will be going now. Remember, tomorrow, after dawn." He hefted Miles's light body to its water-curled feet.

"One last thing," said Toede, raising a hand.

"And that is?" said the undead creature.

"Do you have a real name?" asked Toede, smiling. "I mean, necromancer is just a title or a job description. What are you called at the Necromancer's Club?"

"Necromancers do not *have* clubs," said the creature, more of its face muscles loosening from their moorings as it gave a scowl.

"You know what I mean," said Toede.

A silence fell between the two. Finally, the necromancer spoke. "Bob," he said.

Toede's face brightened. "Bob?"

"It's short for—" the necromancer quickly put in.

Toede waved him silent. "Bob will do. Now we have something that only you and I know, so if you send a message, say it's from Bob, and I'll know it's not a counterfeit." The undead kender nodded, but the remains of its face muscles evidenced suspicion at Toede's reasoning. "I'm going now," the creature said at last. "Prepare well for tomorrow's battles."

"I wasn't counting on sleeping," said Toede, as the undead kender knelt and slipped under the back of the tent.

"I wasn't counting on you sleeping, either," said Miles's corpse with a smile, and then was gone.

Toede cursed and set up his camp chair again. The idea of escape had all the appeal of a cold shower. Cutting his losses and fleeing at that moment meant heading into the woods, where the necromancer likely had undead sentinels. The safest place for Toede at the moment was at the head of an army about to assault Flotsam.

Bunniswot stuck his head in the opening. "Are you alone?" asked the flame-haired scholar.

"In a manner of speaking," said Toede testily.

"Did Taywin tell you about Charka and Renders?" queried the scholar.

"Why aren't you back in Flotsam?" Toede asked sharply.

"I guess I never thought about Renders, you know, as being a romantic individual," continued Bunniswot.

"Why aren't you in Flotsam?" repeated Toede, verging on a bellow.

"I bring bad news and good news," said the scholar, smiling. Toede suddenly missed the straightforward threats of the necromancer.

Toede sighed. "Bad news first," said the hobgoblin.

"They know you're here," said the scholar.

"Small surprise," muttered Toede.

"And Groag has sent a messenger out to the dragon

highlords, to ask for reinforcements."

Toede stroked his warty chin. That meant Groag was either unsure about the size and ability of Toede's forces, or was strapped for cash and in danger of losing some of the mercenary units. "And the good news?"

"Said 'messenger' is me," beamed Bunniswot. "Therefore, no message."

Toede was silent for a moment, then said, "You left by the North Gate?"

Bunniswot looked confused for a moment, then said, "No, by the Southeast Gate. That is closer to here."

"Closer to *here*, human," said Toede, "but in the opposite direction of where you should have been heading. Perhaps Groag is stupid enough not to have noticed, but probably by now he realizes you're at best a coward and at worst a traitor."

"You're saying I made a mistake," said the scholar defensively.

"I'm saying your career in Groag's court is probably over," said the hobgoblin, "so you'd better hope that we win. Or better yet," he said, jumping off his chair and pacing, "head out first thing tomorrow, before the battle. If you reach the highlords, you can at least claim you were delayed."

"I could leave now," said Bunniswot.

"You'd be eaten by zombies," said Toede. "You have a horse?"

"Yes," said the scholar.

"I don't," said Toede. "I'll need yours for tomorrow, so you take one of the kender ponies."

Bunniswot stood there for a moment, looking at Toede.

"Yes?" said the hobgoblin.

"You meant it," said the scholar. "About the zombies. And about not going back to the city. You care about me. You don't want me getting into real danger."

I don't want you showing up during the battle with half your face eaten away, replied Toede mentally. It would be distracting.

"So I have a soft spot," Toede lied. "Maybe I'm getting old. Maybe." He patted the open tome. "I guess I feel I have to live up to the reputation I've acquired in my absence."

Bunniswot gave Toede a look that he could not read, a combination of admiration and fear and something else. It lasted for only a moment, then the scholar stammered and said, "Ah, so you want my report, then?" His face was drained of blood as he reached into his vest pocket.

"Report?" said Toede, arching his eyebrows.

Bunniswot's hand hovered in his vest. "Groag's troop positions," he explained.

"Only if it's different from this," said Toede. "Mercenary troops across the holes in the wall, with militia elsewhere. The gates securely barred and barricaded, a minimal force in the north and west, and Groag's elite guard manning the Rock Wall, to be used as auxiliaries if our forces break through."

The young scholar jerked his empty hand back out of his vest as if he had discovered a venomous snake in there. "How did you . . . ?"

"Groag is strapped for money to pay his mercenaries, and in any event is a cheap little cuss, so they will be placed in the position of the greatest potential loss of life. Dead mercs don't draw paychecks. He then gives the less well-trained militia defensive posts they can cower behind, so they'll fight to protect their positions. Lastly, the elite guard is not intended to reinforce, but rather to protect the highmaster of Flotsam at all costs."

Besides, Toede finished to himself, Groag was there when I set up the bloody plan over two years ago.

Bunniswot's look changed to one of amazement. Shakily, he nodded. "That's right. It's all right." He started for the entrance. "If you want me, I think I'll bunk by the fire."

Toede walked to the entrance, watching the young scholar walk haltingly over to the campfire. Renders was telling yet one more Tale of the Lance to Charka and Taywin. Charka had apparently heard this one before, because he (no, *she*) was interjecting appropriate sound effects.

Bunniswot reached into his vest pocket and pulled out the papers detailing Groag's not-so-secret battle plans. He looked at them a moment, then tossed the plans on the fires. The flames glowed a brilliant green as they consumed the parchment, then dimmed.

Toede shook his head. He hadn't been all that hard on Bunniswot, but sometimes even scholars had to be taught that others knew things that they themselves did not. Still, Bunniswot was quite the nervous nelly, always swooning right and left. Better to get him out of the line of fire, before something bad happened to him, or more importantly, to those around him.

"He's a traitor, you know," said a small, delicate voice behind him.

He turned to a small, elfin figure hovering gently over the pages of Bunniswot's tome of Toede-advice. It was dressed in shades of blue and silver and white, with features so sharp they could cut glass.

Toede raised his eyebrows. "Doesn't anyone knock anymore?" He pulled his chair up to the open book so he was almost nose to torso with the small apparition. "You said Bunniswot was a . . ."

"Traitor," repeated the apparition in a high, melodic, singsong voice. "He works for Highmaster Groag. He means you harm."

"Uh-huh," said Toede. The small figure hovered there, its small feet barely grazing the pages of Toede's book.

"He seeks to catch you unaware and slay you, or failing that, to plant unsound ideas in your mind, hoping you will cause your own death," said the apparition, which looked like a cute pixie, a redundant statement most of the time, but applicable here.

"Uh-huh," said Toede, putting his hands on his knees.

"And you would be?"

"A spirit of wisdom," said the pixie. "A warning from the future. A voice of reason. The animated urge of learning."

"This is a multiple-choice test, I assume," said Toede.

"Mock not," said the spirit in blue and silver and white, "for he does mean you harm."

"So you say," said Toede. "Perhaps I should have Rogate take care of him."

"Trust not Rogate, either," said the spirit, "for he means you ill as well."

"He is a traitor too?" asked Toede.

"Only to himself," said the pixie. "For you scrambled his mind in your first meeting, in the tavern in Flotsam. With every moment he spends with you, his mind clears, and soon he will realize that he was given the holy task to kill you."

"Hmmmm," murmured Toede, "then perhaps Charka and Renders can take care of them, but I suppose they are also . . ."

"Traitors," piped up the small creature. "They have been compromised by the necromancer, who also means you harm."

"*That* I never would have guessed," said Toede sarcastically.

The spirit pixie overlooked his attitude. "They have been promised dominion over Flotsam if they arrange for you to die in battle. Renders is to remain at your side, and slip a dagger between your ribs during the heat of combat."

Toede rubbed his chin again. "Then perhaps we should get the loyal kender rabble to throw these dastards into a makeshift brig, then execute the lot of them at dawn."

"Alas!" said the pixie.

"Let me guess . . ." said Toede. "The kender mean me harm, too."

"The girl is loyal only to her father, who reserves a deep and abiding hatred for you." The pixie bowed its head remorsefully. "You are surrounded by treacherous servants."

"And to think that they don't realize they are all traitors," said Toede. "If only they were organized, they could have killed me days ago."

If the pixie was aware of sarcasm, it did not show on the being's delicate elfin features. "There is but one hope," it said, and Toede could almost hear inspirational music rising up around it.

"You must leave this place," the pixie said sternly. "Take the horse that Bunniswot brought, and ride to the south and east. You will find a small inn, with a single light in the window. Knock on the door and ask for shelter. They will take you in. With you absent, the attack will succeed, but the alliance will fall in upon itself, and the city will be wracked by civil war."

"You're saying I should flee like a coward," said Toede, leaning forward.

"It is the only way." The pixie nodded.

"To save my own hide," said Toede, reaching up and curling his fingers around the edges of the book. "At the cost of my good name."

"You must leave now if you are to *avoimmmmph*!" The pixie's voice was stifled as Toede slammed the massive volume closed. He counted to ten, then opened the book. Only a small singed spot on the pages reassured him that it had not all been a dream.

"Surprisingly," he said aloud to the smoking scorch mark, "I've been thinking the same things myself. Why would these good and, yes, noble people throw in with one such as I? I have been assigning them all sorts of evil motivations and reasons, and my guts have been twisted trying to figure it out.

"But your appearance, dear little singe," said the smiling hobgoblin, "confirmed my hypothesis. Twice now I thought I had things locked up to retake my throne, and twice now something materialized to swat me away. This time, my common sense says flee, and it is bolstered by a supernatural apparition. I have reached a decision."

Toede closed the book again, softly now, and took it with him as he left the tent. He padded back to the fire. Renders was finishing some saga involving gnomes and boats and gold dragons. Charka and Taywin were listening intently, while Kronin and Rogate were sketching lines in the dirt to hone battle plans. Bunniswot, one of the many accused assassins present, was curled up on his side, snoring softly.

Toede kneeled by Taywin, and asked quietly if she had a perfume bottle. She looked at him oddly, then nodded. He sent her to fetch it, along with whatever passed for a priest of the True Gods among the kender. Then the former highmaster handed the massive tome to Renders. Toede returned to the fire and built it up with a few logs, raising a shower of sparks.

"It's going to be a long night," said Toede. "For a lot of people here, it will be their last one. If we're not going to sleep, we might as well know what we're fighting for."

Renders nodded and picked up the tome, starting to read where Toede himself had recently left off. The old scholar's voice started shakily, but soon he caught the cadence of the writing, the words falling from his tongue like petals. Bunniswot awoke with a snort and wiped the sleep from his eyes. Rogate and Kronin stopped their dirt-scribbling, and gnolls and kender, themselves unable to sleep, began to filter back into the glow of the campfire. Taywin returned with the holy kender and a spray bottle of perfume, and Toede spoke with the priest briefly and softly, then sent him to carry out his appointed duties.

Toede spent the remainder of the evening looking into the flames of the rebuilt fire, throwing on another branch or log whenever Renders reached the end of a parable. It seemed that the former highmaster was only half listening, but rather searching for something that could only be read in the dancing tongues of the flame.

Chapter 25

In which the battle is joined, and the diverse elements of the rebellion demonstrate their weaknesses and strengths, both physical and ethical, and Our Protagonist confronts his former ally. Then the Abyssal Plane breaks loose.

By the time dawn crested the overcast bay to the east, Toede had his unified Allied Rebellion entrenched in the last hedgerow, about a hundred yards from the broken-toothed south wall. Toede had no doubt that the Flotsam defenders had seen his men (really, gnolls and kender), for there was a massing movement along the walls and in the gaps, both southern gates had been hastily closed and shuttered, and no wains or other traffic were visible on either road.

Beyond the walls, the Rock rose on the far side of the city, and from the Rock a new architectural monstrosity. It looked like something out of an elven tale of old, for it glittered like a ruby in the ruddy dawn. On the site of Toede's old manor there was now a castle of classic proportions, with tall, needle-thin spires that seemed to bob and weave in the wind like woozy drunkards. Toede wondered if the swaying spires had been erected as watchtowers, and chuckled at the thought of the constitutions of the poor fools who were obliged to man them.

The clouds broke for a moment. A single ray of light crossed the skies, glancing against the topmost spire and refracting it like a beacon across the surrounding farmland.

Toede covered his eyes for a moment from the intensity of the red-hued beam, and when he refocused them, saw that there was a growing consternation across the field. Some soldiers were moving away, others digging into more defensible positions. Then the first shouts reached his ears, and he saw columns of smoke rising from his left, on the north and west sides of the city.

The necromancer's troops had made their assault against the most heavily protected section of the city, the part lined with solid walls. Toede had to admit he was impressed by the undead horde engaged in what was fated to be a suicidal charge. Toede would have to pick up some of the unusual warriors for himself for his next war.

And thinking of suicidal charges, he had his own to direct. He spurred Bunniswot's mount, a coal-black gelding named Smoker, to the front of the hedgerow, and spun the horse around, facing the troops.

He had half a hundred good speeches stored up, invigorating words he'd heard proclaimed by dragon highlords in order to goad their terrified troops into battle. Glory, loot, the advancement of their way of life, threats, the entire gamut. But as he spun about to face the troops—the gnolls in their war paint and the suddenly somber kender—the lines of communication between his mind and mouth were suddenly cut, the conversational bridges vanished, and the mental cues seemed to scatter on the cold dawn breeze.

Toede's mind went blank.

He sat on his horse, regarding the troops, and could have heard the proverbial pin drop along the entire line. He could feel the strain of the gnolls, as if they were swimmers preparing for a diving start, and he could sense the pent-up eagerness of the kender.

"For . . ." said Toede, his thin voice cracking. "For glory! And for good government!"

He was welcomed with a resounding "*Huzzah!*" as the

gnoll troops boiled out from the hedgerow, and the kender, bent forward, their hoopaks slung over their backs, began a scurrying flanking maneuver to the right.

The gnolls' charge broke in front of Toede and reformed beyond him. Rogate was in the vanguard, waving a sword in one hand, a crudely painted green banner in the other, a bow and quiver of green-feathered arrows on his back. The banner read "TOEDAIC KNIGHTS" and sported a picture of a frog.

Renders clopped up on one of his small horses. "Ah, good speech," he said dryly. "One for the ages."

Toede ignored the review. "Did Bunniswot slip away?"

Renders shrugged and said, "I assume so. Shall we join the battle?"

Toede scowled and wheeled Smoker around. "Right. Stay a comfortable distance behind the main body, and keep up. I don't want to have to explain to an irate Charka how I let you die."

The hobgoblin dug his heels into Smoker's flanks, and the gelding broke into a brisk, uneven trot behind the screaming gnolls.

They were halfway across the field before the enemy responded with a hail of missiles. Toede had instructed Charka to have the gnolls raise their heavy shields over their heads, since the arrows would have to take high arcs at this range. Those that survived the first volley were the ones that remembered to do so, but one of every ten gnolls fell to the ground and did not rise.

The charge continued to within forty yards. Toede could make out the colored uniforms of the foe—colors not found among Toede's livery or those of his successors. Mercenaries then, as he had guessed. A front line of spearmen, grim-faced and at the ready, with a row of bowmen behind. The walls were sprinkled with city guards and the odd crossbowman. Most seem to have been pulled away by the diversion.

The kender, moving faster and wider than the gnolls,

were in flanking position on Toede's right, and already were laying down a fire of small stones against the archers. Although the militia were driven from the walls, the mercs were well trained and did not break under the rain of pellets. Instead, the enemy troops repositioned their aim at the kender, while the remaining archers fired straight ahead at the advancing gnolls.

The kender scattered under the returned volleys. They would reassemble quickly, but time would be lost. The effect on the gnolls was pronounced, as many of the swamp gnolls forgot to hold their shields aloft. Another one out of ten collapsed, wounded or dying.

More importantly, the charge ground to a stop thirty yards from the walls, and the surviving gnolls had to take cover behind their shields, their fallen comrades, and whatever low brush they could find. Toede bellowed orders, but they could not hear him, and the mercenary bowmen returned to their primary targets, hammering the grounded gnoll offensive.

Toede felt a presence close to his right, and heard Renders say, "Ah . . ."

Toede cut him off, interrupting. "We're being cut to ribbons, be prepared to . . ."

The next word was going to be "run," or perhaps "flee," or even "surrender." However, at that moment, the gelding whinnied and rose on its hind legs, almost tossing Toede from his saddle, then bolted.

Forward, toward the withering arrow fire.

Toede pulled his sword with one hand, clinging to the horse's neck for as much protection as possible. He was over the front line now, Smoker clearing it in a single bound.

Directly behind him, Toede heard the roar of the gnolls as they regained their courage and rose to follow their leader in his impromptu charge. There was another cheer, this one of childlike voices, as the kender also joined in.

Toede turned in his saddle, motioning for the kender to

hold their ground. Without decent cover-fire, they would all be cut to shreds. He realized that Smoker was wounded, a long red smear of blood dripping from the animal's flank.

What the kender thought they saw, however, was the general of the Allied Rebellion waving them on, his sword glistening in the dawn. Those who survived the day would speak of the valiant spirit of the hobgoblin.

He was right on top of the enemy line, the gnolls behind him, the spearmen in front of him, when Smoker hit a chuckhole at high velocity. The horse cartwheeled forward, pitching Toede over its head.

And over the heads of the spearmen in the front line. The archers loosed one more volley at the gnolls (and at Toede's mount that screamed as the arrows riddled its broken, twitching body). Those closest to Toede dropped their bows and drew their swords, short wide blades that could gut a hog with one swipe.

Then the stones struck among them, and two out of ten archers fell to hoopak accuracy. The remainder moved back a few paces, and Toede scrambled among retreaters and the bodies. Pain gripped his shoulder—the same one Rogate had shot over a year ago—but he was otherwise unharmed. He touched his breast pocket, and found his secret weapon still intact.

The mercenaries wavered but did not panic as the gnolls slammed into their lines. Toede had to scramble again to avoid being trampled by the human troops falling back. The archers had mostly abandoned their missile weapons and were slashing at those gnolls who had pierced the line of mercenaries.

Still, Groag's mercenaries did not break, and Toede had to wonder exactly what the smaller hobgoblin had promised in exchange for their services.

A particularly burly mercenary swaggered toward him and was rewarded with death as Toede cut the man off at the ankles. The hobgoblin then spun and sunk his blade into another merc. Apparently the missile troops were better with bow than with sword, and lightly armored to boot.

A cry went up, this time from human throats, and Toede could see fresh enemy troops pour into the fray. At least fresh in that they had not yet fought Toede's kender/gnoll army. Many of them were bloodied and had the look of men who had fought the undead, and were now glad to battle flesh-and-blood opponents who have the sense to lie down and die.

Slowly, the mercenary line stiffened, then began to drive the combined gnolls and kender backward, away from the wall. Toede was still trapped on the wrong side of the lines.

And then the dead whale appeared, and everything changed.

It was even larger than in Toede's memory. Most of the skin had peeled away, and the rotting blubber had turned a sickly yellow-green. The ribs poked out one of its sides, and its massive eye was a runny pustule of white ichor.

It had erupted from the beach, where Toede's men had buried it long ago, leaping about two hundred feet in a high arc toward the battlefield. Alas, it would not clear the entire distance, but the airborne necro-whale did cause three things to happen:

Some (not all, but enough) gnolls gawked at the great mass of animated cetacean flesh in midleap.

Some (not all, but enough) humans turned to see what the gnolls were looking at with such fascination and awe.

And some (not all, but enough) kender took advantage of those humans with their backs turned.

The spearmen's line crumbled in a dozen places as the humans toppled, either from daggers set squarely in their backs or calf tendons severed, bringing their unprotected necks closer to the ground (and nearer to kender swords).

Toede was pressed to the ground by a toppling human. He rolled with the body, struggled, and pushed it off him at last. He rose to find himself alone in the gap of the wall. Alone in the sense that he was the only one present who wasn't dead or close enough to death to deceive the casual observer. He did not recognize any of the dead except Smoker, who had sprouted a double-dozen arrows in a deadly bouquet and lay there, open eyes staring at Toede accusingly.

Toede cocked an ear and heard distance shouts, battle cries, and the clash of metal against metal. It was all around him, throughout the city, the battlefront broken into a hundred clashes, fought in alleys and plazas and storefronts. The kender would be in their element here, an entire terrain of places in which to run and hide.

The gnolls would make for the Rock Wall, and Renders and the other battle leaders with them. Toede picked through the bodies and moved toward the headland, noting in passing that none of the mercenaries wore the gold disks he had seen in his last incarnation.

He had to double back twice as his path was blocked by intense fighting, and once had to redirect a bloodstained unit of kender to a likely battle scene, but at last he made it. He had no idea how long it took him, but Toede reached the headland wall.

The wall was undefended, the gates to the Rock open. It was comparatively quiet, the battle raging elsewhere in the city. The defenders had abandoned their posts, but had they fled out of fear of flying whales, or plunged into the heat of battle? Or were they lurking in ambush?

Toede strode cautiously up to the gate as a large shadow appeared on the other side. It was gnoll-sized, but had the head of a great ox, and carried a massive, double-headed axe.

It was a minotaur, but this one's skin was the color of paper left in the sun too long, its eyes as sightless as Smoker's or, for that matter, the dead whale's.

Toede sighed and stepped forward. "Hi, Bob," he said.

"Greetings, Toede," said the undead mix of human and

bovine traits. "You seem to have expected me."

"Sooner or later," said Toede in a conversational voice, slowly closing the distance between them. He reached back and slid his bloodied sword back into its scabbard. "How long have you planned this, working for both sides?"

The minotaur zombie managed a shrug. "Since before your return. And while it would have been easier had I captured you before the kender did, fortune allowed me to turn that happenstance to my advantage."

Toede smiled. "So you appeared to Groag and offered to protect him in exchange for . . ."

"For the dead," said the minotaur zombie, "same as you. And of course, *everyone* will be the dead soon."

"So you wanted Flotsam for yourself, eh?" said Toede, now standing all of five feet away from his opponent.

"As a start," said the zombie. "Even now the first of your battlefield dead are twitching as the bones reknit and the flesh empties. They will be my new army, to slay the survivors of the city and further swell my legions. Then, when I have sufficient ships, I will launch raids along the entire coast, until I have a small nation of undead humans, kender, ogres, hobgoblins, and even dragons under my control!"

Toede sighed again, reaching into his short jacket as if trying to physically slow his beating heart. "Dream no small dreams," he said. "Well I have news for you, Necromancer. *Murrurrurume!*" His voice had dropped to an unintelligible mumble.

The minotaur zombie cocked its head for a moment, then said, "You said something?"

"I said . . ." Toede again dropped his voice. "*Murrurrurume!*"

The minotaur zombie managed a smile and dropped to one knee to hear better. It kept its axe in one hand, to gut the hobgoblin should he try to pull anything. "Once more," it chided.

"I said *have some perfume!*" said Toede, and pulled Tay-win's atomizer from his jacket. Before the minotaur zombie could react, he sprayed the contents full-force into the undead creature's face.

The minotaur zombie screamed as the holy water, pre-pared by the kender priest, boiled away what remained of its face, revealing the skull beneath the flesh. Toede's sword flew from his scabbard as he brought it in a neat line across the minotaur's shoulders, separating its head from its body.

Toede smiled, but the smile was short-lived, as the now-headless creature tottered to its feet and hefted its axe.

"Oh, come now," gurgled the remains of the minotaur-zombie skull, "you of all people should know that death is not a career-ending injury around here."

The zombie brought its axe down, hard, and splintered the pavement as Toede jumped to one side. The minotaur was still mighty dangerous, albeit blind.

Blind? No, Toede corrected himself. Rather the mino-taur's skull was still relaying orders, although at a disad-vantage due to its lowered vantage point.

Toede lunged out and kicked the skull, hard. It went flipping end-over-end to one side of the gate. Maybe that will slow down its reaction time, he hoped.

Or not, as Toede's left side exploded in a flash of pain. Not the axe, but a kick from the minotaur zombie had caught him fully in the side. He dropped the spray bottle and heard it smash. Toede flew five feet and hit the wall, not far from the decapitated head.

"Gotcha," gurgled the zombie.

Small stars novaed in front of Toede, but he could make out the shadow of the headless necromantic puppet tow-ering over him. He heard the necromancer's laugh as the minotaur zombie lifted its axe above his head. Then the minotaur stiffened, jerked three times, and fell at Toede's feet.

There were four green-feathered arrows jutting from the minotaur's back. Rogate ran into Toede's view. "Milord!" he shouted. "Are you all right?"

Toede nodded and rose painfully, pointing to the fallen axe. "Hand me that, will you?"

Rogate gave Toede the axe. The hobgoblin limped over to where the minotaur skull gurgled. Bob the necromancer had apparently abandoned it for some other body, since it had no last words as he chopped the skull into pieces.

Toede turned. Rogate had replaced his bow and arrows and picked up his tattered banner that now only read: "TOE   KNIG ."

"You can't conquer the world," said Toede to the skull pieces. "You don't even have your own book." To Rogate he said, "How's the battle going?"

Rogate nodded. "Better than expected. The kender are excellent in house-to-house ambushes—Kronin calls this 'a stonework forest' and you know how good they are in the woods. The gnolls are at a slight disadvantage due to their size, but make up for it with their strength. We've also had some natives join in, though most are in hiding. And we've had some reports of the necromancer's undead in combat with our own troops, but that might be a mix-up."

Toede pointed at the minotaur's arrow-dotted corpse. "No mix-up. The necromancer's playing both sides against the middle. Get back into the battle, spread the word that all corpses should be burned immediately, on both sides. And see if you can get word to the human mercs as well. They may lose their will to fight if they know their deaths guarantee them eternal bondage as revenants and zombies."

Rogate grunted agreement. "And you, milord? What are you going to do?"

Toede walked shakily toward the crystalline palace sprawled on the site of his home.

"Me?" said Toede, sighing. "I'm going to end this, once and for all."

* * * * *

The headland was empty as Toede stalked through the streets, the guards engaged in battle elsewhere, the bourgeoisie and burghers either hiding in their basements or hightailing it to the hinterland. Occasionally, from the Lower City there would be the shouts of men and gnolls rallying for battle, or the crash or explosion of a house caving in on itself. But that seemed half a world away, for the breeze from the sea swept the smells of battle inland and far from Toede's mind.

Toede felt strengthened as he walked. His left shoulder was useless, but the pain had subsided to a dull ache. Same for his side, though the bruise might be permanent, and if he breathed deeply he could feel a loosened rib sliding against its neighbor. Still, he was ambulatory, so he stalked forward, sword in his one good hand, minotaur axe clutched in the other.

Up close, Groag Hall (at least, that's what the carving along the granite frieze announced) looked like three or four architectural styles that had not really merged, but collided in the dead of night at some unmarked crossroads. Parts of the old gray stone front remained, but this was bolstered by a white granite colonnade in the High Istar style. Some glasswork of the Hopsloth period survived, ornamented by a set of needlelike spires that rivaled Silvanesti. A dome hung over the center building like a crystalline turtle glued to the roof.

Ugly as sin, Toede thought, and definitely an improvement.

The broad steps, replaced after Jugger's ruinous charge, were some type of tinted concrete, but made of shoddy material and already flaking.

The original doors were still present, and Toede pulled

them open, expecting Groag's honor guard to be waiting for him. Instead, nothing happened, and Toede wandered into the entry hall.

The hall was a suitable restoration of the original, complete with balcony and stairs winged to each side, framing the large iron doors of the central court. Groag must have had it rebuilt.

Still no one, not even a zombie.

Toede pulled open the last doors, the heavy iron ones (apparently pulled from wherever Hopsloth's priests had stashed them). The audience hall was similar to the one Toede had presided over. The furnishings were as rich, at least, and dominated by a great handwoven rug in the center, directly before the throne. The only major change was the dome above that cast a wide circular pool of light on the rug. For the first time the brightness made Toede aware that it was nearly midday.

On the far side of the light, a small figure was bunched up on the throne. "'Lo, Toede," said a familiar, small voice.

"'Lo, Groag," said the former highmaster. "How's tricks?"

A deep sigh came from the shadows. Lord Groag leaned forward. Toede saw that his former lackey's face was now lined and careworn, his form nearly skeletal, and his eyes bloodshot. Such an appearance cheered Toede tremendously.

"So it comes to this." Groag motioned weakly. "Come forward. We need to discuss what happens next."

Toede took two steps forward, to the edge of the handwoven rug. Then he hefted the axe painfully in his left hand. "As a sign of goodwill, I leave my most dangerous weapon behind." And he threw it on the rug.

The axe and the rug both vanished as the trapdoor beneath flung open. Toede heard a splash.

He tilted an eyebrow and circled the pit. "*A* for effort," he said.

"F for phooey," responded Groag sulkily, and settled back into the shadows.

"Sharks?"

"Crocodiles," said Groag. "Give me credit for some imagination."

But not much, thought Toede. Instead he said, "We're alone?"

Groag nodded. "When word spread that the undead were attacking from the north, that our ally the necromancer had double-crossed us, the loyalest of the loyal headed to battle, while the bulk headed for the docks. But the captain goes down with his ship."

"That's a myth put out by those who are not captains," said Toede. "And the necromancer did not double-cross you so much as double-cross everyone. He's on nobody's side but his own. He hoped to turn Flotsam into a necropolis, a city of the dead."

Groag leaned forward. For a moment Toede thought the smaller hobgoblin was going to take a leap into the pit. Instead, the lord of the manor rocked back and forth, sobbing. "I tried so *hard!*"

"Sometimes effort isn't enough," said Toede coolly, circling around the pit, his sword poised. "Remember how hard I tried, the first time, only to be laughed at and goaded?" He was three steps away from a sword thrust good enough to end Groag's whining once and for all. Two steps. One step.

"Would it help if I said I was sorry?" asked Groag suddenly.

"Pardon?" said Toede, staying his hand for the moment.

"About leaving you in the hole," sobbed Groag. "And exploiting your name to take over Flotsam. I'm sorry. I mean it. I was angry at you for deserting me, and wanted to hurt you. Badly. And then that vision, that angel in blue, appeared and told me of my destiny. I thought I finally had been recognized for my own ability. Of course after I made it to the top, that dratted book turned up, and

I was afraid you'd come back early and were planning to have me killed. I cut all these deals and plotted with the necromancer and hired mercenaries and now everyone is going to die, and it's all my fault."

Pity touched Toede's heart, pity that Groag, a natural follower, had made the mistake of seizing leadership. Perhaps it would be better to let him live, to just let him leave. Still, that would make Groag a live enemy, as opposed to a dead martyr. "I . . ." He hesitated for a moment, then continued, "I don't think it's entirely your fault."

Groag was silent. "I suppose you want your chair back."

Toede heard the groaning of iron hinges and cast a glance back toward the door. "I think we'll have to put that off," he said, "at least for a little while."

The doors had swung backward to reveal a dozen shambling forms: gnoll, human, and kender. Rogate had been too late to spread the warning. The necromancer's spell had already spread through the city. The undead had multiplied, were everywhere.

Groag's eyes widened as he saw the necromancer's minions shuffle forward. "Know of any good miracles, Lord Toede?"

Toede hefted his sword. He wondered how long he could last in combat before his damaged rib slid into his lung. "I'm fresh out, Lord Groag," said Toede. "Wish I had one handy."

That was when the lightning struck, and *she* appeared, floating in a ball of brilliant light. Her flesh was mirrored silver, and she was carrying a blade so dark it hurt to gaze at its ebony blackness. Her hair was the color of flaming blood; her eyes gleamed. Toede, Groag, and even the zombies had to shield their eyes from her feral appearance.

The world held its breath. Judith had arrived in Ansalon.

"When will you learn," Toede heard Groag say, "to stop saying things like that?"

Chapter 26

A being of extradimensional power materializes. A star chamber is called, witnesses are brought forth, the matter of betting is discussed, and a judgment is made, all in a manner of speaking.

"I am Judith," said the silvery figure in a booming tone that caused the glass walls and dome to vibrate. "Lieutenant and servant to her Dark Ladyship, Takhisis. Let all who witness me quake in peril!"

The hell-maiden spun, regarding the two figures by the throne with an icy glare. Words dripped like acid from her lips. "Where is the one named Toede?"

Toede wanted to point to Groag, but his wounded arm stopped him. Groag in the meantime had pointed at Toede, and taken two polite steps back.

Toede sighed, meekly stepping forward. "I . . . am . . ." He cleared his voice and tried again. "I am Toede."

Judith regarded the hobgoblin crossly. "Are you not supposed to be dead?"

Toede nodded. "I tried, but it wouldn't take." He managed a weak smile that withered under the hell-maiden's glare like a fresh posie tossed into a maelstrom. She looked insulted at the very idea that anyone would dare to jest in her presence.

One of the zombies behind Judith tried to lunge at her,

only to pass through the multicolored sphere surrounding her and disintegrate into myriad pieces.

Judith seemed to take notice of the undead for the first time at that point, and waved a hand dismissively. The zombies exploded. Not with a roar of fury and streaming of rotted intestines, but with large holes erupting from their chests and soft puffs of air that sounded like popcorn roasting over a fire. The zombies slumped silently to the floor.

"These are yours?" she asked crossly, apparently looking for more evidence of Toede's impertinence.

"Uh, no!" said Toede quickly, passing a hand over his heart to ascertain that it was still beating. "They . . . er . . . belong to a rival of ours"—he indicated himself and Groag—"who is overrunning our city with his undead."

"Please, most powerful lady!" interrupted Groag, falling to his knees. "Please save our city! The necromancer's forces will kill everyone! I was a fool to have trusted him, but they'll all die unless you help."

The shining maiden of the Abyss did not deign to smile. "Why," she asked, "in the name of the Dark Lady herself would I want to stop the undead from slaying every living being here?"

"Because . . . ah . . . because . . ." Groag stammered to a halt.

"Because you are letting one small evil destroy a greater potential evil," put in Toede. "This city is the greatest repository of malice and mischief on the Blood Sea. No bloody-handed madmen, mind you, no great armies of foul-spawned warriors, no megalomanic world-conquerors, but petty evil, venal evil, and greedy evil. This town has been a haven for pirates, con men, thieves, and all manner of ne'er-do-wells and outcasts, along with crooked merchants, mercenaries, and yes, a few madmen, or mad-beings. It is a spawning ground for ill will and evil activity, for hatred and corruption, and unless action is taken and taken quickly, it will be replaced with the silence of the grave, and the shambling of the zombies' tread."

Toede was winded from his long exposition and had to bite the inside of his mouth to avoid saying more. Judith had closed her eyes halfway through his discourse. Now she opened them, and Toede saw they glowed with the crimson fire of the hearth. "Your argument has merit. Evil turns on itself all too often in this world. The appeal is granted."

She waved a hand. The two hobgoblins heard the sound of popping corn in the courtyards outside, growing in intensity as it swept outward, and reaching a crescendo with a loud bang that sounded like the detonation of a gnomish invention.

That would be the whale, thought Toede.

Judith's steely gaze returned to the former highmaster of Flotsam. "As I stated before, you are supposed to be dead."

Toede nodded. "Yes. I have died. Three times now, each time in painful fashion, and each time was restored to life again. Are you the agent of my recovery, the torturer whose task it is to send me here time and again?" he asked.

Then Judith did something very surprising. She laughed. It was not the merry laugh of the party-goer, or the demure chuckle of the debutante, but loud, rollicking laughter that seemed to start in the Abyss and work its way to the surface with the force of a mounting earthquake. Toede took two steps backward. Groag moved for the shelter of the throne.

"I am *not* such an agent," said Judith. "Witness those fools responsible for your reanimation."

There was another sphere of multicolored lightning, and two twisted and shackled figures materialized in the throne room. They were manacled together, the metal bands around their wrists and ankles still glowing from some recent die in the furnace.

The pair were in obvious pain, yet still capable of standing upright. They looked like some type of winged lizard men or draconians with long, horselike faces. They sweated and smelled like burned blood. Though of similar breed, they were different in that one was tall and rail-thin, the other short and portly. Their appearance tickled something deep within Toede's memory.

"Witness the agents of your reanimation," repeated Judith. "These are two petty bureaucrats of the Abyss. The Castellan of the Condemned, and the Abbot of Misrule. They are charged in this court with shirking their duties, abusing their positions, idleness, gambling, and unauthorized return of the dead to life. All are serious crimes."

Toede looked at the pair and remembered the two shadowy godlike forms—Mountain-tall and Sea-wide—from his dreams. "They told me to live nobly," he said.

"Live nobly," hissed Judith. "And they gambled on your success. So tell me, my petty fiends, who won your bet?"

Both abishai looked embarrassed. The Castellan ventured meekly, "I think I did."

The enraged hell-maiden regarded him harshly. "And your reasoning is . . . ?"

"Ah, well," said the Castellan, sounding a little like Renders. "He has embarked on a noble mission, as you can clearly see."

The taller abishai chuckled, and Judith turned her attention to him. "And what are your reasons for saying this Toede has not learned nobility?"

The Abbot blanched and stammered. "Why, his very failure, repeatedly and continually, where he backstabs his allies and cheats his supposed friends. He would have turned on the very people that had helped him regain his throne had we given him another day. Indeed, he was at the point of killing his old comrade, here, one of his own species, when we interrupted."

"No, he wasn't," put in the Castellan.

"Was too!"

"Was not!"

"*Silence!*" bellowed Judith. "And to think that this foolishness would have continued, had not an elder juggernaut returned to our fold with stories of strange and unorthodox happenings in this land."

Jugger, thought Toede. She's talked to Jugger. He wondered what the fiendish siege engine had said about him.

Judith pressed on. "Answer me this question, then. What is nobility?"

Both of the abishai were quiet. Then the Castellan meekly ventured. "That's what we were hoping to find out."

"I see," said Judith, her eyes becoming slits. "So you began your experiment without the slightest idea of how to measure your results?"

"Well, we . . ." started the Castellan, then stopped when he looked into her angry face. "No, ma'am," he finished.

"Then I declare the bet over, the experiment finished," said Judith. She brandished her ebony blade and strode toward Toede. "Let this spirit return to its rest."

Toede felt his stomach drop out of his body entirely at these words. This time, he thought woozily, death would be for real and final.

"Hold!" shouted a voice from the iron doors.

Judith hesitated.

Rogate strode into the audience hall. He looked even bloodier and more tattered than his banner, which now read: TO   NI . Behind him stood a small party of survivors from the battle. Renders was limping and leaning on Charka; Kronin and Taywin were bruised but otherwise unharmed; and even Bunniswot was with them, looking suspiciously untouched by the mayhem that had taken place.

"Dark envoy of the depths!" greeted Rogate. "If there is any question as to nobility, then let us have our say."

Judith regarded Rogate coolly. "Does your testimony

have bearing?"

Rogate nodded. "We have fought alongside Lord Toede and can vouch for his noble deeds!"

Judith drew her sword back, and Toede felt his heart resume beating.

"Proceed," she said.

"Well, ah . . ." said Rogate. He was reduced to stammering, apparently having fired all his brain cells to get this far. Then he seemed to be thunderstruck by an idea. "I am of the Toedaic Knights!" he proclaimed. "And one cannot be knighted unless by a lord, so therefore Toede is noble!"

"Fallacious argument," said Judith. "If Toede is not noble, then you are not a knight. And I see more merit in arguing for his nobility than your knighthood. Appeal denied. Anyone else?"

"Wait!" puffed Rogate, reaching inside his vest. "I have this, as evidence." He pulled Groag's disk from its chain and approached the evil minion. He dropped to one knee, presenting it.

She took the disk from his hand, turning it over in her palm. "He died nobly," she read. "This is a trinket anyone can make." The disk warped and melted in her hands, dripping to the floor in thick globules. "Did you inscribe this?" she asked Rogate.

"No, sir! Uh, ma'am," said Rogate, bowing and moving backward.

"I . . . uh . . . did," said Groag meekly, from his position by the throne. "Toede lured Gildentongue off just as he was about to kill me. When it seemed Toede had perished, I had the medal inscribed in his memory."

"Did you believe him truly noble?" asked the Castellan nervously, for he had dared to interrupt his superior.

"I . . . I think I did," said Groag, emerging slightly from his shadow position.

"And do you now?" pressed the Abbot, more assured in his voice than his comrade.

A moment's thought. "I . . . I don't know." said the hobgoblin. "I don't know what would have happened this time if you had not arrived."

"So your argument therefore states that Toede is only noble in repose," said Judith. "Dead, he was noble. Alive, he is a wild card."

"I . . . I guess," said Groag, not looking in Toede's direction. "We do have our falling outs now and again, you know."

Toede felt the room closing in on him.

Kronin, shaking off Taywin's hold, stepped forward. "Nobility is wisdom," he began, "and Toede's parables and sayings demonstrate his wisdom, even if his actions always do not."

Bunniswot stepped in. "You cannot rely on the words that may . . . uh . . . have deeper sources." He shot a wary look toward Judith, but when she neither interrupted nor corrected, he continued. "However, Toede showed kindness to me on a number of occasions, including directing the juggernaut elsewhere when I might have been killed.

"Last night I was supposed to kill him for Groag. Yet, Toede warned me of the necromancer's treachery. I was supposed to strike him with a poisoned needle, hidden within some false plans. And Toede realized this, for he knew Groag's true plans, and kept me from drawing my false ones and attacking him. Then he insisted on me remaining safely in camp, when he could have let me ride to my doom. Kindness and forgiveness in the face of adversity. That is nobility."

"Bravery!" bellowed Charka, getting into the swing of the discussion. "Toede is smart, but many cheats and fools are smart. Toede is brave, because he spurred battle-charge, leaped forward on his horse, and led by example."

"Ah, he had no choice," put in Renders softly, "for the necromancer contacted me and promised me great scholarly knowledge in exchange for Toede's death." Renders looked at his feet. "I'm afraid I missed and struck his horse instead."

Toede shook his head. The little spirit (who he now strongly suspected had been one of the abishai) had been correct about all the closet traitors. "It's all right," Toede muttered. "It hardly matters now."

Bunniswot pointed. "See! Kindness and forgiveness!"

"I know naught of that," Renders put in, "but I can say that the Toede I have encountered is very different from the one I told of in the tales. He is smarter and cannier, and perhaps a little wiser."

"He *is* different," interrupted Taywin. "Had I known it was Toede we captured a year ago, I would have had him slain, for he once endangered my father with foolish and cruel games. But this Toede risked his life for others. True, his life seems easily lost and easily restored, but it was risk all the same."

"Risk is not nobility," said the Abbot.

"Wisdom," put in Kronin, "true wisdom."

"Kindness and forgiveness," said Bunniswot.

"Honor!" shouted Rogate.

"Bravery!" bellowed Charka.

"*Silence!*" shrieked Judith, and the walls bulged outward at her fury. "This is a testimony of fools. You cannot agree among yourselves what nobility is, yet you prattle on about how Toede is one way or another. I render my judgment against all of you . . ."

"Please," said Toede quietly.

The words lacked the unctuous, haughty tone that had been heard so often inside these walls. Even Judith was silenced by the sudden hush in Toede's voice.

"A testimony of fools is still a testimony," said Toede, feeling the blood drain from his face as he spoke, "and I thank them for their kind words, even if they are sometimes misguided. However, their crimes and follies ought to be punished in their own times. They should not be judged for appealing on my behalf."

Toede felt his knees give way and the hard impact of them striking the floor. He continued, "I have been sent on a fool's errand, and that errand is done. If I am more noble dead than I was alive, so be it—few get a chance to rewrite their own eulogy. I am ready to return to my eternal rest."

Behind him, he heard Groag say softly, "Toede, I . . ."

Toede shook his head. "Sort out for yourself, everyone, who's running the show after me. Groag, if you apologize, and quit trying to imitate me as I was, you might just get good at the job. The rest of you, clear out. Her ladyship might not agree with me, and you'll be the next to go."

Toede closed his eyes. "Let's get on with our lives. And our deaths."

Judith looked at Toede for a long moment, as Toede swayed, waiting for the blow to fall.

Then she held her sword out, touching Toede's shoulders lightly with the ebony tip. "By what powers, I grant you your nobility. Arise, Lord Toede of Flotsam."

But Toede did not arise. Instead, he pitched forward in a dead faint, and would have tumbled into the crocodile pit if not for Groag.

Epilogue

Wherein final matters are sorted out, and Our Protagonist finally becomes Our Hero.

Flotsam was alive with cel-ebration. The Lower City danced with pixie lights and congratulatory fires. Most of the buildings wrecked in the battle were now the sites of large bonfires, and smaller flames rose up from torch-light parades. Every now and again, a magical illusion would stride across the sky, or a gnomish smoke-rocket would spiral up over the city and burst in half a hundred streamers.

Mobs milled in the streets as the survivors partied and compared war stories. Were the tales to be truly believed, Toede had wrestled bare-handed with the undead min-ions, while the rest of the population cowered in their hid-ing places. In the main courtyard before Toede's (formerly Groag's) manor, gnoll and kender and human mingled and bragged and drank. The defeat of the necromancer seemed to have unified the races and dimmed more recent memory. The gnolls and kender were now seen as rescuers, not invaders.

Bunniswot was highly visible, encamped next to the fountain, reading Toede's volume on government to three very interested young ladies. Kronin wandered through the crowd, smiling, and if a piece of jewelry or a coin pouch suddenly came loose in his proximity, he "found" it very quickly, then moved on. A large fire had been built in the center of the court, and over it two huge oxen were spinning slowly on iron spits, turned by gnolls. Groag stood on a slightly raised platform of green wood and basted the rotating carcasses. He looked up toward the outer balcony and smiled, raising his ladle in salute.

Toede returned the salute with a heft of his mug and took a long pull of the Jetties' best ale. The Jetties had survived both Jugger and the Undead War, and instead of leveling it, the highmaster of Flotsam had proclaimed it official alehouse of the Toede Restoration.

Lord of Flotsam, he corrected himself. Ordained by the pit itself, and recognized by the people. Let the dragon highlords argue with that.

Toede took another pull, his nostril hairs bristling at the scent of burned blood, which was not coming from the ox-roast.

He did not turn around. "You've come at last," he said. A statement, not a question.

Judith responded in her steely voice. "How are your injuries?"

Toede's entire side was bandaged, his left arm wrapped tightly to his body. "Several ribs are cracked. One's pulled loose entirely and is nudging my lung. My shoulder's separated in three places."

"Meaning?" asked the hell-maiden.

"Better than usual," said Toede. "A priest of Shinare patched me up fairly well, and in exchange I gave him the part of town where the whale landed to set up a church. So I get full-time healers and a clean-up job."

She moved closer to the seated hobgoblin to observe the festivities, the flames reflecting darkly off her polished skin. If any of the revelers saw a silver-skinned Abyss-spawn chatting with the new Lord of Flotsam, they thought better than to mention it. Ever.

"I've been expecting you," said Toede. "You've changed your mind?" Again, a question but phrased politely.

"No," said the enforcer of Takhisis. "I gave my judgment and stand by it. You have your life until someone else chooses to take it."

"Did you have the power to make me a lord? Really?" asked Toede.

"Did you have the power to make Rogate a knight? Really?" responded Judith.

"A Toedaic Knight," corrected Toede, and forgetting his bad arm, he tried to gesture to a tattered banner on the wall. "And chief bodyguard."

"And the others?" said Judith. "Have you meted out suitable rewards and punishments?"

Toede set down his ale and ticked off things on his good hand. "Bunniswot has been made chief historian and head scribe, since there has been a huge demand for 'Toede's Wisdom.' Kronin has been made chief game warden, with Taywin as his assistant. The first thing they did was deputize the entire kender clan. Charka has been officially recognized as the master of the swamps and given access to the surviving libraries, while Renders has been made chief librarian emeritus."

"They all tried to kill you," said Judith. "Multiple times."

"Yes, but better the devils you know," said Toede. "Pardon the offense."

"None taken. And Groag?"

"He's become quite a decent cook in the past two years, so he will continue to serve as my chef," said Toede, then added with a smile, "He is also my food-taster."

"I see," said Judith. "Most suitable arrangements. Each gains what they desire, and the responsibility that goes with it."

Toede swore there was a hint of amusement in her voice. He ventured, "And what of your 'punishments'?"

"The quality of enlightened mercy is underdeveloped in the Abyss," said Judith. "It turns out that Old Jugger was one shy of his quota. So I had the Abbot and Castellan bound to a mile-wide expanse around a near-empty landmark, and turned Jugger loose in that area."

"You think they can outrun Jugger?" said Toede.

"I think they are concentrating on outrunning each other," said Judith dryly.

There was a silence between the two, hobgoblin and hell-maiden. Then Toede ventured a question. "If you are not here to pull me back . . . ?" He let the question drag out.

"I thought I should explain," said Judith quietly. "About nobility."

"Am I noble?" asked Toede.

"Do you feel noble?" she responded.

Toede thought for a moment "No. At least not in the terms of what I once thought was nobility: title, rank, prestige. And definitely not in terms that everyone else talks about: honor, wisdom, kindness."

"Don't worry. You are as black-hearted as they come. Your newfound nobility only provides a larger array of resources and allies. If anything, you are more dangerous now than you were when that dragon ended your first life," Judith said.

Toede gave a sigh. "I'm glad you said that."

The pair watched the mob swirl beneath them. "It's not over yet," Toede said. "The necromancer's attack unified these people, and he is still out there."

"I do not think that a major problem," said Judith. "You know the near-empty location I spoke of? The necromancer's castle was perfect for my needs, as zombies do not count in Jugger's total." Another pause, broken by the distant howls of the gnolls.

Judith put a silver hand on his shoulder, and Toede jumped at the soft warmth. "We look forward to your return to the Abyss."

Toede reached beneath his chair and pulled out a small silver tube. He turned in his seat and presented the tube to Judith.

"This is?" she said.

"A small scroll made from the metal of the amulet you melted," said Toede. "A souvenir of our encounter. It has a full and accurate account of my accomplishments and actions, my strengths and desires, and hopes for the future, in the hopes that I may be of service to you."

Judith turned the scroll tube over in her hands. It did not melt at her touch. "What you're saying," she said, with a hint of amusement, "is that this is your resumé?"

Toede smiled broadly. "If Abbot and Castellan are typical of your middle management, you need talented servants badly. Just don't rush my recruitment."

At that Judith broke into a smile, and out over the city several gnomish skyrockets exploded at once, illuminating that silver smile into a beacon that could be seen far out to sea.

And deep within the Abyss, there was another smile, one that threw new mountains upward and dislodged half a hundred fiends, as the Dark Mistress herself was amused by what was to come.